FATES
DIVINE

FATE
OF
GODS AND FIRE

BOOKS BY SHANIA SCICHILONE

The Fates Divine Series

A Fate of Smoke and Ash

A Fate of Gods and Fire

READERS DISCRETION

A note for readers,

A FATE OF GODS AND FIRE is a New Adult novel; however, it should only be read by mature readers. This book contains sensitive content, and it is advised to review the list of potential trigger warnings provided. You can find the list on the author's website at www.shaniascichilone.com under the tab "BOOKS: TW - Fates Divine Series". Readers discretion is advised.

CHARACTERS

- Shivalri Acadia Grimsbane-Gray (Shih-v-all-rEE Ah-kay-dEE-ah Grim-s-b-ay-n Gur-ay)
- Raidan Grimsbane-Gray (R-eye-den)
- Eden Grimsbane-Gray (EE-d-in)
- Archer Gray (Arch-er)
- Diego (DEE-y-egg-oh)
- Satyra Grimsbane-Duke (S-ah-tEEr-ah D-ooh-k)
- Enya Grimsbane-Duke (Ehn-Yah)
- Olliver/Olly Duke (All-ih-v-er/All-EE)
- Sabine Grimsbane-Cormier (S-ah-b-EE-n K-or-mEE-ay)
- Moira Darkmore (Moy-r-ah Dark-more)
- Sora Fujin (S-or-ah Fyoo-jEE-uhn)
- Ember Blackwood (EM-ber Bl-ah-k-w-UU-d)
- Damek Lagunov (Dah-mek L-ah-g-uh-n-aw-v)
- Nesrin Mehra (Neh-z-r-in M-ay-r-ah)
- Baaz Mehra (B-ah-z)
- Pyre Malum (P-eye-er M-ah-l-uhm)
- Drakovyr (D-r—ay-k-oh-v-EE-r)
- Alriq (All-r-ih-k)

- Nor (N-or)
- Ombrose (Aw-m-b-r-oh-s)
- Dramael (Drah-mah-el)
- Tasphen (Tass-f-en)
- Reaver (R-EE-v-er)
- Gerimor (G-air-ih-m-er)
- Wulfric Hallows (W-ull-f-r-ick H-al-oh-s)
- Kaede Rin (K-ay-d R-in)
- Nihility (N-ih-hih-lih-t-EE)
- Esther (Ehs-th-er)
- Izra (Ih-z-r-ah)
- Marisole (M-ah-r-EE-s-oh-l)
- Matrine (M-ah-t-r-EE-n)
- Greivos (G-r-EE-v-ô-s)

CONTENTS

1. Freefall   1
2. Surface   9
3. Uncover   15
4. Shadows   17
5. Umbra   23
6. Starlight   31
7. Cypress   38
8. Peril   44
9. Intruder   48
10. Hidden   51
11. Suffocate   57
12. Dice   63
13. Équivoque   69
14. Mountain   73
15. Under   77
16. Thaw   84
17. Blueprint   90
18. Unearthed   97
19. Divulge   102
20. Tea   109
21. Imagine   116
22. Descry   119
23. Insomnia   125
24. Clue   134
25. Return   136
26. Proctor's Ledge   142
27. Obscurum   145
28. Passage   150
29. Unpredicted   153
30. Hush   157
31. Pledge   168
32. Impart   181
33. Làérxo   189

34. Leave — 202
35. Foray — 206
36. Lieutenant — 217
37. Base — 225
38. Advance — 229
39. Helm — 239
40. Creux — 247
41. Mirror — 254
42. Ôhrtum — 259
43. Summit — 264
44. Amity — 268
45. Idle — 273
46. Enigma — 281
47. Numb — 285
48. Lull — 289
49. Lethal — 292
50. Entice — 301
51. Bare — 305
52. Clean — 314
53. Steam — 323
54. Laced — 333
55. Displaced — 346
56. Muse — 355
57. Ruse — 366
58. Bound — 375
59. Insufferable — 398
60. Seed — 405
61. Game — 420
62. Venture — 426
63. Unite — 431
64. Sōrza — 438
65. Chosen — 449
66. Red — 454
67. Treasure — 467
Epilogue — 470

Salem

Salem
Witch House

Proctor's Ledge

House of

Enchantment

Grimsbane

Manor

Essex

Fishing Dock

Osbuvïa

Orsimm Cave

Varakane Grotto

Palace

Emorïa

Dr

Castle Fortress

Under

Larweïa

Desert

Dhetrïa

Ephlumeldegôr

Ondalôr

Obystrus

Realm

1

FREEFALL

SHIVALRI

"I will save you, and only you," I heard Pyre Malum, God of the Dead, rumble from a far-off distance. I could feel the heat sweltering all around me.

"Nor will die! I will die!" I sobbed, looking down at the doom that awaited me, clinging to the ledge of the fault of my own making. It was such a long fall. I could vividly imagine the feel of my stomach dropping into my chest at the freefall. The River of Pain beckoned my name.

"No, my goddess," Nor whispered. "You will finally live." I would not. There was no way to survive the fall. I knew that. Surely, I would die.

"What about you?" I asked, not really feeling the voice that came from my mouth. A warm prickling sensation touched my face. He had kissed my cheek. Nor had *kissed* my cheek.

"I am already lost," he whispered, and it echoed over and over again. "*Lost, lost, lost...*" pounded throughout my head. I clenched my eyes shut, pain throbbing in my brow bone.

"*Wake up, Goddess,*" a voice tried to sooth. All it did was add to the massive headache that staunched my breathing.

"Leave me alone," I murmured, unable to stop my lip from trembling. I felt a cold hand press against my back, and I shot up in an instant.

"Hey, you're fine," a familiar voice, much louder than before, declared. My eyes darted around me, not quite seeing my surroundings as clearly as I would like to. It was dark as I looked up into the trees that covered the entirety of the skies. The cold hand moved lower on my back as I tilted my head up, and I gasped, turning around, to find the God of Nightmares knelt behind me.

"What are you doing?" I choked, voice dry from ruinous, agonized screaming. His eyes widened, and he quickly removed his hand from my person.

"You were having a nightmare," he said. "I was just trying to help you."

"Help me?" I shook my head in confusion. Where was I? The forest behind the God of Nightmares was thick with fog. Pyre Malum, God of the Dead, had told me that nothing grew here in the Under Realm. Was this some sort of trick? There were bushes, warped and shady, covering the grounds. There was no end to the wooded area that caged me in. There was nothing more to see, but I was absolutely sure of the forest I saw. Was it possible that I had made it out of the castle? Was I finally back on Earth? "Where are we?"

"We are in the Forest of Lost Souls."

I crinkled my nose, a myriad of chaotic thoughts tumbling through my mind. I winced at the ache that came with the facial expression.

"The what?" I rubbed at the pain in my forehead. Clumps of dirt fell from my face, and I quickly realized that I must have been sleeping face-down on the ground. No wonder my face hurt. I lifted my other arm to dust the dirt from my hand, but soreness and something tethered to my arm stopped me from the movement.

"Careful." The God of Nightmares went rigid. "Your hand is fairly damaged, Goddess. I wrapped it in cloth and slung your arm out of harm's way."

"Oh," I mumbled, looking to my poorly wrapped arm. The crushing memory of Pyre's weighted foot atop my hand made my stomach curdle. My neck felt clammy beneath my hair as the recollection came rushing to me. Looking away from the bandage, I inhaled deeply, blinking away the hurt. My eyes were dry as deserts. Even if I wanted to cry, I didn't have it in me. "Thanks." I groaned, more to myself than to the bat-winged, creepy-eyed God who knelt behind me.

"My pleasure," he said, nodding at me. This was so strange. What had happened after my fall? Where was I? Why was I sleeping in the middle of a forest with the God of Nightmares?

"I'm sorry. What the hell is going on here?" I tried to stand, but my legs were too weak to push up from the ground.

"Steady, now." He reached out to hold me in place, and I flinched at the movement.

"Don't touch me," I spat. "I don't know you, and you don't know me, so keep your paws off." He blinked at me, then looked at his hands.

"I'm not sure what you're seeing, Goddess, but I can assure you, I do not have paws."

I rolled my eyes, a shock of pain following their movement through my skull. "Where are we?" I demanded. "Where have you taken me?"

He stood then and held out a hand for me to take. I didn't budge. He quirked a brow up at me, scoffing, and shook his head. "You are going to be a handful, aren't you?"

"Why won't you just give me an answer?" I growled in frustration. "Why am I in the middle of the woods with you?"

"To keep you safe, Goddess," he said, rubbing at his temples. His voice made it clear he was annoyed with me. I glared at him, pressing for additional information. "Nothing more."

"Am I back on Earth?" I asked, not wanting to show too much of my hand. I didn't know how much he already knew about me. I didn't want to give away exactly who I was if he didn't already know. He threw out his hands, gesturing to the forest around us.

"Afraid not."

"There are trees. We're in a forest," I stated, entirely confused by the situation.

"That is true," he supposed.

"I was told that nothing lives or grows in the Under Realm. If we're not on Earth, then where else could we be?"

"We're still in the Under Realm." He shrugged. It was the most infuriating gesture he could make.

"Why are you being so damn enigmatic? Just tell me where we are!" I boomed. The leaves around us rustled in the air.

"Keep your voice down," he hissed, crouching down to meet my level. "This forest is an illusion, created by my father to ward off the dead. The trees aren't real."

"Why do you need to ward off the dead? What could they possibly do?" He shook his head at me, grinning. "What's your problem? Why are you looking at me like I'm senseless?"

"You don't seem senseless, but you do ask a lot of questions."

"So, I've been told," I ground out, gritting my teeth. I wanted to cross my arms, but the sling prevented me from doing so. The God of Nightmares laughed at my expense, and I wanted to curl in on myself. Instead, I picked up a rock from the ground and hurled it at his gut. When the rock met with his chest, it bounced off quietly and rolled onto his lap. He glared at me with his black eyes.

"Interesting." I wanted to rip out my own hair.

"Stop looking at me like I'm a study and help me out here!" My patience was entirely lost to me.

"You're quite cute when you're angry." My eyes shot up to his. He grinned at me as he enjoyed my surprise. "Like a feral kitten."

"You're comparing me to a feral kitten?" Who was this guy and what was his problem?

"It only makes sense." He shrugged a shoulder.

"How?" I griped.

"It's none of your concern."

"What?" I scoffed. He was really starting to piss me off. I had just had the worst night of my entire life, woke up in the middle of a dark forest with the God of Nightmares, and this was what I was dealing with. "You are ridiculous."

"And you are fascinatingly irritated." At that, I finally mustered the strength to lift myself up off the ground. My bare feet screamed beneath the sharp pebbles and dirt. I'd gotten used to walking barefoot in the castle. The floors were smoother from having been worn down with use. This, a poor excuse of a getaway, was a quagmire. I blew out a frustrated breath and started walking away, ignoring the sting in my soles. "Oh, I don't think you'll want to go in that direction, Goddess." I turned on my heel, hair whipping across my face.

"And why is that?" I spat, eyes piercing through him like tiny knives.

"That way,"—he pointed behind me with his index—"leads toward the God of the Dead." I blanched as a memory of Pyre Malum's beautiful, terrifying face flashed through my mind. I shook off the chill and planted my feet in the dirt, one after the other, and passed behind the God of Nightmares.

"Fine," I muttered. "I'll go this way."

"Alone?" he hollered over his shoulder. "Without me?"

"Yes," I gritted out, continuing my stride.

"And just what will you do when you come across the forest's terrors?" My gait halted in place, eyes flying up to the tops of the trees. I saw nothing but leaves and branches. Still, I did not move. I could hear footsteps behind me, slowly making their way to meet me. "Frankly, I don't know who you are or what you're capable of, but no one makes it out of this particular forest unless they are of Orsimm blood." He came up beside me, and I finally turned to look at him.

"What are Orsimm?" I asked with little to no emotion. I felt so uninformed. So out of place.

"My father and his children. We are the creatures who personify dreams. This is our forest, created to shield our home from the wandering dead, and any rogues who might try to visit."

"You have siblings?" I wondered aloud, considering his words. "And a father?"

"Yes, I do."

"Who are they? What can they do?" My mind started spinning stories as I considered the possibilities. If he was Nightmare personified, then who were his family, and were they just as unnerving?

"Why don't you wait and ask them for yourself?" he suggested and started walking ahead of me.

"Wait, what?" I stumbled and started forward to follow him. "I'm going to meet them?"

"Yes."

"When?" I prodded. Excitement and fear washed over me

as I quickened my pace to match his. He was so tall that his long legs took one step for my two.

"Soon."

"How soon are we talking here?" I questioned, not wanting to be caught off guard by their presence.

"So many questions." What a senseless reply.

"Not enough answers," I held, and he tilted his head up to the skies.

"We are on our way to them," he snapped, "The less you question, the faster we'll get there. Now please, if you will, try to be quiet." Who was he to tell me to be quiet? I had every right to question where this god was taking me. I had already been taken against my will at a great cost. I was not eager to partake in another kidnapping. Though the God of Nightmares had managed to save me, there was no chance of my trusting him. No matter what, he was just another captor, and this forest felt like another form of prison.

"I thought you were going to help me escape the Under Realm." I observed him, trying my best to keep my alarm at bay. "Why are you taking me to meet your family?"

"Is that your final question for the hour?" My jaw dropped at his disrespect. He quirked a brow, jutting his pointed chin out. "Well?" I let an exasperated breath loose and blinked unhurriedly, struggling to reign in my frustration.

"Yes," I ground out. The god sneered, his wings stretching then folding behind him.

"I am taking you to my family because I don't know how to get you out of here on my own. We will take my father's council in attempt to plan your escape."

"What?" I hissed, curling my hands into fists, wincing at the pain in the one that was bandaged. "You mean to tell me you stole me away without a plan?"

"Ah, ah, ah." The god tsked. "No more questions."

"But—" He cut me off with a stare that told me not to push him further. "Fine." I settled. I wouldn't drop this entirely, but I would give him the silence he thought we needed. I would use this time to reflect on my situation.

As we walked through the woods, leaves crunching beneath our feet, I managed to keep my mouth shut in avoidance of truly aggravating this nightmare god. Though the banter between us felt almost familial, I knew better than to fully let my guard down. I had seen what he could do. I had looked into the bottomless blacks of his eyes.

When the God of Nightmares had spoken in my mind, pleading me to let go of the ledge I had been dangling from, I hadn't had much of a choice. I wish I could say that I had chosen to let go, but the truth of it is that I was a coward. My desperate begging stung my heart as I remembered my thoughts as I hung over the Ondalôr. I had wanted Pyre to save me. I hadn't wanted poor, sweet Nor to die. I would have never wanted that. But as I recalled clinging for dear life on the broken rocks of Pyre's castle floor, I remembered that *I* had not wanted to die. I was scarcely worried for anyone but myself. And that would eat away at me for the rest of my life.

When I had let go and fell into freefall, the shadowed tendrils had wrapped around me, slowing the descent. Before I could even blink, the God of Nightmares had caught me at the waist and flew us both up and out of the crater. The last thing I saw before flying out of the castle was Pyre's twisted face. Though Alriq's sword pierced him over and over again, his eyes never moved from mine, pain emanating from his gaze. He had called out to me, despair flooding his voice. And then he promised that he would find me again, just as I was lifted out of sight.

2

SURFACE

SATYRA

Darkness swept around me as the howling wind sounded from this way and that. I was weightless in the woods as I floated forward, eyes ensnared by the cloaked figures that trudged ahead of me. Where were they going so late in the night? Why was the High Council making their way toward the tree of my nightmares?

I looked down at my hands to find that they were not my own. Dark fingers curled around my cousin as I held her limp body to my chest—the chest that was, equally, not mine.

"Shivi?" I called to her, but she did not move. Panic swirled around me as I realized where I was and what I was doing in the woods. "Who are you?" I screamed, but no one heard me. No one ever seemed able to, as no one ever answered when I see-walked. When this person, the witch who showed me their sight, would enter my dreams at night, I was never able to see them, and they never once spoke to me.

I watched through the eyes of another as I made my way closer to the tallest tree I had ever seen. I remembered the eerie feel of my past see-walk well. The cloaked figures that huddle around the tree's trunk in the past were now clearly the same as the one's I was seeing in this moment. The past dream had been a bloodbath. Cloaked figures held on to the flesh of their fresh kills and drank their blood before sloshing it to the base of the tree—my cousin Shivalri's name the last thing spoken from their lips.

I was a fool for not having recognized the cloaks when my family had met with the High Council at the Salem House of Enchantment. It was so blatantly obvious. They were the ones who chanted Shivalri's name the last time I see-walked. They were our enemies, and I was watching them again, as a gift, or a curse, from whomever had been seeking me out. Voices buzzed around me as I found my focus again. I looked down to my arms to find that I was now standing empty-handed. Where had she gone? Despite how desperate I was to find Shivalri, my eyes would not move. I was only able to see what the see-walker allowed. He was looking at the crowd, filled with people of all shapes and shades. If I didn't know any better, I would think we were standing amongst creatures of another world. Then again, maybe we were, and the darkness of the night sky did not allow me a close enough look.

My head shifted to the giant tree now, and my heart sank in my chest. "Shivi!" I gasped as my eyes landed on my cousin, bloody and full of muck. She lay on the ground at the base of the tree, buried in the dirt, all but her head. Thick, perverse roots infolded her as she screamed bloody murder. The earth that covered her turned to ash, and the roots blistered and sparked around her wrists and feet. The sound of lightning struck, and I thought perhaps it came from Shivalri's screams. The tree, in all its might, cracked in half in tune with the thunderous sounds. A pit of fire burst through the bark, flinging pieces of wood and dirt at the cloaked figures that stood watching tentatively. The tree splintered and tore, and the fire made its way up and up until I couldn't see any further. Smoke and ash fluttered around the forest, and all I wanted to do was run to save my cousin from this vile nightmare. I tried to go to her, tried willing this body that didn't belong to me to move, even just an inch toward Shivalri. It did not.

Hands tipped in long, sharp claws burst through the trunk and tore their way forward—tore their way to her. My heart sunk through to my stomach, sickened by the scene. A strong armed figured emerged from the fissure in the tree, and my insides befell an acidic demise. Dark feathered wings lifted above the man's head, making me think the worst. He was *terrifying*. Terrifying didn't even begin to describe it. He looked like sin incarnate. My mind raced, and all I could do was watch him approach Shivalri, and bend to rip the roots from her exhausted frame.

"Get up," he boomed, voice carrying over to where I stood. "Get. Up," he repeated. The roots around Shivalri vanished into nothing. I watched as she pulled herself out of the dirt, and I wanted to cry. Her hands and feet were dripping wet with blood that could only be hers.

"Welcome, Redeemer," I heard Moira stammer. The winged man didn't answer her. He was too entranced by the weak-bodied form, who he held firmly in his grip. He looked at her like she was a meal he hadn't had in decades.

"Goddess, you have released me," he said, looking over Shivalri's face. A chill ran up my spine as all I could do was watch.

"We, the High Council, your children, have released you, oh, prevailing Redeemer," Moira boasted and knelt before him. The creatures that skittered around us instantly dropped to the ground. Some even lay their arms flat to the dirt in high respects. Suddenly, my body lurched forward, and I, too, knelt to the ground.

"No! Stop it!" I hissed at the body that moved me. "Let me see her!" I strained as hard as I could, but my head did not move to look up. "Why are you doing this? Help her, gods damn it!"

"I have been anticipating this evening for thousands of lifetimes," the winged man said, voice deep and unnatural. "I have great plans." The creatures surrounding us resounded in answer.

"We are here at your command," said Moira, still grounded on her knees and head bowed low just ahead of me.

"You bitch! You fucking bitch!" I shrieked. My head finally lifted higher, and my stomach spoiled as my eyes landed on the scene again.

"I do not require your service," answered the man, or *thing*, who held my best friend in his grasp.

"What?" Moira snapped, scurrying forward.

"You, Goddess," he boomed. His eyes burned red, outwardly enthralled by the woman he held in his arms. "I need you." Suddenly, he scooped her off her feet and up into his arms. Shivalri tried to push off of him, but nothing she did changed the man's grip on her. She tried, bless her heart, even when her head bobbed from side to side at the limitation in her body. Her head flew backward, and I thought her neck might snap from the force. Flame upon flame whooshed up and over her, and my breath hitched.

"Shivalri!" I called to her. Even if anyone could hear me, she would not. She was entirely engulfed by the flame she called forth.

"Impressive." Her captor growled, only holding her tighter in the fire. And then. Oh, *what the fuck?* My eyes must be failing me because I think I just saw him *lick* her face. He licked her face and the flames died out...

"No." She whimpered, looking around. Her eyes landed

on mine, and I so badly wanted her to see me for me instead of whoever's body I occupied.

"I am built of fire, Goddess. It does not impair me." The man seethed, licking his lips. "Cinnamon..." Shivalri shifted away from him at his words, but the man was stuck in place. Her movements did nothing to help her. In fact, I could almost see him pull her in closer. "My divine, mischievous goddess... You are going to bring me so much pleasure."

"Wait—" Moira started, but the creature she called Redeemer slammed a wall of fire into the ground around him and my cousin.

"No!" I screamed. "Please, do something! Help her, you bastard!"

"She is of no use to you!" Moira groveled. "She was meant to die. A sacrifice for you!"

"A gift," the man rumbled, flames brighter than ever. He turned around, Shivalri in his grasp, and faced the towering tree that splintered and blazed in the woods I stood in. He was going to take her away.

"Stop him! Don't you dare let him take her!" I begged.

"Don't hurt her!" I heard myself shout in a voice that did not belong to me.

"Don't!" Shivalri cried out. I wanted to go to her. I needed to save her, but my body would not move!

"Move! Please, fucking do something!" I screamed as I watched the winged man whisper something inaudible to Shivalri. He lifted them both over a hole in the ground that I hadn't noticed until now. I hadn't realized just what the break in the base of the tree was. It was a portal. And in this very moment, I was wholly certain that it led to *Hell*. Within an instant, the two of them fell into the hole, and the tree closed behind them.

"Show yourself, you coward!" I could feel the stinging in

my eyes, even though I couldn't produce the tears. The utter rage I felt toward this see-walking stranger consumed me. "You will answer me. You will tell me who you are, or so help me, I will find you myself and gut you like a fish!" I wanted to beat my own brains in from this folly. Whoever this was that walked me through this dread was the worst kind of person. They had known that this was going to happen. They had known and not done anything to prevent it. They did not move a muscle when my best friend stood helpless in the clutches of evil.

UNCOVER

SATYRA

Waking from the see-walk had my blood boiling. I was sweating from head to toe, but cold from the vision's bite. Why had they shown me this? Now I knew that they were a part of the scheme. I knew that they did not try to help my cousin. Worst of all, now I knew where she was, and I didn't know how to wrap my head around it. Shivalri Grimsbane was descended into Hell.

I ripped the blankets off my body and ran out my bedroom door without a second thought. From my doorway to Grams, I had but two seconds to come up with a way to explain what I had seen—What I knew.

"Satyra?" Gram called, not coming from her bedroom, but from the top of the staircase. Her eyes grew harsh as they landed on my face. Unable to mask my terror, she read me like an open book. "What's wrong?"

"It's…" I trembled and felt the quiver in my lip begin.

"What's going on?" Raidan asked, rubbing the sleep from his eyes as he emerged from the bathroom. He looked at me closely now, face blanching as he waited for an answer.

"What is it, my sweet?" Gram beckoned, still standing at the top of the stairs. Her hands gripped the railing, paling the knuckles that glinted in the morning light.

"I know where Shivalri is."

SHADOWS
SHIVALRI

"How much farther are we going to have to walk?" I asked, breaking the silence in which we were submersed. "I'm not sure about you, but I for one could use a break."

"You've just woken from a nap." My companion grumbled.

"I think there's a difference between being knocked unconscious and napping." I pointed.

"You weren't knocked unconscious. You simply slipped into it."

"Same difference," I mumbled under my breath. He chuckled at my reaction and heaved a long sigh.

"Unlikely," he mused.

"Seriously, how much longer is this going to take? My feet hurt." The god stopped us in our tracks.

"Shh." He pressed, eyes squinting at the trees around us.

"What is it?" I wondered, heart pounding in my chest. He threw a hand over my mouth, and I bit the inner part of his palm. He shook out his hand and glared. "Don't touch me," I spat, and he threw his hand over me again.

"Be quiet, Goddess. There's something here with us." I gulped under the weight of his covering. My eyes widened as I searched, trying to find the thing in question among the bushes. He released his hand from my mouth and quickly pulled out a blade the length of my forearm. Where the hell was I? A blade? What in the medieval times was happening? Ice prickled the back of my neck as I watched him step forward, ever polished. As he held the short sword in front of him, I could tell that he knew how to wield such a weapon. As he moved further away from me, the bat-like wings he bore between his shoulder blades covered my view of the sword.

"Where are you going?" I whispered loudly. He slowly turned his head around, lifted a finger to his lips, and shushed me. Before my eyes could register the dark, a black fog drifted up and over him, swallowing his entire body. "Where did you go?" I gasped, voice coming out much louder than before. The clouds of darkness swarmed the forest's expanse, and I could barely even see the trees. A faint glint of light shone several feet away from me, moving in a slicing motion. It was the blade, and the God of Nightmares was fighting something off.

"Be gone!" I heard him over the whistling of the wind. I surged forward, not thinking of what I might find beyond the fog and entered its cecity.

"Um, hello?" I called, unsure whether to speak or stay silent. A loud huff blew out in front of me, a heat following suit. I froze in place, unable to see the creature that stood before me. The dark fog seeping through the air whirled about, slowly unfolding before my eyes. The darkness became shadowed whisps. Piercing red eyes were staring down at me.

"Goddess, look out!" the God of Nightmares thundered,

hurling his sword toward the shadowy shape. The glinting blade flew, flipping over itself in a fast whipping of the air. Though it was made to blow the creature, the mark was missed, as the fog parted itself around the weapon—the weapon that was now coming for me. In the swiftest effort of my life, I dodged the blade just in time, hearing the *thwack* it made after landing in a tree that stood behind me.

"Are you trying to kill me now, too?" I squeaked, eyes finding the trunk. The God of Nightmares hurried for his sword, ripped it from its plunder, and aimed it back to where I stood. "Great. You *are* trying to kill me."

"Move," he commanded, but my feet would not budge. As I looked to where he pointed, the red eyes stared back.

"Hello." I squeaked, voice a little shaky. The shadows shifted, forming a more solid appearance. It was strange, the way it moved. Like smoke dancing on the wind. Who was this being that stood before me? Though the God of Nightmares had been trying to run it down, it had not made a move to strike either of us.

"Step away from the cauchemæra," the god warned. *Cauchemæra...* That sounded so like the French term for nightmare. Was it the god's doing? I was so confused.

"Are you doing this?" I asked, feet planted in the soil.

"I most certainly am not." He grunted. "This thing has come here without invitation." *Thing.* So, it was another being... But why was the God of Nightmares feeling so antsy? Though blackened smoke was never a welcome sign, I didn't feel like I was in danger.

"I don't think it means any harm," I stammered, never leaving my eyes from the shadows. As my words left my mouth, the blackness solidified into a hazy form I could recognize. What stood before me was not a human. It was not a person at all. "It's a horse." I looked to the God of Nightmares in confusion. He still held his weapon high, eager to use it against the creature. Why had he been so scared of a horse?

"Oh, no, no," he said, gritting his teeth. "Don't let that thing fool you. She is not good company to keep."

"She?" I wondered, involuntarily taking a step closer to the jet-black steed that stood before me.

"Nihility. She's a beast of prey. The Under Realm's cavalry."

"Well, no kidding," I scoffed. "She is a horse. We are in the Under Realm."

He rolled his eyes and scoffed in my direction. "That is not how things work." He blew. "The things I have to put up with..." he muttered and strutted forward, hand wrapped around the hilt of his sword. Seeing his marked desire to make use of his weaponry, I quickly stood my ground at the head of the horse. Her nose landed atop my head, as if telling me that she was on my side. "Don't let her touch you!"

"Leave her be," I demanded. "She's just a horse. She's not going to hurt me," I said, and lifted my head up to meet her muzzle. She lowered her head, and the warm heat of her fur brushed my cheek. I turned back to look at the God of Nightmares and found him utterly dumbstruck. "If you leave her be, she won't hurt you either. Trust me. I can feel evil, and that, she is not."

He shook his head at me in disbelief. "Nihility is a killer. Trust *me*. I would know."

"Well, she's not going to kill either of us," I assured him, turning my back to him to face the black horse. Her bright red eyes lowered in confirmation. It was almost as if she could understand me and my words. I held up a hand and she nuzzled it with her nose. "You're a sweetheart, aren't you?" I cooed, and she huffed in my palm. A small laugh left my lips and her eyes burst into flames. "Whoa!" I gasped, taking a step back. "What was that, girl?" Footsteps crunched behind as I held the horse's stare. The red in her eyes were made of fire. *Real* fire.

"I told you," the exasperated god hissed. "She's a horse of this inferno. The cauchemæra are terrorizers, made to show you your worst nightmare to keep you in place for their kill. I'd kindly advise you to step away from the horsey." I grimaced at his choice of words and whirled on him.

"The *horsey* is nice," I spat. "You on the other hand…" I trailed, looking him over. His short sword was still aloft in his right hand.

"How would you possibly know Nihility's true nature?" he threw at me.

"I can sense these kinds of things. Especially with animals." I shrugged, then pet the horse's muzzle again. "Call it intuition."

"Intuition, my ass…" he muttered.

"Oh, come on." I sighed heavily. "Just come see for yourself. She won't bite."

"Says she who bit me only moments ago."

I threw my hand on my hip and slouched in annoyance. "I warned you not to touch me." I tsked.

"Noted." He met up with me in front of the horse and gave her a once over. "This is strange." He held. I furrowed my brow at him, entirely confused by his revelation.

"What's strange?" I wondered, and he turned to look at me.

"What does it say of you that this creature of evil has taken a liking to you?"

I grimaced, feeling the weight of the past few weeks burry itself deep in my core. "It seems there are many evil creatures who are prone to liking me. Or so I thought…"

"As I said," he muttered. "Strange." At that, the horse in front of us lowered its head, her body following suit until she was lying on the ground. She whinnied up at me, and the God of Nightmares held up an arm to stop me. "Don't even think about it."

"I think she wants me to," I said, awe apparent in my voice. I moved past the arm in front of me and reached out a hand to stroke the horse's mane.

"It's not a good idea," he warned.

"Oh, would you relax?" I shooed him away, then gave the horse a good pat down her neck. "Hi, Nihility. It's nice to meet you," I said, smiling down at the horse. In a quick move, she spun her muzzle toward me, shoving me onto her back. "Nihility!" I giggled as I righted myself onto the horse. I had never ridden a horse before, and I wasn't quite sure how to hold on. As if hearing my thoughts, Nihility's shadows curled up around me, holding me in place. She was soft and warm, feeling like a nice, cozy blanket wrapped around my legs. Her muscles moved under me as she stood up from the ground, and in all but a few seconds, I was sitting six feet high in the air.

"Be careful," the god cautioned as I settled in my seat.

"I am!" I laughed, rolling my eyes at him.

"Not you." He sneered, looking at me with bewilderment. "The horse."

5

UMBRA
SHIVALRI

Nihility was calm as we walked through the Forest of Lost Souls. When the trees stirred and sounds flitted by, she didn't spend a moment of her time worrying. She was rather tranquil for the cavalry of the Under Realm. Though, of course, I had no idea what the temperament of this species of horse was expected to be, I could assume merely by examining the God of Nightmares' reaction to her. I thought it odd for a god to fear such a thing. Nihility hadn't shown an ounce of hostility toward us, even when the god had charged after her.

The God of Nightmares had been walking quietly alongside us, never once slowing down. When Nihility sped up into a trot, he kept pace. It almost seemed as though the horse was testing his limits. She appeared to find amusement in the way the god would start running to catch up to us when we got too far ahead. Though the walk hadn't been too long, he seemed to grow tired from the game of chase.

"Are you all right?" I asked, looking down at him. The top of his head was level with the tops of my thighs as he trudged beside me and the horse.

"Fine," he barked, looking away from me.

"You seem tired," I held, watching him trek alongside me. His bat-like wings were spread out behind him, the wind appearing to hold him back. "Can you fly?" I wondered aloud.

"You already know the answer to that."

"I mean right now. Couldn't you fly now?" I asked.

"I could, however, flying would make me travel faster than you. I'm keeping pace."

"So, you're tiring yourself out by slowing yourself down," I supposed. "You are tired, aren't you?" I watched him glower at my words.

"Of course, I'm tired. We've been walking all day. Rather, *I've* been walking all day." He huffed loudly.

"Are you sure you don't want to ride with me?" I prodded. "I'm pretty sure there's room. Nihility's a big, strong gal."

"I'm good on the ground," he answered, and it occurred to me then that I didn't know his name. I kept thinking of him as the God of Nightmares, though I remembered Pyre and Nor calling him something else when we were back at the castle. I called Nihility by her name, but I did not call this god by his.

"Hey, can I ask you something?"

He turned to look at me, eyes landing first on my legs, then up to my face. "More questions?" he mused, one eyebrow raised in query.

"I promise this one will be beneficial to the both of us." I smirked. "At least, I would think so." His brow furrowed as he considered this.

"What is your question?"

"Well, I was wondering if you might tell me your name?" I asked, suddenly feeling shy and looking down into my lap.

"I know the horse's name, yet I don't know what to call you."

"Oh." He stammered. "I didn't realize that you didn't know it." When he didn't answer, I looked at him to ask again. He looked at me now and gave a small smile. "I'm Ombrose." The name rang a bell in the form of Pyre's voice. Yes, that was what he had called his cousin.

"Ombrose," I repeated. "Cool."

"Cool?" he questioned. "What does that mean?" I looked at him in puzzlement.

"The word, or my using it?"

"Both."

"Cool means…nice. It's like saying that's neat," I offered, trying to find an explanation.

"Temperature, neatness, and my name have commonality…" He still looked ever the bit confused.

"You have a good name. I think it's a nice name. A *cool* name." He looked away from me then, and I stared at his profile. I found that his lip quirked into a slight smile.

"I knew what it meant," he answered, shaking his head. "I just wanted to make you say it."

I scoffed, feeling the heat rush to my face. Of course, he knew what it meant. In fact, I was beginning to notice that Ombrose seemed more familiar with Earth's present-day lingo than Pyre was. Perhaps, because he was the God of Nightmares, he'd learned through the night terrors he'd created for us all. Surely, he must hear the voices of those he sees within the nightmares. For the first time since learning of him, I pondered his existence and what his responsibilities might entail—what he might know. If he was the God of Nightmares, the implication meant that he had reach in all realms. I wondered what it might be like to experience other worlds without ever truly entering them.

THE AIR GREW COLDER AS we made our way further into the forest. I wrapped my left arm around my right in its sling and rubbed at the goose bumps that formed on my skin. It had been hours of journeying into this unknown territory with no end in sight. I was glad to have Nihility to ride and felt guilty as I watched Ombrose walk at our side. Though he had chosen not to climb on, I still felt bad that he had to walk this whole way. When the god stopped his sauntering, Nihility slowed and lowered to the ground.

"Whoa…" I stammered, looking for something to hold on to as the horse's body dipped us low. "What are you doing?"

"It's late," Ombrose replied off to the right of me. He removed his blade from its sheath and began cutting away at the shrubbery before him. "Time to set camp for the night."

I blanched at his words. I hadn't thought for one second that we would be stopping tonight. Surely not in the middle of the woods, surrounded by the creatures of the Under Realm. Though we hadn't come face-to-face with any monsters, their scurrying through the nearby trees had been all I needed to stay on the path and clear from the darkened areas of the forest. Recollecting the nightmare that I'd had at the castle had my stomach in knots. The feel of a snake slithering down my throat as claws ripped at my skin. I shivered, my goose bumps increasing. As quickly as the eerie chill had come, it evolved into a new sensation—one that heated the core of me. The intense memory of Pyre, consoling me as I sobbed in his embrace had my heart thumping in irregular repetitions. The way he'd lain beside me, a single finger rubbing the curve of my side in comfort.

I shook my head, forcing the thoughts from my mind. I turned my attention back to the present. Ombrose now collected the wood he'd cut in his arms.

"Won't a fire attract unwanted company?" I asked as he placed a pile of sticks in the middle of the trail we'd been walking.

"Most creatures are afraid of fire," he told me, stacking the branches into a messy version of a pyramid. Nihility eased her shadowy hold on me, and I hopped off her back. The muscles in my glutes burned at the change in my body's demand to hold me upright. I sluggishly walked to Ombrose, who now trailed his fingers through the rocky path.

"Looking for treasure?" I tested, then winced at the flash of my brother's face in my memory. I remembered him searching his head for a trace of his scar and telling me he struck gold. Oh, Gods… My brother. My family. What was I doing out here in the woods when my family could be hurt? When it was entirely possible that they were dead because of me. If I hadn't have ripped a hole in the veil, none of this would have happened. *Damned Fates.*

"Are you all right?" I heard Ombrose ask from afar. I shook the thoughts from my head, yet again trying to focus on the here and now. I buried the guilt and melancholy as far back as humanly possible, and gave Ombrose a small shrug.

"Just cold," I said, looking away.

"You'll be warm in just a moment," he promised. "Just as soon as I get this fire started." He stood from his crouch and extended his hand to show me the rock he'd lifted from the rubble. I said nothing as I watched him make his way to the pile of sticks. I knew that I could help him make the fire. I knew that it would take but an angry thought in its direction and flame would burst from the bark. But for some reason, deep down in my gut, it didn't feel safe to reveal this power of mine. I didn't want him to know who I was. He didn't need to know what my destiny foretold. I didn't need yet another god trying to use me to their advantage. So, I watched as the God of Nightmares tried to build us a fire.

Pulling his blade up over his head, he grabbed at a lock of dark brown hair and sliced a piece off.

"What are you doing?" I gasped, looking to find the patch of missing hair on his head.

"I needed a starter," he told me as he folded the hair around the rock he held. Holding his sword by the blade, he tightly gripped both objects and threw the sharp force into the rock. A small spark flew and sputtered out as he hit the stone repeatedly with his weapon.

Over and over, he smashed blade with rock. Barely any real heat made its way from stone to starter. Minutes had gone by, and nothing had come from his efforts. With the cold of the night biting at my toes, and the frustration emanating from Ombrose's stance, the need to speed things up tugged at me. If I could just call upon the smallest of flames without him noticing, we could be warm within seconds of my workings.

Cautiously, I concentrated on the sharp edge of the rock that lay in Ombrose's hand. If I could time things right and send a spark to the hair that wrapped around the stone just as the blade hit it, I could get away with using my power unnoticed. I took a deep breath, eyes strictly focused on the starter, and when he made to swing again, I blew out the breath, and with it, fire.

"I did it!" he boasted, and Nihility whinnied just behind me. I giggled and allowed myself to rest as I sat cross-legged near the pile of sticks. Ombrose blew on the smoking hair and slowly lowered it to the stack in front of me. "I was beginning to think it would never work." He huffed.

"Me too." I laughed, and Nihility came up from her spot to find me. She lowered herself behind me and nestled her side into my back. "Thanks, Lity," I said softly, stroking her fur. With her warmth seeping in, I was happy to be near her, and sank into her comfort. Ombrose took a seat opposite to me and rubbed his hands over the growing flames between us. I stuck my feet out toward the pit and wiggled my toes in the heat. When I looked past the flames, Ombrose's eyes were roaming over me. When he caught my gaze, he shook his head and cleared his throat.

"Are you warm?" he asked, examining the fire he'd proudly started.

"Yes, thank you," I answered. His shoulders shivered and he grimaced. "But you're not," I held. "Come sit next to Nihility. She's very warm."

"No, thank you," he replied. I scoffed at his unwillingness to get over his fear of the horse.

"Come," I demanded. "She won't bite; I won't bite. You'll be perfectly safe." When he didn't move, I sighed heavily. "And you'll be warm and won't freeze to death." He shot me a look of incredulity and finally gave in to my offer. He sauntered over to us, cautiously approaching the mare, and sat a couple feet away from me.

"There," he muttered. "Happy?" I shook my head at him. How immovable was he?

"Lay back," I insisted, and surprisingly, he listened to my instruction. I watched the tension in his shoulders ease as his wings made contact with Nihility's soft fur. "Happy?" I retorted his same question. He closed his eyes and smirked.

"You are very stubborn," he decided, eyes still closed and facing forward as he settled into the horse.

"That isn't news to me." I watched the grin grow on his face. It was subtle, but I saw it flicker from grimace and back to grin.

A muscle ticked in his jaw before he said, "You're staring at me." I quickly turned my head from him, suddenly very interested in the flames ahead of us. "You didn't have to look away," he added, somehow aware of the things my eyes were doing. My skin heated from the slight embarrassment, but I shrugged it off quickly.

"How do you know what I'm looking at?" I questioned, gaze still fixed on the fire.

"I didn't." He shrugged, a smugness in his voice trilled past me. "But you just admitted to it." I picked up a small rock and chucked it at him, aiming for his knee, and striking true.

"Ow." He groaned and moved a hand to rub at his leg. It was my turn to smirk now as I watched the god's childlike behavior. He gave me an unappreciative scowl and threw the rock from his pantleg into the woods.

"Baby," I muttered under my breath. The daunting look he gave me confirmed that he'd heard my insult.

"This is how you treat the one responsible for saving you?" he interrogated me, lifting a brow in question.

My stomach turned at the recollection of the events. Memories swirled into muddied images across my mind, and I wished desperately to grab them and rip them apart. I wanted to shake them out and make things clear. I wanted to know so much of what I didn't, and it troubled me to think about it.

"Did you?" I asked, trying to pick up the pieces of my strange abductions. "Save me, I mean. Am I safe?"

"Go to sleep, Goddess. We have a long day ahead of us."

6

STARLIGHT

SHIVALRI

Pyre Malum's face appeared to me in my dreams, his form wavering, almost a liquid haze. I knew this was a dream, my mind lucid as I walked toward the God of the Dead. I knew that nothing could truly happen in here, and that I was within my mind's limitations. Though I knew that none of this was real, it felt achingly tangible as I stood in front of him. We were almost chest to chest, barely any space between us as I tilted my head up to look him in the eyes. I wasn't afraid to do so. I knew that this was a dream. I could do anything in here, and it would be of no consequence.

"Your eyes..." I whispered, mirroring a true memory from within the castle's walls. My hand inexplicably lifted to his face, and I found that this time around, I wasn't frightened by it. I wanted to explore, needing to feel for proof that he was real. To prove that when he looked at me, he, in fact, had the most beautiful eyes to ever exist. Eagerly, my fingertips landed just above his cheekbone, and he hitched a breath at my touch. The pigment of gold that swam in his irises seemed to brighten at my action. Every bit of his presence was captivating, the dream wildly vivid as he stared back at me.

"*Your* eyes," he murmured, voice guttural and cracked at the end of his speech. "So very blue," he spoke, searching my gaze. "With a ring of gold." My mind twisted and bent, this way and that, forcing me to look down at my hands. It was raining now, the shoes on my feet were drenched in a puddle. The gold ring of my eyes drifted out from its place in my face, hovering in the air, until it drifted onto my finger, turning into my mother's band I'd been wearing. It shone brightly, as if coming alive on my very finger. The shine was becoming too much, blinding me as if it were made of the sun in the skies above. My finger began to heat, and through crying, burning eyes, I watched as the skin on my hand melted away, revealing ebony bones. I tried to scream, but there was nothing in me to give. I tugged at the ring, ignoring the pain as it seared through my fingertips. Finally, removing it from its killer grip, I threw it as far as I could. As I heard the plunk, I watched it bounce atop a black casket that lay just beside a muddied hole in the ground.

"Daughter..." a nasty, hallowed version of my mother's voice drifted through the rain and slapped me in my chest. The coffin slowly creaked, the door lifting open and revealing the rotten corpse that was my mother. I couldn't move. I couldn't look away. I could only stand there and watch as my mother's head twisted around on itself, bone snapping and crackling under the unnatural forcing of movement. "How does it feel to know you've killed me?"

"No!" I screamed, my tongue tasting of blood.

"*Wake, Goddess...*" My eyelids stretched and pulled, begging to be unglued from the horror playing behind my eyes. My mother's corpse still hung in the back of my mind, but I was slowly drifting up into the stars. As I got closer and closer to the clouds up above, I couldn't keep my eyes off the ground. I watched as the casket grew smaller until finally, it disappeared from sight. *"Open your eyes, Goddess,"* I heard the voice say, purer now more than it ever had been during my night terrors. I surged forward, eyes widening as I sucked in a deep, clearing breath. I still had the shakes as I came back to consciousness, Ombrose hovering over me like a nervous animal, unsure of what to do with me.

"I'm awake." I shivered, bitterly swallowing the fear and humiliation.

"Are you okay?" he asked, deeming it safe to sit back down beside me. I was still sitting against Nihility, having passed out with my back and head resting on her belly.

"I'm fine." I groaned, rubbing the sleep and weariness from my face. Regarding him carefully, begrudgingly, I asked, "Why did you do that?"

"Do what?" he questioned, visibly confused.

"Why did you give me that nightmare?" I questioned, groggily scrutinizing him.

"Oh," he flinched, frowning. He seemed ill-prepared for the question. "I didn't do it on purpose… It's not something I control. It's something the sleeper falls into."

"Bull."

"What?"

"I know you were in there with me," I stated, accusingly. "I can hear you talking to me. I've heard you talking to me in my nightmares for a long time now." It was weird to voice this out loud. It was the strangest thing to come across, but I knew it the moment I'd slipped into unconsciousness earlier this morning. The soothing voice I'd heard for months now had always belonged to him. He was the God of Nightmares. He was the reason I could barely sleep.

"I—" he faltered, and my eyes burned into him as I willed him to offer the truth. "I don't know where to begin…"

"How did you find me?" I pushed, asking the most important question I'd had for him. So much had happened between being retrieved, landing unconscious, finding Nihility and getting to this moment. I'd asked as many questions as I could during our journey in the Forest of Lost Souls, but he'd been entirely avoidant of giving me proper answers. Now, having established my knowledge of his meddling, he'd have nowhere to escape my interrogation.

"That's a loaded question." He blew, leaning into the horse. "With many complicated answers."

"Spill it," I demanded. I was oddly composed as I sat beside him, challenging a god from the Under Realm.

"I'm not sure how, but I think we have a connection." I stilled at this. I hadn't expected anything of the sort to fall from his lips.

"I'm sorry. What?"

"You could hear me? Truly hear me speaking to you?" he asked, turning his body to face mine.

"Yes. Didn't you hear me?" I wondered, now considering whether it was a two-way connection or just one.

"I did." He nodded. "Every time you started to scream, I heard your plea." Swiftly mortified by my cowardice, I looked away from his study. "You never seem able to wake yourself from your terrors." I considered his words cautiously. That wasn't entirely true. Before the worst could be done to me, I'd always woken.

"I do, though… You always change my dream at the end."

"Normally, that's not something that I can achieve," he admitted. "When I visit the nightmares of mortals, I can do nothing but watch and coax them into fighting their fears. I think the difference with you is that, well, you're not entirely mortal, are you?" he questioned me.

"Recent events would prove otherwise..." I grumbled, considering what this could mean for me and the God of Nightmares. Was this a good thing, this connection we shared, or yet another strange curse I'd have to face in the forthcoming future?

"I believe that your cries call out to me. Somehow, I hear you. All I have to do is listen to your voice, and I'm instantly transported into your world of purgatory."

"How do you take me into the skies?" I wondered, remembering the stars that glowed around me, melting away the heat of fright.

"I don't know..." he supposed, confusion wearing out his lips. "I watch you, speak to you. When the nightmares become too much, I turn to sooth you in whichever way I can. It's something that has never once worked for me. I can't give good dreams, only nightmares. But you heard me. You responded to my voice. I think your willingness to connect with me tied us together, allowing me to show you whatever I wished to display." I held on to his mention of our connection, storing it safely as a possible lead to the enigma of my being, then considered the display he'd always shared.

"Why the stars?" I asked, trying to get an understanding of this god.

"All I could do was show you my favorite memories from a time when the world was whole. I showed you the moon and all of its stars." I watched as he tilted his head up to the night skies and frowned deeply. There were no stars here in the Under Realm. No moon, no genuine light. Nothing but the fire for guidance. Ombrose let his head fall down, his chin lowered along with his eyes. I thought I read a bit of sadness in his gesture, and I couldn't blame him. The stars on Earth were a beautiful thing to witness. To live in a realm without their light was a sin. I cleared my throat, and it made him turn his gaze to me.

"I hadn't had a nightmare in quite some time. Before a few days ago, my mind hadn't slipped into any." I paused, searching his eyes. "Where did you go?"

He sighed a long, heavy breath, and I could tell it was full of details I didn't have. "In search to find you."

"Really?" I prodded. "I know you say that the answers are complicated, but I need to know. How did you find me?"

"Through a nightmare." He spoke as if this were answer enough.

"Explain."

"It was the nightmare in which you were being beaten. I felt it… Your soul. It was as if the minute you'd entered the Under Realm, the connection between us was stronger, more alert. I knew you were here, and I knew that you were dreaming of being tortured here. When you couldn't show me the face of your torturer, couldn't tell me his name, I knew I had to do everything to find you again. I tried sorting through nightmares, searching for a connection here in the Under Realm, but I couldn't find you. No matter how hard I tried, I couldn't find your soul."

"Why not?" I wondered. "Why did it take so long? That nightmare was during my first night at the castle. I've been here for weeks."

"I know." He blew. "And I'm sorry for it, but I didn't have the tools to find you. Frankly, I assumed you were deceased, and so I searched almost all the grounds for your soul. No matter where I looked, you weren't there. Ultimately, I became impatient and gave you one last nightmare. That's when you showed me the castle's throne room. I immediately left the nightmare and flew to find you." My mind scratched and clawed at the words he spoke, and I realized Ombrose had made an error. He *gave* me a nightmare... He'd just finished telling me that nightmares were not given, but slipped into by the sleeper. So, which was it? I assumed position, pretending not to have heard his blunder and concentrated on the rest of his speech. "My shadows found you through the arrow slit. I couldn't reach you."

"Hmm..." I hummed, studying his words with heavier attention. "What happened with the pythrants?"

"Oh, yes," he acknowledged. "The one that... Well, the one that jumped onto your back during the fight found me outside. He'd smelled my magic, apparently on guard at your door. He told me that you were good and didn't belong in the Under Realm. That was something we'd both agreed on, and he made the decision to work with me to aid in your escape." A well of tears filled my lashes as I blinked the sadness away. I'd only had a few weeks to know Nor, but still, I grieved over the life he'd lost. I wondered now, if he was among the dead in the Under Realm, and if perhaps I could one day see him again. I wasn't sure how it worked for creatures such as the pythrants, but I desperately hoped he'd found peace in death.

"Nor was good," I replied, hiding the tremble in my lip.

"He died so you could live," said Ombrose, watching me carefully. My breath hitched, and I curled away from him, turning into Nihility for comfort. "Rest well, Goddess," Ombrose whispered. "And dream of the stars."

7

CYPRESS

SHIVALRI

When I woke from the sound of wings flapping, cool air flowed over my face, my hair stirring. I had had a rather restful night's sleep, and my muscles and bones were thankful just as much as my mind was. Nihility's weight shifted around me as the sleep evaded me, and I turned to follow the heat of her body. Just a few more moments in the sweet comfort would feel like bliss. Aside from the one night I'd slept at Pyre's side, I hadn't felt anything like this kind of comfort in the Under Realm. I hadn't had this warmth in ages, and I wanted to relish in the moment, but the horse started moving away from me. I flung out my good arm and clung to the muscle of her leg, begging her to stay close. She stiffened under my touch, and I wondered if perhaps I had grabbed her too tightly. A hand gently folded over mine, and when it pulled me from the grasp, I froze in place. When I finally opened my eyes, a wave of embarrassment took over my entire body. There I lay, arm outstretched over Ombrose's legs, head tucked into his lap. My back had been warmed by his chest, and it was him that lay on the horse for support.

"Oh, my gods!" I gasped, trying to pull myself up. My arm wrapped in sling made for an awkward lift as I pushed myself up using Ombrose's thigh to push off. He grabbed at my shoulders and hoisted me upright, seating me next to him. He gave me a wide grin and rubbed at the back of his neck. He almost looked discomfited, but the smugness in the grin told me it was not his first emotion.

"When you said no touching, I didn't realize that it only applied to *me* touching *you*."

I scoffed and punched at his shoulder. "I'm sorry, okay?" I heaved a deep sigh. "I can't control what I do in my sleep."

"Excuses, excuses," he chimed, and I made to give him another punch. "Okay, Bobcat. Enough with the fists. Let's take a look at that other arm of yours, shall we?" I frowned at him, feeling both mortified, useless, and a little peeved that he'd called me a cat—again. *What the hell was that?*

"Be my guest."

Ombrose took care not to tug at the wrap around my arm and hand too hard, and I was happy to find that my hand didn't hurt as badly as it had when Pyre had crushed its bones. I understood that in the Under Realm, I was immortal, and my body worked very differently. I did not need to eat, I did not need to sleep as much as I used to, and my body was able to heal much faster than that of a typical human. Though my rheumatoid arthritis hadn't escaped me, the injuries I'd received during my time in this inferno were incredibly quick to heal. Scratches and cuts took only minutes to mend, bruises could last up to a day, but I wasn't sure about how my bones would react.

"Your hand is mostly restored," said Ombrose as he examined the hand in question. When he removed the bandage from my fingers and palm, dried bits of blood lifted away with it, allowing the fresh air to cool my skin.

"It feels good," I reported, and flexed my fingers. They were slow to move, and I could feel the swelling bubbling in my joints. But aside from the slight discomfort, my hand was back in working order.

"Would you like to keep the sling on?" he asked, pulling at the material to move it back into position.

"No, that's okay." I shrugged. "It's just my hand that's hurt. I don't think I ever needed the sling."

"You don't remember?" he questioned, looking at me with furrowed brows. His dark eyes studied my face as he removed the material from my arm. I, too, was confused.

"Remember what?"

"Your rather entertaining landing?" he said.

"My what?" I hadn't the faintest clue what he was talking about. I tried picking up the pieces of my memory from the night of my escape from the castle, but my mind was drawing a blank. "I don't know what you're talking about, Ombrose." I crossed my arms over my chest, waiting for some kind of explanation. He laughed lowly and shoved a hand in his pocket.

"When I tried to land us safely after our escape, you insisted on flailing yours arms this way and that until I lost my grip on you." My stomach dropped. I had no recollection of this. "You fell from the skies at an alarming rate and fatal height. When I made it to the ground, you were lying in the woods, your arm bent unnaturally underneath you, and you were entirely unconscious. That is, until you started reliving the battle in your nightmare and woke in a frenzy." He looked at me for a reply, but I was utterly shocked at this revelation. How could this have happened to me, and I not remember it? Was I concussed? At this point, anything was possible, and I wasn't surprised that I had survived the fall. If falling into the oubliette taught me anything, it was that my body could recover quite miraculously from such things. "You truly do not remember?" He blew, and folded the old material of the makeshift sling, shoving it into his pocket.

"It must have been quite the fall," I supposed, and got up from the ground. Ombrose followed suit and began walking down the path, just as we had the other day. I opted to attempt boarding the beautiful black horse, and she willingly obliged my request.

"Where are we, Ombrose?" I asked as we neared the edge of the forest. There was a small clearing just ahead of us, and Nihility and Ombrose both seemed set to go there. Was this where we were headed all along? Where did it lead to? He hadn't exactly answered me the night before when I had asked where I was, aside from telling me that I was not back on Earth.

"We're walking alongside River Osbuvïa." *That's strange… I haven't seen any water while traveling.*

"Where is it?" I wondered aloud.

"It's adjacent to this wooden trail we've been following," he told me.

"Are we going to go to the river?"

"Oh, absolutely not," he asserted, turning to meet my gaze. His jet-black eyes were stern, and the ring of light blue was cold as ice.

"Why not?" I asked, looking away from him. It was hard to look past the strange eyes he bore. I didn't want to stare and make my curiosity apparent.

"Osbuvïa is the river of oblivion. If but a drop of its waters set root in your mouth, you would forget your entire existence." My eyes widened at the notion of such a horrific possibility.

"Why would that even exist?" I blew. "That's awful!" He

shook his head, grimacing at his feet as we continued our walk.

"You'd have to ask its maker," he supposed. I wondered about that, too, now, as I considered the mind that might have created such a river.

"If it's as dangerous as you say, I'd rather not discuss its creation with its maker," I held, pondering how that conversation might take place. "Hey, Ombrose?" I called, pulling his attention from the ground he glowered at.

"Yes, Goddess?"

"My—" I stopped myself from speaking the name that sat on my tongue. I wanted to correct him and insist he call me Shivalri, but sharing my name might mean more than simple comradery, and I wasn't sure if I should test it. Instead of correcting the title he used, I cleared my throat and decided I'd better not. "I was just wondering," I stammered as he looked to me with a cocked brow.

"Wondering what?" he pushed.

"Why are we anywhere near Osbuvïa? Wouldn't you want to steer clear?" I questioned. "I don't necessarily feel comfortable knowing it's so close by." He threw me a courteous smile and pointed ahead of us now.

"Osbuvïa borders my and my family's territory. We follow the river, and we will never be lost." I nodded, understanding. It was helpful to know this, and I was glad he so freely told me. I was happy to learn of the Under Realm's terrain, trails, and traps. It was not a bad idea to have this information in case of emergency. In case I might need to flee from this god too. "See that?" he asked, pulling me from thought. When I focused on the tree line again, I started to see more clearly. I had been trying to see farther to decipher our destination since the moment the clearing appeared through the tree trunks ahead. Now I could see the empty field more prominently, noting the giant tree that stood alone in the center.

"I do," I answered.

"That is our sign that we've made it to my home. Once we pass that giant cypress tree you see in the middle of the field, we'll have almost arrived."

"Almost?" I grunted, feeling my tired muscles ache in displeasure. He chuckled deeply at my complaint, and I scoffed at his ridicule. "Hey, my butt hurts!" I ranted. "Nihility is beautiful, but man is she ever sturdy."

"Would you prefer to walk?" He smirked up at me. I shook my head fervently. I absolutely did not. My knees would beg me to end them. I patted the mare's neck in gratitude, and she tilted her head up in pleasure.

"I am happy and thankful for the horse." She snorted in response.

8

PERIL

SATYRA

"Hell?" Raidan boomed, looking livid as ever. Gram looked like she'd seen a ghost, and I, stuck with the task of delivering this information, felt weak in the gut.

"That's what I saw, Cuz," I answered, voice weedy from having recounted the see-walk I'd experienced overnight. Gram had guided us into the secret sanctuary far faster than I'd ever seen her walk. I had tried telling them of my dream while we were still upstairs in the hallway, but she insisted that we make our way down to the basement so as not to have spies overhear. I had always thought her silly for being overly cautious of these kinds of things. After having discovered that we were a family of witches, I didn't have to question any further. When we were drugged and Shivalri was taken from us, I learned that Gram had been keen in being guarded.

"Are you sure?" asked Gram, pulling me back to the conversation at hand. "Was there any sign that this might have been a foretelling, rather than a see-walk? Are you sure you were being shown a moment that has already happened?" I swallowed hard and nodded in her direction, which elicited a tight whimper out of her. I thought that seeing my grand-mother like this, white as a sheet in her old, worn robe was the saddest thing to ever witness. I shrank back from that thought, replacing the title winner with Shivalri being dragged into Hell by that monstrous creature. I couldn't shake the image of him. He was huge, larger than anyone I'd ever seen. He had claws wrapped around my cousin's body, sharp and deadly. His black feathered wings made me want to recoil in my seat, but the worse thing of it all was his piercing red eyes. I thought perhaps his gaze had afforded the misfortune of looking straight into Hell. It was more than a sinking feeling that Shivalri had gone into Hell. I *knew* it. I saw it with my own eyes. She had not gone through just any portal. My cousin, by the High Council's hand, was on a different plane. Whether dead or alive, I wasn't entirely sure.

"There's no way that this is possible!" Raidan blew. "She's my sister..." His voice cracked, and he sniffed hard to avoid more tears. "It had to be a dream. It's not real, Saty. It can't be." He looked to me with red-rimmed eyes, and I wanted to shrink under his regard. I tore my eyes from his and fiddled with the string of my sweater. Though I hadn't caused it, it felt like a burden to deliver the details of the scene.

"I'm sorry, Rai..." I whispered. "I wish it weren't true, and I really wish I hadn't seen it..." I looked back up to him now, trying to convey the guilt I was feeling too. He was not alone in feeling this hopelessness. This damnable peril. "She's my best friend. You don't understand... She couldn't see me, but *I saw her*. I saw every bit of her anguish and felt every ounce of terror, and I didn't help her."

"Why didn't you stop it?" Raidan hissed, face reddening. I knew that I didn't have to explain myself. He understood why. He knew that I wasn't really there and that I couldn't have done anything to save her. But she was his sister, and he was her protector through life. He wasn't upset with me for not having done anything; rather, he was tormented for not having been able to help her himself.

"She could not have done anything, dear," Gram spoke softly. She was still so pale. She had been so silent during my retelling that I had nearly forgotten she knew how to speak. "You understand this, don't you?" She redirected to me. "You could not have done anything, Satyra. You must accept this." My breath shuddered in my chest, unable to keep steady through the mess.

"Why?" Raidan muttered, more to himself than me and Gram. "Why my sister?" He traced a line down the dusty book that Shivalri had compelled, then opened it to the pages we had learned of during our familial discovery. When Shivalri had called her book to her here in the Grimsbane sanctuary, Gram had been so terrified. Raidan and I both kept mostly quiet during the reveal of Shivalri's prophecy. I had felt a tinge of jealousy at her importance. My cousin was always quiet with her nose in her books. She was never one to venture out into the world. She even had a fear of driving, let alone traveling. I was the one who wanted adventure. I craved magic and journeying more than anyone I had ever known. Yet she was gifted all five elemental powers, and she was the chosen one written in this old tome that we looked through now.

"Could there be anything in here that might help us get her back, Gram?" I asked as I watched Raidan and her reread Shivalri's fate. Gram's eyes crinkled as she focused on the riddled text.

"If there were answers in here, I think I'd have found them by now," she replied, voice dim. "I've known about this prophecy for the entirety of my witch-hood. All who practice magic know about this prophecy, and yet none of us have ever known the answers."

"That can't be the end of this." Raidan huffed. "There's got to be a way. There has to be something you've been missing."

"What about your other books?" I wondered, looking around to the bookshelves that lined the cavern walls. "Are there any other clues in the rest of your stuff?"

"No, perhaps not my ancestral volumes, but it is possible that there would be more information elsewhere..." she trailed, face grim. It clicked in my head then, what she was referring to. I felt the pattering of my heart as I came to understand where we would be heading.

"We're going back, aren't we?" I hesitated. Though I was always up for adventure, this was not the kind of entertainment I was looking for.

"Oh, no we're not," Raidan held, his fingers curling into a fist over Shivalri's book.

"It is the only place I can think of that might give us a clue. It might be all that stands between us and saving your sister."

"If we go back there, we could get killed," he hissed back at Gram. But that was not what I feared most.

"Or worse," I added, limbs going numb.

"What could be worse than that?" Raidan snapped.

"We could end up like Shivi."

9

INTRUDER

SATYRA

W inter Solstice announced itself loud and proud this morning as I opened the curtains in my room. Looking out the bedroom window to find wet, packed snow lining the lower roof hadn't been much of a surprise. It was December twenty-first now, Yule, and the cold had been prominent in the last couple of weeks. It was strange to think that Christmas was just around the corner. Ever weirder that Shivalri's birthday was coming up, and we were expected to ring in the new year without her.

Exactly fifty-one days have gone by since my cousin was captured and taken. Gram has been searching high and low for signs of Shivalri's location, asking spirits from the other side for aid. She had told me to keep an eye open for any visions I might receive in see-walks. It was unfortunate to find that when Shivi left us, the see-walks were no longer given to me, and I was entirely useless. Until, that is, I saw her the night before, being abducted by a black-winged creature from Hell.

When Shivalri left, the world seemed to darken further than before. Though she had been the cause of the most eerie-looking sky known on Earth, unnatural in its red hue, it was not her only magic trick. When the world started shifting into constant storms and decline, we knew that it was Shivalri's doing. When the windstorms rose, breaking trees and houses all over the country, I was sure that it came from my cousin's manifestations. As we listened to the news for more signs of Shivalri's vengeance, we quickly learned that her powers were getting stronger, and she wasn't reigning in whatsoever. Rivers overflowed, some places turned to drought, and the earthquakes delivered had done some significant damage to the planet. It was terrifying to think she held so much power in her. Moreover, it horrified me to my core that she did not have a handle on it. Had it been me, I would've surely found a way to protect Earth, rather than destroy it. Then again, if I were the one trapped in the Hell, I can't say how I might react.

When I tried to think about Shivalri being held in that other world, I was never quite able to picture her there. Not only was I unable to imagine what Hell might look like, I was unable to determine whether or not she was all right. I thought that maybe the storms up here were a sign that she was alive and well, angry in her cage. A small part of me wondered if she was dead, and if this was the world's way of telling me that she was gone. She had been selected to protect and rule over the Gates of the three realms. If she was gone, who else was left to do the job? Would the prophecy rewrite itself and choose another? Would the original Triple Goddess have to go back to being in charge as she was all this time? I never understood why the Triple Goddess would ever want to give up such a position. It seemed to me that it would be quite the feat, and something to be proud of.

When I made my way down the stairs after getting

dressed for the day, I was surprised to find Raidan standing stiffly, back barricading the front door.

"What's going on?" I asked, just as Gram came out from the foyer adjacent to the entrance. "Gram?" I questioned, following her with my eyes. She looked to be angry, hands out in front of her in an unyielding point.

"Step away from the door. I will deal with this rubbish," she spat and moved Raidan out from the doorway.

"Who's at the door?" My heart stopped dead from shock.

"It's that asshole from the council," Raidan ground out, baring his teeth.

"What?" I gasped, eyes flying to the long, thin window that lined the right of the door frame.

"Please," a voice called from outside. "Just let me explain."

10

HIDDEN

SHIVALRI

"Once we pass the cypress, not even the Ruler of the Under Realm will be able to find you," Ombrose told me, voice hushed in the open field we'd entered. "The cave just ahead conceals all odors and all light." He pointed, gesturing to the abysmal opening in the mountain ahead. As he slowed his steps, I dismounted the horse I'd grown fond of to stretch out my legs. A lot of the journey we'd made hadn't been clear in the logistics of things. I didn't understand how Pyre Malum, God of the Dead, wouldn't know where we are. If I knew him like I thought I might, I was under the impression that he was sure to find me like he had promised, and that our location was compromised all throughout the escape. Not only had I kept my eyes on the trees for the creatures Ombrose swore were terrible encounters, but I was also incredibly engrossed by the sounds around us, waiting to hear the flapping of large, feathered wings. Every time I heard the tiny flutters of what sounded like birds, I jumped out of my own skin. An unforgiveable part of my heart was almost excited at the sound, tightening in hope to see him again.

It was inexplicable, this war between my head and my heart. I had grown to care for Pyre, feeling empathy where it was due. But my brain knew that his morals were corrupt. I knew that I needed to free myself from him from the moment he had a hold on me. I still didn't know how I would do that, but I trusted that Ombrose was a pawn in my game of getaway. Whether I could trust him or not, I didn't know. I was admittingly unable to trust anyone at this point, still not entirely forgiving my family for hiding my witch-hood. Had they warned me, I might have been able to prevent my downfall and the world's doom.

"Won't he know where you've taken me, given that you're his cousin? He must know where you live," I presumed. "Wouldn't that be his first guess?"

He shrugged at me, disregarding my fear. "He is well aware of my father's home, yet he has never once visited."

I looked at him with distrust. "Never?" I questioned. That sounded unrealistic. For having lived so long in the Under Realm, I would think he'd have visited the family that remained here with him.

"My father's duty is important. He doesn't normally leave his place, and the God of the Dead doesn't seek those of no use to him. There is also the fact that my father has put a ward up over the cave's entrance, making it so that no one may enter unless granted access," he explained. "My father is a primordial deity. He's powerful in that way."

"Primordial?" I repeated, wondering just what that might entail.

"One of the first," he replied. I could see the pride in the way he talked about his father. He was gratified to be of his descent. Though he said that Pyre had no use for his father, I could tell from the way he spoke that this primordial deity was significantly important, and that I should pay close attention. I wondered who this god was, contemplating the role he played in the universe. It made me feel small to think that I was here, beholding those from the beginnings of the world I'd grown to know and love. I had had several weeks with the God of the Dead, I had spent two days traveling with the God of Nightmares, and now, as we crossed the cypress's threshold, I was *en route* to being introduced to a primordial god.

"Who is your father, Ombrose?" I asked, curiosity piquing in the rush of adrenaline that surged through my veins. He smiled back at me, the ring of blue-white in his black eyes lighting at my interest. Before he could answer, my foot snagged on a thick rock and I tripped, falling flat on my face. Nihility whinnied and fussed around me as I lay on the graveled area. The hot sting in my nose made my eyes prickle with tears, and I couldn't help them from streaking down my face. Embarrassed, I wiped at my cheeks to find that blood was leaking from my nose.

"Staunch it! Quickly!" Ombrose hissed, turning me into his chest.

"What are you doing?" I squealed, squirming to free myself from his hold. His body grew rigid against mine, and I suddenly felt the change in the air around us. Nihility reared up onto her hind legs, releasing hot steam from her nose in a frenzy. Her mane turned wispy, ash floating around her face until she herself disappeared. As if life had been removed from all surroundings, the wind turned stiff and unmoving. It was stale on my tongue, and the foul odor came up my nostrils soon after. A putrid draft smelling of the juices in a compost wafted over us, and it took everything in me not to clamp down on my tender nose.

"If I tell you to run, you run," Ombrose growled in my ear. The sound of his distress rang true through my bones. "If I tell you to do anything at all, you listen. Got it?" I nodded my head against his chest. "Good." He grunted as heavy, abundant, footfalls resonated throughout the field. I couldn't have counted the amount of feet I heard even if I had all the time in the world to try. They were coming from everywhere, and even louder ones came from behind Ombrose's back.

"Ombrose," I whispered, hardly able to speak the name. Two sets of overly large wings came around the giant cave, and I swore their angered black eyes were set on me. "Behind you." I gulped, trembling in his arms.

"Nice of you to announce your presence," said the exceedingly tall beast of a being. Ombrose's head whipped around, and some of the tension actually released in his shoulders.

"Brothers." He clucked, wings snapping behind him. "Perfect timing."

"Brothers?" I shook, sizing the two newcomers. It was clear now as they approached that they matched so much of what Ombrose looked like. Leathery wings, jet-black eyes, and dark, tanned skin—bronzed to perfection. Though there is no true sun in the Under Realm, these three remind me of the sun-tanned Mycenaean Greeks, a vision of strength and hard features like Ares from Grecian myths. Where Ombrose was clearly very muscled, the tallest was burly in compari-son, and the other who hadn't spoken was of the same height as the God of Nightmares, but the slightest bit slenderer.

"Who's this?" said the tall one, examining my face. "Your nose is bleeding." He pointed, and Ombrose blew out a heavy breath.

"Thank you, Reaver, for pointing out the obvious." He rolled his eyes, arms still folded around me. "But I think we have more pressing matters to deal with at the moment." My heart lurched at the loudening footsteps that approached us from all sides. I had almost forgotten about the rest after spotting Ombrose's brothers. I thought that we were preparing to fight the pair off, but it seems I was wrong in judgment. The strong, winged men took a stance on either side of me and Ombrose, ready and willing to brawl with whatever horrid beasts were snapping our way.

As if crawling straight from the most abominable depths of Hell, nasty, hirsute bulbous spiders emerged from all corners of my vision. The rushing abhorrence churned my stomach.

"Oh, you've got to be kidding me," I whined as the volatile arachnids scurried forward. They were the size of Nihility herself, their mouths as big as my head. "Giant spiders?" I groaned into Ombrose's chest, and he released me from his hold.

"Varakane," he spat.

"What the hell are varakane, and what are they all doing here?" I trembled, unable to focus on any of the beings. There were just so many.

"They are exactly what they look like," said Ombrose.

"And they're here for your blood," Reaver grunted and handed me a small piece of cloth he'd pulled from out of nowhere. "Here," he insisted. "Pack your nose and pray to the gods they don't get their hands on you." I took the fabric gladly and shoved it up my nostrils, heat flaring under the force to the tender area.

"Are they going to try to eat me?" I spluttered, not wanting to commit a look to the foul creatures headed our way.

Reaver barked a laugh my way. "You'd be so lucky."

"Why?" I pushed, not wanting to know the answer.

"Again, with all the questions," Ombrose marveled. I gawked at his response.

"Hey, I think I have reason to—"

"Move!" he shouted, and I ducked behind him and away from the spider that now stood only a foot away from the group of us.

"Holy gods, that thing is fast!" I yelled over the clawing in the dirt that scuffled in the field.

"Stay out of their path and away from our swords," Ombrose ground. "When I say so, leave for the cave and do not look back."

"But—" I hesitated, though Ombrose and his brothers would not have heard my refute. As quickly as the spider had lunged for me, the three gods of the Under Realm flew into the skies, sending spider after spider away from my range.

"Now, Goddess!" he roared from above. My mind and my feet collided as I tried to decipher which move I should make. Could these brothers manage to fight all of these creatures off? There were so many. I could hover above the spiders and use the powers I'd learned to wield against them. I could only assume fire would instantly burn the varakane to a crisp. But that meant that I would have to show my hand and reveal just how powerful I was. It would unveil *who* I was. I looked up to the skies finding that the men who flew above me were covered in sweat, muscles glinting in the light. With each slice down the gut of the spindly legged creatures, exertion adorned the gods above. But as they dove down to fight, I noted their teeth, sharp and flashing. They were enjoying this feat, exulting in the battle as they smiled fiercely against the wind. That's when I decided that I could let them fight the beasts on their own. They would do fine without me, and I would take the chance to flee.

11

SUFFOCATE
SHIVALRI

R unning away from the spiders and into the mountain's mouth seemed like a good idea at the time. That is, until my debilitating fear of the dark settled into the top of my spine and halted me in my tracks. I wasn't sure how many steps I'd made into the blackness of the cave when I stopped to realize I was living my absolute worst nightmare. Every time I dreamt of the dark, the worst kinds of things would poke and prod at me, never allowing me to see what was out there. As my toes curled under me in the dirt of the rocks, the instant feel of suffocation knocked the air out of my chest, leaving me breathless and vulnerable.

A loud explosion reverberated around me, causing my knees to thud to the solid surface.

"What was that?" I gasped, choking on air. My voice echoed through the walls, dizzying my mind. Again, a boom rang, not helping my fright's cause. I wasn't getting any real air in. My lungs were hot with flame, collapsing in on themselves. I couldn't breathe. Without ever having to look down at myself, I knew that I was alite with fire. The cave was blasted by the light I emitted, sharpening the stalagmites adorning the ceiling. The world seemed to topple over as the rest of my body sank into the limestone, warping in and out of blackness. I had to breathe, had to take back my oxygen. When the next rumble resounded, shaking me to the core, I went under, and the darkness I found was anything but inviting.

Coming in and out of consciousness, the unknown wrapped around me, constricting my body with ease. Every part of me itched from the touch of gangling limbs, lithe, slithering forms, and thin, bony skin. I was entirely surrounded by the things I could not see, but that I knew were there, enticing me. I was trapped in a mess of cobwebs, awaiting to be consumed. I wanted to scream, wanted to beg for mercy, but my mouth was covered with soft, silken strings.

"So precious," a foul, timeworn voice sang. My eyes widened in fear, but still, I couldn't see a thing. "Please, make yourself comfortable," it crooned. "How you choose to endure this is entirely up to you." I searched and searched for evidence of the creature that watched me, but everything was blank. I needed to see. I needed my fire back.

Calming my thoughts, I shut everything off. I closed my eyes, focused on the worst parts of me and my existence, and pushed them to the center of my mind. Images of the red skies from Earth flitted under my eyelids, my mother's limp body against the steering wheel of the crashed car. I could feel the anguish building in my gut. It was going to work.

A cacophony of voices and clicking whirred and stirred about, pulling me from the focus I had found.

"She is perfect," a voice sounded, enigmatic in its tone.

"She is more than perfect," the older one sang. "Scent her, my lovelies... What do you smell?" I tensed under the scrutiny of whatever surrounded me, feeling them approach at the hoary one's command.

"Can it be?" one shrieked, sounding pleased even through the rancid voice.

"Truly alive?" said another. My gut sank at the implication that they had wanted me whether I was or wasn't dead. What were these things doing with the souls of the departed? What did they want with me?

"Isn't it marvelous?" The crone beamed. "With the deceased, we may only fertilize once. With the living, we will spend an eternity making children."

"No!" I tried to scream, but my mouth was still covered in the binding. Skittering echoed as my senses honed in on the creatures. They were coming even closer than before, and gods only knew what they planned to do with me. Their mention of fertilizing and making children made me want to hurl the contents of my stomach, but I swallowed it down, and used all my strength to spark a flame.

Rage scintillated at the forefront of my mind. I grew hotter and hotter, skin prickling under the fulfilling feel of blaze that begged to come out. I gritted my teeth, smiling in delight as Pyre's words rang through my mind. *"When you conjure fire, it frequently stems from anger. It correlates to your pain."* And pain, I had felt. In just a couple of months I had experienced enough pain to last me a lifetime. I clung to the rage that burned through me, clung to the strength that Pyre's words had afforded me, and lit the world on fire.

"No!" the gritty voice cried out in anger. "Don't let her remove my silks!" When I caught sight of the ghastly varakane in the light of my flame, I flashed it a wicked smile.

"You took me when I was down, when I was weak and oblivious," I ground, feeling the power roar through my veins. The flame went higher as I rose, dusting the webbing off me. "Now let me return the favor." With a move like lightning, I whipped a torrent of fire across the room, slashing through bodies like butter. They would not take me alive. They would not use me as their personal incubator. They would not live to see another day.

I didn't even need to look where I was aiming. I knew that if I let my intuition guide me, I was sure to hit every mark just by sensing their sinful presence. Alive in the power that seeped out of my being, I flourished in my triumph. With each thud to the ground, I savored the feel of death that flooded me. This was what I was capable of. I was the Fates' creation, destined to wield this supremacy. A guttural laugh escaped my lips as I relished in my accomplishments. Giant spiders, spanning miles and miles down a deep cave, lay limp and lifeless. It was a glorious feat. I would revel in this act for a lifetime, and with pleasure.

The darkness of the cave no longer frightened me. I knew now that my elemental power would shield me from all darkness for the rest of time. So long as I wished it, the fire and I would unite.

"Not so precious now, huh?" I grumbled, sneering at the lifeless bodies. I heard faint skittering leaving the cave's entrance, and everything in me wanted to throw myself at them to finish the job. I had never felt so powerful. So delightfully in control. But I was tired, and I had made a huge dent in the group of arachnids that assembled to witness whatever they planned to do with me. I was content with my triumph. It was enough fighting for now.

Before moving to leave the cave, I turned around to regard the remains of the snare I had been fixed in. Most of it was ash now, settling into dust. Some of it remained, glowing iridescent in the light of the fire I still held in the palm of my hand. I lowered to the ground, moving my hand forward to better see the material. It was in fact spider silk, and it was thick like rope. In the glow of my flame, the pearlescence of it danced along the floor and halfway up the ceiling. Something about it made it seem of importance, and the urge to shear some as a trophy itched my fingers. Perhaps it would come in handy, whether to use as rope or a reminder of my strength. Deciding to collect a ribbon of the silk, I twisted it over my hand, collecting until I had a fistful of material. I extinguished my fire, shoved the silk in the pocket of my pants, and headed toward the dim light that shone from the cave's entrance.

When I emerged from the cave, three tall men stood before me, bat-like wings rigid, and bodies entirely out of breath.

"Good gods, woman!" Ombrose barked. "What the hell were you thinking?" I looked at him in puzzlement. Was he upset with me for having fought the spiders? Oh, *fuck*. Had he seen me use my fire? Which would be worse, or harder to explain, I did not know.

"Are you well?" asked Reaver, taking a step closer to examine me. I took a step back, holding my hands in the air.

"I'm good," I stammered, unsure what they knew or what they were thinking as they watched me.

"Why would you run into a grotto full of varakane?" Ombrose hissed, rubbing at his temples. "I swear it's as if you're looking for trouble." He shook his head at me, and I instantly knew that he hadn't seen me fight. If he had, that would have been the first thing to fly from his mouth.

"You told me to run into the cave," I argued, then turned to point to the cave's entrance behind me. "That's exactly what I did."

"This is a *grotto*," he grunted, emphasizing the last word. "We live in a cave, a giant cave with a door!" he bellowed, then grabbed me by the shoulders, turning me to look in the direction of the mountain I had somehow missed. I swatted his hands away and blinked when my eyes adjusted.

"Oh," I muttered. "*That* cave." A light laugh startled me in place, and I turned to look at the other brother, unsure if I was imagining the sound coming from him. He smiled at me, and without a word, he made to walk toward the obvious home of the three brothers.

12

DICE

SATYRA

Rich, dark skin stood in contrast to the lightly falling snow just outside the window next to the front door. I instantly remembered the man who was freezing and waiting for a welcome into our house.

"Mr. Blackwood?" I hesitated, remembering who the face on the other side of the window belonged to. The dreadlocks atop his head were dusted in white, powdery snow. I couldn't fathom how long he'd been out there to have collected so much of the flurry on his person. "What's he doing here?" I asked, looking to Gram for an explanation.

"Better yet, where are the rest of the jackasses?" Raidan barked. Gram stood firm in front of the door, keeping it locked by deadbolt and a tricky magic that seeped from her hands.

"I'm alone, and unarmed, Mrs. Grimsbane. I won't hurt you or your grandchildren," he called to my grandmother. His deep English accented voice was a shock to my system. He was *here*. A member of the High Council was here at our doorstep.

"You are a traitor, Blackwood. Whether a common man or a member of the High Council, we do not tolerate your kind in this home. Leave now," she demanded. "As you well know, this hearth is protected against the wicked." Energy stirred between her open digits, seeming to radiate with her words.

"Please, I mean you no harm," he implored. "Satyra, let me explain." Confusion fuddled my mind, and Raidan whipped his head to me in abhorrence.

"Why's he talking to you?" he snapped.

"It's me," said Ember, growing louder as he pressed his forehead to the window. "Satyra, it's me." Raidan stalked forward now, face going red as I watched his mind twist and turn with assumptions.

"Raidan, chill." I hesitated, torn between wanting to escape my cousin's scrutiny, and figuring out why the member of the High Council was talking directly to me. Wondering why he spoke my name as if he knew me.

"Saty, you'd better tell me what's going on right now, or so help me." Raidan was livid.

"Hey, hey, hey!" I heard a shout from outdoors. "Leave her alone. It's not what you think. It's my fault. Just let me in and I'll explain everything." Raidan spun on his heel, heavy footsteps thudding with each step he made back to the door Gram guarded.

"Move," he told our grandmother.

"You will do well not to test me, Raidan. Back away."

Raidan scorned Gram with a look, then leaned against the window that stood between us and the man who poisoned us at the Salem House of Enchantment. "What are you doing here?" he demanded from the man.

"She told me to come," he replied. "Called me a coward and demanded I make my presence known." I walked forward, the words feeling familiar. "I'm here. It's me, Satyra." My hand flew to my mouth in response to the gasp that crawled from out of me. It was *him*. He was the seer who had let me into his mind. Rather, he was the one who had entered mine and forced the images upon me. I remembered Gram explaining how the power worked. After being told that I was unable to tell the future, rather I was being shown images of things that had already happened, Gram explained that being able to see-walk was a gift that many seers had. It was used among like-powered individuals—ones such as Ember Blackwood and me.

Though I was almost certain that he was telling the truth, I wanted to know for sure. I had to have some proof before letting my guard down. If he really was the seer who had been spying for us, and showing me the images, then he was our secret ally.

"Prove it," I demanded, approaching the window. Raidan, a whole foot taller than me, made to block my path, but I shoved him aside. "Let me through, Rai. Gram's holding the door anyway." He grunted and allowed me to fully pass. On the other side of the window, Ember Blackwood stared back at me with guilt and plea wrapped in the frown of his face. The scar along his jaw and up his ear crinkled at the movement.

"Show yourself, you coward. You will answer me. You will tell me who you are, or so help me, I will find you myself and gut you like a fish." He repeated the words I'd sworn at him during our last see-walk. Chills ran over my arms as I wiped at the lone tear that escaped my eye.

"Gut you like a fish?" Raidan barked back his words, that were actually my own. "Now you threaten her?" No... It was I who had threatened Ember.

"You didn't help her." My lips trembled, never moving

my eyes from his. I wanted to see his reaction, wanted him to see the pain he'd caused.

"Please, you don't understand…" he trailed, placing a hand on the window. I backed away, feeling the full force of the memory I'd been given of Shivalri's capture.

"You stood there and watched," I whispered, unable to hold in the shaking. "You did nothing to stop that monster from taking my cousin! You wouldn't even let me try." The tears were hot now as they came pouring down.

"It wasn't happening in real time, Satyra," he explained, voice soft. "It was a memory of mine. Something I wish you didn't have to see, but I knew that it was the only way to warn you of what happened."

"Why now?" I choked.

"What?" he asked, and Raidan came to put an arm on my shoulder. I felt the slightest bit of tension release as he aided me in healing my emotions. His healing powers were helpful, and he was becoming more attune with them with each day that passed. I didn't want to repress my feelings, but as I thought of Shivalri's face as she was swept away, I knew that Raidan was only helping reign in the pain so that I could focus on the task at hand.

"Why now?" I spat, angrier. "If it wasn't in real time, then why did you give me the see-walk now? Why didn't you show me the minute it happened?" I was screaming now, aware, and not, of the cracking in my heart. "We could have been looking for ways to free her! All this time, you've known that she's in Hell!" Raidan's grasp on my shoulder tightened as I shook, seeing woods in a blaze and claws of a monster.

"I can only do it when I'm alone," he explained, voice still kind. I wanted to punch him in the throat to harden that weak voice of his.

"Bullshit."

"No, my sweet," Gram said beside me. She lowered her hands and came to stand in front of the window with me and Raidan. "If he truly is the one whose been giving you see-walks, it is true. Moira has a gift of keeping tabs on minds."

"What?" I questioned, still seething in my own skin.

"Moira Darkmore is evil, and eager to scratch at the minds of us all. That includes the members of the High Council," said Ember. "She keeps a claw in my consciousness at all times. It's only when I'm left to spy in the night that I have any time to let go and share my sight."

"It's been fifty-one days," I argued. "Fifty-one days since she was taken. You mean to tell me that you couldn't have gotten away in all this time?"

"I swear." He sighed a heavy breath. "I could only do so much. You must trust me."

"Trust you?" I ground. "How could we trust you? You poisoned us, sacrificed Shivalri, and gave her to a demon!"

"No, I didn't! I didn't do any of that. I stood by and watched it happen, and for that, I will never forgive myself." He shook his head fervently. "Please, you must trust that I did what I could. I could never take on the witches and warlocks of the High Council on my own. They are too big of a collusion to stand a chance in winning this extensive battle. I've been trying to warn you for so long. Long before anything ever happened. I swear it." He looked down and away from me and my family. "I just couldn't do it in person."

"Too many eyes," said Gram, voice wise and weary. A long pause stilled in the air as I watched the member of the High Council drown in his culpability, Gram studying him through the window. A loud click jolted me out of my dimness as Gram unbolted the lock from the door. Hands down in sign of acceptance, she opened the door and gestured for Ember Blackwood to enter the Grimsbane home.

13

ÉQUIVOQUE

SATYRA

G ram's tolerance toward Ember Blackwood was alarmingly quick to come. She must not have realized just how involved he was in all of this. I didn't trust him for even one second. Though I knew he had been the key player in giving us clues in the case of Shivalri's prophecy, I wasn't so keen on inviting him into my home. Raidan was clearly on the same page as me, grabbing Ember by the elbow and dragging him through the entrance.

"Hey, man!" Ember coughed. "I'm fragile." Raidan didn't so much as blink at Ember's words, only grabbing him even harder and shoving him into the coatrack. I was suddenly very glad for Raidan's inheritance of Gramp's height and build. He could've been a bodyguard in the way he moved around us, seeming to put himself between me and Gram and the trespasser.

"Don't even think about making a move out of place," Raidan warned. "Your fragility will be useful when it comes time to kick you out."

Ember cocked his head, and slowly removed his shoes,

one at a time. "No need for the aggression," he answered coolly. "I'm not here to hurt anyone. I'm only here to help."

"How are you going to help us with this if you can't get anything past the rest of your clan of ass wipes?" Raidan retorted.

Ember's dark face lit with a smirk. "Ass wipes..." he mused. "Haven't heard that one before."

Raidan snarled and took a step closer to him. "Watch yourself. You're in one piece only because my grandmother's allowing it." He swore and folded his arms over his chest.

"And what about you?" Ember questioned, eyes landing on me.

"What about me?" I grimaced under his watch.

"Would you like to see this ass wipe ripped to shreds by this—" He paused and lifted a hand to my cousin. "What are you, exactly?" Raidan scoffed, furrowing his brow. "Are you even a warlock? Or are you just here to play the macho bodyguard?"

"Fuck off." Raidan grunted, seething in place.

Ember shook his head in what seemed to be amusement and looked to me again. "So, what will it be?"

"I—"

Gram walked forward then, taking the coat from Ember's hands and placing it on the rack behind him.

"All right, children," she began, her tone filled with impatience. "That is quite enough banter. Let's take it downstairs." Raidan and I both whirled on her in sync.

"What?" I gasped, eyes wide and matching my cousin's look of shock.

"You're letting him into the basement?" Raidan choked in disbelief. Ember's look of confusion swarmed his face as he looked at me and my family.

"What's so special about the basement?" he wondered

aloud. Gram shook her hands in the air, lodging the deadbolt back into place and lifting the spell back over the door's threshold.

"Come, come." She gestured and left to find the entrance to the top-secret Grimsbane sanctuary. The rest of us hadn't moved yet, merely watching her trek the halls.

"Is she serious?" Raidan asked. Ember scowled then made to make a move, but my cousin blocked him immediately.

"Look," Ember started, but Raidan threw out a hand, commanding the intruder to wait.

"Do you trust him?" Raidan asked, not bothering to look at the man in question. Why would he ask *me* that? It was Gram who knew everything about this life. It was she who had invited him in. If it were up to me, I'd have stayed far away from the guy who helped knock us out with drugs. I would stay very, very far away from the person who stood silently by as Shivalri was taken into Hell. But then I remembered that it was I who had confronted the seer, demanding that he show face. His arrival, in the end, had been my doing.

"I don't," I said, and Ember's gaze forced me to look his way. His eyes were downcast. Whatever hope he might have had was gone. He hardened his face and looked back to where Gram walked.

"So, we don't let him in then," Raidan decided. "If we weren't allowed into the sanctuary all of these years, then he's not getting access so quickly either." He made to grab Ember again, but something in my heart told me that even if I didn't trust him now, I was supposed to try.

"Actually, Cuz," I countered, stopping him in his tracks. He tried to read my look, and I sighed heavily, letting go of the tightness in my chest. "I don't trust him, but I think we need to listen to Gram. If she says it's okay, then, I guess we listen. I guess we try." Raidan nodded once and left to meet up with Gram.

"Thank you," said Ember, voice soft and quiet. When I didn't answer, still feeling all the hatred and guilt in my heart, he walked ahead of me to join the others. I took a second for myself, allowing myself the briefest moment to remember the main goal. It was hard to train my mind to ignore the flashbacks of Shivalri in the woods, but I would have to for the sake of saving her. I would have to put my own feelings aside to find a way to work with the man who stood by and did nothing to help my best friend.

14

MOUNTAIN

SHIVALRI

A darkened bronze door the size of an overhead garage entrance stood before us as we reached the entrance to the Orsimm cave. It was an ornate portcullis with images of clouds and stars trailing along the dull bars. I thought it odd that Ombrose had ordered me to run into to the cave when we were under attack by varakane. I would have never made it through the door. The memory of him informing me of the ward placed over the cave's entrance suddenly entered my mind, making it really unclear as to what Ombrose was thinking when he had made that command. He had told me that his father had created a ward so that no one may enter unless granted access, and I surely didn't imagine my trying to barge in would have worked against its magic.

"So, um, when were you going to tell me that I was meant to run into the absurdly large door prohibiting me from entering?" I asked, turning all attention on me. Ombrose shook his head at me, sneering in amusement.

"I was planning to swoop down in time to grant you access, but you decided to take your own path, *prohibiting me* from doing so." He lifted a hand and touched a large stone that appeared to be indented in comparison to the others. In an instant, the portcullis moved upward and into a slot in the mountain.

"We couldn't find you," said Reaver. "We didn't realize you'd go into their grotto. We should have known sooner." Ombrose tapped his brother on the shoulder and let out a low laugh.

"Don't worry yourself, Brother. It is not your fault. She is quite capable of landing herself in trouble all on her own." I grimaced at his words, and he grinned at me.

"What manner of woman have you found, Ombrose?" Reaver sighed.

"A goddess," he answered. "A well wanted one, at that." His brothers spun on me now, blades in hand and ready for battle. I tripped over my feet, trying to back away from them.

"Hey, what's your problem?" I gasped, feeling their unease.

"Are you sure?" asked the quiet one, head cocked, trying to unravel my truth. "There are no live goddesses left here."

"See for yourself, Tasphen," Ombrose insisted, taking a small step toward me, feeling like solidarity.

"It's true." Reaver blew in disbelief. "I don't know how I didn't sense it before…"

"Her blood," said Ombrose. That was an odd thing to say.

"What about it?" I asked, the brothers seeming to wonder the same of his report.

"You bleed the blood of a mortal. That's what drew so many varakane to you."

"Impossible!" Reaver exclaimed.

Tasphen approached and sniffed in my direction. "You are mortal, aren't you?" He examined.

I wasn't sure what to say. Acknowledging my human side

to the people of the Under Realm meant that they would question my being here. It meant that I was a strange phenomenon to analyze. It meant more trouble for me than I would like, but there was no avoiding the truth. I was mortal. But somehow, some part of me, allowed me immortality in both the Under Realm and the Celestial Realm.

"Sort of," I murmured, still trying to come up with a lie to cover my true identity. Then it occurred to me that perhaps these immortals also had the gift of scenting lies, and I stopped the wheels from turning, deciding to simply avoid the subject all together. "That's not really important right now though," I added. "Ombrose, the pythrants said that you'd help take me back home. Please, if we're done here, I'd like to accept the offer."

"It's not so simple, Goddess," he replied, face grim.

"Pythrants?" Tasphen looked angry as he turned on Ombrose. "Do not tell me you went into *his* territory." Ombrose huffed in annoyance, nodding in admission.

"Seriously?" Damn, Tasphen really seemed to dislike Pyre. It was evident in the way he'd spat *"his."*

"You did this intentionally?" Reaver snapped, joining in the scrutiny. "You willingly brought a live mortal to father's abode? One that, undoubtedly, belongs to *him*."

"Uh, excuse me," I cut in, placing a hand on my hip. "I don't belong to anyone."

"Tell that to him," Tasphen replied.

I ground my teeth, trying my best not to argue with these gods.

"Whatever, or in your case, *whoever* is found in that territory forfeits their fundamental freedom the moment they step foot on the soil. Gods, never mind his home territory. The Under Realm itself belongs to him." Reaver turned his worried eyes from me back to his brother. "And *you* know that. So why, pray tell, did you think to have the nerve to steal her?"

"I had no choice, Reaver. She needs our help. She needs to get back to Earth."

"And how exactly do you plan on getting her there?" Ombrose shrugged and took a step into the cave.

"I was hoping she might have an idea and that father would have a way to execute it."

"Me?" I gawked. "I haven't the faintest idea!" This was not a good start to my escape.

"You are stepping into matters that aren't yours to deal in. You know this, brother." Reaver tsked in disapproval.

"You have no idea," Ombrose answered over his shoulder. Following him into the dim lit cave, I took a deep breath and tried to ease the tension from the knowledge that both Reaver and Tasphen held blades at my back.

"*Yrdôs*," a voice boomed, dizzying my mind instantaneously.

"No, Father!" Ombrose thundered.

What was wrong? Where did that voice come from? A hypnic jerk, a heavy head, and a lulling pull drew me over the edge and into slumber, and I was no longer conscious in the Orsimm's cave.

15

UNDER

SHIVALRI

A faint trickling noise ticked in the forefront of my mind, woozy and uncomfortable in a head that swam through thick sludge. I counted the ticking, *eleven, twelve...*, then dove back into the quiet.

"She is not meant to be here," I heard a far-off voice murmur. I wondered who it spoke of. Who was not supposed to be wherever they were? *Eighteen, nineteen...*

"I know, Father. You must understand. She was in *his* castle."

"And this is an excusable reason for your insolence?"

"What shall you do with her?" said another voice I could almost recognize.

"I cannot harbor her here. Not now. If the king would discover my withholding her, it could lead to a war far too soon."

"She has nowhere else to go?" asked a softer voice.

"I don't think so. She's important somehow. He'll come for her the minute she's free from these wards."

"Ombrose, what exactly are you implying?"

"He knows I took her."

A grumble came from an angry soul. "How?" it bellowed.
"I took her from him."

"Brother," said the rational voice. "Why would you put yourself in this situation?"

"He is a fool with poor timing," said the loud one. "Inserting himself where he does not belong." There was a pause after this, and when the most familiar voice sighed at my side, I felt my body wake in time to consider the conversation a little clearer.

"Do as you see fit, Father. I came to you for your decision. She means nothing to me. I took her because it felt like the right thing to do. I see now that this was unwise." Alarm rang through me at those words, my eyes straining to break through the REM I'd been placed in.

"You shame me, Ombrose," said the loud one. "Nevertheless, it is done now. I will think on this further before coming to a decision."

"Yes, Father," he replied.

I heard movement cross my path, and I managed to open my eyes. It was lighter in this section of the cave I'd carelessly walked through. There were jars of glowing liquid mounted on rocky ledges along the cavern walls that allowed a blue-hued light to filter through, the specs within them looking like stardust. Three bat-winged men stood over me as I lay on a slab of rock.

"She wakes," said Reaver, and I blinked, feigning having just woken up.

"Where am I?" I asked. "Is everything all right?" A stirring, dark shadow appeared from behind the three brothers, and my breath caught in my throat as I peered up at the man who'd made my heart stop. I had never seen nor imagined a being quite like this one. He was bound by several strips of leather, winding around his shoulders, torso, and down his arms. A bronze plating covered his pectorals, and up over his collar bones the sculpted metal wings were the showpiece. There were markings all across his armor, etchings burned into the leather from head to toe. His skin, which was only bare around his head and hands, was tanned, just as the three who stood around me. Had I thought the Orsimm siblings resembled the Greek God of War? I was a fool to think so. This man, this being, was battle wrapped in leathers. Where the brothers all had a glowing ring of lightning around their jet-black eyes, their father did not. I felt myself trying to crawl into my own body, but that was not something I could do.

"State your name," he demanded, voice sounding like the grinding of two heavy rocks.

"I—" I fumbled, unable to make my voice work. He was frightening in every way possible. When Ombrose told me that his father was a primordial god, I had not expected to feel this way in his presence.

"Now, child," he boomed, and I flinched away from the sound.

"Father, patience," said Reaver, but the look in which his father held told me that he did not know of such a thing.

"Shivalri," I stammered, feeling lightheaded both from having been put under and the immense fear that washed over me as I looked into his black eyes.

"A peculiar name." He hummed. I just stared up at him, trying to decipher his intentions. I knew from the minute I stirred in my sleep that it was his voice that had impelled me to collapse. If what I had overheard while trying to wake was any indication of his character, I knew that I wasn't safe with him, and I was definitely an unwelcome guest. What felt even worse was the confirmation Ombrose gave me in not being able to trust him. Assuming that I was still asleep, he had told his father and brothers that he didn't care about me. He had said that it didn't matter what his father chose to do with me —whatever that may be. I was so alone in this infelicitous life of mine. I could never trust anyone. Not for a minute.

"What are you doing here?" asked Tasphen, voice assertive having gotten the air from his father.

"I'm not quite sure," I muttered, taking them all in. "Ombrose brought me here," I added, looking to him for help.

"Not here, in this cave, child," the primordial deity bellowed.

"What do you mean?" I gulped as he forced me to look upon him. His eyes darkened even further, if that was even at all possible. I shrunk under the intimidating stare, feeling small and weak in his otherworldly presence.

"Why have you come to Mortades?"

"Mortades?" I choked, eyes widening at the title.

"As if you do not know where you are," he answered, moving his face in closer, allowing me to see the wrinkles set in his brow and frown line. "What sorcery have you used to enter the Under Realm unscathed?"

"I didn't come here," I croaked, unwell as the word *Mortades* screamed in my mind.

"Blasphemy!" He roared, teeth sharp and spittle landing on my cheek. "The child spits in the face of a god?"

"No," I stammered. "I'm sorry! I didn't mean that. I mean—"

He cut me off with a thud to the slab I still lay on. "Out with it!" He snarled.

"I was taken against my will!" I yelped. "I didn't come here of my own volition. I swear. All I want is to be left alone and for my heart to finally end its aching." I cried, a downpour of tears flooding my face.

"What is this?" Reaver whispered as they watched my fragilities unfold. Wave after wave of tears came rolling through, and when I thought I might have used up every ounce of water to exist, another wave came thrashing from my mouth, a storm of water choking me as it poured down my chest and onto the floor of the cave.

"Stop it this instance!" the god commanded. "*Yrdôs!* Sleep, now!" he thundered, but nothing he could say or do would end this. It was up to me to decide when the waters would stop. I needed to bring my thoughts into good memories before they took my outburst as a threat. I needed to reign in the emotions of weakness and fear and replace them with happiness.

Raidan appeared to me first, moments from our childhood playing in the yard together appearing in my mind. Satyra and I playing make-believe with Gram made my heart leap in my chest. I felt it now, the water starting to ease in pressure as it left my mouth and eyes. It was working. All I needed to do was continue this path, and I would be able to shut it off. I watched as Pépère gave Gram a kiss on the cheek, relishing in the summer sun. Mom and Dad, both happy and well, smiling at me in the comfort of our living room.

Too quickly, I remembered that my mom had been murdered. My mother had been killed in order for the High Council to trigger my powers. In doing so, I had ripped a hole in the veil between realms, allowing the other realms to see into our home. I had all these damned powers, yet felt so powerless.

I felt the surging of waters heat under my skin, boiling me alive in this wicked torment. Wind whipped from out of me, and my head leaned back as the weight of my body lifted into the air. I was spiraling out of control with no end in sight.

"It *is* her!" the primordial god shrieked over the wind that whooshed around us. Rocks and debris soared this way and that, hitting against the cave walls, but forever missing me. I could barely see out of my tear-filled eyes as the god latched on to me, trying to pull me down. But I was at peak elevation within myself. I could feel the storm coming to life in my gut —a seed well-watered. With the god still holding my feet, a fire came forth in a blast of heat. I needed to free myself from him. I needed to free myself from everything.

"Let go," I demanded, and watched as his eyes widened. He'd heard me, though I hadn't moved my lips. It was my mind speaking to him. It was not a power I was aware of, but in this moment, it was only natural. I felt the might of my demand force him off of me, even though he tried his best to hold on. *"Back away, and I will end this,"* I thundered, intention set on speaking to all their minds. *"I will make it go away."*

Then a familiar voice echoed through my memories, feeling acquainted and earnest as it instructed me. *"Why on earth would you want it to go away? You are glowing."* Pyre Malum had admired the power that coursed through my veins. He had taught me to value the strengths I had, and to use my weaknesses at an advantage, rather than treat them as a curse. His eyes were alite with gold as we leaned into what I had and learned to wield it. A memory of his lips kissing my forehead swam in my mind, and I couldn't help but let it wander into racier thoughts of being held in his arms, our kiss ravaging the tension between us.

"It's working," said Reaver, clearing my honied recollections. The tears abruptly ended with a last splatter to my lap, and I wiped away at the wetness on my face. Without truly meaning to, I had stored away my elements earlier than planned. Where was my mind? What had happened to my heart?

"Sorry." I gulped, voice dry.

"Who are you?" Reaver whispered, jaw dropped. He and his brothers were drenched and dirty from head to toe. His father came forward placing a hand on his heart.

"The Bringer of Worlds," he marveled. "Welcome, Goddess of Three. I am honored to behold you."

16

THAW

SATYRA

The basement was just as we left it as we escorted Ember Blackwood into its sanctuary. The lavender pots hung above our heads, accompanied by the dozen herbs Gram had grown and nourished down here. The feel of the dirty ground was familiar now as I walked behind my three companions, watching for any sign that Ember might strike against us.

He appeared to be surprised by the underground cave that rested under the Grimsbane house. I couldn't blame him. When I had first seen it, albeit with Gram hovering in the air, I was completely shocked by this place. First, offering a feel of wonder, now providing a sense of protection with the knowledge of Gram's fortification spells guarding the place. It had been my great-great-grandmother who had created the safe place for us Grimsbanes. She made sure we were safe in life, and even in death, with the option of finding ourselves in the waterfall's mausoleum.

Gram took her seat in the old, high-backed chair. Scooting closer to the marble table, she sat upright and pulled the prophetic book toward her. Ember made to pull out a chair for himself, but Raidan grabbed it from his hands and sat in it, facing our grandmother who gave him a stern look. I sighed heavily, reaching the lot of them.

"Here," I said, and pushed a chair toward the seer.

"Thanks," he muttered, and sat opposite me. He stared at me hard, never blinking away from the awkwardness of our eyes catching. I, too, would not fold in this staring contest. He wouldn't win the feat of making me uncomfortable. I would be doing the intimidating from here on out. I was powerful in my own way. I had no reason to cower now.

"Mr. Blackwood," Gram began, and it jolted both of us out of the stare. When he moved to look to my grandmother, I couldn't help my eyes from wandering over the lightning-shaped scar that traced the side of his face. As it glowed in the light of the torches surrounding us, I wondered what had happened that he'd obtained such a scar. I wondered how he felt about it, and realized that, with no authority to feel anything at all about him, I found him incredibly sexy. Gram spun Shivalri's book in his direction, and I was thankful for the waking. "Assuming you are indeed on our side, I will allow you to read the prophecy my family has found in collections. I know that not every family of witches has the same text, and it would be beneficial to have all the pieces. That being said, I expect your participation to be of use to us too. If you know anything else, out with it now."

"Of course," he said, clearing his throat, the apple bobbing with the motion. "Unfortunately, I don't have any records here with me, as that would require me to slip them out from under Moira. As you may know, that is quite literally impossible." Gram nodded, face hard and grim. "But I am happy to answer any and all questions you may have regarding the prophecy, Shivalri's whereabouts, and most importantly, what the High Council's intentions are."

"Let's start there," said Raidan, pushing his elbows onto the table and leaning forward. "What are their intentions?"

I looked at him in bewilderment, scoffing at his ignorance. "What about Shivalri?" I scoffed. "Your sister?"

He shook his head at me, a look of annoyance written on his face. "You of all people should know that we already have her whereabouts, Satyra."

"But she doesn't know everything," Ember interrupted before I could disapprove of my cousin's statement. "She wouldn't know who took her, and that is an important piece of the puzzle."

"You know who the winged man is?" Gram spoke, shock and hope lighting her appearance.

"Yes," he answered. "I do."

"Who is he?" Raidan asked, shaking the solid table as he leaned even further toward the seer. He's a heavy, sturdy guy, and it seemed his stature unnerved Ember. Ember looked away, seeming both a little anxious and at war with his thoughts.

"What is it, Mr. Blackwood?" Gram begged. "Who is he that he has got your mind in a twist?"

Ember looked up now, and I could've sworn his eyes were liquid in the dimness of the torches. "Mrs. Grimsbane, I fear it is not what you wish to hear…"

A hand settled on her heart, and I felt my own crumple under the view of Gram's torment. "Please," she whispered. His eyes were grim and lit with sadness, and I knew nothing good would come from his lips when he made to speak.

"He is the Redeemer of souls. The God of the Dead." Gram's body collided with the back of her chair, eyes blank and staring up into the ceiling.

"Gram!" I cried, running to her side straightaway. When I

made to push her head back up, I swore I saw a swift movement behind her, folding in over her shoulders.

"Aunt Eden?" I gasped, making out the glimmer of spirit. Before I could blink, the hazy form disappeared, and Gram's eyes were expressive once again. "Gram, are you okay?" She swung her head to Ember now, who sat rigid in his seat, waiting to be struck.

"We have to get her back." Gram swore. "We have to." She and I both began to cry, unable to stop the emotions from coming out.

"We will," said Ember as he slowly moved to take the book that lay in front of him. I stayed put at Gram's side, calling Raidan to come near.

"What?" he asked, voice worried.

"Just come here," I insisted, and he got up from his chair to stand beside me.

"What?" he asked again, concern covering his frown. I gestured for him to move in closer, and when he was close enough for me to whisper in his ear, I spat my nonsense, almost not believing myself.

"I think I saw your mom." He froze over me, and I felt a wave of frissons.

"What?"

"Oh, my gods, Raidan. Stop saying *what* over and over again. I saw your mom," I said, voice louder than I intended.

"Satyra, my sweet," Gram spoke. "Did I just hear you correctly?" I stilled in my spot, Raidan appearing to match my stance.

"What did she say?" Ember asked, lifting his eyes from the book, and peering at us.

"Saty?" Gram prodded. I swallowed hard, feeling cold all over.

"I, um…" I hesitated. "I think I saw Aunt Eden hug you."

Gram smiled softly, lowering her eyes, and folding her arms into a hug around herself.

"Oh, sweet girl." She sighed. "Thank you, daughter."

"It's true?" Raidan blew, throwing a hand over Gram's shoulder. Her smile widened at his touch, and she let out a small but precious laugh.

"Two healers at my side…" she hummed. "How lucky am I to be in such remedial company?"

"You're a healer?" Ember asked, turning Raidan's attention to him now. My cousin nodded at the seer, unable to hide the grin from forming on his face. "That could really come in handy," he said, considering Raidan's power.

"In *hand*-y," I added, remembering when Shivalri had made the joke first. The memory was bittersweet, in that I was happy to remember my cousin in good times, but knowing where she was and what manner of monster held her made me want to cry all over again. Raidan smiled grimly, seeming to be on the same train of thought. Gram patted his hand, which still sat upon her shoulder, and Raidan took that as a sign to go back to his seat.

"Are you going to be okay, Gram?" I asked, not sure if I should move back to my chair or not.

"Yes, my sweet. I will be just fine." She took the book back from Ember and lifted a querying brow at him. "So? What say you about this version of the prophecy?"

He huffed a breath and straightened his posture. "It is as it says in the books we have in the High Council's collections. Whether now or later, your granddaughter was meant to fall into some form of worldly chaos. No one is ever gifted such immense power without having to prove they're worthy of it."

"Naturally," said Gram, apparently in full agreement with his statement.

"That's ridiculous!" I interjected. "Shivi never wanted any of this. It wasn't a gift in her eyes. She shouldn't have to prove herself to receive something she never wanted in the first place."

"I agree," Raidan responded, joining the argument. "It doesn't make any sense to me."

"Of course not," Ember muttered under his breath. Glad for the fact that Raidan hadn't heard him, I turned to look at Gram for justification.

"Shivalri was born to have this destiny, Satyra," said Gram. "Whether she wanted it or not, it is who she *is*. Now, what she does with it is entirely in her hands."

"But we can help her, right?" Raidan asked, alarm written across him.

"We will do everything we can to help her. Starting with Mr. Blackwood telling us the intentions of the High Council, and just what they thought the outcome would be after offering her off to the Redeemer himself."

17

BLUEPRINT

SATYRA

"**M**oira Darkmore has been working toward this goal far longer than one might think," said Ember as Gram, Raidan, and I listened for clues to help save Shivalri, and ultimately, the world.

"How did she know to look for Shivalri?" asked Gram.

I, too, wondered about this. It wasn't as if my cousin had been parading about her powers, flaunting her prophecy for all to see. She hadn't even known about her witch-hood up until now.

"She sensed it in the magic," he told her. "Shivalri had been using her powers for quite some time now, unknowingly. Something happened to her that made her very down, which we concluded was the source of her ascension."

"So, you know about her mom then," I supposed. "That was the incident."

"No, actually." He frowned. "That wasn't the cause of her ascension. Though I am sorry for your loss," he murmured, head bowed.

"What was it then?" I wondered aloud.

"I don't know for certain, but it was not around the time

of her passing. It was shy of a year ago, just before summer began."

"Hmm…" Gram hummed. "I cannot think of anything bad happening to her in that time."

"I can," Raidan remarked.

"What is it, Raidan?" Gram prodded. He gave her a passive look and shrugged his shoulders.

"We moved."

"That can't hardly have been so terrible," Gram stated.

"Really, Gram?" Raidan questioned. "Do you not know her at all?" He huffed a short laugh and shook his head. "Leaving you and the home she grew up in wasn't something either of us wanted to do. We grew up here, got used to being around you and Saty." He looked to me briefly, trying to hide the emotion that was clear in his eyes. "Shivi hated going to public school, didn't like being moved to a new state, but most of all, she felt like she was leaving you guys behind. The day we moved, she told me how guilty she felt. I know we don't talk about it much, but the loss of Pépère, your mom, and Uncle Olly was really hard on you two. On all of us. When we left, we felt like we were leaving you both alone to grieve. It really weighed on her that she couldn't stay here with you guys." Gram put a hand to her heart and exhaled lovingly.

"It is not yours or her burden to take on. We are strong, Saty and me. We can care for ourselves." She squeezed my hand, then patted the top of it. "Isn't that right, my girl?" I nodded in agreement. It was true. I lost my parents, my grandfather, and my aunt in this short life. With death following at my heels, I had to be strong to survive.

"We're fine, Rai," I told him. "I only wish I could tell Shivi the same." I turned to Ember again, who was studying me like my book was wide open. I cleared my head from the negative thoughts and leaned back into my chair. "Now that we know where Shivalri's ascension started, could you please explain how Moira even sensed it in the first place?"

"I would also like to know about this," Gram added.

"Absolutely," he settled. "During the incident, the weather picked up storms, sending them across oceans and valleys high. Within them, the feel of powerful magics were potent. I personally couldn't feel it, as that is an inheritance Moira herself was given by her family. The minute it came our way, I was tasked to find the source of the magic, with the assistance of Moira's mind device guiding me along. Once I found your granddaughter, my job became spying on her. I was forced to report back anything suspicious or of worth. I don't know how she knew that Shivalri would be the one to take the place of the Triple Goddess, but I am sure that confirming her suspicions was her highest priority."

"Do you suppose Moira might have the ability to fore-tell?" Gram asked, and my mind sharpened on the lessons I'd briefly been given about witches who had the spirit affinity. The entire line of women in my family were gifted this power, including me, Raidan, and Shivalri.

"She is able to make small predictions, but nothing so far off, and surely nothing of such importance," Ember explained, and I found myself wondering about him and his powers. Gram had taught us that Ember Blackwood had the fire element in his family heritage, but with him having given me see-walks, that could only mean Gram was not as informed as we all assumed.

"Can you?" I asked, turning his attention on me. I couldn't help but trace the lightning pattern with my eyes as he squinted at me with a confused look on his face.

"Can I what?" he stammered, and I thought I might have caught him in one of his secrets.

"Can you predict the future?" I clarified. "You know, seeing as how you're a seer."

"Oh!" Gram gasped, clearly not having registered that he was more than he seemed. We knew that someone was coming to me in my mind to show me the imagery, and we knew who he was now. "That is right," Gram mumbled, looking first to me, and then to Ember. "Mr. Blackwood, I think you have some explaining to do, as I know the line of Blackwoods are fire wielders—not seers." Ember gulped at the heat of the focus we put on him, and Raidan seemed enlarged in the corner of my eye.

"Before I explain myself, here, I would just like to inform you all that I did not predict Shivalri being the Triple Goddess incarnate. But, yes, I know that it is odd for me to have more than one affinity, and you are probably wary of me because of it. It is why Moira placed me so high in ranking. Both for my power, and to keep her eyes very close on me."

"Good to know." Raidan grunted. I watched my grandmother's face grow more worried as she took in the information.

"Are you absolutely certain that the leader of the High Council does not know you've been helping us?" she asked, and a chill ran down my spine at the thought of what that implied. If Moira had been keeping a close eye on him, that could potentially mean she was on her way here to strike us down when we weren't looking.

"This isn't safe," I spluttered, feeling a new sense of panic rise within me. "We can't be working with you, whether we trust you or not."

"Please," he started. "You have to let me help you. I need to make this right."

"We are way past that, Blackwood," Raidan barked.

Ember's eyes grew wide in alarm. It was the first real sign

he'd shown that he truly did want to help us and atone for his mistakes. "Please," he begged, turning his gaze on me. "You, of all people, know what I did, or rather, what I didn't do to stop it." His eyes were solemn, lips curling into a snarl of distaste. "I cannot live with myself knowing I stood by, never able to help make it right."

My gut twisted at the agony he portrayed. "Why couldn't you have done something to help her before it was too late?" I pressed, eyes searching his.

"Because if I did anything at all to raise suspicions about where my loyalties lie, I would be dead before lifting a finger, and you guys would never have received any information about the corruption of the High Council. With my playing it slow and safely, it gives us a chance at putting an end to the High Council's corruption, and great hope to save Shivalri from the impending doom."

"She's already in the doom, Ember!" I hissed. "You watched her enter a portal into Hell," I cried out, feeling the tears heat my eyes. "You showed me…"

"She is in Hell, but she is not lost," he decreed. "Not yet."

"How do you know?" Raidan asked for me, but it was Gram who answered him.

"Because the world is still coming to an end," she declared. "And that would be the proof of your sister's wrath. She is still alive, somehow. We will get her back."

"How?" he pled, needing the answer just as much as me.

"By retracing our steps. By doing our research and trusting that this is not over, rather, it has just begun."

"When do we go?" I asked, remembering the plan to go in search of more books on the prophecy.

"Go where?" Ember demanded. I watched as a nerve ticked in his jaw, unease emerging.

"The House of Enchantment," I answered. His eyes flew wide with incredulity.

"It is not safe to leave your house, let alone show up at your enemy's doorstep! The High Council has more than one spy to account for." He blew out in frustration.

"So, we take them down." Raidan hissed, outwardly searing in the thought of vengeance.

"It's not possible," Ember rebutted, but Raidan only scoffed.

"We're not going to take them down," Gram said, and the rest of us looked to her as she stood from her chair, demanding attention. Raidan got up and took a place next to our grandmother, voicelessly affirming allegiance.

"What's your plan?" asked Ember, already out of his chair and pushing it back to its spot.

Gram started walking toward the staircase, and without warning, she blew out the torches with the twist of her wrist. "We trick them," she sang, voice low in the dark of the basement.

I was still in my seat, not expecting the lights to go out. I could barely see the table that sat in front of me. I heard feet ascending the staircase, and my heart hammered in my chest. I didn't want them to leave me alone, so I hurriedly stood from my perch, feeling around for something to latch on to. A steady grip took my elbow, and I spun toward the heat of the person standing close to me. Before I could land a punch, another hand grabbed my fist, catching me off guard.

"Please don't hit me," I heard from behind my ear. A hot groan melted down my neck, making the frizz in my curls cling to my skin. The hand holding my elbow let go, and I saw a tiny flame just as I heard a small snap, simultaneously taking my breath away. Ember stood behind me, his right hand just in front of my face as his index held fire like a personal lighter. I immediately moved out of his reach, feeling terrified and excited all at once by the strange encounter. "Shall we go?" He chuckled lowly. He held the small flame between us, considering my palpable nervousness. I swallowed hard, finally catching my breath, heart still thundering violently in my chest.

"Lead the way," I mumbled, unsure who the unreliable voice belonged to. He swung an arm out for me to go forward, and even though I didn't want to turn my back to him, I desired getting out and away from him far more. Taking a steadying breath, I huffed in annoyance, and made my way up the creaky stairs—Ember and his flame trailing behind.

18

UNEARTHED

"Y ou're the Triple Goddess?" Ombrose blew, his
lips twitching as if unsure whether to smile or
frown. "I had no clue!" He threw a fist in his hair
in frustration as he paced back and forth. The way he'd said
that felt like a forced line. *What was with him?* Reaver and
Tasphen stood with mouths agape, clearly unsure what to do
besides stare in my direction.

"To your knees," the primordial commanded, and one
after the other, the Orsimm knelt in front of the slab of stone I
was sat on. The black-eyed god following suit.

"Hey, there's no need for that," I offered, feeling heavily
uncomfortable with the change in attitude. It did, however,
beat the harsh terror I'd felt only seconds earlier.

"You are the gatekeeper incarnate, Goddess. We hold you
in the highest respects," said the primordial. "Please, forgive
us for our insolence." This was exactly what I didn't want to
happen. I didn't want them to hold this over me. Them
knowing who I am puts me at risk of far more danger. The
less people knew the better. If this information kept spreading

as it was, the whole world was bound to know who I was by the end of the year. I took a deep breath and sighed out my frustrations. I could do nothing about the fact that these four knew who I was. I would have to play things differently, and to my advantage. If they truly held me in high respects, and knew just how important I was, they might help me leave this place for good.

"All's forgiven, so long as no one else finds out who I am," I said sternly. "You must understand how vital it is to keep my identity a secret. Not only for my safety, but for the safety of the realms."

"Of course," said the primordial. "You have my word."

"Why can't others know about you?" asked Ombrose. His father shook his head as if his frustrations with his son were far from few.

"Those looking to use her against others would be happy to get their hands on her," he explained.

"Well, then she's certainly not safe here with Mortades." Ombrose gave a discouraged look.

"*With* Mortades?" I choked, coughing on tough air. "Like, the person?" Ombrose looked to me with brows furrowed, the rest of them gawking at me like I had two heads. "What?" I asked.

"Are you all right, Goddess?" asked Reaver. "Are your memories intact?"

"My memories?" I shook my head fervently, not quite understanding.

"Do you not remember where I found you?" Ombrose asked, trying to prod the memories from my mind. Of course, I remembered. My mind wasn't hazy at all.

"You found me at Pyre's castle," I told him, concern written across my lips.

"Pyre?" he repeated, eyes dull. "Pyre Malum is what he has you calling him?" Ombrose scoffed, brushing a hand through his hair in disbelief.

"That's who I was with," I said, knowing I was sure but feeling less confident as I said it.

"Such a poet," Ombrose chimed. "To use the titles in which the Fates bestowed him upon arrival in the Under Realm, rather than his given godly name."

My gut plummeted as I fully grasped what he was saying. "It's not just the land that's called Mortades... Pyre *is* Mortades..." I whispered; a high ringing throbbed in my ears at the comprehension.

"That, he is," the primordial confirmed. "Mortades, the Ruler of the Under Realm, God of the Dead."

"He didn't tell me..." I shook.

"You didn't know he was the ruler of the Under Realm?" Tasphen asked.

"I mean, yes. I knew that. I just didn't know his real name... So much of folklore and religion I learned about on Earth is terribly mixed and uncertain. We humans don't know what's real and what isn't. But Mortades... The sounds within that name are so like the word *death* in French and Latin. And Hades, which is something most of us grew to fear."

"For good reason," Ombrose scoffed. "Have you met the guy?" He shrugged and kicked a loose pebble on the ground. "Oh right. You have." I grimaced.

"Ombrose," Reaver cut in. "Though the myth of Hades is centered around Mortades, he is only feared for his title. Do not trick the girl into forming her opinions of him based on your feud with him."

"What do you mean?" I asked, prodding for more.

"He is the one to face upon death. That is where the fear lies. But he does not cause death, nor does he wish it upon those who aren't ready for it. He does respect the Fates and their strings. He respects all lifelines." This was a new angle, though I wasn't entirely filled with shock. It was new to think of him as considerate and wanting to respect the lives of others. For all my time with him, I had found that his wants came before the needs of others. But he did seem to appreciate the magic that the Fates held. I could believe his respect of them.

"Do you know him well?" I wondered, remembering that they were family in some form.

"Not I," Reaver replied. "Though my uncle is quite fond of him, and I, fond of my uncle."

"Who's your uncle?"

"Gerimor," he answered. "God of Death."

"Death?" I blew, my heart racing at the mention of their relation. "Like, he causes death?"

"My brother is the Bringer of Peaceful Death," said the primordial as he stepped closer. "I am the Bringer of Sleep." He bowed his head to me and lifted a hand to take mine. "I am Dramael, and these are my sons. We are happy to help you in whichever way we can, Goddess. Our home is your shelter for however long you may need it." I stood up from my perch and held out a hand to him. He took it without reluctance, and that gesture alone surprised me.

"Thank you, Dramael. I appreciate your help." He shook my hand firmly, black eyes meeting my gaze.

"We appreciate you keeping us safe. It is not an easy fate to face, having to take the place of our dear gatekeeper. We commend you for it." Reaver seemed to agree with his father and fisted a hand over his heart.

"To you, Goddess," he spoke. Tasphen and Ombrose repeated his motions, each nodding in my direction.

"To getting me the hell out of here," I added, and the room grew heavy in magnitude.

19

DIVULGE
SHIVALRI

"Tell us everything," said Dramael who sat behind an old Victorian-style desk in the dimly lit cavern. We all sat in unexpectedly comfortable chairs knit closely together. They were styled differently, the legs and back posts extremely curved in comparison to modern furniture. The material and structure were curved to contour the body while seated. There were tufted seats, which felt as if I were sitting on a cloud, and it felt nice to ease the ache in my tailbone from having ridden Nihility for the last two days.

"What would you like to know?" I asked, not sure how much I really needed to divulge. I avoided his gaze by toying with my mother's ring, which still took its place on my right hand. It melded to my fourth digit, lightweight, feeling as if it were always meant to be there.

"Start from the beginning," he said, and a rush of panic started my heart. I didn't want to tell them about my family. I didn't want them to know anything about Earth, nor the exacts of how I'd gotten here. I knew I'd have to give them something on the subject, but I wanted to avoid putting anyone else in danger. Though I knew that these gods couldn't leave this realm without me, I had the feeling that if they understood that I could potentially bring them through with me like Pyre had planned to, they might take advantage of the opportunity.

"How long had you been with Mortades?" asked Reaver, and I was glad to have him cut in. It was the perfect escape route, the perfect way to start from a different beginning.

"Since October thirty-first. Samhain," I told them. "Pyre never told me what day it was, but I'd been counting, trying to map out a timeline since being down here." I suddenly realized that perhaps these gods would help me clear that confusion up. "Do you guys keep a calendar? Do you know what day it is?" The hope in my chest was rising fervently. I knew that I was close in my guessing, but I was quite desperate to gauge my time in the Under Realm. Keeping count of the days felt like something normal I could hold on to. Having the exacts would be a small piece of considerate humanity I'd be very thankful for.

"It is December twenty-first in your home realm," said Dramael. "That you've come to me on the day of Winter Solstice is a fitting sign."

"December..." I whispered, trying to swallow such an actuality. I counted, using my fingers, trying to calculate how long I'd been away from Earth. I must have lost track of time while with Pyre... There was no way, yet why would these gods lie to me about the date? Somehow, it must be true. I had been in the Under Realm for fifty-one days. Fifty-one days away from my family. Fifty-one days entirely surrounded by gods and monsters. Fifty-one days was all it took for my affinities to take root and flourish within my veins. I could hardly imagine what another fifty could do.

"You've been away from your realm for a long while, haven't you?" Dramael affirmed.

"It's quite hard to believe," I told him, playing all those long days in my head.

"What did you do in Mortades's castle?" he asked. That pulled me out from my slump and back into protecting my mind.

"We trained," I said, not wanting to give away too much too soon.

"Trained?"

"Yes," I confirmed.

"In what way?" asked Ombrose. His look of concern was heavy on my shoulders.

"Like, running and dodging his attacks."

"He attacked you?" he boomed, standing up from his seat. He turned to his brothers and father now, fists tight at his sides. "You see, Reaver? What have I told you about Mortades? Time and time again, you've defended his behaviors, favoring your beloved Gerimor, never seeing my opinion as a valid thought. Yet, here stands the Triple Goddess reincarnate, another of his victims, and even now, you do not speak against him?" Reaver didn't even flinch. Dramael was still in his seat, but I saw the rage melting off his mask with each word Ombrose outwardly launched. "We cannot sit idly by and allow him to continue ruling the Under Realm."

"Enough," Dramael thundered, the sound ricocheting throughout the domed space.

"Father," Ombrose began, but Dramael's eyes were enough to silence him.

"Mortades may rule morosely, but he is still our Lord, and we will respect his title."

"He is not evil, Brother," Tasphen spoke, surprisingly defensive on Pyre's part.

"He is vile," hissed Ombrose as he swung his head at me. "Tell them." He demanded. "Tell them what he did to you. Tell them what I saved you from." It was then that I realized all that Ombrose saw. He had seen into my nightmares and watched the horrors I'd dreamt—being beaten and scolded by Pyre. Though he'd never done so, Ombrose could have taken the dream as a reflection of my reality. Ombrose had also seen how Pyre had treated me in the throne room. Though the nightmares were not real, and after the oubliette, Pyre himself hadn't ever truly hurt me until the day I'd left, Ombrose must have assumed otherwise. Pyre Malum had used his strength against me, that was true. But the infliction of pain on my part had only been in small doses to scare me, to fill me with anger so as to conjure my fire affinity. Though I hated the method, I could admit that it was the fastest way to stir my magic into waking.

"What did he do to you, Goddess?" It was Reaver's turn to question me now. His eyes were soft, offering empathy in the way he asked. But his jaw was tight as he waited for my reply. It was his duty to ask, whether he cared to or not.

"He stole me away and forced me to work with him."

"Toward what?" asked Dramael.

"What did he *do* to you though?" Ombrose prodded, skipping over his father's question. *Gods, would he never let it go?*

"For the most part, he wasn't all that bad."

"Wasn't all that bad?" Ombrose was livid now, eyes narrowed, the ring of light blurring over the edges.

"In the beginning, he was horrifying. He'd locked me away to see if I'd survive starvation and madness in the oubliette tower of his castle."

"You were tossed into an oubliette?" Reaver asked, doubt and concern clouding his face.

"That bastard!" Ombrose spat.

"You will do well to mind your tongue, Ombrose," Dramael ground out. "I will not tell you again." Ombrose grunted, then sat back into his chair.

"What happened afterward?" Reaver asked.

"How did you manage to escape the tower?" Dramael added. "It is next to impossible... Did you use your affinities?"

"No, actually," I said, grimacing, "He just let me out."

"He let you walk out. How peculiar," Dramael remarked.

"Mind games," Ombrose muttered under his breath. None of us turned to look at him, but his words did sink uncomfortably in my gut. Had he been tricking me all along? Had Pyre been pretending with me? No, it couldn't have been a ruse. He didn't have to let me out of the oubliette, didn't have to give me the comfort of my own room. No, I didn't think his treatment of me had been a ploy. When he let me into his mind, allowed me to search for truths about him, I had seen his growing attachment to me. That hadn't been fake. Certainly not after the kiss.

"What did you do after he let you out of the oubliette?" Reaver's question brought me back to present.

"Like I said before,"—I shrugged, trying to seem casual in hopes to hide my half-truths—"we trained."

"That cannot be all," Ombrose snapped. "I saw the way he treated you when we fled from the castle. I saw the way he looked at you as if you were the only thing in the universe he'd wanted to devour. My taking you was like stealing a huntsman's prey."

I swallowed hard at that, suddenly feeling like the air around me was far too thick to breathe.

"Are you all right, Goddess?" asked Reaver. Tasphen stepped out from his chair and made his way closer to me.

"Your heart is beating rather fast," he murmured, scrutinizing me where I sat.

"I just don't like thinking about it," I explained. "It doesn't do well to my nerves."

"Understandably," said Dramael, who was rifling through parchments on his desk. "We will not dwell on it much longer. We just ask that you are patient while we piece the mystery together."

"Okay," I agreed, nodding once. He looked up from his desk now, looking to the four of us who sat in front of him.

"I have a proposition for you. It may help acquire more knowledge in hopes of assisting you toward your goals." I stilled in my seat, heart thundering in my chest. He was a primordial god. Surely, he knew of a way to let me out of the Under Realm if there ever was one. "It will require you allowing another god into our assembly," he supposed, squashing my hope, and churning it into dread. I didn't want anyone else to know about me. I didn't want anyone else to get involved.

"Who?" asked Ombrose, clearly on the same train of thought as me.

"My dear brother, Gerimor."

"You can't," Ombrose rebutted, flailing his arms frustratedly in the air. "Whatever you tell him, he will tell Mortades."

"I agree with Father," said Reaver.

"It isn't safe," Ombrose argued.

"Uncle is trustworthy," Reaver spoke. He was sure in this, in the way his tone was clear and stable.

"More than that, I believe out of everyone, he would know the most about the Triple Goddess." I gawped at

Dramael, more curious than ever as to who his brother was and what he had to do with the goddess before me.

"You are right in that, Father," Tasphen agreed. It was then that I realized that on most things, Ombrose's judgments were the odd ones out. His brothers and father were combined in mind. At this point, I didn't know whose side to take. Either I sided with the God of Nightmares, who had saved me from Pyre, or I could side with the other three, who appeared to have a more level-headed approach.

"What say you, Goddess?" Dramael bellowed, ultimately leaving the decision up to me. I was still undecided. Too much had happened to me in the blink of an eye to make any rational decisions for myself. I wanted to disappear. What I truly coveted was the avoidance of needing help from anyone, but at this point, my wants were not a part of the plan.

"May I think on it?" I was unsure of myself, and unconvinced that I'd be given this courtesy.

"You may sleep on it," he decided, and I found a sliver of relief wash over me. "You will have the night to think it through, though I'd suggest you make up your mind quickly. I do not suspect Lord Mortades to sit idly by, knowing you're here with me."

20

TEA

SATYRA

"I really hope you've got some kind of idea forming in there," I whispered to Gram, tapping my temple. Raidan and Ember took to the foyer while she and I made tea for the group of us. I watched her carefully as she spooned the loose-leaf tea into the pink flowered china cup, waiting for her to divulge her plan. I knew better than to question her intelligence when it came to these things. After discovering witch-hood, I'd finally realized just how cunning she was.

"I have an idea, but it will all depend on everyone's approval of it." She poured the steaming water into all four cups and pushed two of them forward for me to carry.

"That doesn't make me feel better about this." I groaned, lifting the cups, and starting past the kitchen island.

"Worry not for the things you cannot predict nor change."

"Easier said than done," I muttered as she passed me by. I followed her lead, unsure where her mind was going, but tried to trust that if anyone were to land on a good idea, it'd be her.

"No, I'm not old, but that doesn't mean I don't know

anything," I heard Ember grumble as I turned the corner into the living area.

"What could you possibly know that my grandmother doesn't?" Raidan pushed. "You're what? Thirty? You've spent how long with the High Council, and still couldn't find a way around poisoning us and sacrificing my sister?" I could see in his face that he was testing the seer, trying to break him into giving him more information. Hoping to force him into dishing out secrets by pissing him off.

"Ouch." He winced, feigning a wounded paw. "Thirty? Do I look thirty to you?" This was actually interesting now. Gram had said that the youngest High Council member was Nesrin Mehra, who'd joined the group at the age of twenty. I'd assumed everyone else was at least ten years older, given that Gram had disapproved of Nesrin's joining at such a young age. That is, until I saw Ember Blackwood. Raidan clearly wasn't seeing what I was… *Though I really shouldn't be looking into him as much as I am.* I shook my head in frustration, my curly bangs bobbing up and down.

"So, you're younger?" Raidan blew. "Yeah, some help you're going to be…" I moved toward the chaise that Raidan always took up and passed him his tea, giving him a look to say I knew what he was doing. He gave me dirty side-eyes and sent me off.

"Thank you," I heard Ember from behind me. I turned to see my grandmother hand him his teacup. Gram took her seat in the rocking chair ahead, which left me to catch the eye of the seer, who was seated on the loveseat where Shivalri usually sat. I took an exasperated breath and plumped down on the cushion, pulling myself to the side and as far away from Ember as possible.

"Now," said Gram, clearing her throat. "Let's talk about tricking the scum who stole my Shivalri."

I swallowed hard at the seriousness in her voice. Raidan let out a small laugh, and I turned to find him snickering at Ember, whose eyes seemed to pop straight out of his head.

"Yes. Of course." He took a sip of his hot tea, the vapor wafting up over his face.

"Do they know you've betrayed them or are they under the impression that you are still a part of their team?" asked Gram, and now, more than ever since he'd arrived, anticipation ate away at me as I waited for the answer that could shift the balance of our chances.

"I am on duty as we speak, spying on the Grimsbane family," he replied, his dark face taking on a pale pallor. "I am meant to discard of you all."

"Well, for all that that sounds like a grand time, I'd prefer to keep my head," Gram retorted, poised in posture, voice lethal.

"And I'd prefer not to remove it from your shoulders," Ember replied, then stared back down into his tea. He passed his cup to my grandmother, and I wanted to swat his hand for having assumed Gram should put away his dish. When I finally understood what he was doing, I relaxed myself, feeling surprised at the willingness and openness of the seer. He wasn't telling her he was finished with his drink. No, he was giving her insight into his life. He was allowing her to read his leaves, baring his past, present, and future to her.

Gram twisted the cup in the palm of her hands, looking this way and that for a story.

"A wash of broken feathers... A hand for helping... And a smattering of wavy lines." She hummed in thought as she processed what she saw. "Your future is uncertain, wavering. It's entirely dependent on the actions you take. What you decide in the next few chapters of your life will determine whether you survive the journey."

"Good to know." He swallowed, tensed in his seat.

"At least I've proof you'll be of help to us, one way or another," Gram supposed, and handed him back the cup. He let it sit in his lap, examining the pieces forming his future's shape.

"I need to." He sighed, dipping a finger into the flecks of tea that sat at the bottom. "I can't sit by and let the world fall to pieces, knowing that I could have tried to help. I need to do this. We all need to do this."

"It's not about what *you* need," Raidan retorted as he sat up closer to the edge of his chaise.

"I have to compensate for my standing by, whether you allow me to help at your side or not," said Ember, squaring his shoulders to meet Raidan's scrutiny. "I will help. If it needs to be from afar, then I will learn a way to do so. But seeing as how we all share the same goal, the same motivation, I think getting your sister back will be much easier if we all work together."

I studied him now, liking the way he spoke with this confidence. I could tell that he meant every bit of what he'd said. He really did want to help get Shivalri back from Hell. I now wondered what kind of punishment he'd receive for doing it. At the hands of the High Council, or otherwise. His tea leaves resulted in a future unknown. Did that mean he could possibly die by making the wrong choice?

"I agree, Mr. Blackwood, and that is why you are here. If I didn't think you'd be beneficial to the mission, you wouldn't be." Gram turned to Raidan now, who was still sitting on the edge of the chaise, face tight. Though he was known to be a tad bit stubborn, this wasn't the cause of his reaction. I knew that he was worried about his sister and was scared that by letting Ember in it could be another risk that puts her in more danger. I was also hesitant to have the seer involved, but I had a feeling that he was a key player in all of this, and we needed him by our sides. He'd allowed me the see-walks, had tried to help far earlier than I'd realized. That had to count for something. "Do you understand, Raidan?" Gram asked now, turning her attention to my cousin, who was still grim in face.

"I trust you," he told her. "I don't trust *him*." He threw eyes like daggers toward Ember, proving just that.

"I don't expect you to," said Ember, forming a frown through his lips. "I just want you to accept the help I can offer. That's all I ask. Make your judgments based off my actions."

"I have been," he ground.

"The past will not be erased, but it will be forgiven if you prove yourself in these coming days," Gram insisted. We all looked to her as she stood from her chair. "Tomorrow, we go to the House of Enchantment."

"How will we get past the High Council?" I asked, now turning my gaze to Ember. He'd know best when it came to their routines and whereabouts.

"They'll be there all day tomorrow, and the day after that, and so on. Until I return with the news of your deaths, they won't leave the building." What? He was truly supposed to kill us. This was a turn of events. Before he'd said so, I hadn't thought that the High Council knew his whereabouts. I thought he'd gone behind their backs by coming here, but as it turns out, it was their plan all along.

"And so, you will do just that," Gram chimed, her shoulders backing to hold her head high. "Tomorrow, you return with the news of our deaths. You will provide a distraction while we"—she gestured to me and Raidan—"rummage through the files and books within the library."

"That's a great plan, but we'll have to find a way in

without them noticing us, won't we?" asked Raidan, his head clear and focused on the game.

"They'll want to see the bodies for themselves," said Ember, spirit and determination flushing his eyes. Most of the color came back to his face, and I thought that in this moment, he looked quite handsome. He finally looked alive.

"It's a perfect plan," Gram claimed.

"I think it's going to work…" he replied, contemplating the steps he'd have to take. "Once we leave the building, you'll have at least an hour to scour the place."

"That's plenty of time." I blew, relieved to know that we could enter the building without the worry of running into the witches who'd poisoned us all. I didn't want to imagine running into Moira. After seeing her face in the see-walk, full of animosity and thirst for power, I never wanted to see that bitch again.

"I can keep guard at the doors to make sure you and the Council don't get back before we manage to find our way out," Raidan decided.

"They'll see you standing at the doors if you wait there," Ember replied, rubbing his thumb and forefinger over his chin.

"I'll risk them finding me if it gives me the chance to give Gram and Saty time to run." He folded his arms over his chest, seeming resolute and settled in his plan.

"I trust that you're strong but leaving you to fend them off alone would be like throwing a rabbit out to the wolves." Ember huffed, looking over my cousin.

"Still, I—"

"A rabbit," Ember continued, "missing its limbs."

"We need a look-out. It's as simple as that."

"What about looking out through a window?" Ember suggested, though his face was still furrowed, unsure. "The one with the clearest observation point won't give you as much of an advance on our return as the doors would, because the rose bushes block most of the view. You wouldn't be able to see us from a far-off distance, but it would buy you enough time to get you all out."

"It will be enough time?" Gram asked, turning Ember and Raidan's attention to her.

"It should be."

"It's settled then," Gram held. Raidan nodded in agreement.

"Tomorrow, we start looking for clues to help save Shivi." Raidan approved.

"We'd better get some rest. Tomorrow will come for us quickly," Gram supposed, and left the foyer to find sleep.

21

IMAGINE
SATYRA

"We have spare rooms from which you may choose from on the first level of the house, Mr. Blackwood," Gram offered as she led the member of the High Council down the hall. I wasn't a huge fan of him staying the night here under the same roof as us, but Gram pointed out that it could mean trouble for all of us if the enemy found him slumped and asleep at the foot of our door. "Towels are found in the bathrooms throughout the house, and you may use the facilities as necessary."

"Thank you, Mrs. Grimsbane. I appreciate it."

"Which will you take?" asked Gram as she gestured to all the doors lining the hall.

"Whichever has a bed and my name on it." He shrugged.

"Very well," she mused. "You may have this one. It's closest to the restroom, and closest to the door in case you grow the urge to run."

"I assure you that's the last thing I want."

"I'm sure." She hummed and opened the bedroom door for him. "Goodnight, Mr. Blackwood. Rest up."

"You as well," he said, then swiftly added, "Thank you." Gram gave him a courteous smile, took me by the hand, and turned us away from our guest.

Once upstairs and in the comfort of my bedroom, I lit a single candle for light while I dressed for bed, feeling the weight of the day press heavily on my shoulders. I crawled into bed, making sure not to move the pillow wall Shivalri had laid out in the middle of the mattress all those weeks ago, and I sank heavily, trying to relax. I knew that I needed to find sleep quickly, needed to give myself every chance for energy, but it was hard to concentrate on sleeping while I knew who lay just beneath my room. I couldn't help but wonder what he was doing, what he was thinking.

I imagined that all of this was hard for him too. Not in the same ways as me and my family, but in a whole different kind of way. I was quick to forget the sacrifice he was making in turning his back on the High Council. Not only could he be killed if caught, but this was his entire life. The members of the High Council were placed there only if their parents had died and given them their spot. The group was made up of witches and warlocks, each holding the power of one of the five elemental affinities. I imagined that Ember had been promised his position in the group his entire life. I wondered how I might feel if the roles were reversed.

I've always wanted to be more, to see more. Before realizing that the members of the High Council were evil, I'd dreamt of someday joining them, or at least working at their sides, relishing in the magic of it all. Now, I thought, perhaps I would make my own assembly of witches in charge of magical law. If the current council was full of immoral assholes, that left the rest of the magic world with no one to depend on. I could see it now; me, Gram, and my cousins fighting for what's right, and helping people with magic in whichever way a High Council might do. I could even picture Ember at my side, determined to make things right, and I ashamedly wished for this fantasy to come true.

22

DESCRY
SHIVALRI

"The fire's taking longer to build than I would like it to." Ombrose grunted. "The number of times I've built the damned thing, you'd think I'd be better at it by now." I was growing impatient with the cold, myself, having only the thin clothes I'd borrowed from Pyre and no shoes to cover my dirty feet. Even the knees of my pants were ripped to shreds from having fallen one too many times. I decided to weave a little fire magic into the wood while Ombrose struck the stones. I had managed to do it while out in the forest with him, aiding him without his knowledge. This time, I wouldn't have to keep my use of the affinity a secret, but I decided I would anyhow. Watching him try and try again only made me wish him his moment of triumph. I flexed my fingers at my side, so as not to have anyone notice my meddling. With barely any effort on my part, I sent a tiny spark to the wood, and waited for it to set root.

"It's working," said Tasphen, who sat close to his father at the far side of the rounded room. "There's a draft of smoke eddying on the wind." I thought it strange that he'd already smelled the fire. There was nothing aglow at this point. I should've been the only one to know of the spark.

"By gods, Son." Dramael sighed. "It was due time." There was a low chuckle beside me, and I jumped at the sound. Reaver had taken a seat on the ground just to the side of the rock I'd sat on.

"Thank you," he muttered under his breath, his eyes pointing to the hand I'd twisted with magic. I tried holding in the grin that came forward, but it slipped away from me when Reaver grinned too.

"I have no idea what you're talking about," I whispered, biting my lip in effort not to laugh. He quirked his brow as if to say otherwise, then turned to look at the fire which now held steady throughout the logs.

Ombrose had found a seat near Dramael and Tasphen, and I was surprised by that choice. I hadn't expected Reaver to join me, yet I did expect Ombrose to come. I had no reason to, other than the fact that it was him I'd known the longest. Though two days in comparison to one was not a significantly longer amount of time, I might have felt the slightest bit more comfortable with a more familiar face.

Reaver did seem kind, though, and the way he'd defended Pyre to some degree made me like him a little more. Why I'd want someone to defend the God of the Dead after our last encounter is beyond me. My mind says he betrayed me, but my heart says he cared for me the only way he knew how. He was trying.

"Tell me; how did you find yourself in the Under Realm in the first place?" Reaver asked, as we all sat around a fire lit courtesy of me. The stack of wood at the center of the cave's floor not only helped with lighting Reaver's face, but it delivered a bit of warmth I'd been missing. The orange hues mixed with the blue glowing vessels made for a weird combination of color all around. As I watched it dance around the room, it shimmered over Tasphen, Ombrose, and Dramael, who were carried away in their own conversation.

"Hey, what's in the jars?" I asked, coming out from my thoughts.

"Answer me first, and then I'll tell you," he insisted.

"My answer is going to take much longer to supply than yours. I fear I might fall asleep before getting mine." He chuckled into the firelight and gestured to the ledge with the most jars.

"They are dreams," Reaver explained, as if that was answer enough.

"What?" I looked at him for more, and he tilted a brow at me. I sighed. "I got here through a portal." It was my turn to tilt a brow at him. He grinned wide, bemused by my willingness to match his game.

"Fair enough." He smirked, nodding. "When I visit the dreams of mortals, sometimes I take bits and pieces from my favorite parts. They're like mementos."

"That is so cool," I admitted under my breath. "Weird, but cool." I couldn't help the splinter of melancholy in my stomach over the missing pieces. Were the lost mementos missed by those who'd dreamt them? "Do the humans notice that the pieces are missing?"

"Do you remember every part of your dreams?" Reaver's words struck me. I never had. It was common knowledge that no one could remember absolutely everything they'd dreamt.

"So, you're the cause of the hazy memory," I thought aloud.

"It's a part of life," he supposed.

"How so?"

"Our posts are that of ruling your unconscious minds while my father guides you into slumber. I oversee reminding the being of its memories and emotions. All of us work to give messages to everyone, but only those who seek them will notice. When the messages are made too clear, we must intervene, and make certain we haven't given too much away to the sleeper."

"You give us messages?"

"Not all the time. We filter through. They are only given when necessary or earned." I was stunned by this information. I had always felt like my dreams were telling me something, had always felt that my nightmares were real. I shivered at the thought of what they could mean. Most of my time asleep was spent suspended in darkness, encased by fire and things that went bump in the night. I wondered now, if perhaps, the Orsimm knew of my fate, and were warning me that it was coming. "How did you get through a portal?" Reaver asked, forcing me to get back to my explanation. I wanted to know more about the dreams, wanted to ask if they'd given me messages. More importantly, I wanted to find out if they'd known about me all along. It seemed rather suspicious for Ombrose to have found me in my nightmares. I sighed, pivoting to sit facing him. Ombrose had given me lots to think about in the days to come. I would be sure to keep an eye out for more pieces to the puzzle that was my life.

"Back when I was on Earth, a group of witches and warlocks drugged and kidnapped me."

"What?" Reaver gasped, shocked by the revelation. "Did they know you were the goddess?"

"Yes. That's why they did it."

Reaver closed his fingers into fists, visibly shaken. "They are disgraceful," he hissed. "To disrespect a goddess is a sin greater than all."

His words rang cold in my blood as he said them. I knew what he was saying. I understood the underlying message.

Not only was he enraged by the fact that I had been disrespected, but he would be equally upset to witness any god or goddess being disrespected. I tucked away the knowledge of this reaction, swearing to watch myself around him and his family. I would do well not to go against them, whether I was powerful now or not.

"They were awful," I replied. "That's certain."

"I can only begin to imagine," Reaver responded, still stiff in his posture; fists held tight. "What did they do to you?" he asked, his voice softening ever slightly.

Moira's face flashed before my eyes, and I remembered how much she'd enjoyed slicing through my skin as if I were her fresh kill on the hunt. I took a moment to breathe through the aches before answering. "They did a ritual," I finally said, feeling a little shaken by the subject. "They were offering my life as a means to be in contact with Pyre."

"You were a blood sacrifice?"

"That was the intention." I sighed, wrapping my arms around myself. I didn't like reminiscing on the attempt on my life.

"They will burn in Obystrus for it," he declared, voice low. Reaver was showing me a whole other side to him tonight. At first glance, he seemed level-headed, a leader in his right. Now, he appeared to have his father's temper. Though the anger was not directed at me, I still couldn't shake how uncomfortable I felt while sitting here with him in this state.

"Where is Obystrus?" I wondered. "Is that your version of Hell?"

"It is the deepest region of the Under Realm. Think low under the ground, and then assume your estimation can be multiplied by thousands."

I gulped at the idea that there could be a place even lower than I was now. "Have you been there?"

"Gods, no." He whistled, shaking his head. "The worst creatures ever to exist reside in Obystrus. I would like to stay as far away from there as possible."

I shuddered at the terror in his glower. I recalled the nightmare I'd had of the creatures attacking me as I ran through the Under Realm. Perhaps my dreams had taken me to Obystrus without my knowing.

"Noted," I muttered under my breath, goose bumps slithering over my skin. Reaver grew quiet, and I stared at the fire, all-consumed by wicked thoughts.

23

INSOMNIA

SHIVALRI

"You're sure you want to sleep here? On the ground?" asked Ombrose, eyeing me suspiciously as I sat close by the fire, warming my toes.

"I'll be fine here where the fire's warm. Really," I assured him, then looked to his father, the primordial God of Sleep. "Thank you, Dramael, for allowing me to stay the night. You're all very kind for giving me this shelter." Dramael dipped his head and clapped his hands. The noise struck an echo through the vaulted cave.

"If there is nothing else, we should be on our way to our dens," said Dramael, bidding me goodbye for the night. I nodded in thanks as he and Tasphen started to leave the rounded room I'd decided to sleep in.

"Are you certain you wouldn't prefer to have my kline for the night?" Reaver offered again. "I assure you it would be no trouble." After I'd been shown around the cave, I'd realized the mountain had only two large spaces. The rest were simply burrows met with dead ends. I didn't want to be wedged in a dirt hole for the night, but it was very generous of him to offer me his bed, and I would remember that benevolence in the days to come.

"You are kind to offer, Reaver, but I am happy to sleep by the fire."

"Very well," he said. Reaver casually stood from the ground and made to follow the rest of his family, though Ombrose was not so quick to go. He was leaning against the wall, leg crossed over the other, and staring at me with a studying expression.

"What?" I asked, meeting his curious stare.

He furrowed his brow further and snapped his tongue. "I just don't like the thought of you meeting my uncle," he decided to tell me. "It means more gods will know of you. I get the feeling you're trying to keep yourself hidden." I stilled at that, trying to keep my face smooth from reaction.

"What makes you say that?" I asked, adding a light laugh to the end of my line. It didn't feel right, but if he'd noticed, he didn't show it. He merely gestured around to the cave we'd been hiding in, and I rolled my eyes. "Well, yes. Technically, I am hiding in here. But it's just because I don't know where else to go."

"Don't you?" he retorted. I shot him a confused look, and he smirked at me. "You have the key to walk through the Gates of all realms. What's stopping you?"

"What's stopping me?" I repeated, frustrated not only by the question, but at myself. "I only wish I knew! You guys don't seem to know a way out from here, and Pyre refused to help me leave without taking him with me."

"Take him with you?" Ombrose's eyes widened. "You could do such a thing?"

I swallowed hard, unhappy with myself for having revealed yet another secret. "He seems to think so," I answered, voice muted.

"How interesting…"

"But not of any use to my plans of escaping," I told him, bringing the issues back to the forefront of the conversation.

"Perhaps," he replied, unfolding his leg, and straightening himself up. "Though perhaps it is the very thing to put to use." And with that suspicious riddle, he left me alone with the fire and my thoughts.

THE EVENING TURNED to dusk far slower than I'd ever witnessed in my life. The winged family of gods all slept soundly in their beds, while I lay achy on the dirty ground. Reaver had surprisingly offered me his bed, but I'd politely declined, having used my being cold as an excuse to stay close to the fire. I didn't want to leave the only light provided in the cave. The darkness rattled my bones in the worst ways, and I couldn't let these gods see weakness in me. Being shoved into a hole underground with only room enough for the cot rubbed me in all the wrong ways. Not only would it be suffocating, but it would be the deepest dark to exist.

I kept the fire running all throughout the night, never once falling asleep. It was a collaboration between the aching pain in my bones and the fear of being unconscious in a place I didn't feel entirely safe in. The gods were mostly polite and seemed to be on my side in wanting to help me. But trusting them wouldn't come easily for me. Not after having my life flipped completely upside down. I didn't know who to trust anymore.

Even my family had lied to me. My grandmother, mother, and aunt all knew about my witch-hood. They'd believed that by keeping it a secret until our magic woke within us would be a sort of protection. But keeping that secret from Saty, Raidan, and especially me, only proved to be the wrong choice. We could have avoided so much turmoil had I known what I was capable of. Though I understood that they didn't know that I was related to the prophecy, I still wished they'd at least told us about magic. Thinking of my family, I lifted my hand above me, watching the soft glow of the firelight cast shadows over my palm and through my fingers. The wedding ring glistened in the gleam, and I wished so badly for a chance to speak with my mother. To ask her why she'd kept this life a secret. To ask her if she knew that I was sorry for being the reason she'd died.

My brain absolutely refused to acknowledge the fact that my parents who'd raised me were not my blood relatives. I didn't want to believe what Pyre had told me, but everything inside me was screaming at the defiance, pushing the truth forward and begging me to accept it. If Pyre was right, my biological mother and father were, or perhaps, *are* celestial deities. I was created by celestials, harvested by a daimon, and sewed into the womb of a human. Thus, giving me ties to all three realms. Everything about my storyline was surreal. It was a fantasy, that if I'd had the choice, I would not have partaken in.

I understood my duty, and I accepted it now. I had caused the tear in the veil. I had been the source of deterioration. There was no turning back from the incident. Though I'd done it unknowingly, it was still me who had dealt the world its doom. It was up to me to fix it. It was always up to me, for I was given the power to do so, long before I even existed.

With the Triple Goddess on my side, giving me all affinities to wield, I would be finely equipped to execute the task. It was all of the trouble I'd run into that slowed the process. I had a feeling, like intuition, that I was destined to face all of these troubles. The prophecy had foretold my working with someone else to seal the Gates. It never mentioned who nor why, but it was clear that I couldn't do everything on my own. That line in the prophecy led me to believe I had to go through the trouble of finding that person, whoever they may be, to finally end this. To keep the realms safe so that I might live out the rest of my life in peace. So that I might fulfill my destiny and protect the Gates for as long as I live.

My thoughts lingered on the mystery of my counterpart. I couldn't help but reminisce on fiery, exciting moments with Pyre. A part of me, far closer to the surface than before, unintelligently wanted it to be the God of the Dead who was meant to help me. We'd been turning a new leaf while working together at the castle. I'd seen the gleam in his eyes as I made progress and became stronger and more confident in my magic. Not only was he visibly happy for my rising power and willingness to learn, but he was also beginning to like me. *Really* like me. Just as I had been learning to care for and empathize with him. He was frightening, and tempestuous, and in our last encounter, completely ruthless. But that last look of desolation in his eyes as Ombrose carried me out of debris, hinted at a lot of things I wasn't sure I could totally handle. I felt a surge of unrelenting need bloom in my core, and twisted in on myself, trying to put out the flame of untamed thoughts. Thoughts of kissing and wanting and electrifying desire.

Clamor from down the curved hall had me sitting upright in an instant, the heated thoughts vanishing completely. I widened my eyes, trying my best to see in the dark. My vision had been off ever since losing my glasses between being in the House of Enchantment and entering the Under Realm. The sound sharpened as it neared the room. I was sitting in the middle of the space between the entrance and the fire, yet still I couldn't see who walked the hall.

"Can't sleep?" a voice whispered, then Ombrose's face appeared in the dim light. My nerves settled as I saw him, and I sighed a long, exasperated breath.

"Nope."

"I thought so," he replied, and took a seat beside me, rubbing his hands over the fire.

"You?" I asked, eyes fixed on the fire.

"It's not easy at this time of night." Ombrose huffed.

I looked at him now, entirely confused. "Is there a specific time of night in which you sleep?"

He laughed quietly, turning to look at me. "We're nocturnal, Goddess."

"You are?" I questioned.

"Yes." That was so strange. They all said they were going to sleep.

"Then why did you guys go to bed?" I asked, bewildered by his statement. He shrugged a shoulder at me and offered a small smile.

"You needed sleep. My father thought it'd be best to have you believe we'd needed the rest too."

"So, you're all just lying awake in your dirt holes?"

He let out a real laugh this time, his teeth shining in the firelight. "Yes, but we're at work during this time of night."

"How long do stay up to work?" I wondered.

"That depends," he said.

"On?"

"Where are you from?"

I wanted to avoid this question altogether, but I had walked myself right into the trap. "I'm from Essex," I offered, unsure of whether I should have told him where I currently lived to hide Gram, Raidan, and Saty's location, or say Massachusetts to hide my dad's location. It was possible Raidan had returned home by now, making him a possible target in both states. I hoped that by giving Ombrose the name of a city, surely, he wouldn't recognize it if he weren't from Earth. There was no winning, so I told the truth. I told him where I was born, and I prayed it wouldn't bite me in the ass later.

"Massachusetts?" He asked. I frowned, then hesitantly nodded. "For you," he started, pulling me from my fretting, "it would be considered between seven in the evening and eleven in the morning. We're able to reach a sleeping period in all time zones in this way." He knew where Essex was, which struck me as odd. It was also upsetting that he had this information now, but I couldn't let on that I didn't trust him. Not while he was finally talking to me about who he was and what he did with his powers.

"That's a long time," I supposed, considering the time stamps. Seven in the evening till eleven in the morning felt awfully odd, but after my calculations, it was merely sixteen hours. It was a healthy amount of time to be awake.

"That's how long we have to be at work," he replied.

"With the dreams?" I asked in hopes he'd divulge in the works of the gods. I was actually curious when it came to this. I found it fascinating that each god held the responsibility of different powers.

"The dreams, the fantasies, nightmares, and sleep." It was easy to decipher who ruled what. I already knew that Ombrose was the God of Nightmares, and Dramael was the God of Sleep. Tasphen and Reaver must be in charge of fantasies and dreams.

"You're not working," I remarked, not a question but an observation.

"No, not at this moment."

"What does that mean for you?" I wondered aloud.

He shrugged and turned to look back into the flames, taking a moment to consider my question. He let out a short breath and tilted his head down. "It just means far fewer nightmares for those who are sleeping."

I considered this and decided it was probably a good thing he was taking a break from working.

"Lord knows I could use a night free from them," I muttered, then stiffened as he turned to look at me. "Sorry. I didn't mean any offense." He furrowed his brow at me in disgust.

"Trust me." He scowled. "I know."

I wanted to look away from him. He had seen my worst nightmares, had possibly induced them. That was as vulnerable as one could get.

"Right…" I breathed. "You would." I suddenly remembered the smooth voice that called to me in the night. The kindness and warmth that echoed through my dreams as my worst fears played over and over in my mind. "That's how you found me…"

"It is," he replied. "I wanted to get to you sooner after realizing you were in the Under Realm, but I didn't know where you were until you dreamt of Mortades's throne room." I remembered it now, the nightmare turned dream I'd had the night before all things went south. I had woken to thorns and roses guarding me in my chamber. "What were you doing with him, anyway?" Ombrose asked, scoffing under his breath, but in a way as to purposefully have me hear it. "If you can produce the kind of power you exhibited for us earlier, why hadn't you left on your own? Why endure it?"

I shrank into myself at the question, not fully certain whether or not I should admit that I was new to wielding such power. I didn't know Ombrose from a hole in the ground. He and his family of gods had given me shelter, yes, but only after seeing that I was strong in my magic. I couldn't help but wonder if they'd only obliged due to my abilities. For all I knew, they could either be threatened by me, or want me for some greater purpose like Pyre did.

Everywhere I'd go from now on, I could assume the worst. Because that's what my life had turned into since my ascension. I wasn't sulking. I wasn't being overly dramatic and cautious. It was the truth. It had been my fate since birth, and it was entirely unavoidable. I still didn't know how I was going to get out of opening the Gates for Pyre, but I knew that my chances of saving the world weren't over yet. There was an inkling inside me that assured I was simply beginning on the path in this game of Fates. Though my destiny had been mapped out for me, I was the key, and it was I who could choose how to play the pieces that led to the finish line. I would repair the veil, and I would close the Gates for good. When and how, I did not know. But I would get there some day. Hopefully someday soon.

Ombrose looked to me for an answer as I sat and contemplated my words.

"You'd be surprised what I would endure to ensure the safety of the world."

"Time will tell," he replied in the flickering of flames. Before the silence decided to swallow us whole, he got up from the ground and took his leave. Before disappearing into the hall, he stopped and turned to face me. "Would you like some help to fall asleep? I can ask my father—"

"No thank you!" I said quickly, swift in declining that offer.

"Goodnight, Goddess." He shrugged and turned away.

"Goodnight, Ombrose."

24

CLUE
SATYRA

I was in a tall building, walls blank with white. It looked familiar, but for the most part, unplaceable. My legs moved without my assistance, and I realized very quickly that I was not in my own body. As I climbed the massive staircase, a black cape billowing at the corners of my vision, I understood that Ember was taking me on another journey.

He looked from side to side, slowly, as if to allow me time to register and collect my surroundings. I was in the House of Enchantment's library now, standing at the top of the staircase. There were so many books lining shelves three times as tall as me, and I felt the wave of discouragement wash over me. There were just too many books to look through. That hour we'd been promised seemed to shrink at the sight of what we'd have to read through. Ember moved us down to the back of shelves where the longest wall was lined with textbooks. We walked all the way to the right of the room, stopping to stare up at a bookcase that read I.I.M. at the top. The letters were carved into the shelf, dating the material all together.

"Is this where we'll find the books we need?" I questioned, though of course, no one answered. My hand, that wasn't really my hand, moved to grab a book from the shelf. It was titled *Το χαμένο αρχείο*.

"Um, yeah, I don't know what that says." The book flipped over, and I tried to read the back, but it was no use. At least he'd given me this much. He'd given me a start.

The book left my point of view, and I felt it tuck into my side. My legs moved, pulling me backward, and I suddenly lurched downward. The dark brown hands now pried at a floorboard at my feet, and I watched as the knuckles turned pink from the strain. With a light pop, it lifted, revealing a small hole and another text already hiding in it. The hands placed the new book from the shelf into the hole, joining the two together, and stood back up. My large boot stepped on the flooring and pushed the piece back into place, sealing the books in for safe keeping. I turned away, still searching the shelves with my eyes as the body carrying my conscious made its way back down the stairs.

"Thank you," I said, and the vision winked out.

25

RETURN

SATYRA

Passing by the exit I'd grown used to taking to get to work brought back the unwilling resentment I held over my best friend. It wasn't that I wanted to blame her for our problems, but it was hard not to point the finger at her. I cared for Shivalri, possibly more than I cared for anyone else in the family. But she had caused this apocalyptic mess, and she, unintentionally, had ruined so much of my life.

I couldn't go back to work after Shivalri was taken. Gram had forced me to quit my job and remain at home with her. She even forced Raidan to stay, telling Uncle Archer that she would homeschool him until Archer was able to start working again. Raidan was happy to stay and was even the one who'd suggested the idea to our grandmother. I could understand his need to help find and save his sister. I wanted to do that too. I wanted desperately for Shivalri to be safe and well. I just didn't like how much this affected me. I knew it was a selfish thing to even question, and I hated myself for it even now, as I scowled out the window toward the docks I'd grown used to working.

The ocean, it seemed, had surged upward in an impressive rise since the storms started brewing. I could just barely see the waves that surfaced inch by inch onto the decking near the boats, making sludge in the dirty snow. Shivalri was going to have a lot of fixing to do when she got back. She was going to have to settle herself and rebuild the disorder she'd produced.

"It's getting worse," Gram muttered under her breath as she sat behind the wheel, focused on the windshield spattering with hail. The storm we drove in switched in and out of hail and snow, making for greasy road conditions.

"I think it's safe to say it's only going to continue getting worse until she's back," said Raidan, folding his arms across his chest. Ember Blackwood hadn't spoken at all during the drive to Salem. Sitting beside him in the back of the car, watching the sticky slush take over the roads, had been eerily quiet, yet full of sound. Every move he made while shifting in his seat made my heart race. The hail hit the ground hard, tires rushing through the slosh, and I couldn't bring myself to speak either, for fear that I'd miss the sound of him bolting out the door. Whenever his fingers inched closer to the handle, I held my breath, waiting for him to jump out of the moving car. It seemed as though he desperately wanted to escape. I could only think how funny it was, that he, too, felt this way.

Ember hadn't mentioned last night's see-walk when we woke and left the house this morning. So many times, between running around and getting ready, I wanted to ask him about the books he'd hid beneath the floorboard in the House of Enchantment's library. But every time I'd approached him, he managed to find a way around me, preventing me from doing so. It was as if it had never happened. As if he hadn't spent a moment of the night with me in my dreams.

Gram took the exit into the snow-filled roads of Salem, Massachusetts. The tires beneath us skidded and swayed as she made her way down the one-way streets.

"Take a right here," said the stranger beside me, making me jump straight out of my skin. He had found me in my dreams yet again, and seeing him in person, knowing that it was him who'd guided me through his sights, was unsettling.

"What for?" Gram asked, flicking her blinker on just ahead of the turn.

"I know another way in," Ember informed us, adjusting his posture into a more relaxed pose. He leaned in forward, moving his head between the front seats to direct Gram. "If you drive past Gallows Hill, there's a warded entryway that will allow us passage without ever having to enter the field at the House of Enchantment."

"I've never heard of it," Gram held, but still, she followed his lead, and turned the drifting car onto the side street.

"The whole building is surrounded by field and then forest," Raidan added, turning to face the backseat.

"That's true," I said, regarding Ember. Unless you know how to fly, I can't picture another way to get in."

"Well, I can fly, but I wouldn't be able to carry any of you with me," said Ember.

"What?" I gasped.

"You can fly?" asked Raidan, eyes wide and waiting.

"Yes, but *you* can't, so my ability to fly is of no use."

"So, how are you planning to get us in then?" I wondered, eyeing him carefully, waiting for him to admit he hadn't been planning to take us with him at all.

"You can actually fly?" Raidan asked again, unwilling to accept this outrageous information.

"Yes, Raidan. I can fly," Ember replied, lips tight. "And the reason you haven't heard of the entryway is because I'm the one who put it there."

"How?" asked Raidan, distrust heavy in his voice.

"With magic."

"Great." He scoffed, and a small laugh escaped my lips.

"What's funny?" Ember asked, turning to examine my mindlessness.

"You're just as vague as my grandmother," I said, tilting a brow at him. He bit his plump lip, then turned his face into a grin.

"Then I must be smart," he supposed. Gram chuckled from in front of me.

"You've got the right idea, Mr. Blackwood. I am the one to whose boots you should lick."

"Ew…" I grimaced, considering the muddied frost under my own boot.

"Hey, I'll do whatever you ask of me if it means you giving me your trust," Ember insisted, leaning back into his seat.

"Trust is earned," Gram retorted. "You are doing well so far. Don't make me regret it."

"Understood." Ember nodded, and looked to me as if to say, he was looking for mine too.

I crossed one leg over the other and turned my head back toward my window. He wouldn't gain mine so easily. Though I did believe a lot of the things he'd said about wanting to help us, I still couldn't forgive the fact that he'd stood by and watched as Shivalri was tortured and taken away. He had been the one to carry her limp body, handing her over to the monsters.

"How do we know you're not just trying to lure us into a setup?" Raidan suddenly questioned, still turned to face the two of us in the backseat. "You could be working with Moira and the rest of those fuckers to pull us in their trap."

I turned on Ember now, trying to read his reaction to the accusation. He was annoyed more than anything. Whether that was a front or genuine irritation, I couldn't quite tell yet.

"I'm risking my ass to help save your sister," Ember snapped. "The least you could do is *try* to believe me when I say that I'm not trying to trick you."

"You're the one who handed her off!" Raidan fumed, Ember having clearly hit a nerve. The truth of it was that Ember Blackwood couldn't ask for these things. He had no right. All he could do was hope we'd taken his word for truth, but he was sadly mistaken if he thought he was owed our trust. Just because he'd given me see-walks and came to us preaching his innocence didn't mean he was off the hook.

"I had no choice," Ember said flatly, but I thought I saw a slight quiver in his jaw through the phrase.

"You did," said Raidan, turning back into his seat to face the front of the car. "You just made the easy one."

"You are heavily mistaken if you think for one second that that was easy—"

"Enough," Gram interjected, voice shrill. "Not while I'm driving."

"Sorry, Mrs. Grimsbane," Ember muttered, then turned his head my way. "Sorry," he said again, low and for me.

I pursed my lips, indecisive as to the kind of reassurance I should give him. I immediately recognized that I didn't have to give him anything and twisted my body to face the cold window again.

The car came to a slow crawl as we neared the small park in Gallows Hill. I looked around at the abandoned construction work that took over the icy parking area and frowned at the lot.

"Is this where the entryway is?" I wondered aloud.

"No, but it is where we're ditching the car," Ember told us.

"Is it far from here?" asked Gram, pulling the car into a parking space.

"Not at all."

"How far?" I asked, pushing for a real answer. He rolled his eyes at me and unbuckled his seat belt.

"It's a five-minute walk up one curved street. We'll get there far quicker than we would have if we'd gone through the woods and up the field."

"I'll take it," said Raidan as he stepped out the door. The engine discontinued its racket, and I pulled my gloves on over my hands, praying the cold wouldn't bite too harshly. I was used to dealing with snow, and on more than one occasion, I'd dealt with the icy air that whipped across the ocean while working at the port. A five-minute walk wouldn't be the worst thing in the world, though this whiplashing storm was bound to be a bad experience.

"Lead the way," said Gram, pulling her fluffy-lined hood over her silver hair.

"Where are we going?" I asked, curious as to where he was leading us. I hadn't ever come to Gallows Hill before, only passing it by briefly on a drive once or twice. The area was unfamiliar to me, even with having grown up in Essex.

"We are on our way to Proctor's Ledge."

26

PROCTOR'S LEDGE
SATYRA

T he rounded rocky ledge, once a broken piece of mountain, was now adorned by engraved stone, holding the reputation of nineteen names on its surface. As we stood in the crevice, staring through the mess of hail and snow, the ghostly weight pressed hard on my back. This, where we stood, was the grounds the executioners had dumped the bodies of the falsely accused witches long ago. It was said that if you'd listen closely, the grieving families who'd long passed since could be heard crying in the night.

"You put an entryway at the memorial?" I asked, bewildered by his choice of placement.

"I did," he answered, and took a step up to the stone wall.

"This is scornful, Blackwood. Entirely disrespectful to the souls of the deceased." Gram's words poked at my heart, and I felt sick at the thought of just standing here.

"The deceased are lying below our feet. We're going straight through."

"Through where?" I demanded, needing him to confirm what I thought he was saying.

"The tunnel."

"I will not," said Gram, clinging to her winter coat for dear life. She looked entirely frozen through the mess of storm that spun around us.

"Then you will freeze and join the lot of them."

"Hey!" I hissed and shoved him into the rock wall. "Watch yourself." Raidan was at my side in an instant, a gloved finger pointed in Ember's face.

"Fine." He huffed, his breath making clouds in the frigid air between us. "If she says we're not going through this way, then we're not going through this way." Ember raised his arms up in compliance, looking over me and Raidan to find my grandmother. "We'll do this however you want to, Mrs. Grimsbane. If you don't trust that this is a good decision, then that's fine. But we should get moving before people start to question why these two are attacking me at a memorial site in the dead of winter." I punched him at that for good measure, and he scowled at me in distaste. "I'm only trying to help. This is how I can help," he insisted, imploring Gram to give in. "Do you accept?" I turned to look at Gram, who wavered on her feet, seeming unsure of whether this was a good idea or not. Raidan didn't take his eyes off of Ember, making sure he depicted the distrust he had for him.

"Give him his space, Grandson," Gram finally said, but Raidan didn't move a muscle.

"Hey, man, just take a step back," Ember added. "I'm not going to do anything unless I'm asked to."

"I'll make sure of that," spat Raidan, though he did step away.

"Are you ready?" asked Ember, looking to Gram for approval.

"Let's go," Gram ordered, taking my arm in hers.

"Stay on my heels," Ember insisted. "It's completely dark

in there." At this, I thought of Shivalri and was glad she wasn't with us. She had always hated the dark. I, on the other hand, relished in it.

27

OBSCURUM

SATYRA

A swirl of color slapped my vision before total darkness exploded all around us. Gram still held on to my arm, Ember ahead of us, and Raidan at our backs. A harsh scrape against my booted ankle caused me to stumble forward, forcing me to find purchase on Ember's shoulders for balance, and letting go of Gram's arm.

"Jesus, Rai!" I hissed behind me, voice carrying through empty blackness. "Watch where you're going."

"Yeah, 'cause that's possible." He grunted, a reverberation of sarcasm. A firm hand clutched my own as I realized I still held on to Ember, and I quickly pulled away. When I threw out an arm behind me, I found that Raidan must've taken my place at Gram's side, not caring that I had been holding on to her. I sighed heavily and continued walking ahead in hopes I wouldn't run into Ember's back, as I couldn't see a thing ahead of me.

My senses were always heightened in the dark. As a child, I'd always tested myself when nightfall came. Living at the Grimsbane house afforded no extra light, and I'd taken it upon myself to use the disadvantage to hone my hearing abilities. I had turned it into a game, pretending there were monsters in my room, waiting to hear their footsteps in the night. Of course, the sounds I'd heard were scuttling mice throughout the walls. I traced their locations, up into the ceiling, with my eyes closed and ears open. I had never seen any monsters. It was all just make-believe. It was all just an adventure I'd made for myself in my head. Now, as I walked through the tunnelled grounds, I was certain I'd be able to identify any sound around us and could tell which direction it came from.

A swishing sound moved close to me at my right, and I whipped my head toward the culprit. I couldn't see anything, didn't hear anything more, but something like intuition told me I was being watched. It was at that moment that I saw a faint glimmer of red just a foot above my head. The glow became more focused, and I quickly realized it belonged to a pair of eyes that were looking directly at me. My breath left my lungs as the creature beside me touched my hand, and my body froze in place.

"It's me," it whispered, and I suddenly realized Ember stood beside me. His voice was quiet, not carrying an echo like mine before. Without the sound of footsteps behind me, I realized that I had been walking a faster pace, and it was only Ember and I standing in close proximity.

"You?" I gulped. Though I understood that it was him, it didn't seem real.

"Me," he replied, not offering much more.

"Ember?"

"That would be me." He chuckled under his breath, and it sent a wave of nervousness through me.

"Your eyes," I stammered, voice almost unheard. The glow disappeared for a second, but then he opened his eyes again, finding my face. "For a second there, I thought there was a demon from Hell standing beside me." My heart was still thundering from the jolt.

"I see in the dark," he said softly, squeezing my hand. "Don't worry. Not a demon from Hell."

"What the fuck?" My body flushed with heat as I understood just what he was saying. The whole time we'd been in the tunnel, he'd been able to see me. He'd watched me fall and cling to his shoulders for support. He had seen my concentration face as I searched for sounds in the dark. He was watching me now, and I had a firm hunch that he was amused by me. "Stop looking at me," I demanded, waiting to see his eyes shift from off me. He only laughed and approached me.

"Never," he answered.

I stared back up at him, trying my best to wear him down. He bore into me, enjoying the production, and I blew out an exasperated breath. "Fine." I grumbled, eyes narrowed in his direction. Though I couldn't see his facial features, that didn't mean he couldn't see mine. In fact, I had the feeling he could see me quite well with his strange, glowing eyes. I hastily pulled my hand from Ember's and started walking again. I heard him laugh again, as if he stood directly behind me, but I wouldn't give him the satisfaction of turning his way. As I trudged down into the darkness, the game turned from listening for sounds to feeling for his breath on my neck like the night before in the basement. I couldn't shake the feeling that he, too, played a similar game.

"About last night," he said, voice even quieter than before, and just behind my ear. I jolted in surprise. After this morning, I'd come to the conclusion that we weren't going to talk about the see-walk. But here we were, in the dark, with no one else around to hear his mention of it. Was that what this was about?

"Yeah…" I spun around, answering into the darkness. "About last night…" I waited for him to say more, watching his glowing eyes lower to my mouth. Only then did I realize I'd been biting my lower lip in anticipation. I closed my mouth, unwavering. His eyes shot back up to mine, and I tried my best not to blush.

"Can I trust you?" he asked, pulling me back to reality. I scoffed at his insolence.

"Can *you* trust *me*? Are you kidding me right now?"

"I am dead serious."

I took a moment to consider his words. I couldn't read his face, but I was able to pick up on the urgency of his voice. I heard the breathiness in his tone, as if this were important, a weighing factor. "I would like to think so," I replied. Not really an answer, but good enough of an offer.

"The book," he began.

"The one I saw you hide under the floorboard," I finished for him.

"No. The other one." I scrunched my brow, wondering why that one was the one of interest.

"Is that the one I'm supposed to get for us?" I wondered aloud.

"Shh," he pleaded. "They can't know." I stilled at his words, the secrecy tasting sour on my tongue.

"What do you mean they can't know?" I hissed, crossing my arms over my chest in means of defense.

"Raidan doesn't trust me whatsoever, and your grand-mother… Well, it's just not time for her to know."

"Know what?" I was beyond concerned, quickly begging whoever might be listening for Gram and Raidan to catch up to us.

"Just—" He sighed, his feet scuttling as if he were nervous. His worry only cranked mine up to high alert. "Get both books. The first is going to help us find Shivalri. But the second…" He paused, as if he were weighing his options. As if he weren't sure whether he should finish that sentence.

"What's in the second book, Ember?" I forced myself to sound as stern as possible.

"Promise me you'll keep it to yourself," he insisted, tension filling his voice. "Just at first. If you want to tell them after, that's fine. But just read it for yourself first. Let me explain. Then you can choose to give them the information inside." Silence filled the darkness as I considered his request. Nothing about this felt right. He was asking me to hide something from my own grandmother, the woman who'd raised me and made me all that I was.

"I get to choose?" I finally spoke.

"Yes." He blew, a touch of relief settling on the air between us. I suddenly heard the reverberating of boots thudding closer and understood that Gram and Raidan had caught up to us. It was time to put away all thoughts of the books, even though, I was hardly able.

28

PASSAGE

SATYRA

"We're here," said Ember, who was still by my side, despite having tried keeping my distance. My entire walk through the tunnel had been filled with goose bumps running through my coat sleeves, knowing full-well that the seer was trailing especially close behind me. I stopped midstep at Ember's announcement and searched around unseeingly.

"Where's here?" I heard Raidan ask just a few steps behind me. I heard the grinding of metal on metal and cringed at the loudness of it. In the tunnel, we'd kept relevantly quiet, making sure not to alert our presence to whoever might be around. A slice of yellow light beamed through a crack in the wall ahead of me, allowing me to see where I stood. Aside from the metal door and its wheel mechanism on its front, the rest of the tunnel was made of stone and dampness. I thought there would have been far more dirt, and maybe even snow lining the floors, but the tunnel was clean from imperfections.

"Stay as quiet as possible," Ember warned, voice hushed. "We're not done passing underground, but once we pass the next threshold, we'll be able to hear anyone upstairs, just as they'll be able to hear us."

"Where is upstairs?" I asked, looking at the rock ceiling.

"Mr. Blackwood, am I to understand that we are beneath the Salem House of Enchantment?" I gasped at Gram's words. I hadn't even thought of that. I was clearly unobservant, and especially ridiculous to have reacted audibly. I truly hadn't guessed where we were going.

"That's correct," Ember spoke, still in a whisper so as not to attract the ears of others.

"Should we expect to find anyone in there?" Gram asked, bringing down the winter hood to show the concern written across her face.

"No. This place was only built as a reinforced shelter. It's only ever been used a handful of times as a bunker. These days it's just a place for storage and rats." I couldn't help but laugh at the irony of rats running through the place.

"How is it that you've gotten away with making an entryway down here?" Gram wondered aloud, peering around the corner of the entry.

"This door, if opened by anyone other than me, opens to a small tool room, no matter the direction the door swings. You need my fingerprint to pass through the ward I've placed."

"How did you manage to dig the tunnel?" Raidan questioned, voicing my thoughts exactly. The passageway had been stone from floor to ceiling.

"I didn't dig the tunnel." Ember rolled his eyes. "It was dug out as a burial mound, but in the end, the city decided against disrupting the dead. They chose to leave the bodies where they are underground and sealed the hole with the memorial wall."

"As they should," said Gram. I had to agree. Digging up bodies just to move them a few feet over was so wrong.

"How will this work?" Gram asked as she and Raidan huddled closer to us.

"Just as we've planned," he assured her. "I'll be the distraction, and you'll go straight to the library to search for whatever you think you may find. In and out. Just like we talked about." He turned to my cousin now, straightening his posture so as to size himself up to Raidan's stature. "Are you still good to stand guard while they look through the books?"

"Good on my end," he answered, voice low and eyes sure.

"Ready?" asked Ember, looking to all of us. His eyes landed on me, a slight lift to his brow. He'd shown me the way to the hidden books. I knew exactly where to look because of him. I couldn't help but worry about his wanting to hide it from my family. It was weird to find that he'd kept this secret between the two of us, as if the see-walk and its contents were for me, and for me only. I gave a curt nod, showing him that I understood, and followed his steps through the groaning door and into the new hall that filtered yellow light.

29

UNPREDICTED

SATYRA

W e'd made it to the last door within minutes of walking. This hall had felt shorter than the last, though it might have only felt that way. When we had walked down the blackened tunnel, I couldn't see a thing, but I knew that Ember was watching me. It made the walk seem to take forever, as I wished for it to end. This time around, we could all see each other, thanks to the several yellow lights that were hung every ten or so feet. The darkness had never bothered me before, not until I knew there were eyes surveilling me.

Ember put a finger up to his mouth and looked up to the ceiling as if to say he was trying to listen for footsteps above us. I strained my own ears, trying to sharpen my senses in an attempt to find noise overhead. I frowned, frustrated by my failure, and looked to him to see if he'd heard anything. By the looks of his face, which clearly matched mine, he hadn't heard anything either.

"It's clear," he whispered, biting at his lip. The scar along his face shone under the yellow light with the movement of his jaw.

"It's a trap," said Raidan, deathly low, eyes narrowed. Ember shook his head, proving his confusion, and tilted his ear back up to the ceiling.

"They should be here..." he told us, and a pang of worry filled my mind. Had they known we were coming? I quickly understood that I now trusted Ember, at least in this. If he'd thought anything other than what he'd told us, it certainly didn't show on his face and worry crept further up into his eyes. "Wait here," he finally said, placing a hand on the door-knob ahead of us. I grabbed his arm, forcing him to stop.

"Are you sure you want to go in there?" I asked. "What if it's a trap for you?" He pursed his lips, searching my face before deciding to go through, nonetheless. I had to hand it to him—secrets aside, he was a brave man. After witnessing the horrors of the High Council, blindly walking into whatever could await only proved he wasn't as cowardly as I'd assumed. The memory of our see-walk in the night forest surged through my mind as I called him a coward, demanding he show his face. As I watched him leave through the door, a small piece of regret formed in my gut. I would hold his faults against him for as long as I lived, but that didn't mean I wished him dead.

The minutes ticked by agonizingly slow as Raidan, Gram, and I waited for his return. Soundlessly and timidly, we listened for signs of his arrival. As if carried by a quiet breeze, light steps sounded ahead of us, and all of our heads shot to the door. Raidan took one steady step closer, putting a bit of distance between the door and Gram and me.

"It's me," said a hushed voice before Ember appeared through the door. A rush of relief filled my lungs as I saw him safe and in front of us.

"What is it?" Gram asked, and I noticed the worry still lay on his face.

"There's no one here," he stammered, appearing just as puzzled as I felt.

"Where are they?" I asked, unsure if I wanted the answer.

"I wish I knew..." Ember opened the door and told us to enter. Raidan took Gram's arm and passed the threshold. As I entered the House of Enchantment's basement, I searched Ember's face, trying to read whether it was a lucky chance to have the High Council gone, or if this was far worse than we could've expected. Something in his eyes confirmed it was the latter, and my gut sank heavily as we made our way toward the staircase.

"Satyra?" Ember called my name, pulling my eyes away from Gram and Raidan's backs.

"Hmm?"

"Be on your guard. Something about this doesn't feel right, but I don't want to scare anyone into leaving."

"But should we?" I questioned, eyes wide in panic.

"We can't afford to."

"What if this gets ugly? What if it is a trap, Ember? If we all walk into this, and we get caught, it will all have been for nothing."

"Then we can't get caught," he contended.

"But what if we do?"

"Then I'll hold them off long enough for your grandmother to weave you far, far away."

I gasped at his words, not having realized he knew about Gram's time-weaving. "You know about my grandmother's powers?" I gawked and watched as a slight grin appeared on his dark lips.

"I know all about your grandmother and the rest of her family. It was my job to know." I stewed in this knowledge as we neared the beginning of the stairs, finding that Gram and Raidan were waiting for us at the top. "I will help you, no matter the cost to me, Satyra." I looked to find that he was sincere in his promise and found myself growing fonder of him by the minute, whether that was a good thing or not.

"I'll hold you to it." I gulped the fear down and trudged up the stairs with the seer at my side.

30

HUSH

SATYRA

We were quiet as we entered through a back door in the House of Enchantment. Everything about this screamed that it didn't make sense. I couldn't trust that the High Council wasn't here. It had to be a trick, a play of the mind. Even Ember had thought it strange, deeming it unnatural for them to leave the building without his knowledge. Moira, Damek, Sora, and even Nesrin, the one I hadn't met yet, were supposed to be waiting here while Ember hunted me and my family down. He'd been given the task of eliminating the remains of the Grimsbane problem. What the High Council failed to realize was that Ember, as it seemed, was conspiring against them.

The room we'd come through was dusted in cobwebs, looking as if it hadn't been touched in decades. There were cardboard boxes lining the walls, looking as if they'd been forgotten. At the front of the room, the wall with the open door was lined with shelves, each easily holding a few hundred jars of gods know what.

"You left the door open?" Raidan hissed, turning over his shoulder to scowl at Ember, who'd been walking next to me.

Gram and Raidan had walked into the room first, both eager to get this over with.

"There's no one here," said Ember as he passed us all, widening the door for us to walk through. "I wasn't joking when I said the place was empty."

"They could have returned," Raidan argued.

Gram nodded her head, seeming to agree with him. She met with Ember and poked her head around the corner, looking this way and that. "They truly aren't here..." she mumbled with worry and disbelief. "I don't sense them at all."

At that, I walked over to the lot of them and passed the threshold, clenching my fists in preparation for attack. I'd half expected a shock or punch to the gut, but the giant room was empty of people. The bright white walls were a slam to my senses as I lifted my head to find the stacks lining the library upstairs. While walking through the underground passage, we'd gone from journey in pitch black, to a faint allowance of light, all the way up to this. It felt almost chemical to be around this anomalous vivid-white.

"We should hurry," said Ember, coming to my side. I'd grown to expect him there, somehow, in the last twenty odd hours of acquaintance. He'd felt almost familiar, which I expected was due to the see-walks he'd shared with me. It wasn't a comforting feeling to have him nearby, only it seemed as if it were predetermined. "You see up there?" Ember asked, pointing for Raidan. His aim landed far left and upstairs where a small hexagonal window stood between two bookshelves. "That's where we'll need you."

"Got it," he answered, immediately grabbing hold of the guardrail, and stalking up the stairs.

"Good," said Ember, turning to me. Gram stood just to my left now, Ember on the other side. "We'll need to split up to cover more ground. The more eyes on more books the better."

"Agreed," said Gram. "I'll take the left near Raidan, Ember you're to the right, and Saty you take the middle."

But I couldn't. In order for me to get the books that Ember had hidden under a floorboard, I needed to get as far right as possible. Ember couldn't get them himself. We all had eyes on him, not quite trusting him just yet. He wouldn't get away with retrieving them and keeping them secret, like he'd wished for. I scrambled, trying to find a way to make sense of my refute, and settled on an embarrassing one.

"Can I take the right, Gram?" I asked, feeling a little nervous, and even a bit foolish. "I don't mean to be a coward, it's just…" I looked to the stairs and twisted my face so as to look frightened. "The stairs are closest to the right."

"You are anything but a coward, my sweet," she said, placing a hand on my shoulder. "Of course. Wanting to feel safe is not something to be ashamed of. You take the right and let us hope we don't need to make use of the stairs in that kind of event." I offered her a half smile, feeling like a shitbag.

As far as Ember went, I couldn't tell if he'd caught on to any of that, or if he'd forgotten, and assumed I really was weak. "Let's go, everyone. We don't have time to spare."

I let Gram go up first, making sure she was far enough away from us to finally turn to Ember. He was wearing a smirk now, eyeing me up and down.

"What?" I scoffed, rolling my eyes at him as I started up the stairs.

"Nice cover," he said, and leisurely followed my steps.

"Whatever." I made to walk faster, but he caught my hand on the guardrail, causing me to stop and spin on him. I was a few inches taller than him as I stood two steps further up. I looked down at him, narrowing my eyes as if daring him to come closer.

"You can't let them see you retrieve the books."

"I wasn't planning on it," I said, slipping my hand out from underneath his.

He let his hand fall to his side and searched my face. It was evident that we were playing a similar game. Neither one of us truly trusted the other, and he was searching to find the crack in my façade, just as I was doing to him. He worried his lip, and I watched as the muscle in his jaw ticked. I felt my own muscles tick in reaction. Damn, he was *hot*. He was a bit of an ass and entirely deceitful, but his face was perfection.

"Put them in your jacket," he insisted, ending his weighing analysis of me. I scowled at him, huffing a breath of annoyance.

"I planned to."

"Good." He smirked.

"Good," I replied, crossing my arms over my chest. Not even a second went by before his eyes landed there, and I suddenly felt all too aware of his gaze. With my coat zipped down, my shirt had lowered enough to show some significant cleavage. As a bigger girl with a lot of curves to offer, I didn't blame his eyes for wandering. I turned around, heat creeping up my face, and quickly fixed my shirt before making my way up the rest of the stairs. If I didn't know any better, I'd think the affect his looks had on me were the same as mine on him. What an interesting turn of events…

THERE WERE a ridiculous number of books in the House of Enchantment's library. I couldn't imagine ever being able to read even one shelf full of these books, let alone the entirety of the collection. I hadn't come up here the first time we'd come to the building. Raidan and I were more interested in scoping out the lower level, while Shivalri had been overcome with excitement to search through the shelves. I could only imagine what her face might have looked like as she roamed the top floor like I was doing now. I traced a line across the spines of books, wondering if she, too, had touched these ones.

I had to shake the sadness from my thoughts while I was up here. It was fine and dandy to wallow in missing my cousin, but now was not the time. I needed to focus. I kept my gaze low, trying my best to look inconspicuous as I pretended to search the shelves for clues. In reality, even if I were looking for clues, I would have no idea what to look for. A lot of these books were written in different languages. I was fluent in English and French and knew a little bit of Latin since Gram was fond of using her family's tongue. But these books, both new, old, and very old, weren't written in anything I could understand.

I walked up and down the aisles, eyes intent on finding books, but ears listening for sounds of Gram shuffling through her section. I didn't like the thought of doing anything behind my grandmother's back, but what Ember had shown me, and said to me, had intrigued me. I figured that so long as I wasn't hurting anyone, it would be all right to keep this thing between us a secret. Just until I found out what was in the books. Then, I could make my own decision on whether or not to involve Gram.

I heard a movement coming from the other side of the aisle I was in and peered through the gap in the books. I couldn't see anyone, but I was sure someone was watching me. I felt a prickle of unease settle over me as I considered this. For some reason, unbeknownst to me, it didn't feel like the presence of Gram, Raidan, nor Ember.

"Hello?" I whispered, moving to look around to the other side of the bookcase. It felt cold in the air, like my intuition was not just my imagination. When I peered around, expecting to find an enemy, I let out a sigh of relief when I found nothing there. I held a hand to my chest, feeling the pounding of my heart beneath my skin. I unzipped the rest of my winter coat and allowed the breeze to cool myself. I'd gotten all worked up over nothing.

"Satyra," I heard a voice from behind me. I whirled around, panic flooding my face, and blew out a hiss as Ember stood there, grinning at me.

"What?" I spat. My nerves were clearly getting the best of me.

"You look like you've seen a ghost."

"Yeah, well, you caught me off guard," I muttered, folding my arms over my chest. "What do you want?"

He came closer to me and tilted his head down to me. "I'm going to distract Sabine. It'll give you enough time to grab the books and hide them." I swallowed hard, my heart rate finally slowing to a normal pace.

"Fine," I said, turning my back on him.

"Satyra?" he called, and I twisted over my shoulder to look at him, questioning. "You're blushing." My mouth fell open, and Ember simply turned around and walked away. What was this guy's motive? Something about his arrogance made my lady parts come to life, and I hated myself for it. I was not supposed to be thinking about things like that right now. I was not supposed to be thinking about *him* in that way.

The floorboards creaked beneath my feet as I neared the

area, I knew I would find the books that Ember had hidden. I glanced over to the opposite section of the library and found that Ember was facing me and talking to Gram, forcing her to look in the opposite direction. He was giving me a chance to sneak down and peel the floor up without anyone seeing me do so. I stepped a little harder, bouncing my weight beneath me in hopes of sussing out the hidden compartment below. The flooring creaked and groaned as I continued, until one of the pieces slid from the contact.

Bending over, I sank my fingers into the gap I'd created by bouncing on the board. I'd expected it to be difficult to pry; however, it lifted with ease. There was a quiet snapping sound that escaped the hole, and I quickly turned to see if anyone else had heard it. To my relief, Gram and Ember were both turned to face a giant bookshelf, Ember reaching up to grab a book. I let out a quick sigh of relief, and turning back to the hidden compartment, I found the exact replica of what the see-walk had shown me. I removed them from their resting place, finding that the one titled *To χαμένο αρχείο* was quite heavy, and the other, untitled, feather light. I wanted to take the time to open them now, my curiosity biting at me. But I knew that now was not the time, and I'd get my chance later. I stood from my crouch and shoved them in between my ribs and arm; zipping my jacket over them. In attempt to be silent, I slid the piece of flooring over the hole and stepped atop it, just as Ember had done in the see-walk. With a tiny click, it was back in position, allowing me to walk away with the knowledge that no one would know I'd found the hiding hole in the first place.

I made to walk back toward my section of the library, when I suddenly felt the cool tension lifting in the air again. I swung my head from side to side, widening my eyes in search of the cause. Still, I was left finding nothing in its wake. Earlier, I'd chalked it up to my nerves being on high alert, but now, I couldn't ignore it. There was definitely something going on. There was someone else here with us. Just as I was about to call out to Gram and Ember, I saw something move from the corner of my eye. I whirled around, trying to find it, but it was gone in a matter of seconds.

"Who are you?" I hollered, stalking toward the place I'd seen the shadow.

"Satyra?" Gram called. I could hear the pair of them rushing toward me.

"What's wrong?" asked Ember, his stance rigid and ready for a fight. I looked to both of them, worry apparent on their faces.

"There's someone else here with us." Gram's eyes narrowed as she looked around the room, and I could hear the gritting of Ember's teeth beside me.

"How do you know? Did you see someone?" Ember questioned, putting an arm out in front of me as if he were putting himself between me and whoever was here. My heart made a funny little jump, but the fear from a stranger being here overpowered whatever his actions had triggered in me.

"I can feel them," I said, taking a step back. The cold air was back again, and stronger this time around.

"Show yourself," Gram demanded, and I felt the cold seeping through my winter coat.

A form appeared before my very eyes, taking on the appearance of an elderly woman, who wore glasses on the bridge of her nose, and all beige clothing.

"Hello, Esther," my grandmother greeted her.

"What?" I stammered, turning to Gram for an explanation. As I stared at her, she didn't seem too surprised, and thankfully, she didn't seem worried either.

"Sabine," the old woman crooned. "What are you doing

with the likes of this one?" she asked, pointing a crooked, bony finger at Ember. He bowed his head in mock shame.

"You wound me, Esther."

"How do you know her?" I asked, trying to get some kind of grasp on the situation. "Gram?"

"She's an old friend of the High Council," she replied, though she herself didn't seem to think of her as a friend.

"A friend of witches and warlocks, and most creatures in between," said the woman, looking me up and down. Her eyes found purchase in the crook of my arm, and she tilted a graying brow at me. I felt the books beneath my jacket heat from the attention and turned my body away from her. I was sure now, that I hadn't been as stealthy as I'd thought I'd been. She had seen me dig up and hide the books.

"Why do you show yourself now, Esther?" Gram asked, pulling the focus of the conversation in the right direction.

"Because I believe I have something your family covets, and I think now will be the only time you'll ever get it from me."

Gram stood up straight, surprise twisting in her gaze.

"Details," Ember insisted, but Esther only scoffed in his direction, wearing out the wrinkles in her pout.

"Your granddaughter," she said, pulling out the words slowly. My face reddened as I waited for her to rat me out. Gram looked to me, questioning, but Esther pulled her attention back. "She is gifted, isn't she?"

"My grandchildren are very new to this life, but yes, they are gifted."

"The one whose eyes shine with golden ichor..." She trailed, and I finally understood that she couldn't be speaking about me. My eyes were hazel, a mixture of brown like my father, and green like my mother.

"What of her?" Gram questioned, voice intent on getting the woman to spill whatever she might have to say.

"Before she and I became acquainted, she was quite entranced by a particular tome…" My eyes widened as I realized who this old lady was. I remembered now. Shivalri had told me about meeting a hobgoblin in the library. I had forgotten all about it up until now. "It's what called me to her. The tome spoke words to her, imploring me to seek her out. I would not have shown myself to her. No, I was content in watching over the books, allowing her to roam the shelves. But that girl… She is nothing of this world, is she? Nothing I've ever known. The tome recognized it in her."

"Where's the tome now?" Ember asked, leaning against a bookshelf, evidently trying to seem at ease. The tick in his jaw told me he was feeling otherwise.

"It is safe within my grasp," she held, looking up to my grandmother with a knowing smile.

Gram pulled at her lips and released a breath of frustration. "What do you want in exchange for the book?"

The hobgoblin's wrinkles crashed into one another as her smile split up her face. "Oh, you know… This and that."

"Out with it, Esther." Gram was clearly impatient, and I was entirely confused. The woman's smile simmered down, turning into a smirk rather than a beam.

"I ask only for a favor. One that can be used at a later time, at my convenience," she insisted. I could see now that she wasn't just a simple old woman. She wasn't frail, and she wasn't helpless. She was wily and calculated.

"I will not freely give any favor." Gram scoffed, and I was glad she'd caught on to that being a bad idea. "However, I will grant you a favor within reason."

"Go on," Esther crooned, pushing her glasses up the bridge of her nose. One gray brow lifted in question.

"So long as your request does not cause harm to anyone, including myself, and it doesn't go against the laws of nature, I will provide you with the favor."

Esther grinned wide, nodding her agreement. "Deal," she said, extending her hand out to Gram.

My grandmother took the old woman's hand in hers, shaking firmly. "Deal," she confirmed.

I was so caught up in the sight of a new creature in front of me, I had hardly the time to swallow what had just happened. Had my grandmother really just made a deal with a hobgoblin without knowing what the request was?

"The book," Ember stated, breaking the cyclone of worries swirling around in my head. Esther held out a fist in front of us, the air around us freezing to the touch. She clenched her knuckles tightly, then released an open hand, the small, leather-bound book lying flat on her palm. Ember snatched it from her grip and handed it over to Gram.

"This..." Gram mumbled, a muddled look across her face. "I do not know this language..."

The hobgoblin shrugged, her beige shawl drooping off her shoulders. "No one of this realm does."

31

PLEDGE

SHIVALRI

"**D**id you manage to rest?" asked Reaver as he entered the room. I wanted to groan out loud from the frustration of having stayed awake all night. My eyes were dry from staring at the domed ceiling for hours without respite.

"Does it look like it?" I grumbled and pulled my stiff body up off the ground with much effort.

Reaver cocked his head to the side as if studying me. "Not a wink, huh?"

"Nope."

"Do you sense it, Father?" Tasphen questioned quietly. I hadn't even noticed him move closer to the hall's entrance in which Reaver and I stood in front of.

"He is near," said Dramael, stalking in quick pace toward the entrance room of the cave.

"Who's near?" I asked, turning on Reaver for some form of explanation.

"Gerimor," he said, his face the portrayal of confusion.

"What?" I hissed. "I thought I got to decide whether or not we'd involve him!"

"Goddess, I thought you *had* decided." He blinked, confused. "My father said that Ombrose informed him of your decision to meet with our uncle."

"I did no such thing!" I grit my teeth, feeling betrayed and confused at the same time. "In fact, Ombrose told me just last night that he didn't like the idea of me meeting your uncle."

"That doesn't make sense…"

"No, it doesn't!" I snapped, delving through last night's conversation and trying to find what might have told Ombrose that I'd made such a decision. But there was nothing. I hadn't said anything of the sort. "I don't know who lied to who, but someone here is being dishonest, and it could be the cost of my safety. It could mean the cost of the world's safety." The mention of dishonesty rubbed me the wrong way as I remembered Ombrose's fumble during our brief conversation about nightmares. He'd told me that he didn't cause nightmares, rather, people slipped into them. Not long after he'd blundered, telling me that he'd given me a nightmare in order to find me in the Under Realm. I was starting to distrust him, the more I thought about it. I'd be right to be weary around him. I'd be right to be weary around all the gods who'd fallen into my life as of late.

"Strange," said Reaver, running a hand through his hair in perplexity. "I don't understand the deceit, but if anything, I can assure you that Gerimor is not one to put the lives of others in danger."

"He's the God of Death!" I spat, whirling on him.

"*Peaceful* death," he corrected, placing a hand on my shoulder. "Try to play nicely. I will help you get to the bottom of things as soon as this meeting is over." I knew he meant well, but nothing of that was reassuring in the slightest. If anything, it only amplified my worry. If he thought it strange, it most likely was.

Dramael and Tasphen had disappeared around the corner of the hall, leaving us only with the choice to follow. We rounded the corner and trailed behind the pair. Tasphen followed the steps of his father, his gait never making so much as a sound. In the short time I'd watched the strange gods, his silence was something that stood out to me. It was as if it were his gift. Perhaps it was precisely that. Just as Pyre and the pythrants had a particularly gifted sense of smell, the Orsimm and their father could very well have similar gifts appealing to the senses. If I were to bet on it, I'd think Tasphen would be quite useful as a spy. He'd mentioned hearing sounds far sooner than the others, and his movements were all quieted in comparison.

With Ombrose and Reaver, I was still unable to pin their talents. Ombrose had his shadows, but I didn't quite know what they could do. With Reaver, I noted that he'd seemed to be the kind of person to be more serious and take charge, but nothing else stood out to me. Ombrose, on the other hand, was the opposite. He was looser in the way he spoke, and from what I'd gathered in this short period of time, he was known to act before thinking. Dramael had said that he was always putting his nose where it didn't belong, and I thought it could be factual. His character was off in some areas. He was mostly kind, his behavior never truly giving me a reason to mistrust him. But my gut told me to be hesitant with him. The way Pyre had acted toward him at the castle was a red flag all in itself. Pyre, who was the ruler of the Under Realm, had been terrified by the thought of his brother being nearby. If Ombrose having Pyre's brother's scent on him was any indication as to what kind of god he was, I was right to be cautious around him. I had almost forgotten about that factor.

Heat pricked my skin as I remembered Pyre's reaction to smelling his brother. For the God of the Dead to be scared, to have locked me up for my safety and charged the pythrants with guarding me at all costs, was a sign to be scared of his brother myself.

Dramael and Tasphen entered the cave's entrance, Reaver and I coming in to join them. Dramael turned to greet me, gesturing a salute over his heart.

"*Bœngï magàntin*, Goddess. I hope you were able to find rest overnight." Those foreign words sounded a lot like the French *bon matin*. I understood that he'd most likely wished me a good morning. But I found the end of that phrasing odd. Shouldn't he have known whether or not I had slept last night? I was made to understand that it was him who sent people off to sleep. I'm sure that if he wanted to, he could've used whatever magic was in him to find out for himself.

"Dramael, Tasphen," I nodded a greeting. "Good morning to you both."

"*Bœngï magàntin*, Father," Reaver chimed in a language that was both unearthly, and yet familiar. He still stood at my side, serious and astute. "Have you any news from Gerimor?"

"Yes!" Dramael clapped triumphantly. "He answered my summons immediately." He turned to me now, a smile warming the face, which held the pair of night-black eyes. "I was pleased to hear of your decision late last eve. I believe it was in your best interest. My brother is very close in relations with our Lord and will be an asset to have on our side." I made to correct him, wanting to tell him that Ombrose had lied to him, but then remembered what Reaver had suggested. I was to play nicely this morning, until the issue was sorted. Ombrose wasn't anywhere nearby, so it could still be possible that it was Dramael who lied to Reaver and blamed it on Ombrose.

"What was Uncle's response, Father?" Reaver cut in for me. "Has he agreed to meet?"

"Indeed. He comes just now, Reaver. In fact, Ombrose is out scouting the tree line."

"I sensed him just moments ago," said Tasphen. "Uncle should arrive within minutes."

"Then we've arrived at the perfect time," Reaver supposed, looking down at me. The look he gave me was as if it were a message to remind me of playing the part.

"Is there anything I should know about the God of Death before he arrives?" I asked, finding something useful to add to the conversation without causing any suspicions. I wasn't sure if I was going along with what Dramael had secretly planned, and he knew what I was doing, or if I was going along with Ombrose's plan without him knowing. I wondered now if Ombrose might remain outside during the meeting, so as not to get caught in the lie he'd spun. Though I did find it strange for him to want Gerimor to come. He'd really seemed against the idea of involving him.

"Nothing to worry your mind about," he assured, assumingly in an attempt to ease my mind, but only achieving the opposite. What was that supposed to mean? Nothing to worry my mind about... Meaning there was something, only I shouldn't concern myself with it. I tried scrubbing the mistrust from out of my head, but its stain was irremovable.

"He is here," Tasphen announced, the words moving Dramael and his cape like a puppet on a string toward the cave's entrance. Panic and excitement traveled like anticipatory jitters, my pulse hammering in my throat. Through the barred portcullis, a wisping white mist spilled through the bronzed metal, pooling at the bottom of the cave we stood in. I first found Ombrose, dark and tall, wings held tight behind him. As the fog parted for me to better see the man at

Ombrose's side, I found myself surprised by his physique. I had expected tall, dark, and handsome, like the rest of the Orsimm. To my surprise, the God of Death was anything but that. Sweeping wings like that of an angel, slim in width but full in white feathers crowned the man waiting on the other side of the gate. His skin was not dark, but more a match to my own coloring. The warm, ivory tone seemed almost golden in comparison to the white tendrils that flowed around him. I'd almost expected a sickly, hollowed man, but he was distinctly made of life. Standing next to Ombrose, Gerimor didn't depict death in the slightest.

"Welcome, Brother," Dramael boomed, placing a hand over his heart, and bowing his head in respects. "Good to see you in well form." Ombrose pressed his palm to the cave's exterior wall, and I watched as the giant metal door slid up into the slot in the ceiling, allowing the pair to enter the room.

A warmth like being under the sun on a beach filled the cave, thawing the tips of my toes, which had grown cold since coming into hiding. Gerimor appeared to carry a light with him, as if he were comfort itself. Without ever having met him, I'd expected to feel death radiating from him. This was a welcome turn of events.

Gerimor quickly lowered to the ground, kneeling before us. Ombrose took to leaning against the cave wall, choosing to stay close to the opening. Looking directly to me, the God of Death found my eyes, locking me into a gaze. His eyes... I'd assumed they'd be black or red or at least otherworldly. But these were eyes I'd seen many times before. They were a pale gray under the cave's dim light, but when he angled his head up toward me, the blue and gold shone brightly—a match to my own.

"Goddess of all realms," he spoke, boring into me. "It is

of great honor to kneel afore you. I give you my oath, here and now, before my brother and his kin." My heart was beating out of my chest, breath tight in my ribs, brain foggy from the nerves pinching me all over. This was the God of Death, bent to my feet, about to swear some kind of oath to me. What did it mean for the one who is death to value me? "I pledge myself to you, alongside the king of the Under Realm. I solemnly swear my protection unto you for as long as you remain in this realm." I blinked in shock at the swearing he'd offered, entirely hazy, forgetting my place. A wisp of white curled out from his chest, threading toward me. Before I could even think to move out of the way, the string plunged into my sternum, splintering, and expanding until every inch of me was strung in a white glow. With each tug, my body felt lighter, weightless.

"What was that?" I blew, rejuvenation swimming in my skin. The god simply stood, and gave a quiet nod of understanding my way, before turning to address his brother.

"Dramael," the fair god chimed, voice like a melody, sweet and soothing. "You were right to have summoned me."

As I looked between the pair, I noticed the differences immediately. Not only were they physically different, the nature in which they held their presence tipped the scales in opposite directions. Where Dramael was assertive, brood, and confident, Gerimor was relaxed, as if presenting ease and amity.

"I am grateful for your acceptance, and I am sure the goddess is thankful for your cooperation," said Dramael, speaking on my behalf.

"I have come to your summons, as it is in the best interest of my lady."

"Lady?" I stammered, not meaning for the words to escape my mouth. Heat flushed through me uncomfortably so, and the desire to disappear brewed rapidly in my gut. From behind the God of Death, I heard Ombrose bite back a hard laugh, and when I met his gaze, I wished for my eyes to burn a hole through his head. Then suddenly, as if looking through a foggy window, the space near the open door stirred. I squinted my eyes, attempting to force them through the haze, trying to find the source of the magic. Was it Ombrose's shadows emerging?

Blowing in the air was the scent of earthy woods and fresh soil, filling my senses with familiarity. In one quick move, a pair of hands lifted in the cave's entrance, holding a helmet forged in gold. With the helmet removed from the head, which now appeared in the blink of an eye, I recognized the body that stood before us.

"Pyre..." I inhaled, taking a step back on quaking feet. He was here, and he had entered the cave, having clearly used some form of invisibility I was not aware he had. Before he could find me, I turned on my heel and bolted for the curved hall. My feet tripped over each other, fighting for footing as I looked back over my shoulder, watching him walk farther into the mouth of the cave. My steps faltered at the sight of his face, heart snagging on my captor-turned-instructor. For all that had happened, for all that he had done, my heart still raced with hope whenever he walked into a room.

"Where is she?" a voice like thunder tore through the cave, my heart lurching out from my chest. "Show her to me, Dramael!" he bellowed.

Pyre was here. It was really him, in all his rage and all his power. Needing proof that I wasn't being fooled and that I truly had heard the God of the Dead demanding my presence, I took a step closer, hidden still by the curve of the hall.

There, standing within the confines of the cave, stood Pyre Malum, ensconced by the glow of fire he held in each hand. He was terrifying in his stance, looking fierce and godly, ever able to conquer whatever he desired. He had always seemed strong to me, but now, in the light, the desperation he held told a whole new story. It was clear that he was not one to cross, and certainly not one to deceive. Gerimor stepped aside, allowing Pyre to come forward, face-to-face with the God of Sleep. He was ethereal in the way he glowed, barely touching the ground beneath him.

"Gerimor?" Dramael stammered. "What have you done?"

"Our king should have been extended the same invitation as I to enter this home, Brother. He has never meant us harm," said Gerimor.

"You have given him admittance, fooling us into welcoming him in. This is our shelter, not his," he replied.

I couldn't believe the nerve he had to speak those thoughts aloud with Pyre standing so close.

"I am not here for you, Dramael," Pyre snarled. "Where is she?"

My breath hitched at his mention of me, my body inadvertently drawing closer to him.

"She is not your plaything." It was Ombrose's turn to snarl, but Pyre didn't pay him any attention. He searched the cave, face tight, obviously uninterested in the gods standing before him. Before I could make to hide my presence, his eyes, red and seething, landed where I stood, restricting my lungs. He ran to me so quickly, crossing the cave in so few paces, I didn't even have time to blink. Expecting some form of outburst or for him to pick me up and drag me away, I flinched, arms up to cover my face. He grabbed my shoulders, and then each side of my face, replacing my hands with his.

"Are you all right?" Pyre searched, frantic in every move. His eyes were sunken in as if sleep had evaded him; a dark black shadow adorned his chin and jaw. "Tell me you're okay," he demanded, shaking me. I was far too stunned to do anything but gawk at him. What was this reaction? I thought the first thing he'd do was lecture me for having left him, but his priorities were far off from what I'd expected. He turned on the Orsimm family, smoke lifting from his shoulders. "Did you hurt her?" His voice was deadly low.

"I'm okay," I assured him with the voice of a mouse, entirely unconvinced I should even be speaking at all.

"If you've laid so much as one finger on her, I will personally deliver you to Obystrus myself." His wings boomed with each step he took. He was ferocious in his right, a force to be reckoned with.

"She is unscathed, Lord Mortades. On my honor," said Gerimor. This seemed to put Pyre at ease, if even just a little bit. I noted it in the set of his strained muscles relaxing ever so slightly. I wondered now how Gerimor would even know such a thing. Perhaps it was whatever Gerimor had done to me when he'd sworn the oath. I hadn't ever met him until seconds ago, but Pyre appeared to trust his word, believing that Gerimor would know such a thing.

"We did not harm her, my lord. See for yourself." It was Dramael who spoke now, evidently at ease with speaking directly to him. Pyre turned back to me, eyes a burning red. I gulped as he approached me again, totally fixed on the gaze marking me.

"Pyre," I stammered, watching the warring emotions he bore on his face. His lips were pursed into a snarl, but his brows were lifted in worry. When we stood just a foot apart, I looked up into his stare, then closed my eyes. "I'm okay." I breathed. "They didn't hurt me."

"Look at me," he ordered, voice deep and crackling. I staunched my breathing and looked up through my lashes, only for the contents of my chest to melt at the sight of his liquid gold eyes. "*Sōrza*," he whispered softly. He exhaled, and my breath fastened at the change in his features, entirely captured by the splendor of not only his appearance, but how he was acting toward me. He had been worried for my safety. This look he gave me was the same I last saw when Ombrose took me away from him. I thought I had sensed the gleam of grief in his face, but I wasn't sure I had read him well. He had sworn he'd find me again, and I didn't know whether that was a threat or a promise. Now I could see that his declaration was a threat to those who stole me away, and a promise to me and my safety—whatever that might look like to him.

"Uh, am I missing something here?" Ombrose ogled from behind Pyre. My face burned with embarrassment as I remembered that we had an audience.

"Mortades?" Gerimor prompted. "Tell me you have not fallen for a mortal." The blood in my veins pumped overtime at the suggestion. Gone were the bad thoughts, and in their spot, anticipation crept through every fracture of my being. I stilled as Pyre looked over his shoulder to Gerimor.

"No." Pyre growled, low and rumbling. My blood went from heat to ice at the sting of those words. I hadn't known I'd wanted him to say yes until he hadn't. I knew that I was unwise for having felt anything remotely close to affection for the God of the Dead, but I couldn't help how I felt. Those days in his castle had led to my learning to empathize with him, to care for him. Even more dangerous than that, I had grown an insatiable desire to kiss him on more than one occasion. As if reading my thoughts, Pyre's gaze fixed on me again, still delectably alive in a golden hue. He searched my face, then lifted a hand to my chin, nudging it up so as to better look at me. "I have not fallen for a mortal, Gerimor. I have fallen for this goddess." My heart thundered at the proclamation, lips falling open in shock.

"And you, Goddess?" Gerimor questioned, voice like wonder carried by the wind.

"She can't possibly!" I heard Ombrose say. I was too busily enraptured by Pyre's gaze that I didn't bother adding to the conversation. Surprisingly so, Pyre didn't either.

We stared at each other for what felt like an eternity, as if he was waiting to see if I'd answer the question. When I didn't, Pyre finally broke the silence between us. Low, so as not to have the others hear us, Pyre whispered, "We need to leave, Shivalri. You are not safe." My face turned from stunned to confusion as I looked to him for some form of explanation. "Please, trust me," he insisted, almost begging in the way his lip twisted in distress.

I didn't know what to do, nor what to say. The Orsimm had helped me, had given me shelter when I needed it most. Even when it meant they'd inevitably face the wrath of Pyre Malum for having done so. Yet I couldn't shake the feeling that there was something odd about Ombrose and the way he acted toward me. He had treated me like he'd known me before ever having met. He'd been involved with the lie this morning too. It was obvious in the way he'd avoided me since walking in. And back at the castle, Pyre had said his brother's scent was on him. And Reaver had mentioned a feud between him and Pyre.

With Pyre, I knew what to expect if I left with him. We'd just go back to the way things were—working day and night on strengthening my powers until he thought I'd be strong enough to open the Gates for him. And I would continue to avoid the truth of never wanting to help him do so in the first place. I could go back and keep working on finding another way out. Dramael and his sons were no use in the matter.

They had no way of helping me, no ideas to offer in aid of my escape. That's why they'd called Gerimor in the first place. And the fact that Gerimor had retrieved Pyre and allowed him entrance to the cave could only mean that he was team Pyre. What was I to do? Whether I fought for my right to stay away from the God of the Dead, the others would inevitably bow to him and offer me over. It was best that I didn't fight him on this. I would roll with the punches and start from the ground up again. Only this time, I was at my full potential. This time, I would be able to use all of my powers at will straight from the beginning. And perhaps that would be my fighting chance.

"Thank you, Dramael, for taking care of the goddess. I am in your debt," said Pyre, waking me from my thoughts and hovering over me in a protective approach. He was thanking the God of Sleep for harboring me? What in the world was going on?

"It is my greatest honor, my lord. It is I who is in debt to her. Her existence is proof of a new awakening. It is proof of a new era, a better world to come."

I blanched at his words, feeling the weight of them all.

"Come," said Pyre, folding my arm into his. I hesitated for only a second as I glanced around the cave for a sign that I might be making a mistake, but none of the other gods expressed such things. Only Ombrose looked upset, visibly unhappy to have given me up to the god he'd been in feud with. We walked toward the group of gods, arm in arm, the air hard to wade through. As we reached the entrance in which they all stood, Gerimor offered me an encouraging smile, then lifted a brow to Pyre as if questioning his rationality, before stepping aside to allow us passage. So, without another thought of hesitation, I took my first step out of the cave since having arrived here, with Pyre in tow.

32

IMPART

SHIVALRI

The air was lighter out here, fresh, and empty of
dust. There was a dewiness to it that clung to my
lungs, but still, it was cleaner than what I'd been
breathing in the cave. It tasted of new beginnings. Pyre was
stiff under my touch, and I realized we'd been walking alone
for a while now. It was odd that he'd kept so silent.

"I, um," I began, trying to find the words to say.

"Shh," he quieted me, and I balked at his response. When
I made to ask him why he'd shushed me, I noticed how tense
his entire body stood. He was rigid in the way he moved,
shoulders brood and head straight forward. His feet never
missing a beat. The tingling sensation of being in danger
plagued my spine as I searched for what he was alerted to,
but I saw nothing of consequence. We were past the field and
almost on the forest path, leaving only the trees and long road
ahead of us. If he were this overwrought, this quiet, was the
storm about to hit me? As we stepped onto the graveled
rocks, he finally dared to move his head toward me.

"What?" I asked, unsure of what was to come. Then

suddenly, quickly, he pulled me into his arms and squeezed. "Pyre!" I screeched, until I realized… he was *hugging* me.

"Are you truly well? They did not harm you?" I heard him ask at my ear. His hand stroked my hair, and I began wondering if this was but a dream.

"I am fine," I answered, my voice a little awkward and shaken. He gave me one last squeeze and then let me go.

"What did you find out?" he asked, his breath heavy in exhalation. My eyes widened, expecting anger, and not this unexpected anxiousness. The way he looked so on edge did not become him.

"What?" I was unsure of what he meant.

"What are they planning? Surely you must have over-heard something of significance."

I shook my head in frustration. "What are you talking about, Pyre?"

"The Orsimm! My cousins!" he whispered harshly. "What are they up to?" he ground out, emphasizing each and every syllable.

"I don't know what you mean," I confessed. "They didn't seem up to anything. They only talked about whether it was a good idea to help me. When they realized who I was, they agreed to give me shelter. That's all."

"That is most certainly not all," he hissed, grimacing.

"That's all I know regarding their plans," I assured, a frown tugging at my lips. "Why are you so worried? What's wrong?"

His eyes pointed into slits at my words as if I had insulted him outright. "I am worried about *you*," he said, swearing under his breath. That turned my thoughts to the words he'd spoken for all to hear in the cave. *"I have fallen for this goddess,"* he'd said, without a care who heard him. My mouth went dry in memory of his confession. Something deep within my soul ached for it to be verity, though, I was shamefaced for even considering it a welcome thought.

"I'm okay," I said softly. "And you seem to be all right, albeit a tad bit on your nerves."

"On my nerves?" He scoffed, turning on me. "Do you know how worried sick I've been? Following you as closely as I could but knowing if I'd made my presence known that you would only want to run from me even more." Pyre scowled, looking away. *I knew it. He had been following me.* "For days I have watched you shiver in the cold, suffer from a badly healing hand, and stiff from riding my horse. All the while, chatting with that vile Orsimm. When you'd fallen asleep in his lap—fuck. It took everything in me not to blow my cover and rip him to shreds for ever being near you." *Oh.*

"Lity's yours?" I asked, changing the subject before Pyre could decide to turn around and do just that.

"Lity?" he repeated, his fury ceasing for a moment. His eyes were stunned, breath coming out in heavy pants until finally calming.

"The mare," I clarified. "She's yours?"

"Of course, you've given her a nickname." He sighed, moving a hand through his hair. "Yes, Nihility is my cauchemæra. I sent her for you." I wasn't at all surprised by his following me. At every turn, I was sure I'd felt his presence around me. Though I never once saw him, nor heard him approach, there was something in the air telling me that he wasn't too far behind. I hadn't expected that Nihility was his though. Ombrose hadn't let on that it was Pyre's horse, but perhaps, he didn't know. I was grateful for having Nihility with me during the trek. It was a sweet gesture on his part, one that I appreciated. My feet and bones were thankful.

"I like Nihility," I said, smiling faintly. "She was very helpful to me. A source of comfort during my travels."

"If only you hadn't run away, then you wouldn't have needed such comforts, now, would you?"

I shrank at the mention of my leaving him, remembering the scene like it was happening again before my very eyes. Anger simmered through my veins, coating me in a violent heat. "You left me no choice," I gritted through my teeth, feeling the prick of warning tears. "You were going to let me fall. You were going to let me die."

"No," he said, voice breaking. A look of anguish marked his face. "I would never."

"But you were," I argued, lip trembling. "And you..." I swallowed hard, the words slicing my tongue. Recalling the shattering of my bones, I held my right hand in the other, trying to rub the memory away. "You crushed my hand..." He grabbed both of my hands in his, clinging to them with a gentle force.

"And it was agony to have to do that and pretend in your face that I did not care."

"I know you didn't care, Pyre," I spoke with a mixture of hurt and appall. "You smiled at my pain." Who did he think he was? The fucking *nerve* of him.

"I—" He faltered. "I did what I had to for your protection."

I scoffed in disbelief, feeling the heat rise up my face. "You call that protection?" I questioned, voice hitching. His eyes were fighting to keep my stare, but everything in me wanted to look away from him.

"Please, you have to understand," he begged, insisting I do.

"Understand?"

He squeezed my hands in his in an effort to drive it through me. "Ombrose is working with my brother. I don't know how, but I am sure of it. Back at the castle, I scented him on my cousin. I didn't know how much Ombrose knew of you, only that if he were to find out how important you are to me, he would tell my brother. With that knowledge, he would do everything in his power to get his hands on you. I couldn't let Ombrose see that I cared. I couldn't let him carry that message to my brother."

"Couldn't you have found another way?" I trembled, suddenly realizing that there was so much I still did not understand. Pyre was so outwardly horrible to me and to the pythrants at the scene. I had wanted to bring him crashing down with me as he relished in my torture. But nothing was ever as it seemed in my life. Ice rippled down my skin as I remembered the anger Pyre had displayed when he'd discovered his brother's scent on me while I slept. He had been bursting with fury, only it wasn't just about hating and fearing his brother. More than anything, it was about my being in danger. He had been awful, a true symbol of cruelty. But to him, he believed he was doing the right thing— protecting me. I understood, but I almost did not want to. It was hard to face the fact that just because I saw something one way, it wasn't necessarily the whole truth—only my personal experience of the truth.

"I'm sorry," he whispered, his voice breaking as he rubbed the tops of my hands. His dark lashes lowered as he stared down where he held me. He looked so tired, virtually despairing. "It was the only way in that moment, but please know, it was the worst thing I've experienced in my life. And I have seen my fair share of horrors." He swallowed hard, misery evident in his look. "I did not know what living without you was like until I lost you. Let me assure you, *Sōrza*, it is not living at all." He looked up at me now, dusted in guilt and shame. And for all that it was worth, I believed him. I could hate him for it all my life, but damn it, I knew it was true. I had played a part in the outcome whether I wanted to admit it or not. I had gone feral, ravaging the castle with my twisted chaos and desperate need for escape. He would always be the underlying reason I'd ever needed to escape, but I pulled the trigger that detonated the disaster.

"What now?" I asked, clearing my throat.

His face hardened as he looked over his shoulder toward the cave we'd just left. "The Orsimm smell like my brother, Goddess. All but Gerimor are untrustworthy. Something is happening. They are working with him, and it involves you. If my brother is a player in this game, it means anything but good and has everything to do with hurting you." I could tell from the face he made just how worried he was. Though I wanted to believe it had everything to do with wanting me safe for my own protection, I knew that most of his troubles revolved around his one true desire. He needed me safe because I was an essential component in fulfilling his greatest plan.

"And you still want me to open the Gates," I acknowledged, discouraged, and outwardly tired of the turmoil.

"I do," he ground out, and blew out an exasperated breath.

"So, what do we do?" I asked, pulling my hands from his and making to continue down the path. Pyre followed me closely at my side, his wings outstretched and shielding our backs. At this, I felt a little less exposed, which struck a match of worry in my mind. Had the Orsimm been listening in? Did they know that we were on to them?

Pyre seemed to be thinking the same thing as he pulled in closer so that only I could hear his response. "It's time we pay a visit to the Fates."

"How the hell are we going to see the Fates?" I gawked at him, questioning his sanity. He'd told me not too long ago that the Fates weren't corporeal beings, which meant they were not something we could go see.

"They have a temple in each of the realms," he told me, shrugging a shoulder. I felt his feathers move with the motion and a tingle ran down my spine. "Although, they are not easily reached, one can approach them so long as the Fates allow."

"What is that even supposed to mean?" I scoffed, shaking my head. A blonde mass of unruly hair fell to the front of my face, and I shoved it behind my ear in frustration.

"It means that we'll have to be careful. It means that we're testing their trust, and we can only hope they'll give us theirs."

"That is incredibly vague and discomforting." He crossed his arms at me, sighing a heavy breath. "Why do we need to go see them?" I asked, disgruntled. "And how are we going to see them if they aren't real beings?" *And when did we become* we *again?*

"Oh, they're real," he assured, tilting his head to the side, considering this. "They are more real than any of us."

"Pyre!" I hissed, giving him a look that I knew he understood was irritation. I wanted to know what I was getting myself into before agreeing to whatever he'd planned.

"We're going to them because they are the only ones capable of telling you your fate."

My eyes widened at that. "You mean they can tell me what I'm supposed to do? Who I am?"

"That is the one thing they cannot tell you. They can never tell you the answers you seek outright. However, they are the ones who've weaved your fate. From the moment you were created, they strung your strings, guiding you to all you are meant to become."

"If they can't tell me what to do, then how are they going

to help?" I was entirely confused by the notion, not at all understanding the logic.

"They will tell you your fate, provide you with your title, and weave the hints to help guide you down your path. One look in their reflection pool and you will hear their call. You will hear what they deem you deserving of knowing."

I was thunderstruck. This was what I had been praying for. I'd been hopeless and clueless in so many aspects of my life, but whenever faced with uncertainty, I'd begged for answers, throwing my pleading to the wind. The concept that we'd be able to find those who held all the solutions was immensely astounding.

"How do you know?"

"Know what?" he asked, one brow slanting up. I stopped walking and lowered my gaze to fiddle with the ring on my right hand.

"How can you be sure that they'll find me worthy of that knowledge?" I asked, voice quiet. I wasn't sure I wanted to hear the answer. I had small hopes for his assurance, but my gut told me that I wasn't from the Under Realm, and that since my prayers were never answered before, they surely wouldn't be answered now. Pyre came up to me, standing with his feet squared only inches away from mine.

"Look at me," he insisted. A pang of emotion ran through me as he repeated my words to me. Not so long ago, Pyre was upset and doubtful, and a part of me wished to comfort him. I looked up through my lashes, finding that he, too, was experiencing this now. Something had changed in him since I'd run away. It was as if that solid wall that he'd built had torn to shreds, allowing me to see further into him.

"I'm looking," I told him, meeting his stare.

"You are worthiest of all."

33

LÀÉRXO
SHIVALRI

Pyre and I had begun walking through the forest, but we were both noticeably on edge. I didn't know all that he was thinking, but I had the sinking feeling that something bad was about to happen. Every now and then, one of us would look behind to see if we were being followed. An unexpected stirring caused me to halt my foot-steps, recollecting that not far off, there lay a grotto filled with an army of rancid spiders that sounded just like this.

"Do you hear that?" I asked, looking around, fighting back the urge to run back to the Orsimm cave for cover. We'd already crossed the field and had been through the woods for a few minutes now. I wasn't sure if we'd even make it back to the cave in time to avoid the creatures on the prowl.

"Varakane." He grunted, face contorted. "But, how?"

"They're close, aren't they? They're coming to get me again." I blanched, considering their bony limbs and giant mouths filled with rows of sharp teeth. I felt the silken webbing wrapped around me again, my insides churning. I stuck my hand in my pocket, feeling that bit of web I'd cut and kept. Why'd I ever think to do that? I quickly pulled my hand out, shivering wincingly.

"*Again?*" Pyre whirled on me, grabbing me by the shoulders. "What do you mean, *again?*" His eyes were turning from gold to amber, ready to set aflame.

"They came out just before me and Ombrose made it to Dramael's cave. I fell, and my nose was bleeding... One thing led to another, and I eventually ended up running into their grotto." I winced, reminding myself of the darkness that seized me. "The varakane had me captured, wrapped in their silks... It was awful, Pyre." I looked up at him, waiting for him to respond. Say anything. But he didn't. His eyes roved over me and landed on my stomach. His hands, rough but gentle, slid down my arms. Alarmingly, he placed his palm on my belly, his chest puffed out as if he were waiting for the world to end. When he blew out a breath of relief, I finally understood what he was checking for. "They wanted to." I exhaled, moving away from his touch. "They said they were going to spend an eternity making children."

"They would sooner die than succeed." He growled, low and deadly. The red in his eyes came full.

"We should leave," I said, turning my gaze from him to the rocky mountains just a couple miles out of reach.

"Yes, we should."

Smoke on the wind brushed through the thicket that lined the forest walls just behind Pyre, and my stomach quickly turned to knots. At first, I'd thought to run away, but remembered the familiar wisps of ash to be Nihility's shadow form. A trickle of relief punctured my lungs, generously allowing me to breathe. The cauchemæra had left me while I stayed with the Orsimm family. When the varakane had attacked, she'd bolted from sight, vanishing into thin air before my very eyes.

"Lity!" I laughed as a thicker fragment of smoke rubbed against my side, sweeping up into my hair. "I was wondering where you ran off to," I told her as her form solidified in front of me. Her giant head bowed down, her nuzzle coming close for me to pet her. I lifted my hand and stroked my palm softly down her fur. She huffed in audible pleasure, leaning into the touch. "I missed you too." I sighed and kissed her on the nose.

"Are you aware that you've just kissed the most dangerous breed of animal to ever exist on this plane?"

"What?" I gasped, looking from him and back to Nihility. "You can't be serious." When he tilted a brow, insinuating that he was, I shook my head at him. "But she's so pretty," I insisted, and pet the horse again. She bobbed her head, seeming to appreciate the compliment.

"She is a cauchemæra. A Hell-horse."

"And?" I retorted, rolling my eyes at him.

"And you are her favorite kind of meal." I took a step back, heart thundering in my chest. The horse merely watched me, then lowered herself to the ground. Pyre came closer to us, his height almost perfectly matching the mare's. I noted how similar the pair looked. Both in build and coloring. The shade of their hair was identical, and the glow of Lity's fire-filled eyes were reminiscent of Pyre's when enraged.

"You know, you guys kind of look alike," I spoke, regarding the pair. Pyre turned on his heel, sharp and mechanically. His eyes met mine, playful and light.

"Do you think I'm pretty?" He marveled, a smirk growing on his lips.

"I—" My voice buckled, realizing what I'd just done. I could feel the heat of embarrassment rising to my cheeks as he turned away from me. "Shut up." I huffed, digging my feet into the dirt. I heard a light laugh fade from his lips as he lifted a leg over the horse.

"Come," he said, reaching out a hand to me. "We should leave." My feet felt rigid on the ground beneath me, but I forced myself forward, taking his hand. Taking me by surprise, Pyre lifted me onto Nihility's back, placing me between him and the horse's neck. I felt the roaring of fire start in the pit of my stomach. Something I'd almost entirely forgotten could even exist. I put a hand on either side of the mare's muscled neck, trying to stabilize myself as she lifted from the ground. I'd grown used to her shadows enclosing me snugly, holding me sound as we walked. Though this time around, no shadow came forth for safety. Was it because Pyre was riding too?

"I'm not good at this," I stammered, trying to find something better to hold on to. Pyre's knees might have done better than the mare's neck, but I didn't want to be so bold.

"May I hold you?" Pyre asked from behind me, and I instinctually moved my back into him, without a second thought. I needed the solidity, and he was offering. We were already so close, what more could it do to have his hands on me? The tips of his fingers found either side of my hips, growing firmer and more demanding as his palms pressed into my waist. The feel of his grip on me sent chills up my spine, and I had to hold myself from shuddering under his caress. "*Làérxo,*" Pyre demanded, voice low and crackling over my head. The horse whinnied and bucked, my body begging for something to hold on to as she picked up into a storm, leaving a trail of dust behind us. The pounding of her hooves was heavy, and with every thud, my body lurched up and down, Pyre's hands still firm around me. The pounding grew faster, stronger, until suddenly the ground beneath us parted, and Nihility's smoke filtered in splinters. We weren't just riding the cauchemæra now. No, we were *flying* on her back, wind full through my hair, and trees whizzing by. Within this moment, the memory of another time filled my chest. Wrapped in Pyre's arms, flying through the castle, exhilarated by the freedom of flying. Just as we were now, racing in the airstream on the back of Nihility. It was thrilling and risky, carefree and desperate.

"Why are we in the air?" I yelled, trying to find my voice over the whooshing sounds of wind.

"She's faster when in shadow," he replied, his voice carrying and finding my ears. Nihility's galloping steadied on the breeze, skill keeping her quick pace, but jerking less with each step on the air.

"Do we really need to be going this fast?"

"We're safe," he assured. "Don't worry." I clung to the horse, hoping to gods he was right. "We need to get to the Fates before things get worse. Even now, I can't guarantee we aren't too late." His seriousness sent a tremor of melancholy through my veins, drying the blood from its flow.

"Too late for what, Pyre?" My voice was so low, I wasn't sure he'd heard me. He moved his hands forward, wrapping closer around me as his head approached the side of my face.

"I have a bad feeling." He sighed, the worry on his tongue audible.

"Tell me," I insisted, trying to turn my face to look at him. I could only glimpse the obsidian haze of his hair flowing alongside mine.

"I think my brother knows of you, wants you," he confessed, voice hushed. "I know you think of me as the worst thing to have ever happened to you, but—" he shifted, his fingers seeming to release a bit of the tension around my waist. Queasiness settled in the pit of my stomach, causing an unwelcome chill to crawl over my skin. I hated Pyre for having taken me. I still couldn't believe he'd thrown me in the oubliette and wasted so much time of my life just to test my mental and physical strengths. I hated how he'd turned to anger and violence when teaching me magic. I hated the red viciousness of his eyes that had stared back at me on more than one occasion. But I didn't think he was the worst thing to ever happen to me.

Despite him being a rather malevolent captor, he had shown me kindness in the ways he knew how. He'd given me my own room and privacy to mull over my feelings and get the rest I required to train. He'd willingly offered his help in building a stronger foundation of power, never once showing that he'd been uninterested in helping me. He'd given me answers to almost every question I'd asked, and more importantly, I'd seen how he'd grown to care for me. In his own way, I'd witnessed the raging heat in his heart melt into a steady stream of calm whenever he saw that I needed it.

He was stronger than me, physically, so when the violence washed over him, I knew that when he'd held me too tightly and tossed me too roughly, he hadn't intended to hurt me. After seeing the God of the Dead, the all-powerful ruler of the Under Realm, cry on my part... He'd become such an enigma while he and I were together at the castle. He was harsh and closed off, but over time, I'd witnessed him soften and worry for someone other than himself—for me. And that was a start.

I had a better sense of who he was now. I knew, deep down, that he wanted to change. I saw it in how he'd been learning to treat me better. I'd felt it in the way he'd caressed my sore hands and watched me with molten honey eyes. I couldn't forgive him yet, but I knew deep within me that I wanted to. I wasn't sure if it was safe to want such things, but a piece of my heart begged for it.

"I don't," I admitted, not only to him but finally to myself. He stiffened beneath me, his fingers still light over my waist.

"You don't what?" he susurrated, voice close, but aim so far away, as if trying to escape my awareness. I blew a shaky breath and moved a hand over his, willing him to hold me again. I could feel his chest come closer to my back, as if he were holding in his breath.

"Is that Osbuvïa?" I asked, veering the subject away from what I wasn't yet ready to discuss. I could just make out the river below us, finding that it glowed a vivid blue. I felt as if I were dying of thirst just looking at the waters, but instantly shivered at the thought of what its power would do to me if swallowed.

"It is," he confirmed, stretching out an arm to point in front of me. "Do you see there?" he asked, and I followed the aim of his pointed finger.

"It looks like a small ocean!" I beamed, happy to see more waters. It felt familiar, like being back on Earth.

"It's the Dhetrïan Pool," he told me, lowering his hand back to my waist.

"Is that where we're going?"

"Yes," he said, though he didn't seem as pleased as me to be nearing the waters.

"Don't tell me the water is dangerous there too." I grumbled, considering the possibilities the Under Realm could provide its rivers with.

"It can be."

"You going to explain? Or am I to take my chances with fate?"

"No," he snapped. "Never take your chances with any

unknown territory. Please assume that every place in the Under Realm is unsafe, and do not test it."

"What will the Dhetrïan Pool do to me if I drink from it?" I asked, rolling my eyes at his commands.

"It's not made to drink from, though I imagine its effects would be the same as when touched. It is the place in which the river Dhetrïa collects its water. Dhetrïa is a river built from hatred. If you were to bath in it, every inch submersed would become invincible. It's a place in which many, before the realms were split, would come to visit to make binding oaths. It's the river Dhetrïa that allows dead souls to enter the Under Realm."

"That's a lot to unload." I squinted my eyes, trying to see farther. "Are there any other rivers I should look out for?"

"There are five infernal rivers across the Under Realm. This realm is built like a loop, each river connecting as it meets the other. In the land of dreams, where we've just left, you'll find Osbuvïa all around it. Continuing forward, just ahead of us and to the right, you'll see Osbuvïa connect with a small pool called Emorïa. Its waters restore the knowledge disremembered in the Osbuvïa."

"Well, that's good to know." I huffed, happy to find there was a reversal to the memory loss.

"It's not very useful if you've lost your memory and cannot remember its existence."

"Well, shit." He blew a low laugh, and my stomach tightened from the sound. It was so good to hear his spirits brighten. I tried to stop my smiling, but it was of no use. Thankful to be facing forward, I welcomed the brief smile. "Tell me more," I insisted, searching the land below.

"Opposite Osbuvïa is the river Larweïa. It borders the length of the deepest part of the Under Realm and grants eternal sorrow." The smile I'd worn only moments ago sank into a frown, remembering when Reaver had told me about the deepest plane. I hadn't thought it'd be so close to the Orsimm's home, considering that Reaver wanted to stay as far away from it as possible. "Further down, nearing the Dhetrïan Pool, you'll find the flow of river Dhetrïa. Just behind it, branching away from the rest of the rivers, is the river Ephlumeldegôr."

"That's a mouthful," I chided.

"Indeed, it is."

"What's its purpose?" I asked curiously.

"That is a place I hope you never live to see." He growled, and I could hear the clenching of his jaw. I could almost hear a hint of protectiveness in his tone.

I shivered, considering what that meant. "Is it the entrance to Obystrus?" I questioned, voice a little shaky. He toughened behind me, as if I'd just shot him.

"How do you know of Obystrus?" he demanded, holding on to me with the slightest bit more pressure.

"Reaver."

"Gods!" he hissed. I felt him rock in his seat, then settle against my back again. He was clearly upset, but I couldn't understand why he'd wanted to keep Obystrus a secret from me. He'd had no problem telling me about the other areas of the Under Realm.

"Why didn't you want me to know about that place?"

He let out a long breath, and avoiding my question, he pointed out to the left of me now. "There is the soul's entrance into the Under Realm. River Ondalôr, River of Pain." A memory flashed in the back of my mind, images of the boiling waters below my dangling feet.

"I don't see your castle there," I stammered, looking around to find it.

"My castle is fast approaching, but you won't see it during our flight."

"But the River of Pain…" I started, not quite wanting to finish my train of thought.

"The Ondalôr flows underground. It happens to travel beneath my fortress."

"Lovely." I grimaced, as I realized we were headed in its general direction. I could tell, now that we were not so far from our destination, that Ondalôr was closely connected to the Dhetrïan Pool. The arches in my feet tingled at the thought of approaching my near demise. I wanted to disremember the feelings that came with the memory of my last day at Pyre's castle. It almost felt as if it hadn't happened, especially now, sitting so close to the one who'd watched me dangle, awaiting my death. "Tell me about your brother." My lips moved numbly, my tongue sticking to the roof of my mouth.

"What of him?" I could almost hear the scowl I could picture on his face. I considered all he'd told me about him and decided to discuss it further.

"Why do you think he wants me?"

"Why wouldn't he? You're the prophecy made true. Your very existence has given life to endless possibilities for our realms."

"What do you think he'd want to do with me?" I wondered, looking to the skies ahead. There was no sun in the Under Realm. There was light casted throughout the planes, but I couldn't for the life of me, find the source.

"Honestly, I'm not sure… But no good would come of my brother retrieving you and your power."

"And what?" I scoffed, shaking my head, and immediately regretting it. The ground beneath me spun, and I tilted forward from the dizzying. Pyre held on to me so as not to let me fall, and I leaned back into him. "You think good will come of you getting me and my power?" I finally finished my train of thought.

"I'm not like him," he replied.

"How is it any different?" I rebutted, but he didn't seem to want to answer. I wondered if he'd ever thought of this. I wondered if perhaps, Pyre didn't realize his incorrigibility when faultfinding others. I didn't know enough about his brother to assume anything worse of him. I could only rely on Pyre's word, and Pyre's own actions. I turned my head, still finding mostly a haze of both our hair. I forced my hip to comply with my need to see him and twisted my torso to find his face. His eyes were heavy as he looked to the skies ahead. There was so much in his face that told me he'd had a life-time of worry sitting on his shoulders now. "Pyre?" He turned his eyes to me now, brows furrowed, mouth tight. "Tell me. Make me understand." He looked away again and twisted me back to the front.

"Hold tight," he said. "We're about to land." Just as I was about to ask where, Nihility lurched forward, and my head lashed backward, butting into the hard chest behind me. My eyes widened in panic as the flying horse soared through the skies, lowering at a nerve-wracking speed.

"Holy fuck!" I yelped as we swerved through the tallest trees in sight.

"*Stathèdï*," Pyre commanded, voice dominant over the wind that whipped around us.

"What the fuck does that mean?" I shrieked, but the horse was clearly in the know. As she ducked and cut through woods and mountain, the speed eased with each of her steps on the air.

"Steady," said Pyre, and Nihility bobbed her head up once. Pyre's grip grew tighter, and I braced myself for impact as we neared the grounds below. Heavy clopping slapped me in the spine, my joints colliding with one another as she galloped on solid land. My bones screamed at me at the impact. I clenched my jaw tightly, teeth aching from the bite as I concentrated on the movement of the horse, trying to find the rhythm to better the pain in my frame. In the air, I'd forgotten the usual pressure and aching. It was as if gravity had afforded me a break from the discomforts of my disability. I sucked in a deep breath, ribs rattling with every step beneath me. I held on to the tension, suffering through a few seconds of the reality of my condition, and finally let it go. The horse, along with my pain, eased up a bit as she slowed her footing into a trot. I finally managed to survey the area and found that it looked nothing like what I'd pictured. When Pyre had said we'd be going to the Dhetrïan Pool, I'd imagined rushing water, and abnormally shaped rocks surrounding it. The body of water was stale and quiet, a large expanse dusted with mist along its top.

"What are we going to do here?" I managed to ask between steadying breaths.

"I told you, Goddess," he said, releasing his grip on me. He grunted as he disembarked the giant horse, then laid out a hand, offering his aid. With the stiffness in my body, I begrudgingly accepted, knowing this was something I did need of him. My hips groaned with the motions, but my feet landed lightly on the ground, as if he knew my bones were aching. He was gentle as he let me go, studying me as I took my first step forward. My ankles wobbled, and I bit back a cry as my feet tried to make use of the ground beneath me. It was squishier than I'd expected. The soil reacted like the wetness of a marsh; my feet sinking this way and that. Pyre offered me his arm, and I gave him a look of incredulity. He shook his head at me, his onyx hair flowing over his eyes and down his jaw. "Let me help you." I blew a quick breath and took his hand, allowing him to fold my arm into his. "Now," he said, turning us toward the water. "Let's go find the Fates."

34

LEAVE

SATYRA

As it were, the House of Enchantment was entirely empty, aside from the hobgoblin who'd decided to make her quick appearance. Gram sent Ember to retrieve Raidan from his looking spot and ordered me to watch her back as she descended the library stairs. I knew she'd said that to make me feel important, and to give me a sense of worthiness in this mission. I was thankful for my grandmother, always, but especially when she made these kinds of efforts.

It was a strange feeling to be walking around the building without profusely worrying for my life. After being here for a rough thirty minutes, I grew less afraid. I knew that I *should* be worried, and that letting go of the nerves wasn't a good sign of my serious-mindedness. But I couldn't help falling into the comfort of ease. There were many moments in my life when I'd felt this. My intuition spoke to me in volumes. If I felt safe, most of the time, I was.

"It's weird that they aren't here, isn't it?" I said to Gram as I joined her in the center of the lobby area. The empty white walls sent a warped ripple of my voice up the building.

"I don't find it comforting," she replied, and I gave her a questioning look. She shrugged and tucked the book closer to her chest. "If they are in their *Domum,* they are less likely to cause trouble..." she said, trailing until my understanding caught up with her thoughts.

"If they're out there, they could be doing something bad." I finished for her.

"Precisely."

Raidan and Ember came down the stairs, two steps at a time, and my heart started racing as my thoughts whirled.

"What's wrong?" I asked, holding a hand to my chest as they reached the bottom of the stairs.

"Nothing," said Raidan, throwing a champion-like grin at Ember. The seer rolled his eyes and scoffed at my cousin, joining us at the center of the lobby.

"No, nothing at all." He breathed heavily, turning toward the front door. "Long legs, here, just wanted a dick swinging contest."

"I beg your pardon?" Gram spat, and Raidan and I burst into a fit of laughter. Ember strode out the front door, not bothering to look behind him as me and my family lingered in the building—Gram appalled, me and Raidan red in the face from laughing.

"Let's go, dick swinger." I huffed through my laughter. Gram smacked me upside the head, and I backed away from her, following Ember out the door. "Are you sure it's safe to walk straight out the front entrance?" I asked, the cold breeze slapping me in the face as I caught up to him. He was still trying to catch his breath, having clearly exerted himself by racing Raidan down the stairs.

"They aren't anywhere near here," he said, still wearing the smirk. Gram and Raidan caught up to the two of us, following our footsteps as we crossed the path of white roses.

Stopping only a few feet from the building, Ember looked up into the skies. Snowflakes drifted onto his lashes in stark contrast to the dark length of them.

"Do you have any idea as to where they might be?" Gram asked Ember, who gave her a look of concern and frustration, then looked back up to the sky.

"I don't know." He sighed, wrapping his arms around himself. "It's not usual for them to leave without me. I may get on their nerves from time to time, but my role in the council seals my presence among them. We don't normally travel apart."

"But you travel without them," I interjected, pointing out the obvious between chattering teeth.

"Yes, because that is a part of my role. I'm a spy of sorts. I get our information and do the dirty work. Then I report back to them," he told me, frowning up into the flurries, and then looked to me. "Which is what I should have been able to do here. They were supposed to be waiting on me."

"To tell them you killed us." Raidan sneered, a look of disgust crossing his reddening cheeks.

"Is that something you normally do?" I asked, my mind drawing to the darkest part of the conversation.

"Report back to them?"

"Kill people," I clarified, not looking in his direction. He paused for a moment, and I thought he might not answer. Releasing a deep breath, he gave me a warring look.

"Don't ask questions you don't want the answers to." He turned back to the building and entered the door. When I saw him reach the other side, his dark hair and coat covered in snow, I took a hard look at the seer who'd entered my life. I'd started to trust him, wanting to believe that he was good behind the mask of evil. But I was wrong to think this. Ember was a *murderer…*

"Still want him to tag along?" Raidan retorted, lifting a brow at me. Gram nudged him forward before walking through the doorway herself.

"I never said I wanted him to," I answered, eyeing my cousin. His lips pursed into a glower as he looked me over.

"You could've fooled me."

I rolled my eyes at him and gave his shoulders a shove through the door. With hands still on him, I followed behind with adjusting eyes. Though the snow outside had been harsh and bright, the crisp shade of white up the walls indoors were even harder to look at. I remembered the first time I'd seen the place. I'd been eager to enter, unaware of the disaster that waited for us beyond the door's threshold. It had been exhilarating and frightening all at once. Shivalri had been terrified of coming here, but she had done it. We had done it together.

As the magic of this place sizzled out, a small part of me sputtered with it. We'd had so many great adventures together throughout our lives. I couldn't help my thinking we may have had our last.

"You coming?" asked Raidan, waking me from despair. I snapped myself out of the gloomy thoughts and decided to never think them again. Shivalri was going to be okay, and we would see each other again.

"Coming, Cuz."

35

FORAY

SATYRA

The trek through the underground tunnel took far less time to journey as we left the House of Enchantment. Before, when first coming through the secretive pass, we'd been cautious and careful to keep quiet for fear that the High Council would hear us coming. Upon leaving, we were eager to get out, and it was far easier to do so without the worry of bad guys catching us in the act. We'd made it through the ward and out the other side, finding the memorial bedecked in snow.

Through the blinding fury of snow fall, we trudged knee-deep in thick, white snow. The car wasn't too far away, since we'd parked in Gallows Hill, which was only a five-minute walk from the memorial. Still, it was an exhausting feat to have to walk against the wind, frost biting at the skin of my face as I clung to my coat for fear I might freeze to death. I was used to the cold, having worked winters at the fishing docks and shoveling the walkways next to the frozen water. But this, this raging, glacial shitstorm was nothing I'd ever experienced before.

We knew that the changes in our weather were due to

Shivalri's outbursts. It was the only explanation for the otherworldly chaos affecting Earth. It was strange to think she had such a strong effect on us all, coming from a whole other realm. I wondered about her, and how she was doing. To set these kinds of changes in motion, to cause the world to turn on itself, was unthinkable. For her to be so upset, or so out of control, was damaging to us all. I wish I knew how she was and what was happening to her for this to come from out of her. I wanted to know if I should feel bad for her or be frustrated with her. It was undoubtedly her fault that the world was coming to an end. I just didn't know if she was doing it on purpose or not. *I hope she's okay...*

Having reached the car, which now sat in a pile of heavy snow, Raidan popped open the trunk and grabbed the scraper to remove the cold, white stuff. Gram shot into the car, and with shaky hands, shoved the key into the ignition, starting the car to life. I got in the seat behind her and tapped my feet outside my door before closing it. The tips of my toes were entirely frozen and the skin on my face heated with a burn from leaving the icy wind. I could hear Gram's teeth chattering ahead of me and could see both of our breath hovering in the space around us. Ember and Raidan finished cleaning off the car, Raidan having taken care of the windows, and Ember having kicked the snow from out of the space between the tires and their fenders.

"Gods damn it," the curse burst from Ember's lips as he blew breath into his hands to warm up faster. "It's freezing out there."

"Thank goodness for the heater," Gram said, moving her gloved hands to the steering wheel before shifting into reverse. The tires squealed under us, complaining in the snow before finally pulling out of the parking lot.

"So, Gram," Raidan began, twisting his body enough to

see her and into the backseat. "Did you get what you were looking for?"

"I believe so," she answered, head fixed in the direction of the road. There was hardly any traffic, and I assumed it was due to the blizzard coming down.

"Did the book have any answers in there to help get Shivi back?" he questioned further, and I could see the hope festering in his eyes.

"We didn't read it yet," answered Ember for Gram. "In fact, I'm not sure we can."

"What do you mean?" Raidan snapped, turning to face us in the back seat.

"It's in a different language," I told him.

His frown softened a bit at my words. "Is it in Latin?" he wondered, looking to our grandmother.

"No, my dear. It's a language I've never seen before..."

Raidan huffed a dry laugh and sank back into the passenger seat. "Well, that's just great."

"It doesn't mean we won't figure it out, Rai," I offered, trying to find a spark to give him his hope back.

"No," said Ember, agreeing with me. "It just means we'll need to work a little bit harder to get your sister."

"It's possible that the language is similar to others," Raidan began. "Maybe if we searched the words online, we'll find comparable writing and be able to understand it a bit better."

"That is an excellent idea," Gram approved. "The minute we get home, we'll do just that." I hummed in agreement, and turned to look out my window, when Ember's hand grazed my leg. I shot him a look of caution, and he widened his eyes forcefully, darting from my face to my chest. *What the hell? Is he outwardly ogling my boobs?* I scoffed at him, and he slit his eyes. It finally dawned on me that he was asking, without having to speak, if I had managed to retrieve the books or not. I nodded my head once, and he nodded back, having understood that I had been successful in our secret mission. Sweet baby Jesus! I needed to get a handle on this strange energy between us.

I tore my eyes away from his, shoulders tight. I was torn when it came to keeping secrets and working with Ember behind Gram's and Raidan's backs. I wasn't sure what to make of it, just that it felt slimy. I let my mind drift off into imagination, envisioning what the secret book might hold within it.

Ember had been very vague, if not completely uninformative when it came to telling me the contents of the books he'd hidden in the floorboards. He had told me that I'd have the last say in telling Gram about the secret one, but I was supposed to read it for myself before showing it to anyone. I took a small amount of comfort in knowing that I was in charge of this situation, and if needed, I could spill the secret the moment I wanted to. But the importance and material within the books was a total mystery to me, and I felt them burn in the crook of my arm, begging to be freed from my jacket.

As Gram pulled into the dreadfully long driveway that led to our house, I felt a pang of relief at the safety the home provided. I was very eager to be back in our basement, where I knew we'd be safe from the High Council. I didn't like that we didn't know where they were. Even more than that, I didn't like that Ember was upset that he, too, didn't know where they were. Something about that rubbed me the wrong way, and I sensed inside my suspicious gut that that would be a cause for problems later on.

The car struggled to get through the thickening snow that lay atop our driveway, and when the wheels started turning without the car moving, I knew we were stuck. I looked away from my window and out the front windshield to see that we were only a few feet away from the house.

"Well," said Raidan as he threw his hood over his head. "Looks like we're walking the rest of the way."

"Hold on to your hats," Gram grumbled. When she opened the door, the drifting cold wind rushed through the car, eliciting a shiver down my spine.

The storm was getting worse now, and I wondered if we might even lose power at some point today. The severity of the blizzard was increasing as the minutes passed us by. Gram was out of the car before any of us, briskly making her way to the front porch. I could tell she was keen on getting out of the storm and into the comfort of our home. She'd never been good on the roads, and having to drive through this weather had made her jittery. I knew this, because every time her nerves worked up, her head ticked to the left. It was her tell. All throughout the drive, my grandmother had been nervous, and I was no exception. Especially since I was relying on an anxious old lady to get us home safely.

Raidan was out of the car and giving me a weird look as if to question my staying in the car alone with Ember. It hadn't been a part of my plan. Somehow, I'd forgotten that the seer was sitting next to me. I was just caught up in my thoughts, something I've done my entire life. My imagination had always gotten the best of me, and I'd been picturing car crash scenarios. I shook the images out from my mind and stepped out of the car.

A panicked shiver crossed my skin beneath the winter coat I wore, and suddenly, unwelcomingly, a bad feeling started to sink in.

"Rai," I whispered, grabbing at his arm before he could get away from me. He looked at me with furrowed brows.

"Something doesn't feel right." In all but a second, Ember was tugging me and my cousin down into the trees and pressed a hand over each of our mouths.

"Don't make a sound," he warned, voice quiet, yet still very alarming. Just like that, as if arriving on cue, a group of cloaked figures landed on the front porch in an ominous sight.

"Gram," said Raidan in a flustered voice. I started to get up, Raidan following suit, but Ember pulled us back again.

"We can't." I spun around on Ember, daring him to stop me. He narrowed his gaze and forced me down, but before he could stop me, I landed a punch to his windpipe. He clutched at his throat, but still managed to stop me, just as Damek Lagunov kicked the front door in.

"We have to go!" Raidan snarled with determination.

"It will do none of us any good," Ember hissed, pointing to the house. "There are four of them, and only three of us. And you guys don't know how to use your powers. We aren't any good against those odds."

"But my grandmother is in there!" I cried. The cold on my face burned where my tears fell. "They'll kill her!"

"No," he said. "They need her."

Raidan grabbed Ember by the scuff of the neck and pulled him up to him. "What do you mean?"

"I was ordered to kill you both but leave Sabine for questioning."

"And you're only telling us this now? We could've guessed where they'd gone far sooner! We could've predicted they'd be waiting to ambush us here!" I punched him again, this time in the gut. A noise caught my attention at the front door, and I quickly turned to look for the source. A stranger I'd never seen before stood on the porch; a hand lifted to their forehead as if trying to see past the flurrying snow. When their eyes landed on the three of us who were still huddled behind trees and a mountain of snow, they lifted a hand and folded their fingers into a fist.

"We have to go now," Ember insisted, tugging at the sleeve of my jacket.

"But Gram!" I shouted, not caring who heard me at this point. We'd already been found.

"Nesrin is our tracker, and she'll have been sent out to find us. She's giving us a running start, and that is not something we're about to pass up on. Now move," he demanded. Raidan threw an arm out in protest, but Ember's warning glare made my cousin shrink back. "We don't have time to argue. If you ever want to see your grandmother, or your sister, ever again, you'll do what's best and come with me." My heart wrenched at the thought of leaving my grandmother to fend for herself, but I knew that we were no good if we were caught too. I had to believe Ember. At this point, it was our only option. Die, or live to fight another day.

I'd never been much of a runner, and it was clear that Raidan hadn't been either. The two of us, both panting through the cold, sharp air, tried desperately to keep up with the seer, who was diving through branches, thwarting them out of our path.

"Faster," Ember grunted as he held a sizable branch out of the way for us to walk through.

"We…" I panted. "Have…" I inhaled sharply, the air feeling like glass against my lungs. "Asthma." I huffed, clinging to my chest for dear life.

"Both of you?" He blew, releasing the branch as me and Raidan passed.

"Yes," Raidan breathed, a puff of white cloud misting in the air at his wheezing. "Are they close?" he asked, turning to look behind us.

"No, but they are fast. Certainly, faster than the two of you. Now let's move."

"Where are we even going?" I spat but followed his lead anyhow.

"Out of state," he answered without a glance back.

"How?" I grunted, trying to pick up my pace. It was no use. My boots were sticking in the chunks of snow, and my muscles felt like jelly.

"I'm going to create a portal out of here, but I can't do it if we're close to the rest of them. Moira will be able to hear our thoughts if we're within her radius. We need to keep moving, and I can't decide just yet where we're going, in case she's listening in."

"You can create a portal?" I gasped with eyes wide in shock.

"You think that bitch is listening right now?" Raidan asked, grunting through breaths.

"Yes, I can create a portal," he answered me, then turned to look at Raidan. "By now, I assume she knows I've betrayed her, and she'll be wanting to get her revenge. I'm sure she's trying to listen right now, and I know she's sent our tracker to hunt us down."

"That woman?" I presumed, remembering the dark hooded figure who'd looked at us like prey.

"Yes, now let's quit this chatter and hurry. We don't have much time."

For once, Raidan agreed with Ember and nodded his approval. "Come on, Saty," he said, reaching out a hand. I took a deep breath and let him drag my feet from their spot, joining in on the run.

Tree after tree whipped past my view, Ember still in the lead, and Raidan just ahead of me. My insides curled in on themselves, not used to any kind of exertion. I wanted to stop running, wanted to just give up and let the witches and warlocks of the High Council drag me out of the forest by my feet. But I kept thinking of my grandmother, and what she might be going through, and decided that she had it worse. My grandmother had been captured by the very people who'd betrayed us, poisoned us, and sent my best friend to Hell with that vile, black-winged man. I could deal with the trembling muscles and frost-bitten skin. I could handle surviving with lungs that took in very little air. I would get through the mountains of snow and cross the frozen forest, because I knew that once I did, the three of us would be safe long enough to find a way to save my grandmother. Saving Gram meant saving Shivi. Saving Shivi meant saving the world, and I would do whatever it cost to achieve that.

When Ember and Raidan finally slowed ahead of me, I leaned my hands against my knees and finally allowed the bile to climb my throat. I had very little time to be embarrassed or disgusted with myself, so I let it all out. I wiped my mouth and met up with the guys, waiting for them to say something about my display. Neither of them even batted an eye, the two of them trying to catch their breath.

"We're good here," said Ember before pulling a dagger from his coat pocket.

"What are you doing?" I squealed, eyeing the knife.

"I need blood," he explained, and withdrew the glove from his right hand. Before I could make sense of the words, Ember slashed a small gash across his palm and let the blood fall to the base of a large tree trunk. What was with the blood and the trees? Gods. I was going to be sick again.

"Not this shit again," Raidan groaned, as he, too, remembered that awful night at the House of Enchantment. When we'd gone the first time, we were forced into performing a blood-binding spell. The High Council members had sliced our palms and poured the blood into a chalice from which we drank. The blood had been mixed with a potion, creating an elixir that held the power to make us tell the truth. My stomach felt sour as I thought about the poison we'd drank, thinking it had been the truth elixir.

"Higher magics require blood," Ember told us as the splattering blood sizzled against the cold snow. "*Concede vecturam. Factio rebellis. Quattuor.*" A rippling torrent of colorful magic blew up in front of us. In the space where the tree once stood, a long, rectangular glow appeared like a mirror, reflecting the three of us. We were all flushed in the face, and my hair was a mess of snow and twigs twisted into my red curls. My glasses were a little foggy, but I could see us well enough to understand that we looked like a wreck.

"Where are we going?" I asked, attempting to remove some of the twigs from my hair.

"To hide," he answered, and walked right through the rippling mirror. A branch cracked from behind us, and when I whirled around to find the sound, I saw the cloaked girl running toward us.

"Go!" Raidan hissed, grabbing at my jacket, and tugging me toward the portal. I could feel the tracker gaining on us as my foot entered the colorful mirror.

"Raidan!" I screamed as I felt someone tug on the other end of me. I tried to shake her off, but it was no use. The girl wouldn't let go, and I was falling through a portal without a say. The girl and I collided, tumbling through to the other side of the portal, and into a pile of snow with a hard thump.

"Holy gods, girl…" The tracker grumbled, trying to push me off her as I tried to scramble to my feet. "Get off of me, would you?" Just as I got a good foothold, Raidan grabbed me by the shoulders and lifted me off the stranger with a hard pull.

"Nesrin." Ember blew and threw his hands out to her. The girl lifted herself from the snowbank and ran into the arms of the seer. I blinked hard, trying to make sense of the hug, when the pair started to laugh uncontrollably.

"I thought I was going to have to make my own portal." The girl scoffed, and turned away from Ember to give me a pointed glare. "Not that you were any help in the matter."

I blanched, looking from her to Ember. "Um… What the hell?"

Ember let go of the girl, giving her one last squeeze as he clasped her forearms. "This is Nesrin Mehra, and she is the daughter of General Mehra, our rebellion's leader."

36

LIEUTENANT

SATYRA

"Why on earth would you have chosen faction four?" the one called Nesrin deplored, throwing a playful punch at Ember's shoulder. "*Buddhu*." She tsked, shaking her head.

"It was a last-minute decision." He groaned, apparently also unhappy with his choice of hideout. "And don't call me names."

"Um, Ember?" I scoffed, pulling his attention from the ridiculously gorgeous woman, who somehow had managed to run through the forest without a trace of debris messing her cloak, nor her perfectly braided dark hair. I looked between him and the girl, baffled by the newcomer. "Care to explain?"

"I'm Nesrin," she answered, extending a hand to me. I took it, wearily, and she shook mine firmly. "A pleasure to finally meet you," she said, before taking Raidan's hand as a formal greeting. I watched my cousin, who was still trying to catch his breath, gawk at the pretty girl who'd fallen into the portal with us. She grinned, a sly look in her eye as she pulled her hand away from Raidan before flicking her thick braid behind her shoulders. Something about her voice was sultry in the mix of her beautiful accent. As I watched her swish her hips, finding a spot next to Ember again, I had a feeling this was something she often used to her advantage. A shield made of her own nature.

"Nesrin is the High Council's Earth wielder. She's the youngest and newest recruit."

Right. I remembered now. Gram had told us about her.

"Not so young that I cannot kick your ass," she jeered over her shoulder at the seer. "Through my father, I was able to achieve superior placement more quickly. Similarly, to Ember, here."

"How old are you, exactly?" I asked, finally having a reason to ask this of Ember too. I'd been wondering for a while now.

"I'm twenty," she answered, and I recalled the summary Gram had given us back when she was teaching me and my cousins about the High Council members. Gram had thought Nesrin far too young to be a superior, and seeing her now, after knowing just what the Council members did, I had to agree.

"And you?" I asked Ember, feeling slightly caught being interested in him, but I looked away quickly, hoping he wouldn't note the new flush in my face. It was freezing out here, and we'd just run for our lives. Surely, he'd chalk up my red cheeks to that.

"Just had my twenty-fourth birthday," he answered, clearing his throat. My eyes widened, not sure which way the surprise was leaning. I thought he was close to my age because he didn't look much older than me. But with his position as fourth in command, twenty-four seemed almost too young. I couldn't decide if he was older or younger than

I'd assumed, because I hadn't quite placed an age in my mind. Now I knew that we had at least four years difference between us. I felt a little weird knowing this, as I wasn't normally attracted to those who were older than me. Ember Blackwood was incredibly handsome, but this age gap and his being a spy and possibly my enemy far outweighed his good looks. At least, it surely should.

"You're both kind of young to be in the High Council, aren't you?" Raidan pondered. He'd voice my comparable thoughts.

"It's not easy to explain how the system works, but the basics are that most of us are recruited to work for the High Council around age twenty-five, depending on our magics levels," Ember explained.

"*We*," Nesrin pointed between her and Ember, "are *in* the High Council due to our lineage. The rest of those working *for* the High Council are emissaries and soldiers."

"And you both are a part of the elite five because of your elemental gifts," I said, remembering what Gram had taught us. "You achieve your positions because of your parents. You replace them." I winced, realizing that these two had most likely lost a parent.

"I replaced my father," said Ember. His jaw was tight, his face unbreakable.

"I replaced my father, as well. According to the High Council, he has passed on. Little do they know, he is well and thriving, as their number one enemy."

"You're a rebel spy!" Raidan gawked at the girl. She smirked, narrowing her eyes.

"So are you," she chided. Raidan furrowed his brows, not understanding the implications. But I understood what she meant. We were going against the High Council. We were conspiring with the rebels, running into portals with two key players.

"What's the goal, here?" I questioned, wanting straight answers. The sooner I understood what they were up to, the quicker I would be able to decide which side to take. Either I join them in whatever their mission is, or Raidan and I find our own path, in hopes to save our grandmother and Shivalri. Though I must admit, the two of us knew nothing of the magic world. Here were two of the most knowledgeable witches, seemingly willing to help us.

"First, we need to get to our refuge. Then we can discuss our mission further," Ember declared, turning on his feet.

"I believe Wulfric is there currently," Nesrin told us. Ember nodded and began trudging through the snow.

"Kaede too," he told her. Nesrin started following Ember, stepping in the tracks his boots created in the thick snow.

"Where are we going?" Raidan asked, still standing by my side. I could tell from the vibe he gave off that he didn't entirely trust our new allies, and neither did I. "Better yet, where are we?"

"That's a good question," I agreed pointedly as Ember and Nesrin turned to face us, knees deep in snow.

"We're in Yukon, Canada. We have a secret refuge in the mountains here," the seer answered.

"A place where no one would think to look. It's not exactly a five-star resort, but it has kept the likes of Moira Darkmore out for several years."

"We're in Canada?" I gawked, looking around us. We were still in a snowy forest. The trees looked the same as those back home. I had assumed we were going to another state, as Ember had insinuated. I didn't think we were going to leave the country.

"Welcome to the great white north," Nesrin said, before promptly continuing her trek.

"This is so weird." I huffed under my breath. Raidan gave me a concurrent nod. We were in Canada, the country our grandfather had grown up in and told us so many stories about.

"Let's go before we lose them," Raidan suggested.

"Yeah," I approved, looking around us.

Catching up with the seer and the tracker, I decided to make use of whatever time this journey through snow afforded us. Raidan and I were both clueless, unsure of what we'd gotten ourselves into. Now would be a great time to make as many interrogations as possible.

"Who are Wulfric and Kaede?" I questioned, trying to steady my breath as my lungs forged on with little to no oxygen. Hiking through a forest was bad enough for my asthma, but doing it in the enervating cold was a fierce reminder that I wasn't cut out for outdoor adventures. By the looks of Raidan, I could see that his struggle was just as bad as mine.

"Kaede Rin is our eyes and ears, for all intents and purposes. They're one of our guides, whose job is to control movement in and out of our factions." I met up with Ember, walking next to him now as I watched him contemplate how much he was willing to tell us. "They work very closely with Cormac Galbraith, who is one of our general's head commanders, and a close ally."

"And Wulfric?" I prodded, memorizing the names and titles of each individual.

"Wulfric Hallows has been with the rebellion from birth. His parents and brothers have served as soldiers for as long as the congregation has lived."

"The congregation, meaning the rebellion?" I asked. Raidan flicked me behind the arm, teasingly.

"Obviously," he goaded, still panting, but wearing a grin on his face as if I should have known the answer. I gave him a pointed look, daring him to mock me further.

"Yes," answered Ember. "The congregation is a group of magic-kind who do not agree with the beliefs and practices of those in command of the magic world. We are the resistance against the cruelty of the High Council."

"Do you guys have a name?" Raidan wondered aloud.

"No," said Nesrin. "We refer to ourselves as rebels or the congregation. Just as the High Council does."

"What?" I hissed, stopping in my tracks. The snow beneath my feet felt glued to my soles as I halted. "They know about you?"

"Of course," Nesrin said with the flip of a hand in the drifting snowflakes. "But they do not know who are in our group."

"Well, that's reassuring," I muttered, lifting a heavy foot through another foot hole, which Ember had created ahead of me.

"The congregation has been active for over forty years. We have hundreds of followers, and yet, we still have not been found," Ember said. "We know what we are doing. As long as you stay within our care, you should be safe."

"*Should* be," I retorted, emphasizing on the first word.

"Look," Ember said, turning to face me. "We'll cover all the bases and get you as informed as possible once we've set up time with the general. Until then, we'll find refuge in the faction hidden in this mountain. It's not much, but it will provide shelter until our general can meet with us."

"How long will that take?"

"He's very busy, but he will make time for this," Ember assured me.

"Um, am I missing something here?" Raidan asked, gesturing around us. I finally saw the forest's line where it ended and realized what was ahead of us. A giant mountain, bigger than I could ever describe, began at the edge of the forest line, the trees guarding its surroundings.

"Where the hell are we?" I demanded, sizing up the mountain in front of us. I met Raidan at the edge, the two of us staggering back by the implication that we were meant to hike up the slippery slope.

"Faction four," said Nesrin. "And no, we won't be climbing it, if that's what's triggered your rubbernecking."

"Is it on the other side of this monstrosity?" I wondered, feeling a little relieved that they hadn't expected us to climb the death trap.

"It's at the very top," said Ember, patting me on the back. "I've got a warded entryway to get us there. Don't worry." He gave me a wink and strode to face the towering mountain ahead of us. Another warded entryway. Would it be darkened tunnels like at the House of Enchantment?

This time, Ember Blackwood didn't need to use blood to get us wherever he intended. It did, in fact, resemble the one at the memorial back home. Placing a hand on the icy mountain wall, a shimmer of light danced beneath Ember's touch, opening for our passage. As Ember pushed the entire length of his arm through solid mountain, Nesrin came up behind him and stepped inside.

"Come on." Nesrin beckoned. "Now's not the time to be shy."

Raidan took her comment as an eager push and followed the cloaked girl into the mountain side. I watched the two disappear before taking my first hesitant step. This was so outlandish, exciting even. Ember's eyes latched on to mine, seeming to read the sense of adventure that suddenly ran un my spine.

"Ready?" he asked, extending his hand for me. I walked past him, ignoring his offer as I submerged myself into the swirl of magic and entered the mountain.

37

BASE

SATYRA

I wasn't sure what I'd expected to see within the Canadian mountain, but I certainly hadn't pictured this. Feeling like an insect with nowhere to walk, my body scraped against the narrow passage of cold rock. Raidan, as big and tall as he was, had to scrunch down in order to keep his head attached to his body. The jagged spikes along the top of the space gave me chills as I imagined them raining down on us. Nesrin guided us with the light of her bulky cell phone —Raidan, Ember, and I closely on her toes.

Nesrin leaned over a railing, and when she reached out to touch the rock wall, a click echoed throughout the space. Grinding metal against rock clanged about as a rickety elevator came to life.

"A construction hoist?" Raidan asked, testing the strength of it with a weighted foot on its ledge.

"It's perfectly safe, but we will have to go up two at a time," said Nesrin, stepping onto the unreliable-looking piece of equipment.

"How is it powered?" my cousin questioned, prodding at

the chains and roping that dangled from its floor to a mechanical winch above.

"Don't ask me." Nesrin shrugged. "I'm not the one who built it." I looked to Ember, expecting him to tell us, but he shrugged, too, in the light cast from cell phone.

"Great." I grunted. Nesrin flicked her braid back and pulled a square box down from a wire rope, which hung in the tattered cage. With the push of a button, a green light lit up between her and Raidan, and the pulley groaned, rattling beneath their feet. Raidan grabbed on to the railing around him, giving me a wide-eyed look of panic. "Um, I'll see you up there," I told him, and watched as he and the stranger glided up the wall inside the mountain. In the glow, I could see their cage floating up into a slim crack in the mountain wall, big enough only for the equipment to slide through. I could feel a pinch of newfound claustrophobia clawing at my skin.

"How high does it go?" I wondered, staring up into the small space. Ember came up beside me, leaning over a railing, which stood between us and dark abyss.

"All the way to the top of the mountain."

"What's at the top?" I asked, turning to face him. He stared into the darkness below, his eyes glowing faintly, like they once had in the tunnels beneath the House of Enchantment. His red eyes stared back at me, and I could see my own reflection in them.

"It's a safe house. Though, it's not one we frequent very often, because it is cold and incredibly outdated."

"I don't find it too cold in here," I noted, realizing the inside of the mountain was far warmer than outdoors. Though it was damp and cool, it was not like the freezing snowstorm we'd just straggled through.

"The house isn't inside the mountain, I'm afraid. There

isn't enough oxygen in here to spend too long sitting about. We had to make do with building this faction at the very top of the mountain."

"Like, outside? On the peaks?" I gasped, thinking of the frigid air and extreme heights.

"It's safe. Warded by some of the most powerful people in the world. It's just cold. And a little gross, but it is safe, and that's what matters for now."

I swallowed hard but nodded in measured agreement. "How many safe houses are there?" I wondered. "And why Canada?"

He let out a short huff of a laugh and shook his head. "The reason we're in Canada is because I waited until the very last minute to choose a place. I wasn't thinking of where, rather, who I was trying to get to." Understanding donned on me as I realized Ember had been seeking out a friend, rather than a refuge.

"So, you were looking for Wulf? Or Kaede?" I assumed, having remembered that the two of them were expected to be here.

"Wulf is my most trusted ally," he answered. "You can trust both Wulf and Kaede on this journey. Nesrin too." I scoffed, rolling my eyes. His brows furrowed as he gave me a questioning look. "What?"

"Nothing." I blew, looking back up to the space where Raidan and Nesrin had gone up.

"Tell me."

I tightened my grip on the railing, trying to keep my cool. "I don't even know if I can trust *you*," I told him, keeping my eyes away from the glow of his. Thus far, Ember Blackwood had been kind and trying to earn my trust. It was evident in the way he'd put himself in danger to help me and my family. But I couldn't forget the see-walks we'd experienced together. I couldn't erase the image of the two of us sharing a body with separate minds, watching as Shivalri was hurt and offered off to a demon. A light touch on the top of my hand had me wincing back as Ember placed his upon mine. I shot him a look, both irritated and flustered. He took his hand back, shoving it into his pocket.

"I'm not going to hurt you, Satyra. I only want to help you and your family. My friends and our mission are in correlation to your familial objectives." He took a moment to think, staring into the darkness below. "We all want the same thing—justice."

"I just want my grandmother and cousin back. I just want everyone to be safe."

"As do we. For their safety, and the world's."

I took a shaky breath, finding that those words stung a little bit. I knew it was foolish, but I wished to have a greater importance in all of this. I wanted to play a larger role in the world's new awakening. I was able to overlook my insignificant powers by focusing on what I was capable of. I was strong of mind, and courageous in heart. All my life, I felt like I was made for a greater purpose. Though it wasn't me who was destined to live out an ancient prophecy, I could be a significant participant. I could be more than what I am today if I concentrated on looking forward. My efforts in saving Gram, and especially Shivalri, were of importance. I would be on the sidelines if it meant saving my best friend, and ultimately the world. I would become the best sidekick anyone had ever seen, if I had anything to do with it. My role in this starts here, with the rebellion. This was my chance to fight for a better version of the world I was born into.

38

ADVANCE
SATYRA

When the rickety elevator made its way back down to me and Ember, the two of us climbed aboard, using the light of his cell phone to watch our step. As the machine stirred beneath my feet, I got a good sense of what to expect from it. Though it looked old and sounded like it needed work, it was strong beneath our feet. The way it glided up toward the gap, which climbed up through the mountain, told me that the machine had been doing this for many years and had stood the test of time.

As the darkness of the gap above swallowed our cage, the light from Ember's phone was brighter, due to the closed quarters. I saw that the seer was staring at me from behind his device. I wondered how long he'd been watching me, as I'd been wholly wrapped up in the safety concerns I'd had.

"What?" I barked, crossing my arms over my chest. I felt the book in my jacket stab at my armpit, and I maneuvered it back into the crook of my arm.

"You're not what I had expected," he mused, lowering the light to level around our waists. The glow lit up his face from underneath, making him look fearsome.

"What's that supposed to mean?" I questioned, taking a defensive stance.

He pulled at his lower lip, shaking his head in confusion. "I'm not sure." I frowned at him. He lifted a hand over his eyes, scrubbing at his brows. "I just mean that, for someone who's life has been rummaged, you're tougher than I'd expected."

Surprise came over me at his confession. Though I'd fought to be exactly that, ever since the day I lost my parents, I had grown to second-guess my strength. When my parents were taken from me, I'd vowed never to let any hurt come my way again. Not that kind. Now, with Gram and Shivalri hanging on by a thread, my might had unraveled itself, if only a little. I knew, deep in my heart, that I was made to be a strong person. With knowing of my witch-hood and coming to understand the power I could potentially hold, I was certain that I was fated to have a difficult, yet hopefully, rewarding life.

"I've had to be tough for a long while," I replied, feeling comfortable with admitting this much, but unsure as to why I might be okay having this conversation with him. Though, he had been the one to bring it up.

"I have a feeling that that will prove useful in the coming days," he supposed. The gruffness in his tone had my thoughts on edge.

"How long have you been a part of the rebellion, Ember?"

"Just short of a year."

I shivered, feeling the colder temperature settling around us as we made our way further up the mountain.

"How did you end up joining them?"

He looked solemn for a moment. The scar across his face glinted as he pursed his lips. "There was a battle, a few weeks before I ever met Nesrin…" He paused, seeming to consider his words. "I am not one for unnecessary deaths. In fact, I've only ever killed one person. And I did not do so lightly…"

"You really did kill someone?" I gasped, taking an unwanted step backward, my butt pressing against the cage.

"I've done many things I am not proud of," he said, keeping his gaze locked to his feet. "The battle was my first ever to participate in, and I fought alongside the High Council. I had trained my entire life, expecting to see a more civilized version of war by adulthood. But nothing could have prepared me for the slaughtering in which the High Council released upon the rebels." When he paused to look for my response, I found that I was unable to read the specifics of his emotions. He looked solemn, and angry. Regretful, and scared. "The rebels wear magical disguises, distorting their faces when in battle. I tried to use the masking to my advantage. Tried to picture them not as people, but an unknown enemy."

"Did that work?" I asked, unintentionally blurting the question. I couldn't help wondering if I could use such imaginings to my advantage in what was sure to come.

"When I was far away, only fighting with my fire element, it did."

I took a moment to consider this, picturing flame taking over, burning the fighters to a crisp. A chill ran up my spine at the thought, but I hid any sign that I feared his power with the casualty of shoving my hands in my pockets.

He nodded, seeming to understand that I wished him to continue. "In the end, when I'd come face-to-face with an attacker, I couldn't pretend that he was not a human, just as I was."

"What did you do?" I wondered, looking to meet his glowing red eyes. I could just make out the dancing blaze within. It was a glimpse into the fighter he had been. It was a warning as to who he was.

"I wounded him enough to have him lying unconscious, before pretending to slay him with my fire sword. The High Council hadn't noticed that the flames I'd wielded did not burn. They'd assumed I'd gone for the kill, and we all moved on to fight another day." *Fire sword... Flames that did not burn... Who was this man? I cleared my throat.*

"No one bothered to check if he was dead?"

He shook his head at me. "There were several dozen rebels lying at our feet. It was easy to assume that none of them were ever going to get back up." He shook his head, a faint smirk playing on his lips. "Besides, the rebel that attacked me could have easily gotten away."

"How do you mean?" I wondered.

"I recognized the man who'd tried to attack me. He was a part of the High Council, a member gone rogue... All he would have to do was remove his disguise and settle back into our group as if he hadn't been betraying us by fighting alongside the rebellion. I knew that if he needed to, he would survive. I understood what I did in showing him mercy, and though I felt uneasy about walking that line, I knew I did the right thing by sparing General Baaz Mehra."

"Nesrin's Dad?" I blew, the turn of events catching my attention. "How did you recognize him if he was wearing a disguise?"

"It was all due to a small memory with him. We'd been patrolling through a forest and fell upon a patch of sunflowers growing in an odd spot. I remembered him telling me that the color yellow reminds him of better days. He was the only one wearing a yellow tie around his wrist, and something about it forced me to look past his mask. Call it intuition or a lucky guess, but the way he struck, not to kill, but only to incapacitate... I just knew it was him."

"You weren't mad that he was attacking you? What if it hadn't been him? What if you were killed?" My mind was bursting with questions, one worse than the other as they roiled through my head.

"Worried about my life?" He held a hand to his chest. "I'm touched."

I scoffed, rolling my eyes. "Buzz off." I grunted, unable to keep from grinning outwardly at his ridiculous performance of appeal.

"Buzz off?" He smirked, lifting a scarred brow. I sighed heavily, crossing my arms.

"Actually, no," I said. "Tell me more about Nesrin and her father." He hummed for a moment, rubbing at his chin as if savoring the fact that he had knowledge over something I wanted to know. "Ember." I growled. His eyes seemed to light at that, and he nodded politely, before shoving his hands in his pockets.

"Nesrin recruited me after her father was *killed*," he said, using air quotes around the last word. "Nesrin knew that her father was both a member of the High Council and the leader of rebels, and when he went out to battle, Nesrin followed, trying to stop him. When she got to the scene of the fight, she watched her father die at my hands."

"What did she do?"

"Foolish woman followed me to my hideout." He chuckled, shaking his head in what I could only imagine was disbelief. "She carried with her the yellow band that her father wore on his wrist, and accused me of killing him, declaring our first meeting the day of my death."

"You fought her?"

"No," he said, leaning against the cage. "I told her she

could kill me, if she could prove he was dead." Ember bit his lip, a small laugh escaping him. In the small light glowing around us, I saw a glint of metal at the center of his tongue. *Did Ember Blackwood have a tongue ring? Gods.* "You should have seen her face when she brought me back to the battlefield." Ember's laugh lightened, pulling me out of my personal gutter. "Only to find that her father wasn't there."

"What?" I stammered. "Where did he go? Didn't you say he was unconscious?"

"Yes, well, apparently I wasn't the only one playing pretend that day." I blew a breath, trying to imagine each of these moments, tying the images together in my mind. "Satyra?" Ember questioned, giving me a hesitant look. I furrowed my brow, finding that he had approached closer.

"Um…" I gulped audibly. "Huh?" His lips quirked into a smirk, and I thought about that potential tongue ring again, wondering if he'd come closer to let me see. But the sombreness in his eyes never moved, and I remembered that these moments were important.

"Can I show you?"

I looked up into the glow of his unusual eyes, trying to understand. He lifted a hand, cupping my face.

In all but an instant, I was in another time, another body, another life. The limbs bedecked in armor walked with purpose, pulling me toward a giant castle in the middle of nowhere. It sat so high in the mountains, I was sure if I wished it, I could reach up and touch the clouds.

"I am not a killer," I said, my voice exactly like Ember's, the beautiful, rich English accent ringing like tin in the head my mind now occupied.

"We will see what my father has to say about this," answered the woman who hauled me up the stairs. Her long, braided hair swung back and forth with each demanding step.

Six guards standing at their posts in front of the giant double doors stood still as we marched. Each of them held two long spikes across their chests, as if daring us to give them a reason to use their weapons.

"Lieutenant." They grunted, each of them bowing their heads to Nesrin.

"I am here to see my father."

"He is in the command core, readying to send troops to find you." I tried to get a look at her face, but my eyes never strayed from the guards ahead of me.

"Lovely," she replied, a hint of sarcasm on the tip of her tongue.

My boots clanged against solid ground as we made our way down bland corridors filled with people, all dressed in black leathers with gawking eyes. The bodies moved out of our way, indicating that they were either scared of Ember, who I was seeing this occurrence through, or my furious companion who marched me toward the red door ahead of us.

Pushing the door wide open, Nesrin shoved me into the rounded room, and I fell forcefully to my knees. Large, dark hands fell to the floor, holding me up so that my face wouldn't plant into concrete.

"Princess?" A tall man clad in royal blue and black called.

"Seriously, Papa? Where on earth did you find the time to change your kameez?" The man burst into laughter and ran straight past me. A grumble came from the girl who had hauled me in here, and I turned to look at the pair who were hugging.

"Princess? Really?" Ember asked, questioning them. The tall man squeezed Nesrin a little tighter before letting go and turning to face me as I kneeled on the floor.

"Blackwood," he said, squaring his shoulders. He stared down at me till I was sure there was sweat beading at my brow, before extending a hand to help me to my feet. He clasped my armored arm firmly, giving it a slight shake. "You spared me," he said, cautiously. "Why?"

"I knew who you were when you attacked me," Ember replied.

"Thank you for that, by the way." The man in blue tipped his head. "That does not answer my question."

Ember blew out a long breath. "I am not a killer," I heard myself say through Ember's voice. "Not only are you someone I consider a friend, but your death was unnecessary, as were the deaths of the others. When my father left me to fill his role with the High Council, I did not sign up for war. Not knowingly, anyhow."

"That is as fine a start as any, boy," the man said, shaking my hand yet again.

The vision left me as Ember stepped away. I blinked a few times to clear my mind as I stared back at his glowing eyes. My mind was back inside the elevator's cage, planting firmly in my own body again.

"And that's how the story began. Mine, at least," said Ember, crossing a leg over the other as he leaned against the cage bars, assessing me. When he'd removed his hand from my face, I didn't know. But I found the spot lacking warmth. "Nesrin and her father recruited me into the rebellion after they explained all of the mischief in which the High Council was responsible for."

"That is so strange…" I murmured, trying to make sense of the play. "How did Nesrin get into the High Council after her father was apparently killed?"

"According to records, her father died of a heart attack on the field, because he did not have any wounds to show for. We faked his death. We put him to sleep, resting his heart for long enough that a funeral was held. The High Council never saw through the façade. With Nesrin's Earth affinity, and as his child, she was next in line for supremacy."

As the elevator made its way closer to the top of the mountain, I felt a slight pressure increase in my skull. I could tell we were nearing the end of our caged-in trip, and something about that made me upset. Though I wasn't sure how much I trusted the seer, I was beginning to understand him the more we spent time together. I wasn't finished with hearing his stories. I wanted to know more, wanted to know everything.

"So, you trust Nesrin," I supposed, finding that that was an important piece of his story, and an important piece in mine too. If saving Gram and Shivalri meant that I was supposed to go into hiding with Nesrin, meet with her father, and ultimately, join a congregation of magic-wielding rebels, I had better make sure that the entire group I'd be staying with were safe. "And the other two who are here. You trust them too?"

"With my life," he answered, seeming to lighten at the new openness I was offering.

"Do you trust me?" I wondered, tilting a brow at him.

He bit his lip, surveying me. "Should I?"

I pursed my lips, then patted the space beneath my arm where the secret books were hidden. "I got your secret books without telling a soul. Shouldn't that count for something?"

"Fair," he replied, taking a leisurely stride toward me as the cage slowed, rattling, and squeaking all around us. "How about we trust each other until we give each other a reason not to?" he suggested. "Does that sound reasonable, Satyra?" The weakening in my knees came quickly as the cage came to a full stop, but the elevator had very little to do with my trembling legs. The way he spoke my name had been electrifying.

Ember took a step into the lighter mountain hall, and I realized that the area was more open than the entrance below. There were large, open cavities just ahead, seemingly leading to the exit as I could see the snow drifting past the hole. Behind the caged-in elevator, I saw the large cylinder-shaped mechanism that had powered the roping that lifted us up the mountain. It gave a loud buzz before shutting off, the heat radiating around it in the frigid air.

"Blackwood!" I heard a voice shout out. I whipped my head around to find Raidan, Nesrin, and a stranger standing in a semicircle close to the exit. Ember gestured for me to follow, and I gladly obliged, wanting to reunite with my cousin as quickly as possible.

"Hiro's Dango House again?" Ember jeered, pointing toward the many white boxes that dangled by slim, metal handles between the fingers of the stranger. "He always gets the same thing," Ember told me over his shoulder.

The man was a head taller than Ember, and he was a giant compared to my five-foot frame. Where Ember's features were deep, dark, and warm, this man had an even darker, cooler tone, on the verge of being obsidian. One of his eyes, bright blue, stood out in contrast to the rest of him. He had shorn hair styled to gradually fade from scalp to a nice top of short curls. He looked a little more worn and tired than spir-ited Nesrin, who stood at his side. Aside from looking exhausted, he seemed quite happy to see Ember as he smiled a bright white beam at him.

"The best of the best," he replied, lifting the boxes before us. He turned his gaze to face me, then lifted a teasing brow toward Ember before finding me again. "Satyra, I presume?" I looked between him and Ember, then nodded suspiciously. He grinned. "I've heard so much about you."

"The Fates are here?"

"Beneath the Dhetrïan Pool," Pyre answered, pointing toward the waters. The sand we stood on shone beneath my feet, the water mimicking the same effect.

"And we're going to go beneath the Dhetrïan Pool?" I was entirely unsure where Pyre's reason had gone, because looking out into the water, there was absolutely nothing in sight. And if we were supposed to find the Fates, underwater, was I meant to hold my breath the entire time?

"Yes." He sighed, running a hand through his wind-swept hair.

"So, let me get this straight," I said, eyes wide and questioning. "You want us to go into the water? Like, swim under it, for gods know how long, and I'm supposed to hold my breath?"

"Precisely."

I shook my head at him in exasperation. "Do you think I'm a fish?" I scoffed, hands out forward. "Not only is holding my breath difficult, but going under, deep… I'm not built for that!" I shivered as I imagined myself struggling to swim downward against the pressure. Pyre didn't seem too concerned about my freak out, only offering me a shrug as he took his boots off in preparation. "Pyre!"

"What?" he asked, tossing the boots into the rocky, iridescent sands.

"I can't go with you."

"You must," he insisted, kneeling before me. This was very familiar territory, bringing back the moment he'd proposed marriage to me not so long ago.

"What are you doing?"

Pyre's eyes met mine, and I saw the flame come to the surface. "I, God of the Dead, ruler of the Under Realm, swear my fealty to you. I *will* protect you with my life."

The air in my lungs whooshed right out of me. "Pyre…" I searched his gaze, finding no evidence of lies or betrayal. A sudden white light burst through his chest and into mine, and I gasped in disbelief. The warm, tingling sensation grew within me until it found its resting place in my heart. What was this magic? "Pyre, what did you just do?"

"Trust me, Goddess. Come in the water."

Wearily, I nodded, accepting this path. Pyre swore his fealty to me, just as Gerimor did. My heart did a funny little jump at the thought. I wasn't sure what it all meant, but I had a feeling he was telling the truth. He would protect me.

Pyre stood and gestured for me to move forward. My toes wiggled underneath me, the grains both brown and glimmering, dusting the tops of my feet.

"Does it feel strange to you?" Pyre asked, lifting my gaze from my toes to him. His arched brows lifted in amusement, while his teeth bit at his grin. Good gods, he was striking.

"Um, no," I stammered, fixing my mind back to the sand I stood in. "It's just strange to feel it beneath my feet after so long. I haven't stood in sand in a long while, and I've certainly never stood in sand that glows."

He nodded at me, seeming satisfied with my response. "It's the magic of the Fates," he replied. "It flows up from under the water caves."

"It's really pretty," I offered, bending over, and picking some up in my hand. It was cool to the touch, just as it was on my feet. As I lifted, I let it slowly sift through my fingers, watching it fall to the ground.

"Very," said Pyre, and so much of his look told me he wasn't talking about the sand. My heart fluttered in my chest, and I felt my cheeks heat. Turning away and looking toward the pool of water, I inhaled deeply. Pyre came up behind me, and I felt the distant heat of his wing nestling.

"I thought you said that the Dhetrïan Pool could be dangerous," I said, scowling.

"It can be, if you are not invited into it."

"And we are?"

"No, but I do have a way around it," he assured. I turned to look at him, waiting for more. I hefted my weight on my hip, showing my impatience. My ass moved against his front, and I tried to move away, but before I could, I felt him harden behind me. *Holy fuck.* A current of lightning lit my veins at the thought of his excitement. *No.* What was I thinking? Dear gods! Why was my body so pleased with his reaction? I managed to straighten myself, leaning away from the heat between us.

"Care to explain your way around it?" My words finally found my tongue.

Pyre grunted, his hot breath passing over my shoulder. "Beneath its surface you'll find that wraiths occupy the waters."

"What's a wraith?" I asked, eyes wide in concern.

"They are deceased humans who've transformed into creatures. They are created by those who've sinned by feeding off anger, fear, and negativity."

My skin froze over as I let that sink in. "And you want us to go swimming in there? With them!"

"Yes."

"But how? Why?" I was shaking now, confused, and traumatized by the thought of joining their ranks. My body compulsorily took a step backward, my back seeking comfort in the warmth of his chest. He didn't seem to mind, as he didn't move away.

"The wraiths are there in order to keep the uninvited out. But they cannot do so if they cannot see the intruder." My eyes swung back to the horse, eyes finding the helmet Pyre had worn earlier to sneak into the Orsimm cave.

"The helmet!" I exclaimed, acknowledging his idea's path.

Pyre walked past me and picked it up from the ground, tossing the gold armor between his hands. "My helm is a cloak of invisibility. Wear it, and your presence is entirely undetectable." He came up to me and held it forward, indicating that I should take it.

"I can't take this," I said, pushing it away from me. "You need it."

"I am God of the Dead," he replied, pushing the helmet back to me again.

"And I'm about two seconds away from fleeing," I retorted, folding my arms over my chest. His eyes widened, dark circles bluer in this light.

"Please, don't…" He swallowed, causing my heart to sink. I stared up at him, eyes unblinking. This was a chance to read him, while he left his book open to me. I took a moment to watch his features, finding that though rage lived in a part of him, he was capable of so much more. He wasn't just the God of the Dead. He was a person, with feelings and remorse. And now, in this tiny sliver of time, he was showing me a glimpse into the rest of who he was.

"I have nowhere to go but up," I said, breaking the silence. "And according to you, I can't do that without you." He didn't answer me as his lashes lowered, darkening his face. "I'm done trying to run away."

He looked up at me then, hopeful, and wary. "If you will not run, what will you do now?" he asked, searching my gaze.

I wanted to say that I had no clue. I wanted to scream it from the top of my lungs. Because that was the reality of the situation now. I had tried to run away. I thought I'd needed to get the hell away from Pyre, needing desperately to escape my prison. But it wasn't entirely him that I'd wanted to escape. He was a curious person to live with. He was temperamental, and full of heat, but ultimately, he was just a god who hadn't had any real companionship in what seemed to be a very long time. I couldn't run away from Pyre, and I can't run away from destiny now.

"What's your plan?" I finally said, causing him to close his eyes.

"We swim to the bottom of the pool, where we'll find the cave. As soon as we enter their cave, we'll be free to breathe and walk per usual. There's an air pocket surrounding their temple."

"And the wraiths?" I asked, far from being convinced that this was a good idea.

"I'll handle them," he replied, and strode forward. He lifted a hand to my cheek, and it took everything in me not to flinch or lean into him. He was absorbed in his focus. Finger-tips brushed over my skin as he pulled my hair behind my ear, and I felt a chill run down my neck from the contact. I blinked, sorting my head from my heart, and watched as he lifted his helmet and gently lowered it onto my head.

I'd expected the thing to weigh a ton, but it was surprisingly light on my shoulders. His hands lingered on each side of the armor, and I lifted mine to remove him from me, when a current of surprise rolled over me.

"I'm invisible!" I yelped, pulling my hands away from his and toward my face. I could see nothing of my body.

"That was the purpose of placing my helm on your head," he said, chuckling.

The lightness to his laugh made my lips form a smile. I made to hide it, then quickly realized I didn't have to. He couldn't see me, and I was free to express myself however I wished without the worry of him, or anyone, seeing me. I bit my lip, eager to stare at him without the hazard of causing trouble. Pyre started forward toward the water's edge, and I hurriedly followed his steps. He reached out a hand between us, waiting for me to take it. I lifted mine to his, making physical contact, even though to the eye, he held nothing but air.

"I still don't know if I can manage to hold my breath very long," I told him, staring at the pool in distaste. "I'm not in the mood to be wraith food."

"I would never let that happen," he swore to me, squeezing my hand in reassurance. I swallowed hard, nodding to no one but myself. In an instant, Pyre spun me into his arms, lifting me so that we were chest to chest. My legs instinctually wrapped around his waist, and my lower region heated in pleasure. Memories of impassioned lips melting into mine came to the forefront of my vision, and my legs impulsively tightened around him. I could feel his breath hovering between us, and I wondered if he could feel mine too. Heart hammering, I loosened my grip and settled my hormones, trying to focus. His eyes were a pool of liquid honey, dripping with pure temptation. "Hold on to me, and no matter what you see, no matter what you might feel, never let go." I gulped and clasped my hands around his neck. His dark, wavy hair brushed against my arm, and I was glad for the fact that he couldn't see me. His hair had grown in the past few weeks, and I'd long since wanted to thread my fingers through it. I let the strands fall on the backs of my hands, finding that this was as close as I'd let myself get to doing so. "Shivalri?" he interrupted me, stirring me from my thoughts.

"Y— Yes?" I stammered, eyes roaming his face, landing on the perfectly sculpted cupid's bow atop his lips.

"I need to hear you say it," he insisted, his hands growing tighter up my thighs. He was so close to my ass that I thought I might burst from the close contact.

"Say what?" I gasped when his grip slipped closer to it.

"Tell me you won't let go." He growled, voice low and heavy. His right hand drifted up my side, passing over my ribs and shoulder until landing on the back of the helmet I wore. His eyes searched mine, even though I knew his couldn't see me. His brows lifted in concern, waiting for my reply.

"I won't let go," I let out. His mouth was only inches away, and it was such a thrilling distraction. His hand lowered my head to his chest, and the intimacy of the hold released all the sexual tension, forming into something far different. When had I ever been held like this in my life? A time when these same strong arms held me after a nightmare, soothing me until I felt safe again.

"Hold your breath, and close your eyes," he instructed, and I nodded into his chest. He took his first steps into the shallow, took a deep breath, and plunged into the deep.

40

CREUX
SHIVALRI

That which signaled my brain's need for survival kicked into gear the moment our heads dove under water. My lungs begged me to turn around, imploring their need for oxygen the second I knew the option to breathe was no longer offered. The temperature of the Dhetrïan Pool was like bathing in a tepid hug. It passed between my clothes and up into the helmet, soaking through my hair. As we lowered at an alarming speed, the waters became cooler the deeper we went. The place where our chests met was the only part of me that remained warm, acting as a tether to life. Pyre's muscles worked overtime beneath me. He kicked his legs as our heads plummeted downward, causing the pressure to increase with every thrust.

The arm that wrapped around my core suddenly ripped from me, our bodies jerking awkwardly in the waters. I tried to pull my head from his chest to see what was happening, but the other hand held firm atop the helmet. A sharp scraping dragged across my ankle, and I jolted at the touch. My ankle abruptly froze, and I let out a short cry, not caring about the bubbles, which proved the loss of air in my lungs. I swung low, grabbing hold of my foot, trying to find the point of pain. My hold on my foot was concurrent with the release of Pyre's grasp, and I was suddenly aware that I'd made a grave mistake. I opened my eyes wide, the kaleidoscopic water stinging as the blur became a scene confirming that I was indeed submerged in Hell.

Wisps of ghostly bodies filtered around me, and I watched in horror, face to face with the reality of how terrible these wraiths could be. Flaccid strips of skin rippled from their faceless skulls, a few sharp teeth barely hanging on. Their bodies were gone, replaced by blackened shadow. Their claws were evident as they swarmed the waters. When they finally cleared a path for me to see past their silhouettes, Pyre swam ahead of me, frantic and furious.

Fists met with cracking skulls as he swung left and right, the water undulating over his arms. He screamed so fierce I felt it move in my body from the force of it. I finally realized his distress was due to his inability to see *me*. My lungs burned as I understood what would happen if we didn't find each other. Ignoring the freezing pain in my ankle, I finally forced myself to swim forward through the thick of it, wincing each time the freezing touch of a wraith struck my skin. But with my eyes on Pyre, witnessing the attack he was under, nothing would stop me from reaching him. A wraith rushed toward me, unseeing, but still on its way to me. My body froze, panic rising up my throat as I waited to feel its claws dig into me. As if the Fates had gifted me luck, the wraith changed course, allowing me to continue forward.

The closer I got, the clearer he was, and the anticipation of our reunion swelled in my heart. When I reached for him, hand meeting his shoulder, his body turned to attack me.

"No," I tried, but the bubbles muddied my voice. I swerved away, just in time to avoid the might of his fist. His eyes widened in shock, his hands desperately swooshing between us, trying to find me. I stretched my hand out again, and this time, when we made contact, he pulled me into him, and hugged me so fiercely I thought I might burst. With one hand on my head, pressing me into his chest, I wrapped my legs around him again as he swatted away the hungry wraiths that surrounded us. With the last punch to the nearest creature, Pyre had us plunging downward again, and away from the mass of terror. I closed my eyes tightly, not wanting to see their chase behind us, as I clung to the God of the Dead for dear life.

Our bodies slowly went from swimming downward, to pushing forward as the desperation in my lungs burned at an unnatural degree. When I felt his arm around me let go, my eyes opened in panic, the water pouring into them with a sting. I clung to Pyre's shoulders, pleading the gods for my grip to be tight enough not to allow him to lose me. When I looked up from his chest and over to his face, I noted that he didn't look worried, and his release of me was intentional. His hands glided down my waist, wetness slipping between us as he hoisted me upward, thrusting through the gravity of the water that was holding us down. When I looked up, I found that there was a glowing light sitting atop the surface I was nearing, and understood that somehow, some way, we'd made it to the air pocket. I lifted my arms above my head, desperately swimming upward.

My head burst through the surface, water splashing all around me as I took in my first delicious breath. My lungs hugged me so tight that my ribs constricted under the pressure. Pyre's head appeared in front of me, his wet hair plastered over his face. He wiped a hand up over his eyes, making an even greater mess of the mane, and a laugh tore out of me unintentionally. I couldn't help it. Whether it was hysteria from having escaped those retched wraiths down below, or seeing him look so misplaced and human, it didn't matter. I laughed and laughed until my belly strained, and a gulp of water rushed down my throat. I coughed harshly, still laughing while choking on the waters of the Dhetrïan Pool.

"Are you all right?" Pyre asked, looking around and trying to find me. He was looking in my general direction, which I could only assume was due to my senseless splashing and loud choking sounds.

"You!" I choked, unable to get the words out. I threw out a hand toward him, offering him a sense of where I was. His eyes met the splatter, and his arms immediately darted out, searching for me. Fingers clasped my forearm, and he tugged me forward, until we were chest to chest yet again. Squeezing my eyes shut, I laughed and laughed in his embrace until the water streaming down my face became tears. The laugh died out on my lips as he lifted the helmet off my head, and his eyes landed on my mouth. He threw his helmet behind him, and it landed with a clinking thud.

"*You*," he whispered, and the air I'd been glad to breathe got caught in my throat. I put my hands to his chest and lowered my eyes away from his stare.

"We should get out of the water," I stammered, voice breathy and raw. Pyre leaned back in the water, my body following his to the point of almost laying on top of him. He never left my gaze as he paddled us backward and toward the cave's rock-strewn opening. When we got close enough for the waters to shallow, Pyre stood with soaked-through clothes, taking me up with him. My legs felt wobbly, my body too heavy after being underwater. "Woah," I mumbled, clinging on to his shoulders for balance.

"Are you well?" he asked, still holding on to my waist. I shook my head yes and removed myself from his person.

"Good." I turned away from him, staring into the mouth of the cave, entirely transfixed by the glowing light that emanated from within.

"This is so…" I trailed, unable to find the words to describe what I was seeing. The walls were rounded up into its ceiling, and the height of it must have gone at least a hundred feet up. I stared in bewilderment as I pieced this information in my mind, understanding just how deep Pyre had taken us into the Dhetrïan Pool. When we were on surface, staring across the water, there hadn't been any sign of land or cave within its waters. For this cave to be so tall, we must have swum double its depth downward. I looked to Pyre in incredulity. He picked up his helmet from the ground and walked over to me, looking around at the twinkling walls surrounding us.

"Pretty?" he offered.

I gave him a quaint grin and lifted a hand to touch the wall. There was an iridescent powder lining the surface, and it transferred its glow to my fingertips. Blue and silver shone on my skin as I stared down at my hand. Pyre mimicked my movement and swiped his thumb down the cave's wall.

"I've never seen anything like this," I told him as I watched the glitter dance. "It feels like it's alive…"

"It's the pure essence of magic," he replied. "It *is* alive."

"How can this exist? Why is it down here?"

"You mean down in this cesspool of a realm?" he corrected.

I furrowed my brows, shaking my head. "The Under Realm?"

"Is it not what you meant?" he questioned, coming closer. I looked up at him through wet lashes, finding a rather intense stare.

"I meant magic in general," I explained. "And I was

referring to the underwater cave we're standing in. I don't understand why magic would live here, and not up there."

He grimaced, his lips thinning. "You'd prefer magic to dwell in the Celestial Realm?"

I narrowed my eyes at him, trying to understand where this was coming from. "What do you mean?" I demanded, closing my fists. "When have I ever said that the Celestial Realm is more deserving of anything?" I couldn't think of a time where I'd ever thought that. Though this was like Hell, it was here for a purpose, and not everyone here was evil. I'd never judged the beings here as inherently evil. I've always believed that even if someone were a bad person, they could change and atone. Everyone was deserving of equal treatment, and if magic existed in the Celestial Realm, I was happy that it also lived on Earth and in the Under Realm.

"I thought...." Pyre lowered his gaze to my fists as his words trailed.

"You thought wrong. Magic belongs to everyone, everywhere," I said. His eyes flicked back up to mine, and I saw his emotions soften in his features.

"Even if some of us use magic for wrongdoing?" he questioned, voice low.

"Let me ask you this," I held, taking a step toward him. "Those who do bad in their lives will die in a place of atonement, no?" He took a moment to study me, scrunching his face.

"No," he finally answered, and my heart fell through my stomach.

"What?"

"No, my Goddess," he spoke softly. "There is no place of atonement in the Under Realm. Only punishment." I felt the sting of tears prickle my overly dried eyes as I considered this new information.

"There's no place here for people who wish to be better?" My voice hitched on the last word because the people I was talking about were the witches in my family, who I knew would be sent here in death. They were good people, who didn't need to become better. I'd assumed that they were sent here to pay for the sins of those with their blood before them. I'd wanted to assume that those who were good, but forced to enter the Under Realm, would have a safe place to live out their peaceful deaths.

"There is not," said Pyre, and my stomach soured at his words.

"That's not right." I faltered, a tear rolling down my face. As I lowered my chin, Pyre lifted a hand and brushed the tear away. I stiffened at the intimacy of such contact, frowning at the goose bumps he gave me.

"There is plenty I question when it comes to what's right. If I could change these kinds of things, I would."

"Can't you?" I wondered, looking back up to him. My lower lip trembled, and I bit it to stop it from showing. He took my fists in his hands, gently coaxing mine to relax.

"Breathe," he implored, and rubbed his thumb over my knuckles. The iridescence dusted my skin where he touched me, and I took a deep breath in as I watched it sparkle. "Are you ready?" he asked. I nodded quietly, and he let go of my hands, my arms falling to my sides. We turned to face the massive cave, stepped away from the side wall, and entered the glowing temple.

41

MIRROR

SHIVALRI

O versized opalescent stones jutted out atop the stream that flowed at the center of the temple. They formed a sort of stepping-stone bridge, allowing us to walk on water. Pyre had insisted I walk ahead of him in case my clumsiness took over my senses. I'd assured him that that was unnecessary, but he'd argued that with me, everything was necessary. I wasn't even quite sure what that meant, but I trudged ahead of him anyway, granting him his request.

Step by rocky step, we made our way up the stream and toward the source of glowing light. As we neared the massive monolith, which stood so high, I had to bend my neck to see its top, a rush of nerves tenderized my skin. It was hard to wrap my mind around what Pyre and I were doing here. To consider this a possibility was unfathomable until only moments ago.

When I'd asked Pyre about the Fates during our lessons at the castle, he'd explained that the Fates are sentient tethers, able to form cognizance through their senses. Entirely made of a magical essence, they are responsible for weaving the strings that make up life itself. To wrap one's mind around the idea that these tethers even existed was a difficult feat, but to grasp my journeying to visit them was a whole other thing to give credence to.

A celeste-blue orb now floated several feet above our heads as we reached the giant monolith. The glowing dusting along the cave walls had come to life here in the center of the temple, floating around the tower like a deer dancing on the wind. It was whimsical in every manner, and I could hardly believe I was here to witness it. No amount of fire magic, or any elemental magic for that matter, came even close to being this mesmerizing. Whatever this was, this raw magic emanating from the stone monument was astounding beyond words.

As I reached the last stepping-stone, I saw the tower ahead of me much clearer. There was a domed shape going into the monolith at its base, as if someone had dug a room into it. It was dark, but I could see enough to make out the plain rock walls, and it seemed like there was nothing inside.

"Where are the Fates?" I asked, whispering over my shoulder as if voicing their title out loud would be disrespectful.

"They are everywhere and nowhere," he answered, taking a leap onto the stone I was standing on. He held out a hand to me, and I instinctively took it, not wanting to make another move on my own. "Come, Goddess. It's time." Pyre took a long stride, stretching his leg over the distance, and I followed suit. The ground beneath us crumbled under our toes, the rocks around shifting from their resting place.

"What's happening?" I yelped, clinging onto Pyre's wrist.

"They are waking." As if on cue, the orb atop us exploded into a million tiny shards of icy silver sparkles, creating a circle around the tower we stood at. Every particle of glowing magic screamed up into the hollow, rattling the underground cave in its wake. The sound was deafening as the air slashed through the sanctum, as if the whistling of magic weren't meant for my ears.

"*Xïeuhresse dhèjl vïhïo, teuhïx vïèmme tyeūx scïyre zōhx sōrza,*" voices boomed, feeling like it came from everywhere all at once.

"What?" I screamed over the chanting, eyes wide and looking to the God of the Dead for answers. His face was stark, whole in this moment.

"It is the old language, *Lôgæva Têrvû.*"

"What did they say?" I asked, feeling dumbstruck for having assumed they'd speak in English.

"Goddess of Three, you come to know your fate." I looked at him with a handful of hope in my heart.

"How do I answer them?" I wondered, considering this language barrier.

"They know all languages, Goddess. Speak to them however you wish. They are all-cognizant. You can even speak to them through your thoughts if you'd prefer." Now *that* was astounding. I took a short breath of courage and looked up to the glowing mass of magic still swimming above our heads.

"Hello," I stuttered, feeling like a complete fool and totally out of character.

"Goddess of Three, your fate awaits you," the voices swirled up and about.

My heart was hammering in my chest at the closeness to the very entities who were responsible for my existence. "My fate… What is it?" I asked, trying to find the source of the voices.

"Look into the mirror to find yourself. Submerge your consciousness in our temple waters."

I looked around us, peering into the domed area in the monolith. We were on dry rock. Did they want me to go into the stream?

"In here," said Pyre, his voice carrying on an echo from inside the tower. I took a step closer, watching as a luminance slowly lit up his face in the darkness. He was looking down, staring into a pond, glittering with the same silvery blue that adorned the rest of the temple.

"Oh, wow…" I was entirely astonished as I entered the space. The walls were covered in the pearlescent dusting, and Pyre was in the center of it all. His massive black wings were covered in the dust, and the planes of his face illuminated, making him appear even more divine. Now, standing face-to-face with the God of the Dead, I could see each individual feather spring to life. The barbules in each were crystalline, and whichever part the light caressed was a beautiful shade of sparkling indigo. His shoulders shifted, wings lifting higher above his head as if knowing I couldn't remove my gaze.

"Are you ready?" he asked, breaking the silence with a voice so gruff I could feel it in my knees. I nodded groggily, shaking myself from the beauty that was Pyre Malum.

"I need to be," I answered, quiet but sure. I turned to investigate the glowing water, but Pyre grabbed at my wrist, forcing me to retreat. "What's wrong?" I shuddered, searching his gaze. He was so entirely transfixed on my face that I wanted to hide it.

"What you find…" he began, his brows knitting together with concern. "You may not like what you hear."

"Oh." I was taken aback. I already knew that whatever was to come from this would have its negative points. I hadn't considered how much it might affect me mentally. Hadn't considered that the outcome could very well be the worst thing imaginable. I'd only thought of the path ahead, needing help to fix the veil, and keeping the Gates sealed.

"Nevertheless," Pyre continued, letting go of my wrist and leaving it cold where he'd touched me. "It's best to know and to have these answers. What you might face in your life-time..." he trailed, shaking his head. "I just know that this will help you along the way."

"I know," I replied, and truly, I did. He nodded at me and clasped his hands behind his back.

"Go to your fate, Goddess. Whatever awaits you, I'll be here to help." My stomach lurched into my throat at his sudden words of kindness. This new openness to him was something of wonderment, and I would not take it for granted. I took one last look at the god with eyes so bright an amber I could fall into them. I turned away before my heart decided it never wanted to leave.

42

ÔHRTUM

SHIVALRI

Swirling, iridescence pooled at my feet, begging for me to let go. I could feel the tug, as if the strings of my life were physically tied to my mind, pulling me into their torrent of magic.

"Open your mind and see your fate," the voices chanted, the hum-like wind-chimes ringing through the tower. I tilted my head down, searching with all my might and willing my fate to come to me.

Abruptly, fire burned all around me, lighting everything in sight. The screams of my loved ones, strangers crying and begging for their lives in a nonsensical fashion. Thunder erupted in the skies above me. Red, red, and even darker crimson splattering the edges of my vision. The skies on Earth were swathed in blood, bearing winged beasts who were ravenous and gloating in the graying clouds.

I looked down at myself, palms drenched in my own blood. I oozed red and gold. The cold hard ground laughed as I fell. My family was dead. The world was dying. I was fading away. I collapsed through the ground and into a swarm of chaos. Massive spiders and ogre-like giants charged toward me as I tried to scramble to my feet.

"*Abrôrta dhèjl Ôhrtum!*" the universe screeched at me. I saw the words written in the burn of my eyes. The tears were hot as they poured from my orifices, my fire element drying them as they came. It was too late. Before I even had the chance to try, the world had come crashing down. The Gates were gone. My fate was *death*.

"*Abrôrta dhèjl Ôhrtum!*" I screamed, my throat searing along with the universe I tore into. Pyre was suddenly before me, eyes wide with horror. He looked at me like I was the destruction of the entire world.

"Goddess," he croaked, before falling to lay next to me on the hard ground. He reached out a hand, and I tried with everything I had in me to grasp it. I tried, and tried, crawling and burning and wishing just to touch his outstretched hand. His eyes grew glassy, and my breaths were shallow as I stared at the God of the Dead's lifeless corpse.

"*Abrôrta dhèjl Ôhrtum! Abrôrta dhèjl Ôhrtum! Abrôrta dhèjl Ôhrtum! Abrôrta dhèjl Ôhrtum! Abrôrta dhèjl Ôhrtum! Abrôrta dhèjl Ôhrtum! Abrôrta dhèjl Ôhrtum! Abrôrta dhèjl Ôhrtum! Abrôrta dhèjl Ôhrtum! Abrôrta dhèjl Ôhrtum! Abrôrta dhèjl Ôhrtum! Abrôrta dhèjl Ôhrtum! Abrôrta dhèjl Ôhrtum!*"

Swiftly, as if my mind hadn't taken enough torment, I watched it all play back again, spinning through the tale backward. Now, when I looked up into the skies, the clouds were glowing gold, a heavenly harp cascaded down from the heavens. All around me, I saw life as it should be. The earth was beautiful. The trees were in bloom and the smell of fresh rain filtered my nose. My grandmother, glowing, stood beneath a giant tree, hugging both Raidan and Satyra in a warm embrace. I reached out a hand, wanting to greet them, but a warm, familiar palm was placed in mine. The body connected to the hand was that of a handsome god, his black feathered wings framing his stature. He smiled down at me and placed a comforting kiss to my forehead. I closed my eyes and relished in the relief from the earlier terror. But when I opened my eyes again, the terror came flooding back tenfold, as I stepped into the deepest depths of the Under Realm, enfolded by the beasts I'd only been able to imagine in the darkly inventive end of my mind.

A sword I hadn't noticed glinted in the light as I held it in my right hand. Pyre still held on to me at my left, and I felt a power surge within me, a power created by the two of us, shared between one another. With Pyre at my side, I could face these monsters. I could bring them to their knees. A burst of elements tore from my skin, and this time, when I screamed it was from pure delight. For I knew what I was capable of, and that was a dangerous tool to wield.

"Can you accept your fate, *Abrôrta dhèjl Ôhrtum?*"

"Shivalri!" I heard, the voice like a fissure tearing into my brain. "Shivalri, please!"

"*Abrôrta dhèjl Ôhrtum!*" I gasped, eyes widening until my vision finally came back to me. I could feel my heart pounding in the back of my throat. My tonsils were raw, and I was leaking blood down the front of my shirt as I stared down into the shimmering waters.

"Oh, Gods," Pyre said, still grabbing me by the shoulders and holding me up. "What did you see?" I looked away from the Fates' mirror and found his face inches from mine. I couldn't answer him. I could only stare. He was here, yet, in there... My body gave out from under me, but Pyre held me up. "Goddess? Shivalri?" He was panicked, shaking my frozen body. "What did you show her?" He roared up into the tower. "What did you do to her?" His grip on my shoulders tightened as he pulled me into his embrace. My head felt hollow as it fell to his chest. Pyre clutched me tighter, smoothing my hair in erratic caresses, and I finally took a breath, not having realized my lungs had stopped working till then.

"*Xïeuhresse dhèjl vïhïo, jèllhe dhèjl tuxhü vïhïo væssiuses,*" the Fates answered him. "*Nûvhe nèïmne èllhre Abrôrta dhèjl Ôhrtum, rûhx jèllhe êhzje zràhl Rumlèle Véhtruiran.*"

"What does that mean?"

"*Abrôrta dhèjl Ôhrtum! Abrôrta dhèjl Ôhrtum! Abrôrta dhèjl Ôhrtum!*"

"Gods, damn it! What did you show her? What is her fate?"

"We cannot show you another's fate. *Nûvhe peuxæn kàlvha jémôntre tûwha zōhx sōrza.*"

"You've already shown me my fate long ago. I am to rule the dead."

"That is not all. Look deeper."

"I don't care about my own life, gods damn it! I just want her safe." A small piece of me woke at those words. Surely, he didn't mean them.

"The answer to her safety lies in your hands."

"How can that be?"

"Look…" Pyre still clung to me, my body feeling numb, and my mind overworked. I felt his body shift so that he could look into the mirrored pond, and I quickly shoved my face into him, closing my eyes as tightly as possible. Pyre went rigid and I felt his heart beneath my ear. It pounded quicker and quicker as he peered into the glowing waters. When he stopped searching, I knew, because I felt the breath in him wash out into a wave over my hair.

"How?"

"*Jèllhe êhzje zōhx sōrza. Jèllhe êhzje zōhx yeiftô rôhdem zràhl Xïeuhrïx*. The gift you have been searching for."

"All this time, I was never meant to leave this realm to find it."

"*Nājch*."

"But I was supposed to be freed..." His voice broke, and my mind flickered in and out of indulgence for his words.

"See with your soul, and not your eyes. You *are* free."

43

SUMMIT

SATYRA

Raidan, Nesrin, Ember, and I shadowed the man carrying the delicious smelling takeout, following his steps through the snowy mountain top. From up here, the trees below looked like a blur of dull brown and white. We were so high up; I could hardly believe this was real. Just a few feet from the mountain's exit, I could see billowing smoke in the air above a dingy log cabin, which sat in the middle of the highest peak. When we'd gone up through the center of the mountain in the elevator, it had taken us directly to the safe house.

The group of us entered the small log cabin just in time to beat a freezing gust of snow that was headed our way. Closing the door behind him, Ember dusted the bits of snow that landed on his shoulders. Raidan and Nesrin were the first to remove their jackets, placing them on the backs of the wooden chairs in what I could only assume was a poor excuse for a kitchen. The outside of the cabin had looked worn down, but it was nothing in comparison to the blackened walls and shitty furniture found inside.

"It's old, but it will do," Nesrin said, trailing her finger along the top of the burnt table. "Couldn't have cleaned up a bit while you were here, Wulfric?" she asked the new stranger. So, this was Ember's most trusted ally, his friend Wulfric Hallows. He only shrugged at Nesrin as he removed his snow-covered coat.

"Did this place catch fire?" Raidan asked, patting the dirty wall. A tiny shadow scurried across the floor from one end to the other, retreating into a hole in the busted wall.

"Rats?" I groaned, clinging to my scarf, reluctantly unraveling it.

"It was burned a long time ago," said Nesrin as she and Raidan entered the living room area. Wulfric, still holding the takeout, walked right into the living room, not caring about the melting snow tracks he let fall to the dirty floor. Nesrin folded her legs under herself and took a seat on the ground.

"Why are you sitting on the floor when there are enough chairs for all of us?" I wondered, grimacing at the grime beneath my feet. She reached up toward the couch and pulled off a greened cushion, shoving it under her butt. Wulfric passed her a takeout container, and she took it gladly, humming to herself. When she began to open her food, thrusting a pair of chopsticks into the carton, she looked up at me with an air of nonchalance. Wulfric joined her on the floor, splaying out the food.

"Habit. It's what I've always done. I like to keep certain familial traditions alive," she explained and threw a lumpy dumpling into her mouth. "This is usual for me," she muffled between chews. "Come; sit." I watched her settle into place, picking up yet another dumpling and plopping it into her mouth.

"You've arrived," a new voice sounded from my right.

"Holy gods!" I blew, holding a hand to my chest as my heart settled its heavy thumping.

"Kaede," Ember told me, gesturing to the figure emerging from the dark corner of the room.

"I didn't see you there." The figure laughed, sliding two slender hands adorned with silver jewels through their bleached blond coif.

"That was my intention," the stranger said, before moving to the kitchen in a gliding motion. Had I not seen the feet attached to the body, I might have thought they were floating.

"As you can see," Ember sighed, "They're quite fond of creeping around. I told you before that Kaede is like our eyes and ears."

"Yes, I remember," I said, eyeing the creeper.

"That's because they're very good at concealing their presence." Kaede snickered before bending into the outdated fridge and pulling out a case of Coca Cola.

"Very good," they agreed, winking at me. I startled, eyes widening at the ease with which Kaede lived and breathed.

Moving back to the living area, they passed out the sodas and cracked a can open. Kaede guzzled the beverage down as if they hadn't had a drink in ages, not caring about the fizz that poured from the sides of their mouth. With their smooth gliding motions, Kaede took a seat across from Nesrin and grabbed a pair of chop sticks.

"The floor for you too?" I asked, gesturing to the area.

"Do you have a problem with dirt? If so, you're going to have to get used to it," Kaede muttered between gulps. "Not that I like it by any means."

I grimaced.

Raidan walked over to the spot where Nesrin, Wulfric, and Kaede made themselves comfortable and joined them on the floor. I could picture this being an intimate form of eating, a way of getting to know one another over dinner. No television, cell phones, or busying around while eating. However, these floors were disgusting and if having seen the rat earlier wasn't enough, there seemed to be tiny, pebble-like droppings dusting the area.

"Let me guess," I said, looking over my shoulder to Ember and sighing heavily. "You'd also prefer sitting on the floor?"

"First of all," he said, jutting out a finger toward me. "Not everyone likes to sit on the floor. Those two just happen to. How they're able to ignore the feces ten feet away from them, I do not know." He strode up behind me and teasingly bumped my shoulder. The books within my jacket stabbed me in the armpit in protest to the movement. "Second, and probably most importantly, I am hungry, and I do not have a preference so long as someone is sharing their dumplings with me." I shared a small smile with him and turned to give Raidan a questioning look. When my eyes found his face, I found him happily staring at a dumpling-starved Nesrin, unconcerned by the rat-infested log cabin. I groaned audibly, unzipping my jacket. Then I remembered the books, and Ember's insistence on keeping them a secret, and pulled my zipper back up.

"Come on, Satyra," Ember whispered in my ear. "The rats won't bite."

AMITY

SATYRA

While we ate the dinner provided by Wulfric, those of us at the scene of the High Council's invasion spent the time between bites explaining what had happened to my grandmother. Apparently, they were already up to date with the information on Shivalri, and knew who me and Raidan were, as it was part of Ember's job in the congregation to inform its members of our situation. It seemed that Ember was a spy in every sense of the word, having worked in this manner for the High Council and the rebellion. He hadn't explained to me how it was that he was so skilled at counterspying, but I figured he'd had a lot of practice. He would have to be very clever to be a mole within a group of highly powerful witches.

I didn't have much of an appetite as I listened to the stories being retold. After running through the woods, I knew I needed some food, so I ate a bit of rice from a carton Raidan passed me. I spent my time with caution, studying the group of rebels as they ate and caught up with each other. It was interesting to watch this group exchange conversation. They appeared to be a strange mix of a family, all from different parts of the world, coming together for a change. The way they spoke with one another was as if they'd known each other their whole lives. The way they moved, so alike, was fascinating to watch. Each one of them possessed a sort of feline grace. From picking up food between chopsticks, to folding their legs beneath them, they almost looked as if each movement were a calculated dance.

"Have you been in touch with Cormac as of late?" Ember asked Kaede, who'd just finished their meal and leaned back on their hands.

"All is well on his end, and so are things at the palace," Kaede assure him. "General Mehra will be available soon for a meeting. Perhaps in a week's time, if all is well on their end."

"Who is Cormac?" Raidan asked as he stretched his arms over his head.

"Cormac Galbraith is second in command, General's right-hand man. He and Kaede communicate daily to ensure all is well at each faction."

"Are you high in command too?" Raidan questioned Kaede.

"Not in a soldierly sense, but, in a security sense. I keep the technology in check and am in charge of keeping safe communications open. I, along with Cormac, also make sure that drops between factions are made safely, and travel too."

"Only the two of you?" I asked, fully intrigued.

"We have a certain level of stealth that others do not possess," Kaede answered. "All we need is us two in this continent."

"Hmm," I responded, nodding apprehensively. Ember had told us that there were hundreds of followers, and I could only assume that most of them stayed within their many factions. How were two people capable of keeping all the movement between factions protected? The rebels must not leave their posts often, I supposed.

"Kaede is made of shadow, girl," Nesrin told me, pointing with a used chopstick. With lightning speed, and astounding grace, Kaede pushed the chopstick away.

"No pointing." Nesrin growled at Kaede's demand, but Kaede only smiled in satisfaction when she lowered her chopstick. "Did you not see Kaede appear from nothing earlier?" I balked at her, then steeled my face into a glower. "Open your eyes, Grimsbane."

That comment alone would have done me in, but the way she rolled her eyes at me was even more frustrating. "I saw," I said, gritted between teeth.

"Hey, hey," Ember spoke, putting a hand in each of our directions as if to separate us. "Play nice."

"I don't mean any offense by it," Nesrin replied, shrugging her shoulders. "It's simply advice. Something you'd do well to consider, for the safety of your life."

"Are you threatening me?" I narrowed my eyes at her, fisting my hands at my sides.

"Gods, no!" She laughed, setting me further on edge. "We're on the same team. I just prefer my allies to be well prepared. I can't be spending any time out of focus, trying to save your ass when you're not paying attention." She took a swig from her soda and set it back down.

"She's new to all of this," Ember said in my defense. "They both are."

"And that is why so many of the Grimsbanes are gone," she countered.

"Don't talk about my family," I ordered pointedly. Her

brows softened a bit at my tone, seeing the match she struck within me. "You don't know anything about us."

"To be fair, Saty," Raidan interrupted. "We hardly know anything about our family either." I whipped my head at him to refute, but I saw the tension he held in his posture and understood that this was bothering him, too, only, he was controlling his temper far better than I was. I sucked in a hard breath and turned back to Nesrin.

"We want to help you," she told me. "You should have noted the way Kaede moves and understood that that was their specialty. I may be blunt, but I am coming from a place of understanding. I want you to be smart. We *need* you to be."

"What she means to say is that we're all going to help you two learn about our world and teach you how to spot dangers and signs," said Ember.

"We're a good team when we need to be," said Wulfric. He was so quiet I'd forgotten he was here. "Trust that anything we say or do is for the benefit of us all."

"And don't take the bruteness to heart," said Ember. "We all treat each other like siblings in this group. We get on each other's nerves more than anything, but everyone one of us would die to protect the other."

"Speak for yourself," Kaede jeered, smirking from ear to ear. Wulfric punched them in the shoulder, pulling a smoky laugh out from the blond. "Kidding," they said, pulling a pierced lip into their mouth. I hadn't noticed the metal looped around the center of their lower lip until now.

"We are in this together," Nesrin said, looking around at the group of us sitting on the floor.

"Now, so are you." Ember seemed determined, looking between me and Raidan.

"Thank you for helping us," I said, turning to look at my cousin. "We can't do this without help." Raidan nodded in agreement, though I saw the distrust in his eyes, a strong match to mine. But we had no other choice. We needed the aid of the rebellion.

45

IDLE

SATYRA

With some coaxing from Ember, I followed him and Nesrin to the back of the house where they told us that there was a washroom and two bedrooms we could use during our stay at this faction. I hadn't wanted to go to sleep yet. I wanted to discuss plans with the rebels, needing to know what the hell they were planning. But our new allies insisted that we should get some rest, especially the group of us who had been running through the snow-covered forest earlier today. I could admit that I was tired. My legs still felt like Jell-O, and when I stood from my seated position on the floor, Raidan held me up by my elbows before I could topple over.

The wooden floor creaked beneath our feet as we sauntered down the dim hallway. They had electricity by generator, so they didn't waste the energy on lighting, rather, they saved it for use of water and keeping the refrigerator on. I noted that they used a wood stove to cook atop, after having passed the fire with two pots filled with boiling water on the stovetop. There was a light coming from the first door ahead, but it flickered up and down the doorway. I was used to seeing by candlelight, as I'd lived with Gram for so many years. She deemed candlelight the best kind of lighting and had most of our house gilded with it.

"The bathroom is in here," said Nesrin, pointing to the glowing area. "As I'm sure you will be happy to hear, the shower, sink, and toilet are all functional." As she said this, I noticed a faint blush appear on Rai's face and wondered how deep Nesrin's spell of beauty had dug itself into his mind. I couldn't blame him. She was very beautiful—graceful and impressively resilient. "Towels are in the cabinet. We reuse the same one for a couple of days, so as not to do too much laundry. There are hooks behind the door to hang them after you've dried off." Raidan and I both nodded, the two of us peering into the room. It was small and outdated but very clean in comparison to the rest of the house.

"I guess the bathroom was lucky," Raidan murmured, rubbing at the clean wall. "No soot."

"It only got the kitchen and living area. We're not entirely sure what caused it, but I think perhaps it was a problem with the woodstove," Nesrin supposed.

"It happened a few months ago, and the report only told us that a warlock with water affinity put it out, and the structure is still sound." Ember grimaced, before adding, "The people responsible made sure to leave out their names so as not to get in shit for it. And Kaede still won't tell us who it was."

"Kaede was there?" I questioned, looking down the hall to the rooms that were now lit up.

"I am everywhere," they said, poking their blond head out of the bedroom to the right. My hand flew to my chest, finding that my mind would most likely never keep up with Kaede's random coming and goings. Ember tugged at one of my curls, and I flinched under his sudden touch. I turned with questioning eyes at him, finding that in this bit of darkness, a small amount of red shone in his.

"There are ten factions across the world," said Ember. "Two of which are in Northern America, one in Latin America, two in Africa, two in Asia, and three in Europe. Kaede is responsible for safe commute between the two factions in Northern America. Kaede and Cormac switch between factions for a change in scenery." Kaede scoffed from inside the other room.

"No." Kaede sneered. "We switch off because this place is disgusting, and the faction in Oregon is far better."

"Oregon?" I questioned.

Ember sighed, dropping his head in his hands. "Nice." He tsked, before meeting my questioning gaze. "Yes, that is where the other faction stands in Northern America. It's our base for this continent. We don't often use this one in Yukon, for obvious reasons."

"You mean besides the fact that it's on the top of a giant, snowy mountain and covered in soot and feces?"

He rolled his eyes at me. "It's not always this dirty. We usually pick up after ourselves around here. It just hasn't been in use for some time."

"I thought you said there was always someone here," I pointed. "Cormac or Kaede."

"On the first of every month, they report to General Mehra in our central training base. With what recently happened in Salem, their stays have been longer. All of us know not to look for safe passage for the first two days of the month, as those days are always marked for the report. But this month, because I was ordered to introduce myself to your family and offer my assistance, the meetings have been longer for time to strategize and plan with one another. Kaede only got back yesterday. Wulfric had informed me that he'd be coming here this morning, and as you already know, that's why I chose to come here at the last minute."

"Okay," I said, sorting through the information. "So, there was no one here for a couple of weeks… What if a rebel were in danger on those days?" I wondered; Raidan hummed in agreement. I'd forgotten that he was a part of the conversation, my mind solely focused on getting as much intel as possible while Ember was readily giving it.

"We find drop-off locations nearby for food rations and clothes and stay with families who are a part of the congregation until the factions are up and running again."

"And you just trust that you'll be safe from the High Council without the safety of the faction's wards? I don't know about you, but I would be scared to be unprotected like that."

Ember furrowed his brow at me, slowly shaking his head.

"Interesting that your concern is for your own safety, rather than the safety of the defenseless people whose homes we invade." I cringed at Nesrin's words.

"I—" I stuttered, looking between them before staring down at my feet to avoid their scrutiny.

"No, Satyra. And we don't take entering their homes lightly either," Ember said softly. "We only do this if we have no other option. We don't eagerly endanger the innocent families of our rebellion."

I was such a fool. "I didn't mean it like that…" I stammered, feeling ashamed. I'd been thinking about my safety over those who were being imposed on. I didn't know what it was like for those who let the rebels stay in their homes. I hadn't thought about what it meant for them, assuming that because they were fine with it, I shouldn't care about their well-being. I felt like an asshole.

"No," he said, putting a hand on my shoulder. "I know."

"Let me show you the rooms," Nesrin cut in, giving Ember a narrow-eyed glare. Without saying another word, Raidan and Ember followed the girl, and I trudged my feet behind them, wishing I had a better filter on what I said and did. I hoped they knew that I didn't mean anything bad by how my mind worked. I obviously cared about everyone's safety. I just hadn't considered the families' sacrifices before worrying about my own protection. I was going to have to unlearn this, I knew. I could tell by the way this group of rebels interacted with each other that their friend's lives, and their extended families, mattered just as much as their own. I worried only for myself and my own family. I would have to learn to extend those concerns to the rest of the congregation if I ever wanted a chance at integrating into their rebellion and saving Gram and Shivalri.

"I'll take the cot in here with Wulfric and Kaede," Nesrin told us, gesturing to the room just after the bathroom, which Kaede had poked their head out of earlier. When we stepped through the threshold, the candlelight gave off enough glow to show the cot at the back of the wall, and bunkbed to the right, which was set up in front of the closet next to the entrance. I noticed the bareness of it. No pictures or knick-knacks of any kind. Just three beds and a few duffle bags thrown on the floor.

Wulfric stood at the far end of the room, putting a clean pillowcase on the cot, which Nesrin was presumed to sleep on. Kaede, at the top of the bunkbed, was sitting upright against the wall and a mountain of pillows stacked around them. They were wrapped up in a thick, fluffy blanket, seemingly made from faux fur, which I knew would feel amazing draped over my cold legs. All three beds had the same style of blanket, only they differed slightly in shade.

"This room has a change of clothes that would fit you," Nesrin told me as she headed toward the closed closet.

"Are you sure?" If they were Nesrin's clothes, they surely wouldn't fit. She was maybe a size four, made tall and lean with muscle. I, on the other hand, feel most comfortable in a fourteen. My left boob is the size of her head.

"Of course. We always have spares in case of people needing safety at all factions." I felt a pang of relief, and a sliver of hope. I could use new clothes. Mine were damp and covered in fragmented foliage.

Nesrin took out a few pieces and handed them over to me. I took them gladly, finding that the snow had completely melted through my pants now, and the dampness on my skin was starting to freeze through to the bone. Turning to Raidan, she cocked her head to the side, assessing him. "I'm afraid I don't have anything for you to change into," Nesrin said, frowning.

"I didn't expect you to." Raidan shrugged, shoving his hands in his pockets.

"We have our fair share of tall soldiers, but you," she ruminated, eyeing him in an almost appraising way. "You're *very* tall, aren't you?" I watched him blush and hide it with a boyish grin. The dimple in his cheek appeared at Nesrin's appreciation.

"Six foot four, if you're asking." Raidan tilted a brow at Nesrin, who met him with a similarly cocky gesture of her own teasing brow.

"I can't help but wonder what we look like to you from your vantage point," Nesrin responded, swishing her hips as she moved in closer. Ember and I looked between each other, the two of us biting a lip with eyes wide. This was weird.

"I can pick you up to show you," Raidan offered, removing one of his hands to brush it through his hair as

Nesrin stepped closer to him. She tilted her head up to stare into his face. I couldn't help but compare them to a cat and mouse. Nesrin, with her swashing poise, being the very confident cat, and Raidan, extremely keen on being her mouse.

"Are you trying to pick me up, Grimsbane?" Nesrin purred. Never in my lifetime had I ever seen my cousin so flustered by a girl. Tonight, was a first as he took a step back, causing Nesrin to grin, flicking her black braid over her shoulder before turning toward her bed.

"Go wash it off," Kaede drawled, rolling their eyes, and gesturing out the door.

"Leave the poor kid alone," Wulfric said to Kaede, but his winking blue eye was far more taunting than his words made him out to be. "That goes for you, too, Nesrin." She only laughed as she went to help Wulfric with the sheets for her bed.

"If you're all right to go shirtless, there's a pair of sweatpants that will surely fit you in the other bedroom. We can wash your clothes in the morning," Ember offered.

"Sounds like a plan," Raidan agreed, apparently eager to leave the room and conversation behind him as he hurried to the other bedroom across the hall.

When we stepped in, I found that this room was the exact twin to the other. There was a cot just ahead of the doorway, and a bunkbed to my right, with the closet facing the foot of the bed. Before I was able to consider which bed I might take, Ember threw a pair of gray sweatpants on the bottom bunk.

"You're probably too tall for any of these beds, but the bottom will at least give you the surety that you won't fall off from great heights," Ember told Raidan. "Satyra, are you fine with taking the top bunk?" I nodded, grateful to be put closer to my cousin. Ember removed three sets of blankets and furs, throwing a package on each of the beds for us to use.

Climbing up the ladder, I started unfolding the sheets that were thrown on the top bunk. I was happy to see a similarly fluffy blanket folded neatly beside the pillow waiting for me.

"Who's first to shower?" Ember asked us.

"You want to go?" Raidan offered me from below.

"I'll go after you," I said, removing the clean pillowcase and shoving the pillow through. "I'll make the beds, since I've already started."

"Cool," he replied, before leaving the room to me and Ember.

Finally, alone with only Ember around to see, I unzipped my soggy jacket and took the books out from under my arm. They had been hidden there for so long, there was a hollow marked into my side from where the hardcover stuck me. I threw my jacket down to the floor with a wet thud. I looked down over the bunk rail to find Ember grimacing at the jacket I'd thrown at his feet. When he looked up to chastise me, I waived the two books in the air, before shoving them under my pillow.

"Read them tonight," he whispered, eyes sobering. I nodded, tucking the blankets around the mattress, and over the pillow that hid the books.

46

ENIGMA

SATYRA

I n the light of the glowing candle that sat on the window ledge behind me, I quietly snuck my hand beneath my pillow and tugged a heavy book free from beneath my head. My clean, damp curls caught around my fingers and the secret book, and with a bout of irritation, I untangled the mess before allowing the book cover to rip the hair from my skull. After freeing it from my hair, I lifted it over my face. In the back of my mind, I warned myself not to drop it, for fear its bulk might manage to break my nose. Having left my glasses on the windowsill, I had to bring it closer, squinting my eyes to see. This book was titled *Το χαμένο αρχείο*. It wasn't the one implied to be most important to Ember, but still, I was curious to know what was in it. He had gone through the trouble of hiding these two books in the floor-boards of the House of Enchantment's library. They were most definitely important. How, I did not know.

Carefully, without making a sound, I opened the hard-cover to find browned pages, all full of scattered writing, written in another language. I grimaced, staring hard at the pages, trying to decipher which language it was written in. I looked over the rail of the bed to give Ember a pointed frown but found him facing the wall opposite me. Apparently, Ember and Raidan were both fast asleep, if the snoring beneath my bed was any indication. I sighed heavily, then remembering I was supposed to be stealthy, I quieted my frustrations and pulled out the other book.

The lighter book came free far easier as I pulled it from beneath my pillow. As I held it above my face, I blew the bit of dust from the untitled cover. What was so important about this book that Ember had asked me to keep it a secret? I was almost hesitant to open it, scared I might unleash a world of problems once undone.

The writing inside was overly neat, almost as if the pen had been used by a machine. But I knew, from the faint differences in letters, that someone had written directly onto the pages with pen in hand. The writing, immaculately well-preserved, was written in a language I recognized. Though I was far from fluent, Gram had taught my mother, aunt, me, and my cousins a few bits and pieces of the Latin language. We spoke English and French in the Grimsbane home. English mostly, but we spoke French whenever Pépère prompted us to. I was glad to have this knowledge and now, more than ever, wished I would have asked my grandmother for more lessons in Latin. With the candlelight behind me, I concentrated on the lines, hoping to find words I might understand.

Septem Filiae Mortifer Fatae. This, I could easily decipher. *Septem* meant seven. *Filiae*; girls or daughters. *Mortifer* was definitely something to do with death, or the dead, but I wasn't sure about the word *Fatae*. I flipped to continue through the book, finding more Latin written like poetry on the lined pages.

Infantes de Grimm's Bane sunt factus ex de primogenita filia primogeniti filia.

Infantes de Grimm's Bane... My eyes widened at the familiar wording, piecing the phrasing together. I tensed, holding on to the book far tighter now as I realized this book might be mentioning my family. *Infantes* meant children. I was sure of it, just by shear similarity to the English word, infants. And *Grimm's Bane...* It was far too close to Grimsbane not to be a coincidence. Was this why Ember didn't want Gram to see it? Why did he trust me to read it if he didn't want her or Raidan to? This was so strange...

Cum uterque generation, septem callidus feminae, natus maledicto infortunatus mortem repetere eorum ordo. In commutationem pro magna potentia, illi abdicare eorum animarum per petitionem de Parcae. Cum potestate septem, Grimm non potest accipere animarum donec uti potentia ripas. Unus posse donare totus potestatis alteri per replere alii ripae. Illi sunt pernicies Grim's vitae, quia illi sunt in potestate eorum funera.

This was going to take me forever to translate if it were even possible to do without a dictionary. I sighed heavily, feeling the exhaustion weigh me down as I curled onto my side into the furry blanket with book in hand.

The words seven, daughters, death, Grimm, and Bane came up so often, I couldn't stop my mind from trying to count the women in our family, hoping to find some clue. There were only five of us alive at one time. Gram made one, and she had two daughters, my mom, and Aunt Eden. Then, there was me and Shivalri. That only ever made five of us. My great-grandmother died before I was born... But something about the mention of seven daughters and Grimm's Bane led me to believe this text revolved around the women in my family. I stared at the paper until my eyes couldn't handle it anymore. Setting the book down beside me, I let the darkness take over, settling into much needed rest.

47

NUMB
SHIVALRI

The God of the Dead held me in his arms for what felt like an eternity, yet when he made to let me go, it felt as if it hadn't been long enough. After having seen my fate, my head was still hollow, a darkness swimming back and forth to fill my mind. I was so very cold without the heat of Pyre's chest and arms around me. My knees buckled beneath me, head lilting backward before his arms grabbed at me again.

"Are you well?" he asked, his voice like a distant hum in my ears. Was I still falling? I couldn't be sure, for my limbs were no longer attached to my body. I felt nothing, both in my body and heart. I thought perhaps I might fall under and never wake up. I knew I smiled, but I couldn't sense it changing my face. Yes. This would be a better death than that of my fate. I could rest in my new companion's arms until the darkness swallowed me whole.

"I think I'm going to sleep," I murmured, my lips frozen and unable to form proper words.

"No, you're not," I heard his harsh voice say against my temple. "Stay with me, Goddess. You must stay awake."

"Why?" I grumbled, clinging to his warmth.

"I can't get you out of here if you're knocked unconscious. You need to hold your breath." A wonky frown set
into my mouth as I tried to open my eyes. We were knee deep
in the Dhetrïan Pool, but I hadn't felt the water that now
lapped at my thighs as Pyre held my body to him.

"We're going swimming?" I asked, blinking in confusion.
Pyre placed a hard and shiny object on my head, and the
weight of it tipped my eyes sideways. No, that wasn't right.
My eyes were in my skull. It was my head that the helmet
pulled. "It's heavy now." I groaned, trying to lift a hand to my
head. My arm didn't want to move. I could feel a spark of
panic in the deep of my chest, but the numbness overpowered
the worry. Pyre's hand gripped the back of the helmet and
mushed my face in the crook of his neck.

"I need you to focus," I heard him say. My mind nodded
at him. "Tell me you're going to hold your breath. I need you
to do this for me, Shivalri. Please." I heard the desperation as
he said my name, and something about it triggered my awareness to stir. He was so beautiful, even when he frowned. His
lips were ravishing.

"You're very handsome," I blurted, feeling giggly and
washed out. "I'm going to kiss you again one day."

"Goddess, please," he grunted. "Focus." He had such
striking eyes.

"It's true," I slurred. "I swear it." His eyes widened, then
quickly went back to being frustrated.

"Hold your breath."

"I'm not breathing," I murmured, drawing in a deep
breath, and holding it in my puffed-out cheeks. Pyre didn't
waste a second of our time. He dove down into the waters
and swam faster than ever possible. With one arm wrapped

around me and his hand still holding my head to his neck, the rest of him powered through the Dhetrïan. Wave after rippling wave pushed past us, but Pyre never ceased his motion.

We passed a blur of blackened seas, but the wraiths hadn't had the time to reach for us. Pyre's need to get us out had obviously given him extra strength. My eyes started drifting closed, my cognizance fighting to stay awake and keep my lungs from working. I didn't feel the need to breathe. It wasn't that at all. In fact, I didn't feel anything. I only knew, in the back of my mind, that to survive I would have to stay awake. My body would betray me if my mind evaded me. Forcing my eyes open, I watched the water turn to air, and remembered to allow myself breath as Pyre walked us up the rocky sands.

"Nihility!" Pyre called to the horse whose smoke billowed around us. The horse whinnied, rushing toward us as Pyre flew into the air before landing atop the mare. "*Làérxo! Âhlve!*" he boomed, and the horse powered through the skies instantaneously.

"We're flying," I mumbled, my head resting on Pyre, chin tilted up by the hold of his hand.

"I'm going to make you feel better," he swore, and I grumbled up at him.

"I don't feel anything at all…" I trailed, looking at him through the wet hair that slapped me in the eyes.

"Exactly."

I was briefly aware of the horse's descent as the gravity tugged Pyre and me backward.

"Are we home?"

Pyre pulled me in tighter, leaping from the horse with record agility. "*Mêzhome êhzje woùhe zràhl qoeurhe êhzje,*" he answered, but I didn't ask him what he'd said. I was too busy falling into the nothing that had been calling to me for a while now.

48

LULL
SHIVALRI

I t was dark in here, wherever I lay. I was slightly aware of Pyre's presence nearby, but I couldn't find the will to look for him. I wasn't sure if my eyes were closed or open, but I didn't need to see right now. A feeling of total bliss coated my entire body. No, not a feeling, for I couldn't *feel* a thing at all. And that in and of itself was a blessing. I could never remember a time when I didn't feel the discomforts of my illness, and I was happy to relish in whatever this was. It should have frightened me, this non-feeling of my body. I briefly considered that I might have died, ceasing to exist, but the smell of Pyre's scent was too real to truly believe it.

"Mmm…" I hummed, my lips numb from the bliss. I heard a movement rustle somewhere around me, and I was vaguely aware of my body dipping and stirring.

"I am so sorry." I heard a voice so quiet and raw, I thought the fragments of it might break me. I tried to ask the sadness what was wrong, but my tongue wouldn't move to try. "I cannot imagine what you think of me, but I swear, I am truly sorry, *Sōrza…* I wish things were different. Gods above,

I wish I had known sooner." I wondered what was troubling him so much that he was swearing to the Gods of the Celestial Realm...

If this was Pyre Malum who lingered at my side, I must not have been hearing him right. He wasn't the type to speak of the ones who were placed in the heavens. Perhaps he thought I was sound asleep, giving him the freedom to speak freely to me.

My body shifted again, fluffy clouds keeping me in place, as a solid warmth seeped through my back. I curled into the blankets, allowing the heat to caress me.

"You are far too precious to be in a place like this," Pyre whispered. My blanket moved up over my shoulders, and I smiled faintly, happy for the additional cosiness it provided. With this warmth and the numb sensation running through my veins, my skin was ecstatic to be the center of attention, enjoying the way comfort wrapped itself around me. "What have I done?" I heard the sadness question behind me. "You were so scared of me that night, but I didn't really *see* you. I didn't *see*..."

What was he talking about? What hadn't he seen? I slowly recalled the terror I'd felt upon our first meeting, the trembling in my palms and feet as the blood evaded my body. I thought I must have looked horrified. A little dirty, angry, and confused... Yes, I must have been visibly and understandably terrified.

The heaviness behind me moved away, taking its scent and heat with it. I grumbled audibly, and I heard the sadness chuckle. The sweet, gentle sorrow came back to my side, and the relief that came with the nearness turned to ease.

"Oh, Fates... You are so incredibly cruel..."

I wanted to ask him what he was thinking. I wished for

him to tell me stories until I couldn't reflect anymore, lulled by the air of his honeyed voice.

"I should have known, my *sōrza*. But how could I have? I am not deserving." I frowned and felt the slightest pressure between my brow, smoothing my concern away. "Don't worry yourself. I have you, and I will keep you safe. Think of spring flowers, the brightest of yellows, healthy and perfect. I must thank you for bringing that piece of life back to me. I hadn't realized how much I yearned for it."

I smiled and tried to reply. Indeed, I was dead now, living a grand dream. I wouldn't mind staying here forever, wrapped in the arms of a man who melted only for me.

I felt a light weight come around my waist, and my body shifted back, nestling in the soft embrace. I found that I really liked him this way. I *really* liked *him*.

49

LETHAL
SATYRA

A shocking feeling of ice slapped my face, rousing me from sleep.

"What the fuck?" I screeched, sitting upright in a panic. Looking around the room, I found that I was laying atop a bunk bed with a heap of snow in my hair.

"Get up, lazy bones." Raidan laughed from below.

"You're an ass," I gritted, before flinging the chunks of snow from off me.

"You slept in," he said with a wave of his hand, as if this were enough of an excuse to throw snow at me while I slept. "Come on, Cuz. There's some oatmeal left on the stove for you."

I threw the fluffy blanket off me and found the book I'd fallen asleep reading laying open next to me. I quickly shoved it under the pillow and started my way down to the floor. "They've been training all morning," Raidan told me as I grabbed the clothing Nesrin had provided last night. I'd been given a pair of leggings and a zip-up jacket made of stretchy polyester.

"Training?" I questioned, rubbing at my eyes as I sauntered to the doorway making my way to the bathroom. Raidan casually trailed me.

"Fighting," he clarified. "They have a weapon room in the back, and once you pass through, there's this giant room covered in spongy floor mat. Ember and Wulfric have been fighting against Kaede all morning trying to get a shot in, but Saty, you should see them move! I think Kaede might literally be made of shadow."

I agreed, finding that that unnerved me. I'd seen the way Kaede appeared and moved about last night. There was something about Kaede that marked them as unique.

"Anyway," Raidan said, continuing, "Go shower, get dressed, and have some oatmeal. When you're ready, meet us in the training room. It's my turn with Nesrin again, but she told me to go wake you before we start."

"You're going to train?" I gawked. "*Again*?"

"I've been training for like, three hours."

"You?" My eyes widened at the thought of my nerdy cousin fighting with the rebels. I didn't doubt that he was strong, as his muscles were apparent in his broad shoulders. But I'd seen him run through the forest with me, just as out of breath.

"Don't you think it's a good idea?" he questioned. I found that when I studied him, he had definitely gotten far more rest than I did. He was full of energy, as if whatever training he'd had this morning had awoken something new in him. Raidan was never an early bird. In fact, I knew from experience that it was incredibly difficult to wake him in the morning. But today, for some reason unbeknownst to me, Raidan's morning energy was bursting from out of him. He almost looked excited about this new revelation. I couldn't help but feel a zing of interest myself as I imagined me and Raidan learning how to fight. I'd always wanted to feel powerful, like nothing was off limits. It was smart to get some training in, and who better to teach us than the enemy of our enemy.

AFTER SHOWERING in the lukewarm water, I towel dried my hair as much as I could before shoving my legs through the pair of pants and zipping the stretchy jacket up my chest. It was a little tight seeing as how I was a curvy woman, and my girls were bigger than average. This jacket had certainly never belonged to Nesrin. Where she was lithe and sculpted like a lean warrior, I had extra padding all around. Not that I have ever minded. I love how I look.

Clean and dressed for the day, I walked into the kitchen to examine the oatmeal Raidan mentioned. When I passed into the soot-filled room, I felt my face go beet red as I found my undergarments drying over top an open cupboard door. *What in the world?* Quickly, heart beating fast from embarrass-ment, I plucked the lacey set from the kitchen and folded them under my arms. As I hurriedly scanned the room, I found my shirt and jeans from yesterday. The shirt I'd worn was dry; however, because I had worn dense jeans, they were still damp. I picked up my shirt and wrapped my bra and lacy thong into it, trying my best to conceal what most had prob-ably already seen.

Passing the clothes that were hung, I left the jeans and made my way to the wood stove to find the pot of oatmeal Raidan had promised. Steam still wafting from out of the lid, I made my way to the kitchen cabinets in search of a dish to put the oatmeal in. I had been looking for a bowl, but all I found were mismatched mugs and a drawer of plastic utensils. It would do. Spooning the oatmeal into the mug, I let the steam drift up over my face as I took a whiff of it. It didn't smell any different than regular oatmeal, and last night our meal had been shared among us all, but I couldn't help thinking to look for poison.

I was beginning to trust Ember more now, even though it had only been a couple of days of knowing him. There was something about the way he spoke, especially when it was just the two of us, that was very genuine. The way he talked about his friends made me believe they were to be as trusted as he was. I stirred the oatmeal with my plastic spoon and finally took a bite of the warm gooey goodness. I hadn't noticed before, but there were chunks of apple mixed into it, giving this winter's day a taste of autumn. I finished every last bite before turning for the kitchen and rinsing out the mug. Today was going to be a big day. If they were training with weapons, I would have to keep my vigilance high and guard strong. With shoulders held back and a lifted chin, I made my way down the hall. As I neared the bedroom where I'd slept, I quickly placed my clothes under the fluffy blanket on the top bunk. Skirting around the door and back into the hall, I found the very last door, which would ultimately lead to my new beginning.

Upon entering the room, I found myself unable to focus on just one weapon, as there were dozens of swords, knives, and long wooden sticks lining the walls of the entrance. Though it was a small room, probably only one hundred square feet, they had managed to stack enough weapons to supply an entire army. There was another door ahead of me, and I could only assume that it must lead to the training room that Raidan told me about. I took a moment to look around at the glinting weaponry and considered just how dangerous these rebels were. I knew they were dangerous. I understood that some of them had battled the High Council at least once, after hearing Ember's story beneath the mountain. But this was like putting a name to the danger, showing me the proof of it. With a steadying breath, I walked through the door, dropping my jaw at the dome encompassing me.

This room was massive. It was quite possibly the size of the entire house I'd seen moments earlier, only this room was domed with a ceiling made of glass.

"Good morning, sleepyhead," Ember chimed from the corner to my left. My heart stilled in my chest as the magnetic pull of my eyes clung to his shirtless, sweat-glinting body. *Holy gods*. He was so hot. From the strong muscular pecs, right down to the six-pack of sculpted abs, which became more and more defined as they lowered to the hem of his pants. A trail of jet-black hair poked out at the point of the V that formed at his lower torso, creating a deeper contour against his dark skin. *Delicious...* I slowly lifted my gaze, eyes adhering to every inch of him. When I found his face, a coy grin and a fiery look stared back at me. He bit his lip before making his way to me. Every part of his physique rippled at the movement as his muscles constricted around him. I had had thoughts about what he might look like beneath his clothes. I could have never imagined he would look this appealing. Abruptly, I realized I was still gawking at him, and he was getting closer to me. I let go of the breath lodged in my lungs and managed a slight smile.

"Hi," I choked, mouth dry.

His grin widened. "Hi, back."

I took a moment to gather my thoughts, removing my mind from the places it very desperately pleaded to go. "What is this place?" I finally managed to say, though my words were stammered.

"This is where we train," he answered. "This is where *you* will train."

"Like, with swords?" I asked, the lust fading from view to be replaced with worry.

He laughed lowly. "Not for you," he replied. "At least, not today, anyway."

My shoulders slumped in relief, and I nodded at him. "Good." I looked around again, finding it odd to see physical combat weapons, but nothing to use from a far-off distance. Did they expect me to fight off bad guys with a knife? "No guns?" I questioned.

He sighed, shaking his head with a grimace on his lips. "They're no use against magic. Did you eat?" he asked.

I took this into consideration before answering him. What kind of magic would repel a bullet but warrant an attack from a sword?

"Yes," I replied, still tasting the apple flavor on my tongue, and I imagined the strange battle scene in my mind. Windstorms repelling bullets before blades sliced into torsos. "Thank you," I murmured, remembering that I was having an actual conversation in the real world. My imagination was good at whisking me away.

"Wulf made it," he told me. "Thank him."

"Oh, okay. I will." Looking around the room, I found Wulf standing on the other side of me. Through heterochromatic eyes, he looked up at us for a moment and gave a subtle wave, though he remained focused on whatever he was doing. Ember nodded at him, while I waved back.

"Come," Ember told me, and I could do nothing but oblige as I tried to absorb the new space.

It was completely bare. As Raiden had said, the floor was made of a spongy black matt. I could only assume its purpose was to cushion a fall while doing whatever it was the rebels did in here. As I examined the floor, I noticed that the room was split in quarters. There was one long line drawn up the middle of the mat from where I stood to the back wall, and another long line in the very center, crossing from side to side. In each quarter, there were different sets of weaponry stations. To the left, where Ember had been standing, there was a punching bag set in the middle, and two rectangular boards leaning against the wall. There was also a rubbery bust of a man standing upright on pole, waiting to be punched. To my right, where Wulfric stood, there was a wall mount that had five spaces to hang the long wooden sticks I'd seen in the weapon room. Only three were hung, because two were currently in use as Wulfric and Kaede danced around each other, swinging the sticks around them. Raidan was right. The way Kaede moved was unbelievable. One minute they were right in front of Wulfric, and the next, they'd spun around him to tap him on the shoulder. I couldn't imagine trying to fight off Kaede. It would be like trying to punch air. Entirely useless.

I looked to the back of the room where I faced Raidan's back. He held a sort of fighting stance as he faced the back wall. Suddenly, he dodged left, and I saw the glint of the sword he held in his hand, right before witnessing Nesrin lunge at him with her own.

"Look out!" I screamed, terror ripping through me. I was about to run to him when Ember caught my wrist.

"He's good," he told me, stopping me in my tracks.

"What are you talking about?" I whirled on him, my temper rattling, asking to be freed. "She just tried to stab him!"

"She won't let it get to that."

I scoffed, tugging at my wrist. "If he hadn't moved, he would have had a sword lodged in his shoulder." I pulled my arm free from him and stalked forward. I could faintly hear a clicking behind me and knew that Wulfric and Kaede had put away their weapons to follow behind me and Ember. I watched as Nesrin and Raidan faced off, both of them with sword in hand. Twin wry grins spread across their faces. When Nesrin made another move, the panic resurfaced as rationality clawed its way out of my head. Nesrin had experience in this. What was Raidan thinking? If he wanted to learn how to train, that was one thing. But to pick up a sword on the first day and dance with the daughter of the congregation's leader was asking for trouble.

Blade crashed against blade, Nesrin's steps never faltering as I watched my cousin dance around the mat, trying to avoid her blow. He was faster than I would have thought, clearly having learned a few moves while I slept soundly in my bunk. I couldn't believe my eyes as he met blow for blow, dodging when he couldn't swing his sword up fast enough. With one swift move, Nesrin ducked down, swinging her leg out and catching Raidan in the shin, knocking him back on his ass. I heard the air rush from his lungs as he tried to sit back up. Nesrin prowled, sweat coating her skin. Slowly, she lowered her blade until the point barely touched Raidan's gut. I went to take a step toward him, but Ember held me back, shaking his head.

"She won't actually hurt him," he assured. I crossed my arms over my chest, hesitant to listen to him. Nesrin grinned and licked her lips, and I wondered if this were all a ruse, a way for the rebels to play with their prey before slaughtering us.

"Do you yield?" she demanded, voice deadly. Raidan only growled back. "Say the words," she taunted, sneering at her opponent who lie on the ground.

"Fine," he gritted through his teeth. "I yield." With feet

planted on either side of Raidan's legs, Nesrin lifted her blade away from him, lowering it to her side.

"We're done for the day," she announced, looking over to Ember, who stood quietly watching the scene, and then to me. She nodded her head once before turning away from the training area. I watched as Nesrin Mehra, daughter of the notorious general, swished her hips, blade held behind her head and resting on her shoulder.

"She's going to be the death of me." Raidan groaned, as he sat up on his elbows.

"Eyes on the prize, Cuz," I replied.

"Oh, trust me," he blew. "They are."

50

ENTICE

SATYRA

"You have to keep your fists level with your jaw," Ember reminded me as I swung at him, yet again finding nothing but air beneath my jab. "Keep your head protected at all times."

"I'm trying." I panted. Gritting my teeth, I focused on his moving body. The two of us circled one another on the mat, our footwork light and bouncing as we faced off. I'd spent the past week learning how to maintain my stance, guard myself, and throw a proper punch. I'd learned the hard way on my first day, that placing your thumb inside your fist was not a good way to injure your opponent. Though my finger had throbbed, it hadn't broken when I foolishly struck the square foam punching wall that Ember held.

Today would make a whole week of learning to dodge and defend myself. Learning to punch with Ember made me realize I was strongest in my legs rather than my arms. These legs had carried me up and down the steep hill of the fishing dock every day, slowly building muscle in my thighs and calves. Though I wasn't accustomed to working up a sweat quite like this, I found that the footwork was far more bearable than the thud beneath my fingers as they met the chest of the rubber dummy.

Raidan and I had been here at the safe house with our new allies for an entire week. It almost felt longer, yet somehow, not nearly long enough. Christmas had come and gone, and I had to admit that it felt weird not to celebrate with my family. Though I was used to missing my parents on holidays, it was still an ever-present loss. When memories surfaced from Christmases past—from times when Mom and Dad were still alive and laughing with me—it struck a heavy chord in my heart. I would always miss them and yearn to see them again. With each year that passed, I found the memories fading gradually, as if dulled by the time without them here. What I would do to see my mom's curly hair framing her face, vividly auburn like mine. Or hear my dad's corny jokes, just so I could give him a pitying laugh.

This Christmas I found that the empty space in my heart was deepening, as Aunt Eden's death weighed heavily on me. I also feared that I might be in the middle of losing two more people I loved, and that did no good for my or Raidan's spirit.

My cousin had taken a moment for himself on Christmas night. He'd gone out into the snowy air and sat in front of the safe house, freezing in the cold. When I went to check on him, I found him crying, and tried to offer what comfort I could. He let me hug him before asking for privacy, assuring me he'd come back inside as soon as he was done clearing his head. When I came back in, I couldn't help the tears that came over me as I entered the bedroom, we'd been sleeping in. Ember was there, understood that I was upset, and offered me a chance to get it off my chest.

It was that night that I found myself not only needing his help but also wanting it. He'd been a great source of comfort, a kind friend to lean on when I had no one else in the moment. The way he'd been there for me that night was something I was grateful for and would remember to use as a reminder of his compassion when I came to question him as I so often did. I had a hard time letting myself fully trust him, but the more I got to know him, the more I saw him for who he truly was. He'd been born into this. He had had no choice in so many things, but now, where he did have that choice, he was choosing to do the right thing. He was choosing me and my family.

"Give one to me," Ember prodded, pulling me out of my thoughts as he tapped the center of his chest. His very bare, very hot chest. I shook the image of licking that enticing bead of sweat that refused to remove itself from his lower abdomen and focused on the here and now. I bounced on my feet, feeling the burn in my calves as I lunged forward, throwing my right arm in his direction. With no surprise at all, Ember dodged my blow, and swatted my arm away as if it were a fly. I threw again, this time, using my left to see if I might trick him. He smiled sadly at me, before shaking his head.

"Stop looking at me like that!" I huffed, my feet slowing on the cushioned mat. He laughed at me, enticingly handsome and wickedly cruel. "Ember!" I groaned, lowering my fists to my sides. He took my surrender as a sign to come forward, and I braced myself for more fighting.

"You have to put your body into it," he told me, voice inflecting compassion. "Look," he said, as he came around me, placing warm hands on either side of my hips. I froze under his touch, unsure of what to do. He rolled my hips, guiding a twisting motion. His mouth was at my ear now, his breath caressing my nape. "See?" He slid his right hand up my waist and over my arm, lifting it in front of my face. My fists remained intact, ready to strike when necessary. He pulled my right arm forward while dragging my left hip behind, creating a stronger swinging motion. Twisting my wrist so that it was leveled for a punch, I felt the new strength this move provided. He pulled me back and repeated the motion, and I quickly realized that punching was something Ember was very good at. It had me wondering what other skills he possessed...

"Saty?" I heard from the back of the room. I snapped my eyes up, finding Raidan glowering at me.

"Uh, yeah?" I shook myself out of whatever trance Ember had placed me in and removed myself from the situation.

"You done for the night?" Raidan questioned, playing with the short sword he'd used all day.

I nodded brusquely, following him out the door, and leaving Ember to the empty training room.

51

BARE
SHIVALRI

Tingling sensations crawled up my feet, nestling under my skin as if wanting to disturb my slumber. I groaned, feeling like a child as I pulled the blankets under my chin, wrapping my fists in the fabric. I felt the area my legs lay on shift, a heavy weight moving toward me.

"Pyre?" My eyes flitted open to find the God of the Dead sitting at the end of a massive bed fit for a king. "Where—? Where am I?" I coughed, trying to find my voice. His eyes widened, but the furrow didn't budge.

"You're awake." He blew, running a hand through his dirty, dark tangles. "Thank the Fates." I got up on my elbows and pulled myself into a seated position, only to realize I was dressed in someone else's clothes. I pulled the black velvety blanket up over my chest, embarrassment flooding my cheeks as I looked around the room. The place was massive, decked with luxurious golden tapestries that hung from each of the walls. There were classic chairs carved with intricately designed wood frames, and rich red upholstered furniture I'd only imagined a royal to have. With the giant fireplace facing the bed on the opposite wall, it was hard to make sense of where I was. This was nothing like the Under Realm I'd come to know. Yet here was Pyre Malum, and something about his character suited the charm of this place.

"How did we get here? Where are we?" I asked, looking away from the beautiful new room.

"We're at my palace, Goddess. You've been asleep for several nights."

"What?" I gasped, trying to shake my mind from the fogginess. "How many?"

"Eight Earth nights. I didn't know if you were going to wake. I—" He exhaled, running his hands over his face. "Are you well?" He searched my gaze, sheer panic in his eyes. I cleared my throat, considering how I felt. I'd thought my sleep had lasted a while, and every time I'd woken to hear Pyre's voice, I'd fallen back asleep, enjoying his presence while I rested.

"I think I'm all right," I answered, looking down at myself. "What am I wearing?" He gave me a pitiful excuse of a smile, the kind that didn't quite reach his eyes.

"Izra, one of the spinstresses made you the nightgown." He put out a hand is if to stop my train of thought. "Don't worry," he said, tearing his gaze from mine. "It was Izra and Marisole who clothed you."

"Who are Izra and Marisole?" I wondered, looking around the room as if they'd appear from thin air.

"They are members of my court. Helpers around the palace."

"I've never seen anyone but the pythrants at the castle." I frowned. "You mean to tell me there have been ladies living with us all this time, and I never once was introduced?"

"We are not at the battle castle, Goddess. Take a look around," he offered, gesturing to the extravagant room. I started to get up, but Pyre's head jerked up at the movement, and he stopped me from leaving the bed. "I wished you to look with your *eyes*." He frowned, wiping his hands down his face. "You're not well enough to stand just yet." I folded my arms over my chest, wanting to challenge him. When he didn't budge, I heaved a heavy breath and leaned back into the pillows.

"What's the difference between the castle and this palace?" I wondered, too curious to let my ego take root. I wanted information more than I wanted to win the superiority contest. He seemed to be thankful for the change in my mood and let himself sink into the mattress.

"The castle was built as a fortress. This," he said, looking around the room, "is where I live. This is where many within my court reside. In fact, just outside this window, you can see the many homes belonging to soldiers and feïnyr."

"Feïnyr?"

"They are spirits of nature. They're the closest thing to life in the Under Realm."

"How do you mean?" I questioned, not quite understanding. If they were spirits, were they not deceased?

"They are the source of the forests you've seen towering the lands. They cannot build life from nothing; therefore, they must use the blood of a god to create their forestry. Most of the lands you see were made from myself and a handful of very talented feïnyr. There are other deities who've done the same, like Dramael, for example."

"Wow..." I blew, imagining these interesting spirit creatures. I took a moment for myself, trying to gather my thoughts and figure out just what happened in the last minutes before I had fallen asleep. A flash of fire burned my retinas as I recalled the Fates screaming at me through their mirrored pool. I shivered in place, pulling the blanket back up under my chin. I'd slept eight Earth nights since having visited the temple. I'd wasted so much time....

"Are you cold?" Pyre asked, pulling me away from the burning fires. When I looked up at him, all I could see was his lifeless face staring back at me like I'd seen in my fate. My heart was still fractured by that threat. I shivered yet again, and Pyre got up to retrieve a woolen throw. I let him place it on me, watching the care he put into the gesture. I could tell that he was unsure about doing it, but I saw through the unease and through the wall he'd let down since being reunited. Something about this action brought forth an exciting and scary realization. Pyre had been talking to me throughout my slumber while I was in and out of consciousness. I'd heard the sadness in his voice as he apologized to me openly, assuming I'd been asleep during it all. I'd felt warm and at peace in his arms. My heart suddenly thumped far louder than before. I watched him carefully as he finished tucking me in.

"What changed?" I inquired, waiting for him to join me on the bed again. There was something intimate about the two of us seated on a bed together. I didn't let the fact that he'd been watching me sleep leave my mind either. Or the fact that he'd been lying beside me, providing me warmth in the night. It was all I'd wanted.

"Changed?" he asked, standing at the edge of the bed, staring down at me.

"You," I said, pointing my eyes at him. "You've changed." He lowered his head and turned on his heel to find a chair. A piece of my heart sulked at his refusal to sit with me again, but I knew that it was better to have some distance. Though true, I didn't *want* the space. Pyre took a seat and crossed a foot over his knee, watching me. I huffed a disbelieving laugh as he crossed his arms and straightened his shoulders. He could attempt to don the mask again. He could try, but it would do nothing to erase the new candor I'd seen in him.

"What?" he muttered, one angular brow lifting into a tease.

"You're a real piece of work, you know that?" His other brow shot up, entirely shocked by my revelation.

"What now?" He growled, his face turning from disbelief to annoyance, though the expression in his eyes looked almost hurt.

"I truly don't know what to think of you." I blew, settling into my pillows. I felt a little brash, needing to air out whatever was happening. I'd had enough time to resent and wallow. After seeing what the Fates showed me and sleeping through eight Earth nights in Pyre's embrace, it gave me the time to think about more than anger and sadness. The sorrows I've felt have been earthshattering, and though he was the cause of my last, it was still him I'd wished to comfort me. After all the death, heartache, pain and loss, I would still want to find him. Though it was written in my destiny without my say, I would still choose to help save the world, and I would choose to know the God of the Dead. He was complicated, but I knew I needed him in my soul. I didn't want to live like this anymore.

"Then don't think of me," he answered. He, too, leaned into his chair, matching my tone. I threw up my hands in frustration and flicked my hair over my shoulders.

"I can't!" My words came out as a hiss as I glared at him. My frustration came from flustered feelings more than his response.

"You cannot *not* think of me?" he questioned, his lips twitching in what seemed to be an uninvited smile.

"I *cannot!*" I groaned, striking the fluffy comforter with

my hands. He laughed casually, and I slowly lifted my eyes to meet his. "What?" I snarled, bunching the fabric of the blankets into my fists. At this point, I just wanted to scream.

"You're entirely disheveled," he said, pointing toward my appearance.

"And you're entirely frustrating."

"I frustrate you?" I found his throat bobbing as he reassessed me.

"Gods..." I muttered under my breath.

"Yes?"

"Pyre!" He let out a bellowing laugh, catching me off guard. He laughed with everything in him, his eyes crinkling at the corners, his perfect full lips parting to show those pointed teeth I'd grown fond of. My heart leapt out of my chest at the sound of joy that came from the dark, haunted man. I thought perhaps if I'd stop breathing, he'd continue on, undisturbed, relishing in whatever joy had triggered this laughter. When he stopped laughing, he shook his head at me, displaying a simmered down version of the smile. "Why?" I asked reservedly, both referring to his outburst of laughter, and the melting in my chest. "Why are you laughing like that, and why in all the realms have I never heard it before?" I swallowed hard, watching as his eyes pooled to honey.

"The Fates work in cryptic ways."

"What do you mean?" I asked, feeling a tug at the mention of the Fates. He got up from his chair and stalked over to me, a new lightness to his step.

"May I?" he asked, and I nodded, allowing him to join me in the bed again. He added another pillow to the wall and leaned against it so that he was sat right next to me. I clasped my hands together beneath the blanket for fear they might wrap about his.

"Tell me what you mean," I insisted, and he pulled the

blanket up over the two of us. I settled into the warmth, having forgotten the cold my skin was feeling. His guard was melting again. To be this close without the walls between us was invigorating.

"It's a very long story, Goddess. One I'm not sure you'll understand, nor necessarily wish to be a part of, but it is the truth."

"What is?" I pushed, entirely impatient and needing to know just what he was referring to. "How am I involved?"

"You were a piece I was promised," he declared, making my skin go from freezing cold, to clammy hot. He looked at me briefly, then turned to face the windowed wall again. "My fate has always been to rule the dead, whether I reside in the Under Realm or not. It is who I am, and what I was woven for."

"The Fates strung your destiny," I remarked, already having pieced that together a long time ago.

"Precisely," he said, taking a moment to gather his thoughts. "When I was forced into this role, I had asked for a favor in return for my dedication to the dead. The Fates promised me that one day, when I deserved it, I would meet the one to set me free. They had warned me of the realms breaking apart, and something in my gut told me that I would be sent to the Under Realm with the dead as soon as the world fell apart. It was my duty, after all... I was told of a prophecy, one where a new goddess, different from all others, would join our worlds and cause a disruption between the realms. I'd always thought that my chance at freedom was to fulfill the prophecy with you, and finally find peace else-where where desolation and horror weren't the entirety of my existence."

"Pyre," I interjected, placing a hand to my heart. "You

know I can't let you unleash Hell upon Earth. I just can't do it," I whispered, a single tear escaping me.

"I've never once told you that I wanted to unleash Hell upon your world," he said, turning to face me. I looked away, wiping the tear from my face, and waiting for him to try and justify his needs. "I would never consider destroying Earth," he swore, placing a hand on my knee. My eyes flickered to where he touched me before finding his eyes.

"But that's what would happen if I were to open the Gates."

"I thought I'd find a way to get just myself out. If we were to marry, I would hold the same power and be able to walk on Earth. But I see now that you won't do that... Marry me, I mean. And I don't blame you."

"I—" I started, but his haunted gaze stilled my tongue.

"Although I want you to know that killing innocents before their time was due has never been a part of my plan. You made that assumption about me the minute you heard my proposal. I didn't correct you because it would have made no difference. What I did to you was cruel and unforgiving, and my words could never change your opinion of me." I looked up at him, considering his words and found that they were genuine. "All I've ever wanted was my own freedom. I didn't choose this life. This godforsaken eternity in gloom and grief and death. I was forced here. The goddess before you gave me and my brothers our tasks through the weaving of the Fates. Ruler of the Under Realm, Ruler of the Seas, and Ruler of the Skies. My brothers were afforded a beautiful existence surrounded by ever-growing life. Can you imagine the life I've lived?" he asked me, forcing me to look up at him. I worried my lip, trying to find the words, but I couldn't find anything worthy of voicing. He frowned at me and looked away. "I do not ask for your pity, Goddess. I only wish for you to understand."

"I'm trying," I offered, pulling his eyes back to mine. He searched my regard, and I let him search for as long as he needed to. It afforded me the chance to do the same with him.

"Can you see why I so desperately wanted to find you?" He grimaced, making fists at his sides. "I've never had freedom a day in my life. Even before the realms split, I was cast aside and feared for my ruling. I just wanted freedom… I just wanted to find life, and all that may come with it."

"Well," I said, after a moment of reflection. "I hate to be the bearer of bad news, but I don't think either of us are going to find life. It's likely no one will be living much longer if my fate has anything to do with it."

Pyre snapped his head to me, worry trapped in his core. "What do you mean?" He swallowed, noting the solemnity I held. "What is your fate? Will you tell me?"

I closed my eyes, wincing at the images presented to me beneath the Dhetrïan Pool. "If I don't succeed in repairing the veil and keeping the Gates sealed, we all die."

52

CLEAN
SHIVALRI

"Tell me everything," Pyre insisted, his muscles clenching in his jaw.

"There's nothing more to tell. The world is going to burn unless I manage to fix my mistake and repair the veil. Something is coming, and the scales will tip drastically in favor of the side I choose. Either I doom the entire universe, or I somehow manage to fulfill the prophecy."

"What did it look like when you didn't succeed?" he asked me, and a flash of glassy eyes burned the back of my throat.

"The skies were red, beasts were gloating in the clouds, and everyone I ever cared for was dead…"

"And the other version?" he prodded, pulling the sight of a tomb-like dawn away from my mind.

I closed my eyes, taking a shaky breath and releasing the tension in my ribs. I was starting to feel pain again, and the sensitivity in my bones wasn't welcome.

"It was me and you, Pyre." I exhaled, exhausted from keeping my thoughts to myself. I was tired of having to hold myself together, and I was finally willing to let go of all the past hurt in attempt to accept new resolve. I wouldn't easily forget how I'd been mistreated, but I would find a way to forgive and let live. I was done pretending that my feelings were mixed at this point. I was falling for the God of the Dead, and the Fates had sealed our destinies together for a reason. That feeling I'd had while holding Pyre's hand in the vision the Fates had given me was like an indulgence of electricity. I had been ignited, feeling my very best, and he was at my side, aiding me through it all. The vision of him dying felt like my own death.

"What about us?" he asked, his features soft and inviting.

"We ruled it all," I answered, and watched his lips part in astonishment.

"You saw yourself with *me*?" I nodded, thoughtfully. "Where? How?" He pushed, his eyes passing over me in desperate need of answers.

"*Abrôrta dhèjl Ôhrtum,*" I whispered, looking down into my lap. "I don't speak your old language, but the Fates showed me the meaning."

"Bringer of Death," he acknowledged, and placed a hand over mine, the warmth releasing the stiffness in my aching joints. "Do you understand what it means? Can you accept it?" His voice cracked on his tongue. I folded my free hand over his, and he let loose a tight breath at my touch.

"It's my fate," I replied, letting the reality of it sink in.

"And *you* are mine," he spoke, a deep resolve of an answer I didn't know I'd needed to hear. "You are my *sōrza.*"

"*Sōrza?*" I questioned, remembering the several times he'd called me that. I briefly remembered hearing the Fates say that word, too, and now I was dying to understand its meaning.

Pyre let out a soft chuckle and rubbed his thumb underneath my palm. "Though I didn't realize the role you'd be playing, I've known you were my fate from the moment I laid eyes on you."

I gasped audibly, my heart catching in my throat. "That's what *sōrza* means?" I gawked, staring up at him. "You've been calling me your fate all this time?"

He bit his lower lip, trying to hide a grin. My heart raced at the sight. "Fitting, isn't it?"

I was dumbfounded, utterly amazed that he'd gotten away with doing so without my knowledge. "I have so many questions," I admitted, trying to find the words to form them. "How long have you known?" I wondered aloud.

"Far longer than I'd like to admit. I just thought..." he trailed, looking away from me.

"You thought what?"

He sighed heavily, still moving his thumb on my hand. "You are exceptionally beautiful," he declared, stunning me on the spot. Feeling the heat creep through my cheeks, I wished I could hide my face from the flush. Did he really think me beautiful? Those kinds of words coming from out of his mouth, directed toward me, were doing unthinkable things to the butterflies in my stomach. "Of course, I saw your beauty the minute I laid eyes on you, but then, you were just a pawn to play to find my freedom. I tried not to notice you in that kind of way. I tried my best to consider you only an asset to setting me free. I know I am cruel and selfish for putting the lives of others at risk for trying to find this happiness I so clearly do not deserve. But please, try to imagine my torture. Day after day of welcoming the dead into my kingdom, seeing them weep so fiercely for having left their loved ones behind. Even worse for my heart was seeing them reconnect with the one's they'd lost before. Even in death, even in an Inferno, they were fine so long as they had each other. It has been absolute agony to watch every single soul experience the one thing I never have… It's been too much to bear. This eternity, entirely alone." Silence stretched between us as I gathered my thoughts. I had been right to question who he was. A part of me had wanted to empathize with him and offer him what comforts and kindness I could during our time at the castle. My soul knew his. It understood him before I could figure it out for myself.

"All this time… you've been looking to find freedom and companionship, not war? All this time you led me to believe you were cruel and ruthless just to keep me from finding what you believe to be a weakness?" These thoughts weighed heavily on my mind, and I remembered his anger, not only toward me, but to his servants too. "What about the pythrants? Don't you care about them?"

"Unquestionably," he said, and for some reason, I didn't need him to prove that. The way he'd said it told me he was telling the truth. It was only that I didn't have all the information.

"You were so cruel to them, Pyre," I held, pulling my hand away from his. "You killed so many." I saw him flinch from the corner of my eye and wondered how he could've killed so many people he claimed to care for.

"The pythrants were in on my cruelty. They were warned not to get close to you, and to only protect you. I needed to create the image of my dominance to make sure you'd follow through with the prophecy. To make sure you'd feel obligated to marry me, in order to save the world." When I didn't answer, he sighed heavily, continuing. "The pythrants were more than eager to play the part of scared servants if it meant their freedom. They knew that the goal was to open the Gates, and I'd promised them that whoever might want to leave would be granted access. Though now I see they cared far more deeply about trying to get to the Celestial Realm than I'd assumed, and I cannot for one second blame them. I certainly don't blame them for turning on me to help get you back to Earth. And I cannot blame them for falling for the tricks my brother has clearly played on the many minds here in the Under Realm. We can thank my cousin for having spread the web of lies my brother fed him."

"That is a lot to take in." I was unsure how much I wanted to get into my thoughts and feelings toward this.

"I knew how wicked, how evil my plans were when I took you into the Under Realm. When the pythrants, my loyal soldiers, betrayed me and chose to fight for you, I knew that I was wrong for allowing them to die. In the end, when I first faced the thought of losing you when Ombrose and the pythrants rushed the throne room, I only wanted to protect you. I know it was a terrible way of doing it, but it was the only way I knew how. Like I said before, I had to seem uninterested in your life in case Ombrose and my brother were working together."

"It—" I shook, remembering the feel of hopelessness. "You were horrible," I murmured, folding myself over my knees.

"I am sorry, Shivalri. You must know I am absolutely gutted by the fact that I so willingly stole you from your family. I know what they mean to you. I know what I did and still I kept you here."

"Why?" I whispered, feeling the heat of my tears between my face and the blanket.

"Please, *Sōrza*," Pyre croaked. "Look at me."

I lifted my head, wiping away at the wetness covering my face. I stared up at him through watery eyes, waiting for the rest of his story. I watched his worry grow stronger by the second. I saw it in the way he greatly wanted to look at me but acted as if he weren't worthy.

"I'm listening," I told him, voice wet and tired.

He closed his eyes, then turned to face me better, so that our shoulders were angled closer when he opened his eyes again. "When you mentioned using you to bleed out at the Gates once all of your powers were stronger, it was then that I realized I'd been falling for you." My heart sank at his words, because this, the reality of this, was the thing I'd been warring with for a long time now. "You were right, gods be damned." He shook his head, lowering his chin so that our eyes were level with one another. "I could have taken you straight then and slaughtered you in an instant. But a tug at my soul told me not to. Something inside me warned me that that would be the greatest regret of my life. So, instead, I kept you here longer, lying to you about not being able to leave without your compliance. Each day spent with you was another in which you wrapped your string around my heart, and I knew that I could never let you go. But now, with knowing my brother has his eye set on you, and with what the Fates have shown you, I know that we must get you back to Earth. You need to close the Gates for good. To do that, you must seal it shut from within the one you wish to stay in."

"Pyre?" I inhaled sharply. The sting of this truth hitting me from all directions. "Are you saying that I can fulfill the prophecy right now? Am I powerful enough to do it alone?"

"Not alone," he told me. "I can sense your power rising within you. I think your ascendency is in motion to emerge in full. Once your divinity takes complete root, you will be powerful enough to do it on your own, but I do not know when that will happen for you."

"Well, then how am I going to do this?" I blew out in frustration.

"You will be able to do as the prophecy says, because I will make damn sure my role is executed. I am your counterpart, your night to the light you emit wherever you stand. You need the strength of two gods; you need to borrow my power to close the Gates with you. When the Triple Goddess was given the gift, she was a fully ascended goddess. With you not being ascended yet, you can't open and close the Gates on your own. I think that's why we were tied together. I'm supposed to strengthen you with my power. The prophecy foretold us working together, our fates tied far longer than one could ever imagine. I will give you anything you need if it means making sure you survive all of this in the end."

A long pause made room for my heart to weaken at the reality of his words. *I could finally leave.* I would get to see my family, save the world, and forget this mess of chaos and despair. But I couldn't shake the feeling that I was now choosing between lives, forced to choose between two paths. I never thought I'd even question such a thing, but now that I was given the opportunity to leave, I wasn't sure that I could leave him behind. My chest ached for the man I'd grown to care for. All this time I thought he wanted freedom, which of course, I could understand. But this? *Love?* Pyre Malum was not at all who I thought he was. He was everything my soul told me I needed to keep in my life. I looked up at him now, eyes filled with tears.

"What about you?" I whispered. "What will happen to you?" He smiled grimly at me and cupped a hand over my cheek.

"That you even care is a gift on its own," he said, sweetly caressing my face. "I will be happy knowing you are safe, and thankful for having had this time with you, whether worthy of it or not."

I closed my eyes, and the tears fell into his hand. A delicate warmth touched my hair, and I opened my eyes to find his lips atop my head. He had shown me this side to him from the very beginning, but I had elected to focus on the evil I'd made him out to be in my mind. He had been rough, cruel, and impatient. Nothing could excuse the fact that he'd treated me poorly on some occasions, most prominently for having ripped me from Earth and thrown me into the oubliette. It was not excusable, but I could understand why he had done it now. He warred with himself over these actions, deeming them necessary to obtain his greatest wish. If only he'd known that kindness from the beginning would have delivered it to him far sooner. Because that was the truth. *I* was falling for *him*. I had been for a long while now, whether that was healthy or not in the initial days of attraction. Something in me had felt the need to show him kindness, to nurture his broken soul. I knew what he needed before even realizing it myself. I would not excuse his behavior, but I would forgive him for it. I had enough strength in my heart to give him this. I wanted it for him.

"Pyre?"

"Yes, *Sōrza?*" he murmured, producing a wave of heat through my hair. I moved a hand to his chest and found a heavy beating heart underneath. My own pulse matched the thunder within him, and I came to realize that he was thinking so many of the same things as me. It was a powerful thing to finally open up to each other. Allowing this vulnerability to flow between us was a blessing. I tilted my head up, asking him to look at me. My chest caved at the sight of melting copper glimmering back at me.

"I forgive you."

His breath hitched at my words, brows furrowing in disbelief. "How could you?" he stammered, his lashes lowered and shadowed over his face. "You can't possibly..." At his exhale, I glided my hand up his chest and around his neck. Brushing a thumb over the sharp line of his jaw, I lifted myself up, and pressed a kiss to his lips.

"I forgive you," I said softly, lips brushing over his. His chest visibly shuttered, and my heart ached at the sight. He couldn't hold it in anymore, this mixture of sorrow and relief. I saw it in the way his body seemed to let go of all railings, walls crumbling down in a heap at his feet. "I forgive you," I said again, stronger now. I kissed him again, and this time, he returned it. Breathing heavily, he released the kiss and leaned away from me. My hand drifted back to my side, feeling cold and empty.

"I am unworthy." His voice was choked, overcome with emotions I couldn't even begin to imagine. "I caused you so much hurt."

I closed the gap between us again, and he turned his face away from me. "So, make up for it," I said simply, and brushed the hair from his tear-filled eyes.

"How?" he asked, a sliver of hope lighting his regard.

"Be your true self with me, do good for your people, make improvements in the Under Realm, and help me protect those I've put in danger. That is what I ask from you."

He nodded slightly and found my gaze. "I will do every-thing and anything for you."

"Thank you," I said, and believed him.

53

STEAM
SHIVALRI

"What do you say to a bath?" asked Pyre as he stood from the massive bed we'd been lounging on.

"A bath? Do you have a wash bin and cloths here?"

He smiled down at me and offered his hand. "I have spare everything here, however, I've sent the spinstresses to fetch you your own things. And as for the bath, I am referring to a hot spring, where you can submerse yourself properly and bathe." I sat up quickly, accepting his hand, but winced as a sudden throbbing jolted through my foot. "Well, perhaps not all of you can be submerged into the waters."

"What's wrong with my foot?" I wondered, lifting the blanket from it. It had been wrapped in a tidy arrangement of bandages, but I could tell there was swelling in the obvious expansion of the area.

"Your foot was injured while in the Dhetrïan Pool." He sighed, running a hand through his hair. "I should have checked you over when we got out of the water, but you seemed to be fine. It hadn't even crossed my mind that you might be injured. I'd assumed we'd gotten away unscathed."

I slowly recalled the stinging slash of pain I'd felt when I'd been separated from Pyre under water. "It was a wraith," I remarked, examining my foot.

"Yes, it was. And a wraith's scratch is poisonous, and deadly if not treated properly." My stomach grew sick at the thought of whatever might have festered in me if it hadn't been treated.

"Thank you for taking care of it," I said, grimacing. "I hadn't felt the pain until just now."

"No, you wouldn't have. Their scratch has a numbing affect in the bloodstream. You're healing now, so you'll start to feel the pain until you fully recover from it."

"That explains how I've been feeling in the last while." I grumbled, rubbing at my arms.

Pyre reached out his hand again, careful to help me keep the weight off my foot as I came up off the bed.

"So, you have a hot spring? For bathing?"

"Yes."

"I kind of want to be mad at you for not bringing me here sooner," I teased, rolling my eyes at him. "But I'm so excited to finally have a proper bath that I guess I'll have to forgive you for it."

"How kind," he mused, folding my arm into his. "Can you walk?" he asked, assessing my stance.

"Yeah, I'm all right," I said, testing the pressure as I let my weight fall on the foot. It was hot and swollen, but it wasn't harrowing.

"Shall we?" he asked, placing his free hand over mine that wrapped around his bicep.

Together, the two of us stepped out of the extravagant bedroom and into a corridor so long I could barely see its end. The floors were draped in deep, red carpeting and the walls were covered with golden décor, which looked to be hand sculpted directly onto the walls.

"This is... Well, this is nothing like I would have expected," I admitted, trailing my free hand over the patterns on the wall.

"What exactly did you expect?" he asked, regarding me with that questioning stare of his.

"Bones and roaches." I shrugged, catching the glint of a smirk tug at his lips.

"I suppose that is only fair," he considered as we strode down the lovely passage.

Several chatting voices became louder as we neared the middle of the hall. Two very beautiful women strode out of a room, laughing and holding each other's hands. When they saw us, they both quickly bowed, then passed us by. I turned around to look at the two of them, and when I did, I found that they, too, had turned to get a better look at me. I blushed, embarrassed for having been caught, and awkwardly waved in their direction. The women giggled and turned away before running down the corridor in the direction from which Pyre and I had come.

"Who were they?" I asked him, still full of flush in my cheeks.

"They are lady's maids. *Your* lady's maids, actually."

I shot him a look of disbelief, and when his seriousness didn't budge from his face, I shot him another look of incredulity. "I don't need a lady's maid!" I said, swatting at his arm which still held my hand.

"They are yours if you do," he supposed, letting me win.

"I won't," I said, matter-of-factly. "I can take care of myself."

He gave me a discerning look, lifting a cocked brow. "Says the woman on my arm whose foot is damaged."

I looked at him through slitted eyes, daring him to try me. Pyre let out a low laugh and turned toward a large metal gate to lead us through.

"Is this the way to the baths?" I asked, too eager to find out.

"Yes, darling." He grinned, patting my hand as if he were dealing with an impatient child. I made to send him a retort, but my breath caught as we rounded the corner and entered the room.

I had never seen a place quite like this. Not in my entire life. The smell of sulfur hit me like a shock to my system as the misty heat washed over me. The cavern, which found itself attached to the palace, was something out of this world. Like the Fates' temple, there was a glowing dust of magic dripping from ceiling to floor. The waters were a florescent shade of blue, which stood out in high contrast to the jet-black mounts of sparkling lava that shaped the pool. It was an incredible piece of untouched beauty. It had naturally formed, and it was breathtaking.

"This is incredible." I gawked, my voice carrying in the hollow cave. I let go of Pyre's arm and dipped low to sink my fingers in the steaming beauty. It was warm and welcoming, and I couldn't wait to let it wash over me.

"It's best you keep your foot out of the hot spring," said Pyre, gently tugging me back. "In case of infection."

"How in the world am I supposed to do that?" I asked, staring at the steaming water amid the wet lava rock.

"I'll carry you in," he supposed, considering the situation.

"You're going to bathe with me?" I blanched, feeling my cheeks heat.

"I will leave you to bathe on your own, and you can call to me when you'd like to come out." He left me for a moment and walked toward a wooden crate near the entrance. He came back with a towel and laid it down on a lower piece of rock. "You can rest your foot on this ledge here. The towel will keep it dry." I walked over to the towel and questioned how many things I'd gone without in the Under Realm, when apparently, there'd been a supply of real towels all along. And a hot spring. "The tub isn't very deep. You should be able to stand on your one good foot and wash."

"I guess that will work, but I don't really feel comfortable with you seeing me splashing around..." I trailed, teetering around the word. When he looked at me with a knowing grin, I knew, for some reason, he wanted me to finish my sentence. "Without clothes," I ground out, crossing my arms over my chest.

"Keep your nightgown on until I leave. I'll have it cleaned and set to dry for you, and it will be ready come nightfall." That would work, but I'd need something to cover myself when Pyre came back to help me.

"What will I wear when I need to get out?"

He breathed heavily, as if frustrated by my needs. "I'll give you a towel."

"In the water?"

He groaned, running a hand through his hair. "Yes, in the water. When we get back to the bedroom, I'll give you another to dry off with. Does that please you?" He looked me up and down.

"Um, yes," I murmured, feeling a little silly, because my body was doing unexpected things to my brain as I pictured him pulling me out of the water in a wet towel.

"Good," he said, and scooped me up into his arms. I shrieked, caught off guard, and clung to his neck as he took his first step into the bubbling hot water.

The heat from the hot spring was like a warm hug that embraced the entire expanse of my body. When I'd felt numb earlier, it had been a lovely relief from the pain I always bore. But here, in the bubbling steam, I could feel everything. All the pain in my joints, the strain in my muscles and tendons easing with every second it soaked my skin. I moaned aloud, exulting in this glorious new sensation. I felt the arms around me shift, and I looked up into the face of a striking God, who was carefully focused on holding my injured foot up out of the water. He gently placed it on the nook in the rocks, and my ankle ached at the contact. If it weren't for the gash through my skin, I'd have dunked it into the water first thing. But Pyre was right. I didn't want to get an infection, and so, begrudgingly, I kept it out of the water.

"I'm going to lower you down," Pyre announced as his arms loosened around me. I reached around with the leg I had under water, trying to find the bottom. "Do you have your footing?" he asked. My toes grazed the bottom, and I pushed up with the pad of my foot, finding balance before nodding my head yes. When Pyre let go, the water seemed to sizzle around the skin he had touched, and I found myself missing him in the places he'd been. My mind no longer fought me on these thoughts. It could never keep up with them even if it wanted to remove them. So much of who Pyre was had been imbedded in my heart, and I couldn't deny the feelings I had for him.

I wrapped my arms around myself, and he shot me a look of apologies.

"I'll be on my way," he said, leaning his hands against the side of the hardened lava. In one swift move, water rushed down his muscled forearms as he thrust his body out of the hot spring. The wetness clung to his clothes, forcing me to stare at the sculpting of his physique. I didn't feel my mouth drop open, but I was aware of it as my breath fogged in front of my face. "There is soap on the towel. It's the one you made back at the castle."

"Okay." I gulped, sizing him up. I couldn't look away. Especially not now as he pulled at his shirt to wring it out.

"Call for me when you're finished," he reminded me, and I nodded, unblinking. His lips tightened, brows knitting together as if he were going to say something. When he turned around and left the room, I couldn't help myself from watching him leave, and wondering what he might have said.

I waited a moment to make sure that Pyre was out of sight before self-consciously pulling my nightgown over my head. It was far heavier than it should've been due to its being soaked through. The water rained on my head, and I let out a sigh of pleasure as the warmth melted into my hair. I had to bend forward, stretching the muscle in my calf until it burned to be able to reach the soap that lay next to my wounded foot. Once I had the jar of fruity goodness, I lathered it in my palms and washed away the last few weeks with the scrubbing of my skin. It was like a rejuvenation, being afforded this real bath after not having had one for so long. The rags and boiling water at the castle were better than not having anything to bathe with. But the scrap bath had been nothing in comparison to the bliss of being submerged in a perfectly heated hot spring.

After spending a ridiculous amount of time enjoying the feel of clean soap passing over my body, it was finally time to untangle the bird's nest that sat upon my head. My hair had grown quite a bit since the last time I'd cut it, and without a hairbrush, it had become knotted. The blonde mass of it sank into the water as I bent backward, trying to dip my head into the warmth. My foot gave way underneath me, toenails scraping against the hard rock as my body sank backward. I flailed my arms around, blood rushing to my head as I tried to get myself balanced. My injured foot held firm in its groove above pool, and it only made it harder to catch my footing again. I reached for the side of the rock, knocking the jar of soap aside as I found a place for my hand to grasp.

I let my heart settle before picking up the jar and setting it back upright. With my injured foot sitting above water, there was no chance of washing my hair today. At least I can take solace in the fact that when my foot heals, I can take care of the tangles then. Something to look forward to.

"Pyre," I spoke, my voice carrying up into the ceiling. I listened for footsteps, and sure enough, they came within just a few seconds of calling his name. Within his hands, he held a towel, and I quickly remember that below the water I was completely and utterly naked. My face heated from embarrassment as I tried my best to cover myself, but I had a whole leg up in the air. Before I could even think of dropping myself into the heat, he stepped into the space, rippling the bubbles as he pushed toward me.

"Your hair," he said, pointing to the obvious mess flowing down my shoulders and onto my back.

"Can you please give me the towel?" I squeaked, feeling far too panicked about my nudity to worry about admitting how embarrassed I was. He tilted a brow and held the towel out to me. I grabbed one end, and it floated atop the water around me. I made to twist and wrap it around me, but Pyre was already there, folding the heavy blanket around my torso.

"You didn't wash your hair," he mentioned again, and moved each strand behind my shoulders, baring the skin at my neck. "Was there not enough soap? I can get you more," he offered, before picking up the jar which sat, half full.

"I, um," I stammered, clearing my throat. "I couldn't tip my head back far enough without drowning," I confessed, shrugging my shoulders. Pyre lifted the jar to his nose, smelled it longingly, and then exhaled, carrying a smirk on his lips.

"What is it with you and always finding yourself in trouble?" he asked, taunting me.

I bit my lip, trying to hide the grin that tugged there. "It's one of my many talents," I affirmed, finding that my mood was better when he was there to tease me.

"Hmm," he hummed, and his smirk turned from teasing to gentle, as he took just one step closer to me. It was enough to close the distance, and I felt very aware of the position we were in. With my foot up, his body was between my legs, and my core was heating in a deliciously bad way. Though my mind became provoked, desire pulling at memories of us entangled in each other's arms, his face remained soft, and it drew me into the moment. He lifted a hand to my hair again, looping a strand between his fingers.

"May I?" he asked, and I had to do a double take.

"What?" I gawked, as he started to move away from my thighs and placed an arm around my back.

"I'd like to help you wash your hair." His eyes were earnest and longing. "If you'll allow it."

"Sure." I gulped, then wrapped an arm around his neck. The towel around me started to fall, but Pyre was quick to catch it, and I took the end from him, tucking it back into place. "Thank you."

The God of the Dead picked me up into his arms and placed a hand under my head as he smoothly tilted me back so that my hair was fully submersed. It felt so nice to have the water pass over my scalp, but the pure indulgence of having his fingers through my hair was far too exciting to even think about the hot spring.

"Tell me what you're thinking," he said, stirring me from counting the strokes he made through my waves.

Well…" I hummed, relaxing into him as he massaged my scalp. "I'm thinking you'd make a lovely coiffeur if ruling the dead isn't part of your long-term goals."

"For you, perhaps, I'll play the part."

I smiled at that, closing my eyes. "Play away."

He let out a low laugh, and the muscles in my stomach tightened at the sound. Feeling this sense of security and naturalness with him was something I'd unknowingly been dreaming of. I'd never felt anything quite like this before, and it was interesting to find all the things I liked about it. What was more interesting was how quickly I'd allowed him to get this close. I hadn't even hesitated, whereas before, I'd have put up a fight, wanting to run away.

"What are you really thinking?" His voice drew me out from my thoughts, and when I look up at him, I found him so entirely fixed on me, and I wondered if he, too, was thinking the same things as I had been. He dunked the jar beneath us, and poured the steaming water down my hair, never leaving my gaze. His brows lifted at the inner corner, and I thought he might be in some sort of pain.

"I think it's possible," I began quietly, a lump forming in my throat at the mere thought of his mind in harmony with mine. The thrill of the possibility hovered between us. "We've been thinking the same things." Pyre let out a breath and tightened the arm, which held my back. I searched his eyes, waiting for a reply. He only nodded, a quick, short nod. His hand brushed down my hair once more, and then he lifted me up into his arms, making sure to care for the leg that stuck out atop the ledge.

"Let's get you dried off," he said as the cool air met with my pruned, heated skin. I let him take us out of the room without saying a word and listened as his heartbeat thundered beneath my head.

54

LACED

SATYRA

I t was mostly quiet in the safe house, though the wandering sound of the radio provided a bit of background noise, the rebels had all gone to sleep. Through the dim candle lighting, I flipped through the pages of the untitled book, looking for clues to piece together. Having interpreted more of the Latin text, I was beginning to come to an astonishing and confusing conclusion. I had a hard time swallowing what might be, but if this book were telling the truth, Ember was right in telling me to read it. I still wasn't sure why Gram couldn't see it, seeing as how this seemed to involve her more than me. There was a lot I was still uncertain about, and I was eager to dive into the book's contents again tonight.

Flipping through the pages, I scanned the familiar lines, making a point to remember what certain prominent words might mean within the texts. I continued through, until I landed on a page near the middle of the book, which had a table chart drawn across it. I halted my flipping to study it, finding that the author had finally written in English. The next chunk of book was filled with these charts, the subjects staying the same, though the dates and numbers changed with each. I moved to the last page marked with a chart and found that the last date transcribed wasn't very long ago.

BLOOD ASSESSMENT: *15h14 08/08/2022*

Biochemical and Hematological Changes During Ascension

Parameters Patient Reference Range

Hemoglobin (g/L)

160

90–170

Red Blood Cells (x10twelve/L)

90 (g/L)

5.5–10

White Blood Cells (x10nine/L)

12.5

6.5–19.5

Lymphocytes (x10ine/L)

6

1.3–8

Monocytes (x10nine/L)

92

0–650

Eosinophils (x10nine/L)

7.03 (x10nine)

0–1,500

Platelets (x10nine/L)

510

300–800

Hematocrit

44%

35%–45%

RA Factor
Present 16IU/ml
P-N/A >14 IU/ml
Thaumaturgic Blood Levels
65%
0.001%–100%

THAUMATURGIC BLOOD LEVELS: Levels of Thaumaturgic blood continue to increase and bind to white blood cells.

Cartilage and tissue continue to weaken in accordance with the flow of idiosyncratic Thaumaturgical cells to join synovial fluid. Inflammation continues its rise as predetermined: RA Factor heightening with the transformation.

Ichor not yet obtained. Ascension not yet complete. Subject does not use magics.

Estimated finishing point by December thirty-first, present year.

THESE CHARTS WERE markers of someone's blood tests... And whatever the author was looking for, they thought it might show up in their blood on New Year's Eve, which was only two days from now, and disbelievingly, on Shivalri's birthday.

A sudden whistle sounded from the hall, and I jerked upright, shoving the book under my pillow. I felt the groan and tug of the bed beneath me as Raidan shifted in his sleep. I peered over the railing that kept me from falling out of the bunkbed and found that my cousin was not asleep. In fact, he was fully dressed and leaving his bed.

"Rai," I hissed through my teeth, so as not to wake Ember, who was sound asleep on the cot adjacent to us. He turned to look at me, face flushed as he shoved his hands in his pockets.

"Go back to sleep," he whispered, turning away. I crawled over to the ladder, making my way down to stop him from doing whatever the heck he was planning.

"Where are you going?" I demanded, stepping between him and the bedroom door.

"Nesrin and I made plans to train tonight," he told me, pushing past my guard. I made to stop him again, but he'd twisted open the doorknob before I could manage.

"It's the middle of the night," I snapped, tugging at his arm. "Tomorrow's a big day. You need to sleep, not train." He removed his arm from my grasp and stepped out into the hall. He tried to shrug indifferently, but something about the flush in his face gave away his train of thought. I'd seen the way he watched Nesrin Mehra. He must be a fool to think tonight would be a suitable time to explore those thoughts.

"Get some sleep, Saty. I'll be back with plenty of time to rest." Before I could protest any further, Raidan shut the door in my face, causing Ember to stir behind me. I slowly turned on my heel to face him, trying my best to stay quiet.

"Are you really surprised?" Ember murmured, voice low and gravelly. I jolted in my spot, feeling the shot of surprise surface my skin as I stared into the glowing red of his eyes.

"What do you mean?" I answered, my voice unable to whisper, yet too weak to surely speak. Ember sat up on the cot and patted next to him, inviting me to sit. I glanced at the spot his hand patted, unsure whether to give into my curiosity. Instead, I took a seat on Raidan's bed, facing the seer in the candlelit room. His brow raised, causing the lightning streak across his face to glimmer in the fire's cast.

"Nesrin is the type to get what she wants. Tonight, she wanted your cousin."

"Like, *want* want?" I prodded, wondering if Nesrin had been as curious about Raidan as he was with her. Ember let out a soft laugh, and again, I thought I might have glimpsed a shining piece of metal in the center of his tongue.

"Yes, Satyra," he replied. The way he said my name so darkly had the lowest part of me curling in on itself.

"I see."

"Are you okay?" Ember asked, surprising me with such a question.

"About my cousin nailing the general's daughter?" There it was again, that glint within his perfect mouth as he laughed louder this time.

"No." He breathed, rubbing his forefinger and thumb across the bridge of his nose. "I meant, how are you doing?" He dragged his hand down the length of his face, then shrugged the fur blanket from his torso, revealing midnight abs. "This must be taking a toll on you. It's not every day one's family is taken into Hell." A flash of memory pierced my mind as the see-walk Ember afforded me resurfaced. Shivalri, wrapped in the claws of a black-winged beast. Her angry and scared tears as she was dragged into nothing.

"It's certainly taking some adjustments," I answered, not wanting to dive into the feelings coiled within me. If I ever opened that can of turmoil, I may not recover from releasing all its wounds. "I've lived with a lot of loss," I supposed, offering this small piece of information.

"I know," he said, lowering his gaze.

"How do you mean?"

He stood from the cot and made his way over to the window. With a hand on the ledge, he peered into the night, releasing a weighted breath. "I know all about your family." He sighed. "Your parents, your aunts… All of it."

"Aunts?"

"Yes."

"I only have one, and she's gone."

Ember's glowing eyes looked at me through the reflection of the window. His face was so serious. In this light, he looked far older than he appeared, as if life had been weighing him down for a while now.

"No," he said. "I'm afraid not."

"What?" I looked back at his serious reflection, wondering if he'd lost his mind.

"Have you read the books?" he asked.

"Yes, but…" Confusion fuddled my mind, and then I remembered the Latin texts I'd been reading. I had assumed the Grimm's Bane legend was about my family, only I'd thought it to be much further down the line.

"The Children of Grimm's Bane…" I murmured, loud enough only for the seer to hear me. Stepping away from the window and toward my bunk, Ember retrieved the untitled book and sat next to me on the bed. "Can we talk about it?" I asked, looking to the door closing us into the dark bedroom.

"The others are asleep, and Nesrin and Raidan won't be listening to us either. Now is the time to talk about it." I nodded, grateful to finally have this time to discuss these burning secrets. "Did you read it all?" he asked, worry plain in his face.

"Not all of it," I admitted. "I got to the end of the table graphs just moments before Raidan got up." I grunted audibly, finding that I was still upset over Rai's eagerness to disappear with Nesrin into the night. "I'll admit I spent a lot longer on the Latin passages than I would like to say. It took me our first few days here to piece a few of the words together."

"And did you?" he questioned. "Piece the words?" I shook my head, wishing I had. "Would you like me to translate it for you?" I gawked at him, surprised, and then feeling foolish, for not having assumed he could read Latin. I'd heard him spit out spells before, but I'd assumed he'd only learned the lines necessary. Gram was fluent, most likely because she was a witch and most of her spells and prayers were done in Latin. Of course, Ember would know the language. He was a warlock, born into importance.

"Please," I stammered, eager to finally understand the message. Every night before I slept, the pages ate away at me. My need for sleep always outweighed the need to satiate my curiosity, as we'd spent all day and night training and exerting ourselves to the point of exhaustion.

Ember patted the pillow behind me, and this time, I did as he requested. Laying my head down, I closed my eyes and waited to hear the story of The Children of Grimm's Bane. I felt the bed shift around me, and to my heart's content, I felt Ember lay beside me. Our arms touched as he settled into place, and it took everything in me not to openly gawk at him. Keeping my eyes closed, in fear of giving away my ridiculous excitement, I lay still, anticipating his voice.

"The legend says that the Children of Grimm's Bane are made from the firstborn daughter of the firstborn daughter. With each generation, seven cunning women, born with the curse of ill-fated death repeat their patterns. In exchange for great power, they resign their souls at the request of the Fates. With the power of seven, Grimm may not take their souls until they've used their power banks. One may relinquish all power to the other to refill another's bank. They are the Bane of Grimm's existence, for they are in power of their own deaths." My mind whirled at the possibilities, this legend unfolding violently. Finally, the words I'd desperately tried to decipher were mine to hear, and they were some of the heaviest words ever told.

"Is this about my family, Ember?" I turned my head to face him.

His proud nose was lifted in the air, glowing eyes seeing through thick, dark lashes as he looked at the book held above our heads. When his full lips parted to answer me, I found my eyes glued to them, waiting to watch them move. He turned his head toward me, leaving but an inch between us. My breath quickened at the nearness, eyes still captured by the allure of his mouth. Swallowing dryly, my gaze drifted upward to find the fire in his eyes a deep, crimson red. He searched my face, as if trying to find an answer in me to a question he hadn't asked. He licked his lips, and I greedily savored the sight.

"Yes," he finally answered, his cool, mint breath rushing over me. Lowering the book to lay atop us, Ember moved closer, about to cross the line I so badly wanted to venture. When his lips landed just barely on mine, a sudden cry of pleasure echoed through the hallway. The seer peeled himself away from me, and I cringed at the sound of what had to be Nesrin and Raidan doing the deed.

"That is not something I wanted to hear..." I groaned, leaving my place on Raidan's bed. As I watched Ember smoothly set the book beneath my pillow on the top bunk, I felt the distancing heat slowly evade the space where I stood. Ember Blackwood was about to *kiss* me, and I was going to *let him*. I bit my lip at the thought of him licking his lips before coming closer.

"Assuming they're finished," Ember said, turning to look at me, "I'm going to try to summarize that book before Raidan gets back in here. Then, in the morning, you can decide whether or not you want to introduce this information to him."

"Sounds fair," I replied, feeling the blush rush to my face

as the seer approached me again. Gesturing to the ladder, he bobbed his head to order me into my bunk. "Ember," I protested, but he patted the bunk, insisting.

"Just lay down," he held, voice calm. I exhaled, annoyed, but found my way onto the bed, nonetheless. Ember came closer, leaning his arms on the rail that stood between us. For just a moment, I cursed the damned bars that stopped me from leaning in to steal a kiss, but then I thought better of it, remembering the purpose of my being here. I was sure that Ember Blackwood would be an exceptionally enjoyable distraction, and I would gladly savor the feel of running my hands down those insatiable abs of his. But I was not hanging out with the rebels for fun or pleasure. I was here to learn, to fight, and to save the world.

Glowing, red eyes stared back at me through the railing, waking me from my thoughts and dousing me in reality. Ember was a complete stranger. Though intriguing, I got the sense that he could be dangerous if he wanted to be. I'd seen him train with Wulfric and Kaede, and he was just as good as them.

"If Raidan comes in, pretend to go to sleep. I'll go to my cot when I hear his footsteps."

"Why?" I wondered aloud. If I was meant to eventually tell Raidan about this, then what did it hurt if my cousin knew Ember and I were discussing things now?

"Because if you decide not to tell him now, it won't give him a reason to question what I'm doing near your bed in the middle of the night." I furrowed my brow at him. "If you decide not to tell him now, then what else would you tell him we were doing?" he furthered, and the heat in my face grew as I came to understand that implication.

"Right." I swallowed hard, pulling my face just a bit further away from the seer. Ember bit his lip, trying to hide a grin. That damned habit of his was going to be the death of me.

Still holding on to the bars, he leaned back on his heels, pulling his body away as if he were considering that implication too. I needed to shut these thoughts down before I ended up where Raidan and Nesrin were. That would be unacceptable. At least, right now, it would be. "So, the Children of Grimm's Bane; they're my ancestors, huh?" My voice was a little shaky from trying to keep my treacherous tongue in my mouth. Ember drew himself closer again and set two forearms atop the bar.

"Yeah." He exhaled heavily. "They are."

"So, what do you know about them?" I asked, shifting to turn my body on my side to better face him. I couldn't help but notice the way his eyes darted to my hips, then back to my face.

"That's the thing—I don't know all that much. I haven't found any records of them, aside from the texts written in this book."

"Well, tell me what you do know." I sighed, feeling my shoulders tense in both frustration and worry. "I'm sorry I'm not fluent in Latin or poetry. I don't think I fully understand what that passage meant," I admitted. Laughing to myself, I rolled onto my back and exhaled heavily. "I mean, I feel like a fool, but when I read Grimm's Bane, I couldn't help but picture the Grimm reaper dressed as Batman fighting off a group of women wearing Bane's mask."

"Oh, my gods." Ember choked, coughing on the laugh that escaped him. The lingering echo of it rattled my nerves as we both fell silent, listening to see if anyone had heard him. When the coast was clear, Ember shook his head at me in disbelief. "You have a beautiful mind, Satyra. Just beautiful."

I slapped my hands over my face and groaned into my palms. "Please tell me what the legend means before I die from embarrassment."

Ember laughed silently, but obliged. "As far as I can tell, your familial line is sometimes able to cheat death."

"What do you mean?" I turned my face to the bars, stunned.

Ember still stood with his arms between us, his face thoughtful. "I think that's where the term Grimm's Bane comes from, and where your last name derives. Your family, at least according to the texts I read, are powerful enough to become immortal without otherworldly creature resources."

I gasped at the thought that my family would be involved in something like that. For mortals to achieve such a thing was unheard of. Whenever I thought of immortality, my mind immediately flew to vampires. Human witches weren't made like that. At least, not the ones I'd read about.

"How the hell does that work?" I questioned, feeling the confusion and panic come and go in waves.

"From what I gathered, there are limitations to this, and rules that need to be followed," he supplied, removing his arms from the rail, and leaning his body against the bedpost. "It's not just about the immortality, but also a very strong affinity for spirit. It began with seven sisters who all had a strong affinity for spirit. Somehow, they must have learned that by giving their power over to another of their sisters it would grant that one a stronger, longer life. And yes, that means that those who gave up their powers must have either sacrificed themselves or were dying just before transferring their power."

"That's disturbing," I muttered. He huffed in agreement. "So, where does the immortality thing tie in?"

"After reading through that book, I think it all comes

down to the eldest daughter retrieving all of her sisters' powers. I think it gives the eldest a stronger, healthier life. If you consider that each sister's power would essentially give whatever time they had left on Earth, it could potentially be hundreds of years. But I think with the seven connected in one body, the strength of the spirit affinity is so great that it turns into immortality for the bearer."

"Woah..."

"And that's not all," he continued, while I lay down with eyes wide and staring into nothing as I imagined the dangers of having such a power. "It's hard to know if any of this is even factual, but I think you should know in case it is... You have a right to know."

"There's worse than sisters killing each other off for power?" I grimaced, wondering if after tonight, I'd ever be able to sleep again.

"I'm afraid so," he answered, voice gruff.

"Just tell me," I demanded, holding in my breath for fear I might choke on the air around me.

"If there are less or more than seven siblings, the option for the eldest to be immortal is nonexistent. However, if I read correctly, all Grimsbane women have this greater spirit affinity, whether there are seven siblings in their generation or not." He paused for a moment, and I had to open my eyes to see what in the world had stopped him from speaking. The grave look he gave me raised the hair on my arms as a cold wash of fear emerged. "For the Grimsbane women to have these powers, as the book says, you are all born with the curse of ill-fated death, made to repeat the Grimsbane patterns. If you don't end up being the one to achieve immortality, you end up dying tragically. You see, in exchange for the great power of spirit, your family made the choice long ago to resign their souls at the request of the Fates. Not only will Grimm retrieve your souls in the end, but you don't get to have an afterlife."

As if I were stuck in a loop of terrors, the haunting words rang as I thought of life after death. *Gone*. I would be gone, never to see Heaven. Never to see my parents again. Did this mean my mother was entirely gone?

"*Soulless…*" I whispered, feeling the freeze in my chattering lips and teeth. I was vaguely aware of Ember placing his hand on my arm, but I could barely feel the warmth of it.

"Satyra," he murmured. "You are not soulless." Just as Ember's quiet words flowed to me, creaking floors sounded from the hall, and Ember squeezed my arm before reluctantly moving away. "We'll talk about this again, tomorrow," he promised quietly from where he lay in his cot. My eyelids closed in a jittery motion as my body convulsed with shivers. Grimm was going to reap my soul. Grimm had been reaping the souls of all the Grimsbane women before me. Except for those who'd thwarted him off, by turning to selfishness and sororicide, and seizing immortality. Grimm's Bane; spirit's supreme manipulator.

55

DISPLACED

SATYRA

"I cannot believe you," I hissed, pulling Raidan into the bedroom we'd been staying in since coming to the safe house. The morning light pierced through the bedroom window, illuminating the clear lethargy on Raidan's face. I squinted through the flooding light as it reflected off my eyeglasses, stinging through my retinas.

"What?" He groaned, rubbing at his sleepless eyes.

"Look at you!" I said, closing the door behind us. "You haven't slept at all." He started to smirk at me, then thought better of it, reigning in his glory. "We're about to go on a quest to meet the leader of a damn rebellion, Raidan." He bristled under my gaze, and I could sense that this was going to become an argument, rather than a casual discussion about his recklessness.

"I'm not senseless. I know," he jeered, scrutinizing me.

I took a deep breath, trying to calm my nerves. I was upset with him, but not all of this anxiety and fear stemmed from his actions last night. So much had been revealed to me while Raidan had been off chasing a fantasy with Nesrin. I was confused and scared and readily eager to cast my frustrations on my cousin. I hadn't managed any restful sleep, as throughout the night, I'd woken every few minutes to remember that I was cursed.

"You know?" I questioned, trying to keep my voice low so as not to have the rest of the house hear us. "Did you know when you snuck off to meet with the pretty girl in the middle of the night?" I scorned, throwing my hands in the air. "Sleep with the enemy? Really?"

"I have no idea what you're talking about," he said between closed teeth.

"Don't think I haven't noticed how close you've been getting to Nesrin since we've been here," I pointed, stabbing an accusatory finger into his chest.

He scoffed at me, peeling my finger off him. "And what?" He laughed, narrowing his eyes at me. "You think I haven't noticed the way you look at Ember?"

I shook my head fervently, letting a sardonic laugh escape me. "Ember is the least of my concerns right now, Rai," I told him, though deep down, I knew that something was growing in the Ember Blackwood department of my mind. I didn't know what it was, but I couldn't deny the instinctual attraction that pulled me to the seer. I knew it wasn't the time to be thinking of anyone in that way. It was better to keep pushing those thoughts down. Better to disregard it completely. I was trying to do just that. My cousin, on the other hand, had given into temptation, and left me alone with Ember last night. "We need to focus and remember that these people were our enemies just a few weeks ago. I will admit that I am starting to trust them, but we can't completely let our guards down."

"You think I've forgotten that?" he hissed, lowering his voice. "Every time I look at that girl, I remember that she is as much to blame as the rest of the High Council when it comes to my sister being taken into Hell. Nesrin left Moira and the others to take our grandmother hostage. Ember did too," he spat, fisting his hands at his sides. "Listen. There's something about that girl that has me in a storm." Raidan laughed disbelievingly to himself, turning his eyes to the ceiling in incredulity. "But I know, Saty…" he said more solemnly. "I know I have to keep my head on straight and ignore it."

"I wouldn't call what you did last night ignoring it." I grunted, eyeing him. He shoved a hand through his hair, still looking up at the ceiling.

"What do you want me to say, Satyra?" He closed his eyes and exhaled with unmistakeable difficulty. "I'm falling for the girl who betrayed our family." My heart fell into my gut at the vulnerability in his admission. I knew that Raidan had been one to enjoy his fair share of ladies, but I hadn't expected this thing between him and Nesrin to be anything more than a fling. I suddenly felt a pang of guilt for tearing into him like this. I could empathize with him. I understood more than I wished to admit.

"You left me alone with Ember last night," I murmured, finding that it was better to voice all my concerns. I needed him to see that I wasn't only upset because he'd slept with Nesrin. Raidan was like a protector to me. With him gone in the night, I hadn't been able to sleep, scared that Ember might find me in my dreams to show me more about the Grimm's Bane legend, or worse, find me in my bed. Of course, the new information about our family's legend had rattled me to the bone. This magic world was far vaster than I could have ever expected. Though it excited me to be a part of something important and fantastical, this world of ours was growing increasingly dangerous, and now, more than ever, I wanted to hold my family close. I missed Shivi and Gram. I missed my parents, and Aunt Eden. I had Raidan now, but who was to say how long he'd survive this world? Who was to say when the universe would tire of giving me a lifeline, and finally take the last piece of family from me?

Raidan's face softened, his brows lifting in a sudden understanding. "Saty, I'm sorry," he said, then took my hand in his. "I didn't realize. If I thought for one second that you were in danger, or uncomfortable, I would have stayed."

I shrugged him off and wrapped my arms around myself. I hadn't been in any real danger with Ember, but how could I have known that? No, I hadn't been hurt or anything of the sort, but me and Raidan couldn't take any chances of letting that happen to one of us. I wanted to believe that Ember wouldn't hurt me, and I thought I might trust him enough to say he wouldn't, but it was too early to assume.

"I wasn't sure if I was in danger of Ember, or in danger of myself. I couldn't stop my mind from racing." I sighed heavily, letting my arms fall to my sides. This much I would say, but I wasn't sure when or if I would tell Raidan about the book and its intimidating contents. It was a weight I would have to carry, but did he really need to know such things? He deserved to know because all the women in his family fell culprit to the Grimm's Bane curse. But since he wasn't going to die tragically and lose his soul, I wasn't sure if he really needed to know. I was torn between him deserving to be told and him suffering with the knowledge when it didn't truly involve him. Sometimes, the truth only hurts. "Looks like neither one of us got much sleep last night, huh?"

"I guess not," he answered, his lip twitching into a curl. I tried, but failed, not to let my grin grow along with his. He shook his head, rubbing his hands over his face.

"I can't believe you slept with her." I gawked, letting that sink in.

"I can't believe she asked me to." He beamed, and I saw

just how excited he was about this new entanglement in the way his eyes lit up. I couldn't help but wonder what it would have been like to give in to the temptation of Ember last night. We'd gotten unnervingly close to sharing our own kind of entanglement. That lingering tingle still hummed on my lips from Ember's indulgent closeness.

"What are we going to do?" I groaned, adjusting the messenger bag so that it lay on the side of my hip.

"Meet the father," he replied, opening the door.

When we stepped into the living area, my eyes did a double take as I took in the group of rebels I'd been living with for the past week.

"Um, what is happening here?" I stared at the now totally unrecognizable people who stood before me. Ember, who'd normally worn a bun full of thick, black dreadlocks above an undercut, now sported shorn, curly hair that revealed even more of his scalp around the sides where the undercut had become shorter. The style matched the same cut as Wulfric, I noticed, as the pair stood side by side. As I approached, I resisted the urge to brush my hand down the side of Ember's considerably visible scar as I ogled him in question. He was magnificent.

"Now that Moira and the rest of the High Council know to look for Ember as well as you both, we thought it'd be best for you to change your appearances," Wulfric explained, and handed a paper bag to Raidan. He took it cautiously, peering inside. "Where they would also recognize Nesrin, and assume she's on your tail, we made her change her appearance too." Nesrin scoffed, her nostrils flaring with aggression.

"They haven't stopped mocking me all morning." She glowered, her squared bangs bobbing with her head. Where Nesrin had had beautiful, long black hair, often worn in a braid, now it was a light, warm brown, monochromatic with her skin tone. The cut was just below her collarbones, which gave her a plainer look. The bangs, however, were terribly cut and far too long for her to see through.

"The bangs!" Kaede laughed, pointing a hand stacked with rings at her. Nesrin scowled and stomped her foot. She made to flick her usual braid behind her and let out a groan when she seemingly realized it was gone.

"I can help you with that," I offered, pointing to my own bangs. I'd been cutting mine for years, and over time, had learned how to frame them without making it bulky. She gave me a look both full of distrust and desperation but nodded.

"Thank you," she said. "I'll help you dye your hair." My eyes widened as I fully realized that the plan had included changes to my hair too.

"No," I blurted, tugging at my curls. I'd had this color of hair my whole life, refusing to ever change it. This was the hair my mother had given me, that my grandmother had given her, and so on. I was meant to have this auburn hair, and I loved my curls like a treasure.

"You're going to need every bit of help in disguising yourself, Satyra," Ember said.

Wulfric nodded in agreement. Reluctantly, I removed the messenger bag from my side and handed it to Ember, who turned to the kitchen to fill it with essentials. "There are a few colors to choose from in that bag. The scissors and electric shaver are still in the bathroom."

"Thanks, Wulf," Raidan said, and even though I didn't like the prospect of the new makeover, I did kind of like the camaraderie and assembly it forced.

"What about you two?" I asked pointedly at Kaede and Wulf, who shot me a warning look.

"Don't get Nesrin started again." Kaede sighed.

"Come on," Nesrin answered. "Where's the spirit?"

Kaede smiled wryly and patted her on the head, making the bangs jut out atop her nose. If looks could kill... Kaede lifted their hands in surrender, sporting a toothy grin. "No one knows Wulf and me. Besides, I can just wear a hat," Kaede supposed, rending a grunt from the moody woman.

THERE WERE four boxes of hair dye waiting to be used in the paper bag Wulfric had handed to Raidan. Black, blonde, brown, and red. Raidan's hair was already black, so he opted for the box of blonde, hoping it would change the hue in some way. I warned him that black hair with box dye blonde was going to turn a bright orange, but until he emerged from the shower with a head full of Archie Andrew's hair, he hadn't believed me.

I had taken the box of black and brown, knowing full well that with my head of hair, one box wasn't going to be enough to cover it. Before playing with the dye, Nesrin trimmed my hair so that when she released my loose curls, they shrank up just below my collarbone, matching the length of hers. After mixing the two colors in a foam bowl, Nesrin and I tackled covering the entirety of my head. I watched as my red grew darker in the mirror, and silently said goodbye to the piece of me that reminded me most of my mother.

While the dye processed on my head, Nesrin reluctantly sat on the toilet cover and allowed me to shape her very ugly bangs into something presentable. She was a beautiful girl, and I saw that better now that we were so close to each other's faces. Her eyes, though quite dark, were a beautiful chocolate brown when seen up close. She was lucky to have thick, healthy hair, and long dark lashes. She was exceptional, I decided, as I shaped the bangs to match her perfectly symmetrical face.

"Is it looking better?" she asked from beneath the fallen pieces of hair on her mouth.

"Much," I assured her, as I slowly and carefully thinned the chunk in the center. Pulling longer pieces from each side in front of me, I pulled all of it to the left and lifted my scissors.

"Wait," Nesrin blurted, eyes wide. "What are you doing? Don't cut the long pieces." She took the scissors from out of my hands before I could make the cut.

"Trust me," I said, throwing out my hand and waiting for her to return the tool to me. She crossed her arms and lifted her chin, refusing to give in. "Nesrin, I know what I'm doing. I've been cutting my own bangs for years. Now please," I demanded, exasperated. "Give me back the scissors and let me finish so I can go rinse this shit off my head."

"I don't want you to cut my hair shorter," she protested.

"I'm not," I groaned, rolling my eyes. This girl was stubborn.

"Fine." She grunted, handing me the scissors. Before she could find the chance to protest again, I lifted the hair, angled it perfectly, and cut. I held the same piece in the opposite direction and cut again. When I let go, I quickly touched up the straggling pieces and dusted her off.

"Done," I revealed, happy with the handywork I'd provided. With the thick chunk of square bang gone, Nesrin was stunning.

"It's so much better than I thought," she admitted, tousling the fringe framing her face.

"It's a curtain bang, and it actually looks pretty good on you," I said while turning the shower on.

"Of course, it does," she replied with a pointed chin to the mirror. I let out a cursed breath at her vanity, and she let out a brief laugh. "Thank you. I appreciate your help," she supplied, before leaving the restroom.

WITH LEGS TUCKED into thick leather pants and the zipped sweater Nesrin had given me, I left the bathroom feeling like an alien. My trimmed hair was a match to the soot that covered the living room and kitchen area, and I was decked in clothing that did not belong to me. Raidan, who now apparently had a shaved head, looked at me in a way I knew was sympathetic.

"Couldn't stand the orange?" I asked, pointing to his head.

"Hard no," he replied coolly.

"Understandable." He grunted in agreement as he passed me my winter coat.

Shoving my arms through the sleeves, I found I missed the books in the crook of my arm. Before leaving, I'd thought about whether I should bring them with me. Deciding that since the safe house was warded, and Ember already knew what was inside, I left them under my pillow to keep protected, rather than have the possibility of losing, or worse, having them stolen.

"Ready, Cuz?" Raidan asked as we followed the others into the cold.

"As I'll ever be."

56

MUSE
SHIVALRI

Being back in the bedroom had been calming. It was easy to forget that I'd ever been to the castle, for the palace had become the place I most associated with Pyre within just one night's sleep. When he'd carried me into the room, he set me down on a tufted bench and left for the ensuite bathroom. I was curious as to what might be in there since the bathing situation was found in the cave's hot spring. When Pyre emerged, holding a large towel in one hand, and a set of clothes in the other, I was very aware of just how bare and wet I was.

"Thank you," I said, taking first the towel, and then setting the clothes on the bed.

"My pleasure," he amended, and walked toward the chair he'd once sat in next to the large window. "I do not have a partition in here, since I've never had the need to hide myself while dressing in my own bedroom." My stomach hiked up at the mention of this being *his* bedroom. I'd already known, but still, it was rousing, nonetheless. "You can dress in the lavatory, if you wish." I paid attention to those last words, letting my mind trail to wherever his might have gone.

Taking the dry items with me, I sauntered off, a little wobbly on my bad foot, into the washroom.

The lavatory was made up of candlelight, brown clay walls and wooden floors. Where the bedroom had been lavish, the bathroom was a toned-down version of it. There was still black and red accented in the grooving of the furniture, just as that appeared to be the theme throughout his bedroom. At the center of the room stood a slim wooden cabinet, which held a black sink made of polished lava rock. Attached to the sink was a wooden barrel, much like the ones Pyre had given me at the castle. There was a pump the size of my forearm attached to it, and I quickly learned that if I pressed down on it, I could use it to wash my hands. There was a golden mirror above the sink; the metal was shaped into twisted snakes curling around the edge. Wooden shelves lined the back wall with mostly towels, and a few odd jars filled with the ginger flower soap I'd made, and others with sticks of wood floating in a clear substance. Near the door, there was a small stool made with a deep, vivid red material. I rubbed my hand across it, feeling the soft velour under my palm.

As I dried myself off, I replayed the moments of our time in the hot spring, his hands a mess of warmth in my hair as he held me gently to his chest. He'd been so careful as he washed my hair. I knew he had similar thoughts roaming around in his mind, but I couldn't help noticing all the little things he'd done to make sure he didn't give off that impression. His words were teasing, but his actions were held back —the way he'd asked permission to touch me in most intimate cases and the way he'd caught my towel before allowing it to slip from my body in the water. He'd gotten close enough to taste but hadn't made a move to devour.

I looked myself over in the mirror, finding that the ring

around my head separating the bleached blonde ends and my
natural red roots had gotten low enough for the red to reach
my cheekbones. It was weird to see my reflection like this. I
wanted to be embarrassed for the growth but found that it
only brought memories of my family closer to my heart. I
lifted my hair up, feigning a ponytail, regarding my features.
The circles under my eyes were dark, unmistakably tired
from the stress and turmoil I'd undergone. My nose still wore
its freckles, even though I hadn't seen a hot sun in months.
My lips, still full and wide, looked like they'd seen a new
world. I pressed my fingers to them, remembering the kiss I'd
had with Pyre. My *first* kiss. When I looked back up to my
eyes, I almost saw a flicker of gold hiding within the blue. I'd
always had blue eyes, with a ring of yellow around the pupil.
Pyre had told me once that the ring was gold. Perhaps it
looked different in the light of the Under Realm.

I let my hair loose and unfolded the dark red clothing to
find that Pyre had given me a dress. When it was folded, it
seemed plain and ordinary, like the clothes I'd borrowed from
him during my time at the castle. But once revealed, the
beautiful pattern of gold came to life in the candlelight glow.

"Narcissus..." I gasped, running my fingers over the
thousands of intricately placed flowers that flooded the dress.
A memory of Pyre holding the first flower I'd grown in the
Under Realm bloomed to life behind my eyes as I stepped
into the billowy material. It was soft and light like chiffon,
fitting to my body like it had been made with me in mind.
The cinch in the waist was flawlessly tailored, and the material stretched to hug me in all the right places. It was perfect
in so many ways, and when I looked in the mirror, I couldn't
help the smile that formed my face. These little things, these
very considerate and thoughtful things, were all the pieces
that made up my mind about Pyre Malum. He was troubled

and hard, but he was worth it. This world was worth it. If the God of the Dead could learn to be loving, then I could learn to be whatever the Fates had decided for me. If the God of the Dead could find life in his heart, then I would find a place for death in mine.

When I stepped out of the bathroom to find Pyre looking out the window, I quietly made my way over to him. I was nervous about him seeing me in the dress. I now knew that he'd had it specifically made for me, and he'd chosen to have it adorned with golden embroidery with me in mind.

A step behind him, I watched the glow of the Under Realm cast shades across his sharp jaw. He had grown a shadow of facial hair since our parting some few days ago, and I found that it made him look older, wearier.

"It's beautiful," he said, voice deep and low. My eyes caught his in the reflection of the window, and I swallowed hard at the look he gave me. He turned to face me, and I looked up at him, inviting this new openness between us to flourish. "*You* are beautiful," he confessed, and held out a single white flower between us.

"You kept that?" I was stunned, thinking on how long he must have taken care of it for it to still be in one piece.

"How could I not?" he spoke, his chin dipping. "It was the first sign of life you've ever gifted me. Though I reacted horribly when first it grew, I found that I couldn't bear to part with it." He lifted it to my face, gently holding it to my cheek. A small petal fell from the corolla, and at the same time, Pyre's eyes drifted shut. I bent to retrieve it and held it in my palm. With a relaxed inhalation, I invited my magic to stir within me. I took the petal, flower, and Pyre's hand between my two, and focused my energy on healing. The texture in our hands softened, and when I smelled the musky, leafy scent on the air, I knew I'd given it its life back.

"As I said," Pyre spoke softly. "Beautiful." He caressed my cheek, then stood behind me as I looked out into the night.

I knew now, deep within my bones, that I was meant to come to the Under Realm and into Pyre's life. The Fates had tied us together so long ago, our soul's binding utterly ancient. I could hate how I got here and despise the circumstances all I wanted, but it wouldn't change the path I was destined to walk. Resenting my power, being hurt by the lies and secrets, and disliking Pyre or even the Fates would do me no good. I'd accepted my fate while looking into the mirrored waters at the temple beneath the Dhetrïan Pool. I saw what it would do to the world if I didn't at least try to save it. I was born to be the Bringer of Death, no matter which path I chose. One path would lead to unnatural and unnecessary chaos: a world's end. The other, with Pyre at my side, would be made of proper death, ruled by someone who would be fair and just in it all. The prophecy had never been about sealing the Gates shut behind me and staying away from the other realms. The prophecy had been laid out for two people, light and dark to work together and create a better, safer, kinder world. I would repair the veil and keep harm from reaching the Earthly Realm. I would make certain that the Celestial Realm remained a haven, and I would come to terms with my role as Triple Goddess. The last line of the prophecy rang true in my heart as I played it over in my mind. It was exactly as Pyre had said to the Fates. He'd believed that he was supposed to be freed, just as the prophecy had suggested. The Fates had answered him in the most peculiar way, allowing me to understand their message. Now, having seen my fate and knowing Pyre's history and truth, I knew what they meant.

"See with your soul, and not your eyes. You are free,"

they'd declared. They could see that his wall had come down. They knew I'd accepted him, loved him. *I love him...* My heart fluttered to life at the deep recognition. I did love this man, this God, my fate.

"Pyre?" I called, noticing that the God of the Dead had turned away from me while my thoughts carried into heavy themes.

"Yes?" he answered from the red chair he'd frequented. The flower we'd held only moments ago sat in a slim vase on a small table next to him. I found that the window behind him was darker, and understood that I'd been standing here, staring out into the Under Realm, for quite some time.

"Oh," I muttered, throwing a hand over my face. "I'm sorry. I didn't realize..."

"It's quite all right," he told me, standing up from his chair. "You've had a rough time as of late. Don't apologize for where your mind wanders. I imagine it isn't easy to navigate." I sighed heavily, letting my arms fall to my sides. If only he really knew what I'd been thinking about.

"I'll admit, my life is a lot to process, but I think I'm starting to get a handle of things." I started walking toward him, forgetting about my sore foot, and winced at the throbbing ache.

"There is liquor in the kitchens if you wish for some numbness. It could help with the pain," he offered, gesturing to my foot. My mind immediately drifted to my drunken father, and I grimaced at the thought of ever taking part of such things.

"No, thank you." I scoffed, sitting on the edge of the bed. I adjusted the material of my dress on my lap, trying to look lady-like while still sitting comfortably.

"Are you sure?" he questioned, coming toward me, and kneeling to better see my foot. It was still wrapped in the bandages, but the swelling seemed to have gone down quite a bit since morning.

"I don't drink," I insisted. "And I don't ever plan on starting."

He regarded me with a look of surprise, then nodded his approval. "I don't drink either anymore. I don't plan on starting again." A sense of admiration warmed in my chest. Having chosen never to drink alcohol had been something I'd been proud to decide. Early on in my childhood, after seeing my dad lose himself each time he'd fallen out of sobriety, I'd sworn to never let that happen to me. I want to be in charge of my actions and choose my words. When Dad drank, he was never in control of himself. To know that Pyre also preferred not to drink was something of a shock, and something I was very glad to discover.

"I like that," I admitted. He grunted his response, still busy examining my foot. I lay on my back and let him unravel the bandages. The removal of compression felt nice, and the air cooling the skin there was pleasant. I closed my eyes and thought more on the prophecy, more on the future.

"Hey, Pyre?"

"Yes, *Sōrza*?" His voice sounded like he'd answered to me for all our lives. I ignored the swelling in my chest and forced my way into the conversation I'd wanted to have.

"You remember what you said when we first went into the Fates' Temple?"

"Remind me," he replied, and I heard the tearing of new fabric between his hands. As he wrapped my foot in new bandages, I recalled what we'd discussed in that underwater cave.

"You told me that there is no place of atonement in the Under Realm. That there is only place for punishment down here. But there are many souls who come here who do not deserve that kind of eternity. There are those who've done wrong but would like to apologize. And there are many sent down here simply for the fact that their blood tells them they're meant for this realm in death."

"That is true," he said, slowing his movements around my foot.

"If I'm to play a part in guarding this place, in keeping the people of all realms safe, I'm going to do it right. And about that place for atonement... One day, I'm going to create it." Pyre stilled at the bottom of the bed, and I opened my eyes, staring up at the ceiling. "If I will there to be a place for such things, it will manifest as I wish. I see now that nothing about the prophecy is about me. I think I was made to make a change in this world, and the realms within it. I was made to create a place for peaceful death in the Under Realm, and I will do it. Even if it takes an entire lifetime, I will do it. Once I repair the veil, and fix what I broke, I will begin the change." Silence ensued my speech, and I was starting to worry that Pyre disagreed with my thoughts, when dark, feathered wings lifted into the air, high enough for me to see without sitting up. As I lay there, flat on my back, Pyre hovered above me before coming over me, a hand on each side of my head. His eyes shone, and I could see that there was awe in them.

"The world does not deserve you, Goddess," he said, his voice deep, and his lips only inches away from my mouth. "You are such a light in this darkness." I felt a heat in my eyes as I looked up to the man who'd been made for me.

"I'm going to need your help, you know," I murmured, quiet, for him.

"I will keep you safe, while you hold the torch." I laughed softly and held a finger up. Within seconds, my element ran up my hand and through my fingertip, a single flame danced between our mouths. Pyre's eyes filled with fire, and he raised his own finger crowned with flame.

Boldly, albeit shyly, I leaned in erasing the space between us. I saw his eyes widen before I closed mine, feeling the light touch of his lips beneath me. I pulled away, my belly full of butterflies, and looked up at his shining face. His angular brows were knit together in awe.

"Pyre," I began, but he closed the distance between us again, capturing my mouth in the sweetest of kisses. My eyes rolled to the back of my head as the heat washed over me. He was so tender, so gentle as he caressed my jaw, tilting my face to deepen the kiss. His tongue lightly brushed against mine, causing electricity to send me tremors.

"I have been wanting to do that for so long," he murmured, voice low and rough as he spoke mere inches from my mouth.

"I'm glad," I said softly, trying to reel in the butterflies. Pyre rubbed his thumb over my cheek, then kissed me lightly before reluctantly pulling away.

"You are…" he trailed, running a hand through his thick, obsidian hair, his lips wearing a shy and yet excited grin. "You are such a wonder. Your heart is so kind to want to help the Under Realm."

"It's going to get difficult." I exhaled shakily, considering all that we would surely face. The fires and beasts from the vision the Fates provided sifted through the back of my mind as I tried to concentrate on creating a plan.

"Especially if my brother is involved."

My stomach sank at his words. I had completely forgotten about his brother, Ombrose, his family, and whatever ties he might have to the Celestial God.

"What are we going to do?"

"Right now?" he questioned, raising a brow. He dipped

his head lower, the fire between us hotter than ever. I nodded, and my nose brushed his at the movement. He got up from over me and lifted the covers from the corner of the bed. Without saying a word, he slid into the blankets. "I've laid out a set of night clothes for you in the lavatory. I think it's time we rest." The flush in me was unsure as I slowly nodded, got up on unsteady legs, and made my way to the restroom.

Quickly and carefully, I removed my new dress and folded it onto the small red stool that stood by the door. I splashed a bit of water on my face, shoved my arms through the black night shirt, then pulled on the loose pants. I took a moment to breathe and looked myself in the mirror before leaving the candlelit room and entering the darkened bedroom.

I hesitated at the edge of the bed when Pyre patted the spot beside him. My pulse quickened at the invitation, and I tried to remain calm as I lifted myself onto my elbows and crawled into the blanket with him.

When he lay down, his wings took up the space I would lay in. I wasn't quite sure what to do, but Pyre folded an arm around my waist and tugged me fast into his side. His wing wrapped around my back, tickling my arms.

"Woah!" I gasped and let out a nervous laugh. Pyre chuckled into my hair, and my core tingled in reaction to his heat. I curled myself into him, remembering how lovely and comforting it had been while I'd slept next time him all these nights. Though I hadn't realized how long I'd been out, I was aware of the god who'd slept beside me. Now, in this moment where I was fully attentive, the feeling was heightened tenfold as the electricity between us thrummed.

"This," Pyre said breathily, "will forever be one of my most treasured memories."

"This?" I asked, my voice a little breathy as I tried to steady my heartbeat.

"I've lain next to you for many grueling nights, worrying about you and spending my time recounting every story I've ever lived, in hopes that you'd hear me and wake," Pyre confessed. I felt his ribs shudder under my touch as I placed my right hand on his chest. "I'm very glad you woke from that long slumber. I am most glad to have you lie next to me, freely, and know that I am here with you." My eyes fluttered closed as I listened to his words and felt every one of them.

"I was just thinking the same," I replied, and snuggled into his chest.

"I am going to miss this the most," said Pyre. I furrowed my brows, trying to find what he meant.

"You won't have to," I dozily assured him, the fatigue catching up to me.

"Rest," he murmured, stroking my hair down my back. I felt the sweet press of his lips atop my head as he continued comforting me. "We will speak come morning. For now, *quïrhta, mïèye sõrza.*"

The sense of evil lurked my dreams as I walked through a cloud of mist. The feeling of being watched marked my back as I pushed through the thick of it. My foot was aching as I stepped through the unknown, forcing me to bend over and rub a hand over it. Instantly, the pain left my bones and I found that my touch had somehow healed my injury. The wraith's scratch no longer left its affects.

Through the thick, dense mist, a crying sound alerted me to the presence of someone here with me, and my eyes widened, frantic and searching for the source. A woman with beautiful copper hair sat with her back against a tree, her arms and head hunched over in her lap. Cautiously, I walked to meet her, taking care to keep my distance as I approached.

"Hello?" I said, and the woman's head shot up in panic. When our eyes met, my guts fell out of my skin at the sight of my mother, frightened and cowering in the mist. "Mom?" I croaked, dropping to my knees, and reaching for her.

"No," she murmured, eyes narrowed and full of worry. "No, you can't be here. It's not safe."

"Mom, what's happening? Where are we? Are you hurt?" I couldn't stop the word vomit as it spewed from my mouth. I couldn't believe it. My mother was here with me, but she had died. "I'm so sorry, Mom. It's all my fault."

"No, baby. It will never have been your fault." She reached out a hand, but when I grabbed hers, my hands fell through, meeting nothing. She flinched, pulling back, and my tears sprang forth like a tsunami.

"Mom, I'm scared…"

"You should be," I heard from a dark and creeping voice from behind me. It sounded almost familiar, yet I couldn't put my finger on it. I turned around, trying to find it, but there was nothing but a cloak of dark mist around us. I spun back around to find that my mother was no longer sitting in front of me. Instead, she stood with her back to me, her arm outspread as if to protect.

"Mom, what's going on?" I grabbed her shoulder, but still, I couldn't feel her body beneath my touch.

"Leave, Shivalri. This is not a place for you."

"Yes," said the voice, powerful and full of spite. "Leave, Goddess. Show me how you do it." My skin went ice cold. Who was here with us, and what did they want from us? What were they looking for?

"I'm not leaving you," I decided, planting my feet. Thunder erupted as lightning cast a light through the skies, illuminating the space we occupied.

"Open the Gates, Goddess," my mother spoke. How did she know about the Gates? Why on Earth would she want me to open them? If my mother knew what it would do, she would have never suggested such a thing. She turned around to face me, keeping her guard and protective stance. I watched her face, the one I'd grown up to believe was family, and found that there was a crack in her façade. A slight twitching in her eyes that seemed unnatural.

"Mom?" I questioned, looking her over. She took a step closer, her face still full of worry.

"Do it, Goddess," she insisted. "It's the only way." And that's when I heard her words for what they truly were. Whoever this was, whether my mother or an apparition, it wasn't truly my mother inside, for she wouldn't have called me *Goddess*.

Understanding sank in as I really, truly studied her. Though my mother had always had beautifully blue eyes, they'd never glowed like this before.

"Ombrose." I ground my teeth, clenching my fists, and calling forth whatever elements would come to me. My mother laughed, a gross and unnatural growled type of laugh.

"So, you know, then?" he questioned through my mom, her voice sounding distorted and all wrong.

"I know enough." I hissed, feeling the fire flow through my veins, becoming available and at the ready for my use.

"Then why don't you make things easy for me and give me what I want?" he suggested, a casual air to his traits. I'd never seen my mother look like that in my life, and I wasn't a fan of seeing it now. "I get what I want, the boss gets what he wants, and you get what you want. You do want to go back to Earth, right?" He shrugged, my mother's copper hair falling forward.

"I want to keep everyone safe," I spat. "And you don't seem to have a similar goal in mind, so I'm sorry, but I'll have to pass."

"You don't understand, Goddess. Either you accept and make things easy for yourself, or we force you, and life becomes a lot harder."

"*You* don't understand," I said, shaking my head. "If I

don't fix what I broke, the whole world is going to end." He scoffed, flicking a piece of invisible dirt from my mother's sleeve.

"The world doesn't end for all. Only those on the wrong side."

"*You're* on the wrong side." I pointed. He lifted a brow, the glowing in my mother's eyes widening with the movement.

"That's of your opinion."

"Oh, fuck off!" I cursed, sending a wash of flame through my fingers. "Just tell me your motives and let's get on with it." He laughed dryly and started to walk away before turning over his shoulder. The shock of seeing my mother in this way had turned my emotions off. I was done with playing and being lied to.

"Open the Gates, Goddess. You have until next nightfall to make your decision. The boss isn't known for his patience, but I will allow you these last few hours to decide whether you're in the mood to be accommodating, or to start a war you won't be able to finish."

"I'm going to end this," I swore, the fire in my hands sweeping over my entire body in the rage. "And when Pyre hears of this, I know for certain you won't be there to watch it."

"Sure, Goddess. Whatever you say." He grinned and started walking away again. "Tell Mortades I said hello."

The mist around me began to fade as I watched the back of my mother leave my dream. It was strange to find that I hadn't been having a nightmare when Ombrose had arrived. In fact, this dream had been like a small gift in a way, allowing me to see my mother. When my dream cleared, and my conscious was back in the bedroom, I found that Pyre had been right to be suspicious of the Orsimm family.

I lifted my head from Pyre's chest, and he shifted upright, looking down at me with concern.

"Is everything all right?" he asked, voice heavy and profound. I stared at the place where my hand rested on him and wondered how I'd ever gotten to be in this position. How was this my reality? "Goddess?" he questioned, pulling my attention to him.

"I think you were right," I said, piecing the puzzle from the dream I'd just woken from.

"That is new," he jeered. My eyes snapped to his crooked grin, and an urge like a storm came blowing through me as I considered biting his lip. He lifted a hand and tilted my chin up, forcing me to meet his eyes. "If you continue looking at me like that, it could very well end me, *Sōrza*." I gulped audibly, and he tilted his head, his face full of endearment.

"Dramael," I said flatly before my mind could wander any further.

"What of him?" he asked, his tone quickly turning from charm to severity.

"All of the Orsimm. I think they're working together to make me open the Gates." Pyre sat upright, pulling me up with him so that we sat side by side, my body tucked in by his warm, soft wing. I stroked a feather closest to my face and watched it twitch beneath my fingers. I took a deep breath and recounted my dream, explaining all that had occurred, wincing whenever I pictured Ombrose speaking to me through my mother. "Ombrose visits in nightmares, but I only started having a nightmare at the end of my slumber. It started out as simply being conscious in my sleep, meaning Dramael must have been involved, right? The sequence went from sleeping, fantasy, and then to nightmare." I swallowed hard before delving into the fantasy I'd lived in my sleep. "Seeing my mother again after she died was something I could only ever wish for, but it was make-believe. It wasn't a memory, which means it couldn't have been Reaver who'd shown me the imagery. I think Dramael, Tasphen, and Ombrose were working together to spin the vision. I can't be sure about Reaver, but I didn't sense him around." I paused for a moment, recalling my and Reaver's conversation on my last day at their cave. "Back at the Orsimm home, Reaver and I shared an odd occurrence."

"Meaning?" He tensed, and I realized that could have been taken in a different way than I meant.

Quickly, to diffuse whatever his imagination had stirring, I explained. "When the Orsimm found out what I was, rather, *who* I was, they figured it would be a good idea to involve Gerimor to help us, explaining that he would have better knowledge to supply for my situation. Dramael had told me that I could choose whether to invite Gerimor to help us. He said I could sleep on it and decide in the morning. When I woke, Gerimor was already on his way. Reaver told me that he'd spoken to Dramael, who'd said that Ombrose told him I had decided to meet Gerimor. But I hadn't ever told Ombrose, or any of them, that I'd wanted that. Reaver was shocked that someone had lied. We weren't sure if it was Dramael or Ombrose who'd done the lying, but Reaver really did seem surprised when he found out. I think, perhaps, there is a lot that Reaver doesn't know about his family."

"It's possible that he is innocent," said Pyre, considering this. "He's always been a very strict follower of the rules. However, I wouldn't trust him. He is a part of their family and oversees the Orsimm when Dramael is in deep exertion. It would be difficult for Tasphen, Ombrose, and Dramael to hide such things from the one whose eyes are always present."

"True," I agreed, imagining all the things that the Orsimm

family could be doing now, and wondering just how far deep into their plans they were. "All I know is that they are working with someone Ombrose called the boss, and he wants to use me to open the Gates."

"My brother, without doubt," said Pyre, his teeth gritting in the clench of his jaw.

"I think that what the Fates showed me in their mirror was exactly what would happen if their boss were to succeed."

"Apocalyptic mayhem."

"Exactly," I said, shifting my weight so that my knees were pressed to Pyre's side. I was somewhat aware that I had my injured foot tucked under the other, and there was no longer any pain. But that was the least of my concerns right now as I watched the God of the Dead.

"We need to get you out of here and safely back on Earth."

"What about the veil?" I asked, dreading what was to come. The problem wasn't finding my power anymore, for I'd never felt as strong and as in control of my affinities as I was now. The reason my heart ached was that I was torn between two lives. I wanted to find my family again and live out the rest of my days with them. But I didn't want to leave Pyre here alone. I didn't want to leave the connection we had between us. It was new to me, but ancient to our souls. There was a reason we'd found each other, whether in a terribly merciless way or not. In the end, my fate would bring me back to Pyre. But I wasn't sure if leaving him would result in the horrific fate or the good one. Either way, I didn't want to leave him, and yet, I would have to if I wanted to get back to my family to make sure they were okay.

"Like I said, I can sense your powers building. I think they're almost entirely set, but because they aren't yet, you need the aid of another god to repair the veil. Lucky for you, and the rest of the world, I can be that for you. And so, tomorrow, we will build you a sacred place where nothing may disturb you and send you on your way."

"Tomorrow?" I gaped, my nerves begging him to repeat himself, my mind not ready to have heard such a thing.

"You're ready," he replied, and stroked a lazy finger down my shoulder. "It's time we take care of the veil. Time, I take care of you."

No… I wasn't ready. Tomorrow was too soon to leave. I wasn't prepared. I couldn't let go now. Not when we'd just begun opening up to each other and learning what we really were to one another.

"Not now," I choked, refusing to allow him to make such a decision for me. "No," I said, my body trembling, but voice strong. "I'm not leaving you yet."

"I will miss you, but—" I sat up straighter, turning my body toward him and cutting him off with a stare of desolation.

"No, Pyre," I ground out, my lower lip trembling. I tried to keep calm, but the rush of emotions mixed with all my elements trying to surface was too much to bear. I couldn't stop the tears from washing down. "I'm not leaving you. I won't. Not ever," I declared, realizing that this was indeed what I wanted. I loved my family and wanted to be with them again. But couldn't I enter the Earthly Realm, ensure their safety, and return to Pyre? I was the ruler of the Gates. Surely, I could travel to them more than once.

Pyre was alone, and the person he was meant to be with was *me*. And he was so willing to throw me away just to save my life.

"We must repair the veil down here, since I need to lend you my power and I can't go with you to Earth," he said quietly, his eyes burning through mine. "But once it's repaired, you will have to lock the Gates for good. When you come into full power, which I *know* will be soon, you will have to summon all affinities and let your blood seal the Gates. You need to be in the Earthly Realm when you do it if that's where you want to stay. You cannot risk opening it again to get home. You need to leave here tomorrow."

"No," I refused, letting my hands fall into my lap. I still had so much I wanted to do for the Under Realm—still had too much I wished to experience with my handsome, lonely god.

"I know," he simply said, and pulled me onto his lap, curling my body into him. He kissed the top of my head, lingering there with his lips pressed to my hair before shuddering beneath me. "I know…."

58

BOUND

SHIVALRI

W hen I woke this morning to find Pyre seated at the edge of the bed, head held in either hand, I wanted to begin crying again.

"Pyre?" I started, voice broken from sleep. His head whipped up in a flash as he turned to look at me. "Oh." I sighed. "Come back," I insisted, patting the empty space on the bed. His eyes grew soft at the invitation, and slowly, he moved to lie back. His wings unfurled, flattening to the mattress. My arm was tickled by the feathers that brushed my skin.

"Did you sleep well?" he asked, staring straight up at the ceiling.

"The best in a while," I admitted, feeling ashamed for having been rested while he had obviously stayed awake for most of the night. I'd stayed awake for a little while, dreading what was to come and replaying the strange dream in my head. But once I fell asleep again, still curled up to the God of the Dead, I'd finally relaxed, having slept comfortably in his arms.

"Good," he said. "You'll need rest for what's to come. It's

going to take a lot from you to repair the veil. Then you'll have to open the Gates and return to Earth." I furrowed my brow at the half-truth. "You're going to be drained by the time you close them Earthside."

"It's going to take a lot from you too," I corrected, looking him over. He was going to have to transfer all his power to me while I exerted my own. "And you don't seem to have slept at all," I pointed, turning my head to better see him.

"We need to set things in motion now. We can't wait any longer. Not now that I know for certain that my brother wants you for himself. I can't trust that he won't find a way to you or doesn't already have a plan in action to retrieve you."

"I think we can wait just another day," I argued, anxiously picking at my fingers. I didn't want to leave now. It was too soon after finally admitting to myself what Pyre meant to me. I needed more time with him. I needed to show him that I forgave him, and that I didn't hold my doomed fate against him. I wanted more nights of warm embrace and longing desire. "Let's just take our time and figure this out. There has to be a better way to do this. I don't want to completely shut myself out from the Under Realm, and I'd like to think I could visit the Celestial Realm too if I am truly the gate-keeper of all."

"No, Goddess," he snapped. "You most definitely should never set foot in the Celestial Realm. You'd be handing yourself over to the enemy." He sighed heavily, shutting his eyes tight. "You need to leave the other realms behind. Repair the veil, shut the Gates, and don't look back."

"What if I don't want to?" I asked, nervously chewing at my lip. He shot up to a seated position now, and I thought he was going to leave, when instead, he turned to face me. Everything in his regard was serious, and it scared me to see him like this—to see his fear. A sudden movement at the base of his shirt caught me off guard, and I realized he was about to undress. "What are you doing?" I asked, feeling flustered. It wasn't like I hadn't seen him shirtless before, but to watch him remove his shirt while in bed with me was a whole other scenario.

"I need to show you something." He grunted, pulling the shirt over his head. He unlatched an attachment in the back of his shirt, and it released the material from around his wings.

"You need to undress to show me?" I gulped, my lip going numb from the force in which I still bit it.

"Come here," he insisted, but I was hesitant to move. "Please," he added, and I found myself moving closer to him. As he turned his body away from me, his wings were at the forefront of my vision. They were always beautiful to me. A symbol of his strength and all he wanted to be. I had never gotten this close to his wings until these past few nights, always having seen them from afar or at a different angle. This was new for me. I marveled at the indigo that shown amongst the many strands of perfect black. I touched a finger to the top of where his wing grew from his back, making my way down to the base. When my fingers met with rough bumps, I gasped in horror at the sight, unable to believe my eyes.

Large welts circled around the base of each wing, as if someone had attempted to carve them out from his body. My hand trembled as I searched his skin, finding that in between each shoulder blade someone had cut out symbols in his flesh. For this to have lasted, for it not to heal, meant that whoever did this to him went deep and to the bone.

"Who did this to you?" I inhaled unevenly, feeling the interchanging rage and sorrow battle for sovereignty of my heart. "Who would carve these marks into your back?"

"My brother once removed my wings, and then seared these words into my skin with his power for lightning," he said lowly, shattering my heart into tiny, grief-stricken pieces. "As you can see, my wings regenerated, but the marks will never fade. I am only showing you this to demonstrate how cruel he is. To show you how vital it is that he never gets his hands on you."

"Why?" I faltered, feeling the sorrow gain weight in my emotions. "Why would he do this?"

"As a reminder of who I am, and what I was made for. To remind me that I am worth nothing, for my worshippers are dead. In the minds of all those living, I am the worst thing to ever exist. This is a kindness in comparison to his tortures. These scars, these symbols imbedded in my skin mean one thing, and one thing only." I moved closer to examine them, and his shoulders tensed at my approach, though he did nothing to stop me from looking.

"What does it say?" I asked, unsure if I should even be asking such a thing. His shoulders slumped, and I pressed a finger to the first symbol grooved deep into his skin.

"*Tyeūx dwahbï dhendœ ôhrtum êhzje tyeūx êrèstro cehluï.*" The words sounded beautiful but stung like poison. "To dwell in death is to become it." I shot a glance toward him, but he was looking into his lap as he said the words. So vulnerable, so defeated.

"Do they still hurt?"

"Only my pride," he answered. I winced, moving my fingers away. I made to get up from the side of the bed, but his voice broke my movement. "No," he whispered. "Don't leave."

"I won't," I swore.

"Please."

"I told you, Pyre, I'm not going anywhere. Not now. Things have changed... I—"

"I meant that I didn't want you to recoil from me. I *need* you to leave the Under Realm. My hopes of you staying with me are unrealistic. I know it's not safe. I just wish that this time together felt like enough to hold on to for eternity." My heart was pounding in my chest, unsure how much to say— how much to unveil about the truths of my feelings. This was all new, the unfolding of my sentiments toward him. But they were strong and fierce, and the need to comfort and protect him took over all of me.

"You can hold on to me," I answered quietly, looking down into my lap. I heard a soft inhale on his part and felt the bed sink in where I sat. A light touch caressed my bare shoulder, and a shiver came from out of my core.

"You are far too good." He swore under his breath, and I turned to look at him again. His eyes were low, lashes darkening over the gold I'd grown to enjoy in his eyes. I leaned back again to see the weight of the burdens he bore on his back. He seemed to notice and relaxed his wings again, allowing me to fully see his openness. I so badly wished to take away this pain, or at least help him carry some of its weight.

"Can I heal this for you?" I asked, trailing along the side of a scar, not wanting to cause him harm. "I think I could if I tried. In my dream, I touched my sore foot and it instantly healed. And I revived the flower too. I think I have healing power, like my mom and brother. I could heal you."

"You —" He paused and turned to face me again. "You would do that?"

"If you'll let me, I would try." He took a moment, eyes searching mine, seeming to be caught between several emotions.

"No," he decided. "I wish to keep them."

"Why?"

"Because it is my burden to carry." He blew, turning his face away from mine. I wanted to see him. Wanted to read his face because he so rarely let his guard down. The withdrawal of his face was torture.

"Pyre?"

"Yes?" he replied, still looking away.

I lifted a hand and gently tugged at his chin, encouraging him to find my eyes again. When he locked my gaze, when he let me in to see him, the ferocity of my emotions tugged at my heartstrings. This man was so much more than he ever let on to be. He was not only hard and guarded, but he was deeply lonely and frightened to have to live out an eternity in death feared, alone, and unwanted. He was all of these things, yet more than that. He was broken, and even through it all, he still held a grain of hope and wished for a better life. Even through the sadness and demise, he cared for his people, and he cared for me. Everything in me wished to relieve some of the trauma and misery he carried with him. Having experienced his tenderness toward me, having heard the truth of his words, I saw the broken pieces within him still trying to mend his soul. Now, I would stop at nothing to comfort him, to hold his hand through this.

Placing a sure hand to his chest, I pressed my palm into his bare skin, feeling the heat under my touch.

"Pyre? Do you trust me?"

"Yes, *Sōrza*." The use of his nickname for me furthered my need to help him, to truly become his equal—the light to his darkness.

"I am with you," I avowed. "I will bear these burdens with you. Always."

His eyes widened, lips parting to protest, but I would not

allow it. I would not allow this man to suffer alone in this. He had not chosen this eternity, yet he took it. No more would he be alone in this world of death. Not if I had anything to do with it.

Flattening my palm against his beating heart, I pulled at my strength, calling forward the power I knew I only controlled because he had taught me how.

"Don't remove them," he stammered. Harnessing my strength, calling to everything in my core, I looked into his golden eyes with steady determination.

"I won't. I promise," I answered through clenched teeth. The pain began worsening with every breath.

"Then what are you doing?" he pleaded for an answer, grabbing me by the shoulders.

I knew that his worried look had nothing to do with what his body felt. I knew I was not causing him any pain, because I wasn't doing anything to him. I had a hold on my elements, and I was finally using them for something worthwhile. The more I pulled at the magic, the more my body grew tensed and fatigued, but I knew I was almost at the point of controlling the intention. I saw the words floating behind my lids, letting their imprint become a part of me. I brought forth my fire, allowing it to surface along my spine, imagining the words, repeating them in my mind like a mantra.

"Fuck!" I screamed, my throat hot and prickling as I removed my magic's protective barrier and allowed the heat to melt into my skin, stripping away at purposeful layers as I worked. I gritted my teeth against the pain as I could physically feel the searing deepen through tissue.

"What are you doing, *Sōrza*?" Pyre asked again, his grip tightening on my shoulders. At his touch, the power exploded from within me, a throbbing, slicing cut through muscle I didn't even know I had. But I was used to pain. I had dealt with it my whole life. This would be no different once I healed; only a lingering ache would follow me where I went. I let the fire ease as I felt the flame leave its mark. Smoke billowed around us, along with the sickening odor of burning flesh. With a wash of my water element, I winced at the contact of frigid drizzle, before calling air forward to blow a cool breeze on my wound. I let my spirit affinity touch my skin, sending healing waves into my back. The burning left me entirely, and I felt my skin pull a little as my body rapidly healed. The hurt was gone, but the knowledge of its presence was a weight I'd never lift.

A single tear fell down my cheek, and I lifted my eyes to his. Terrible dread pooled in his dark, copper eyes, demanding an answer. He was so damn beautiful that it was hard to see him this way, so outwardly concerned for me.

"It is our burden now," I whispered, another tear making its way down my face and onto my lips. He gasped at my words, seeming to understand what I did only in this moment. His fingers were stiff as they descended down my shoulders, lightly grazing my back. I recoiled, scared the pain would come back, but it didn't. He shook his head fervently, and my heart crumbled at the slight trembling in his lip.

"No!" He growled. "No, no, no…." He abruptly lifted himself off the bed, wings upheld over his head. He paced back and forth in front of me, a storm of dust following his upset. I immediately went to him, grabbing at his hands to slow his pace, slow his mind in this racing.

"Hey," I spoke softly. "It's okay," I assured him.

"No, it most certainly is not!" He blew, running a hand over his face. "I refuse to believe you've just done what I think you have. You would not have sullied yourself in such a manner. You are not like me."

"I am more like you than you'll ever know," I said, voice

a little shaky, but intentions sure. "Though I may falter here and there along the way, I see so much clearer now. I *am* like you. The Fates have spoken truth to these words, Pyre, and I am more than willing to carry this legacy if it means lifting the load off from you, both symbolically and lawfully. I chose to do this." He took a step closer, looking down into what I knew was my sure and steady regard. He trailed the line of my jaw with his finger and leaned in close enough for me to smell his woodsy scent.

"Shivalri, I *love* you, gods damn it. I am utterly, desperately in love with you. Having you carry any part of my burdens is the last thing I would ever want," he whispered, lowering his lips so that if I willed it, I could simply tilt mine up and meet with his. *He loves me... He is in love with me.* My heart felt like it would explode at the thought. Pyre's throat bobbed as I stared at his lips, the need to kiss him strong and despairing. I took a step back, but he grabbed my hand to stop me. I smiled down at his gentle touch and rubbed my thumb over his knuckles, like he had often done to mine. I removed myself from his hold and turned away from him, facing the fireplace. "Please," he begged. "Don't go. I won't force you to stay with me, but I wish you to." My heart thundered in my chest at his words, for they only intensified the need to do what I had intended. I was not going to leave him. Certainly not now as I carefully curled my fingers under my night shirt and slowly lifted it over my head. I heard the rustling of his feathers behind me in time with the nervous breath I released. I dropped my shirt, and I heard him take a step toward me, but he did not close the distance. My fingers shook as I lifted my hands to move my hair to one side, baring my back for him to see. He needed to see what I did. He needed to know how serious I was about taking on this role in which the Fates had decided for me. He needed proof of my acceptance and willingness to join him in this. I would not simply walk away from him, leaving him alone in the mess.

I slowly turned to face him, unable to look at him just yet. With my head down, I saw my own naked skin in the heat of this room. It was like living in a bottle filled with lightning. Pyre's feet were planted only a meter away, yet still, it felt too far. I took a long, deep breath and settled the rattling in my rib cage.

"*Abrôrta dhèjl Ôhrtum.* I am the Bringer of Death," I said, repeating the Fates' declaration. I finally looked up from staring at his feet and found heart-wrenchingly beautiful eyes staring back at me. He saw me, not only the body I now showed him but the person inside who was destined to face eternal death at his side.

"Gods." He breathed, never leaving my stare.

I gulped and lifted my head in certainty. "If you have become death for dwelling in it, then it is I who carries the burden of knowing I am responsible for your trammel. It's only fair that I walk with you through it." I blinked the heat from my eyes, burning through the glow of his. "Allow me this." My voice wobbled as I spoke those last words, searching for a glimpse into his thoughts. In one swift movement, Pyre closed the distance between us, lifting me off my feet, and driving our bodies together. My lips parted in a quick gasp of surprise, and I no longer felt my legs that swung in the air, as he kissed me with a ferocity like none other. His lips were full against my own, sinfully delicious as they moved over mine. The low tightening in my body begged to let loose in a way I had only felt once before. This was everything I'd dreamed of with him. He pulled away from me, breath hot and heavy. A waft of sugar and spice lifted in the air, and I suddenly realized that somehow, I was smelling Pyre's desire for me. Was this what he'd smelled on me before? Was I learning these new abilities as my power took root in me? It was exhilarating to consider what this meant. I had shown Pyre my body, yet he hadn't been aroused until *I* had grown desperate with desire. I only scented it now. He was fixated on me before, entirely focused on what I had done to my back and why. My chest ached at this revelation, as my surety of Pyre's heart and intentions grew stronger by the minute. I clung to the back of his neck, imploring him to give me more.

"My *sōrza*," he whispered, inches away from my mouth. "I do not deserve you."

"That's where you are wrong." I shuttered, fully realizing just how strong our tether was built. "That is where *I* was wrong before." I trembled in his arms as his eyes studied my lips, desperately clinging to my words. "I was made for you." I inhaled, exasperated both by the admitting of our link, and the burning desire taking over me. I pulled his head forward and pressed my breasts into the hardness of his chest, feeling every place in which, our bodies aligned. He growled deep from within his core, lighting the fire inside me. Our lips fell into madness, tapping into the raw desire that thrummed between the two of us.

He lowered me onto the bed, arms and legs braced over me as he relished the sight of me. A tremor rolled over me, and I physically shook under his predatory gaze. Pyre slowly lowered his head and pressed a delicate kiss below my sternum, his hair grazing the sides of my under-busts. A small whimper escaped my lips, and a heavy laugh brushed my skin.

"Gods." He blew, a laugh still lingering in the back of his throat. "That sound…" He lifted his head and lined himself over me, a hand caressing the side of my hip. I could see the devilish smirk was out to play. He lifted himself up to stand in front of me at the edge of the bed, and the air around me chilled instantaneously. The hand that lingered at my hip was the only warmth that remained. I watched him trail a path down my hip bone and over my pants. My stomach knotted as he neared the band around my middle, and I swiftly learned that his touch over fabric was a tease in comparison to the bare skin he'd stroked.

I tore my gaze from his fingers to his face and found that he was waiting to see where I would take this. He waited patiently, though jaw tight, to see what I would decide. Because that's what he'd always done when it came to this. He wanted me to tell him that I wanted this. And Gods help me, that's all I wanted.

"Yes." I choked, voice shaky and surprisingly full of rasp. His claws sharpened over my pants, but he reigned it in immediately, making sure not to leave a mark. Though I was positive those claws should have scared me, I quickly discovered that his might only fueled my need of him.

"Yes, what?" he demanded. I could see in his stance that he was trying to remain strong, trying to put up a shield to protect himself from rejection. It was what I had done the last time we'd given into our fantasies. But this time was different. This time, I knew what I wanted. Before, when things were fresh, I was broken and confused, unable to make anything right in my mind. Now I was stronger. I knew who I was and what my purpose was. Even more than that, I knew what I wanted, and what I wanted was to lose myself in the one good thing the Fates had promised me. I wanted *him*.

"Yes, to you. Yes, to all of you." His dark black wings widened at my words, and his fingers gripped around my pants. When he made to pull them off me, I threw out my hand, stopping him quickly. His eyes flew to mine, confusion and hurt swimming in the gold.

"What's wrong?" He stilled, holding on to the fabric.

"You," I said, and the hold on my pants loosened a bit.

"Me?" he questioned, and I suddenly realized I'd just accidentally said that *he* was wrong.

"No!" I shouted. "What I meant to say was, what about you? Do you want this?" I clarified, terrified that I'd just ruined our moment.

His chest deflated with the breath he let loose, his ink-black hair falling forward into his face. "You are all I've ever wanted, even before knowing I'd ever wanted you," he confessed.

"Pyre..." I inhaled sharply, and his hold on me tightened.

"Absolutely sapid," he said, voice guttural. "My name on those enchanting lips." And with that, he tugged at the only clothes remaining on my body. I lifted my hips up toward him, the heat growing hotter in our room. As he dropped my pants and undergarments to the floor in triumph, I couldn't help my blush from rushing to my cheeks. I foolishly covered my eyes, suddenly shy and realizing that was a silly thing to feel after having so boldly removed my shirt in front of him. He had already seen most of me. But this was different. This was all of me laid bare for him to see—laid bare for him to *have*. I felt the bed move again, feeling his weight shift the mattress beneath me. He slowly peeled my hands away from my face, and I reluctantly opened my eyes. His brows flew up in surprise at my stare, lips turning into a frown. I was startled, wondering what might have triggered this expression.

"What is it?" I asked, a hand immediately finding a place to rest on his cheek. He leaned into the touch, rubbing his face in my palm, and a welling of warmth filled my chest.

"You're glowing," he whispered, soft and awed. "You

are so beautifully bewitching." His words lovingly wrenched my soul from my body. He sat up then, kneeling over my legs to show that he, too, was undressed. My mouth watered at the sight of the divine length of him as he bared himself to me now. He was perfect in every way, hand carved by an artist so gifted it hurt to look. His skin was alabaster, smooth over the mass of muscle that made up his sculpture. His face, strong yet too beautiful to belong to any man. Those eyes, raving over me, like a surreal dream I'd be happy to lose myself in time and time again. Nothing of his physique seemed real. Everything about him was magic.

Pyre's hands clutched either side of my waist, accentuating the ample hips my body offered. His touch drew my gaze to my own body, and I found that I truly was glowing. A golden hew cast highlights over my hips, abdomen, and breasts as I looked upon myself. Pyre rubbed his thumbs across my skin on either side of my hips, tenderly offering warmth. Every moment of gentleness and vulnerability he shared with me was a gift like none other. My insecurities and nervousness were far gone now. Now, all I saw was him.

Pyre curled his left arm under me, leaning on his elbow for support. There was an electric wave of magic between us as our bodies aligned. He was finally closer, finally at a distance in which I could plead for another kiss. He took his other hand and brushed a strand of blonde hair from out of my face.

"May I love you now?" he asked, the brim of his eyes glistening. My heart raptured at his words, entirely ripped open by the truth of them in his eyes. His face lit with gold as my magic reflected upon his skin.

"Please." I whimpered, and he lowered his head to mine, pressing our foreheads together.

"Tell me if it hurts," he murmured under his heavy breath. "Tell me what you need, and it will be yours."

I tilted my head up and pressed a delicate kiss on his lips. "I need you," I told him, and he lowered himself onto me. The hand under my back held me tightly as I let him get closer, pulling my legs on either side of him. The hand that stayed near my face caressed me tenderly, gliding over my cheek with such affection I could burst entirely from that touch. When he kissed me now, I felt a pressure at my core as he pressed against me. Though I'd never experienced anything like this before, I knew that I needed it now, and solely from him.

"Tell me." He groaned in my mouth, a shiver eliciting pleasure throughout my body. This was pure torture. I wanted all of him. I wanted it all now.

"Love me," I begged, unable to withstand the teasing heat that grew between my legs.

"My pleasure." He growled, his rumble matching the tremor coursing through me. It was like a thunderbolt— ecstasy in its heat and bliss—a thrilling ache. I gasped at the tug inside me as he pulled away.

"No," I rasped, nails digging into his back.

"What's wrong?" he asked. "Do you want me to stop?"

"Gods, no." I panted. "Never." A guttural sound escaped his mouth, and he kissed my neck. I pulled at the back of his hair, forcing him to meet my mouth. I needed to kiss him. I needed to feel every inch of his skin on mine and relish in the moment of bliss. Our tongues clashed, sweeping over one another in a desperate fight to stay in this fever forever. The more the kiss deepened, the more he delved into me, my core pulsing in tune with his thrusts. It was all passion and heat, a deliberate, desperate act. I was going to lose it, going to explode from this intoxicating pleasure. When I tore my mouth from his to look down at us, Pyre growled low in my ear.

"I've never seen anything fit more wholly than us." He blew, his fiery breath tangling in my hair. I couldn't agree more. Where he was sturdy and sharp, I was curved and supple. He fit into me, and I fit onto him, the two of us a lustrously merged power.

"This." I inhaled sharply. "Is the one thing I thank the Fates for. *You* are the only thing I will ever thank the Fates for."

Pyre roared in delight, my words stoking his need. "You are my *sōrza*," he declared. "My life, my everything." His declaration unlocked something new within me as my biology rippled in time. He was *my* life. He was my everything. *Mine*.

"Mine," I whispered, looking into his honey eyes. "Mine." I growled, feeling the claim more fiercely than ever. A desperate need to mark him as such clawed at my skin, tore at my gums as I felt a set of new, pointed teeth protract in my mouth. The wildfire within me completely ignored how strange this was, relishing in how good it felt.

"Yes," Pyre moaned, brows lifted in awe. "Mine." And with that declaration, I sank my teeth into his shoulder, tasting the hot blood on my tongue as I lay claim to the one who was woven into my soul. Pyre moved his face to look at me for a moment, his jaw dropped and eyes wide in wonder. "You claimed me." He blew. Before I could even think of a response, he released a tortured moan before he, too, descended on my shoulder and bit to claim me. My hips bucked in response and a molten pleasure racked my body. I let go of my bite to cry out as liquid pooled between my thighs at the rightness of this animalistic proclamation.

Nothing in this world could ever tear us apart. He was mine and I was his—in body, mind, and soul.

Removing his mouth from my shoulder, Pyre kissed me from collarbone to throat before finding my mouth again. When his lips captured mine, the taste of our blood mingle in the blazing passion of our kiss. My core tightened as he quickened his pace, my hips meeting his every demand.

"You are mine," Pyre roared, and I shattered in time with him as he tipped us both over the edge and into euphoria. A harsh white light rippled through the air as my body trembled and quaked. The muscles in my back tightened to the point of pain, and I winced as I felt the itching of my new scars tearing my skin. My bones buckled in the space between my shoulder blades as a sudden burning forced them apart. The pleasure quickly turned into pain as the release from our claiming ended, only to become something far more overwhelming.

"What's happening?" I screamed, the earlier passion turning to fear.

"Look at me," he demanded, pulling my face between his hands. He kissed me fiercely, and I felt some of the pain leave my body as the bright light continued to spread. A sharp thrust of liberation came from the middle of my back, and I gasped, finally feeling the agony ease. I felt heavier, exhausted, and let my head fall to the bed. My eyes flew to the white surrounding my body, not believing what I saw. Not only was my blonde hair now a shining silver brightness, but beneath me, spread out on the bed, was a pair of white glowing wings, the feathers dusted in a shimmer.

"What?" I gasped, marveling at what had to be a hallucination. When the wing twitched and I felt it through the muscles in my back, my breath halted in my chest. "What the flying fuck is that?"

"I'm assuming birthday wishes are in order," said Pyre, staring into my soul in a way I'd never felt before. I blinked, feeling confused but somehow aware of what had just happened.

"Huh?"

"How old are you now?" he asked, tugging my attention away from the wings.

"Is it December thirty-first?" I asked, finding that the time had gone by too quickly. There was no way several months had passed me by.

"The last day of Earth's calendar year."

I shook my head and felt a tug at the new extremities beneath me. "How is that possible?"

He shrugged a shoulder, then bent down to nuzzle my nose with his. A swarm of quieted butterflies rustled yet again in my belly. He kissed the tip of my nose before pulling away to look at me.

"Time moves differently in the Under Realm. What feels like a week could well be two or three on Earth. In this realm, we measure time by observing the light's placement in the sky. The seasons change at the same time as your Earth's equinoxes and solstices." I took a minute to attempt understanding, remembering bits and pieces of Gram's seasonal celebrations. My grandmother had always celebrated the equinoxes and solstices of the year. Gauging the time frame became a little easier as I remembered the traditions she upheld while I lived with her.

"I think I understand," I said, trying to digest all of this.

"So?" Pyre questioned, eyes still trained on me. He was so very alive in the moment. The gold in his gaze told me so.

"So, what?" I asked, befuddled.

He chuckled and brushed a strand of hair out of my face,

tucking it behind my ear. I shivered as I felt it slide over my shoulder and touch the sensitive wings I'd grown.

"How old are you?"

"Oh." I blew, shaking my head. "I guess I'm nineteen now."

"Nineteen, and fully ascended," said Pyre. "You are far stronger than I would have guess." I wrinkled my nose at him.

"What do you mean?" He smiled wistfully, regarding me in that knowing way.

"I was made to rule an entire realm, and I only ascended to full Godhood at age twenty-one. Your magic is stronger, quicker. You've become a full-fledged Goddess at nineteen. That's quite impressive."

"I see," I replied, the reality of my ascension sinking in. I was not going to go through the changes my family had gone through… Of course not. They were human witches. They would continue to age once their affinities manifested in full. But I was different. I would change like Pyre, like the gods. Pyre had stopped aging at twenty-one, and I would now remain nineteen forever. I wasn't sure how to feel about such a thing, as just a few months before, I'd have never thought this to be possible. More and more I was growing used to these immense changes. Whether it was healthy to digest such things so quickly, I did not know. So long as I was accepting my reality, it would be a good start to healing from all these life-altering changes and traumas.

Pyre leaned down and pressed a soft kiss to my forehead. "Welcome to godhood, *Sōrza*. It truly becomes you."

"I'm different," I murmured, tugging a strand of silver hair in front of my face. "My hair…"

"Is spun of moonlight," he told me, tugging the strand out of my hand. "And your eyes, forged by the sun."

"My eyes?" I gasped, foolishly trying to curl my eyes inward to see them. Pyre laughed and lifted himself from the bed. I tried to sit up, but the weight and pull of the wings that protruded from my back held me down. *My* wings. Pyre scooped a hand around my waist and lifted me into his arms, a hand firmly placed on my bare ass. I jumped at the touch, an embarrassing squeak leaving my lips as he carried me toward the bathroom.

He was careful not to brush my wings against the doorframe as he passed sideways through the door. In front of the mirror, our bodies reflected as he held me to his chest. Naked and heated, my eyes widened as I took in the sight of my new form. I hadn't realized that there would be any physical changes to my appearance. Gram hadn't mention anything of the sort, and from what I'd seen, my family all kept their looks throughout their lives. I hadn't considered our differences, but now, it was clear just how dissimilar I was. My family, the one I'd grown to know and love, were made up of cunning, powerful witches. But I was not a witch like them. I was a goddess—immortal. Here I was, living in the Under Realm, wrapped in the arms of its ruler. We stood in stark contrast to each other, the prophecy ringing through my mind. We were the embodiment of dark and light, and we would work together to keep our world safe.

My wings fluttered, almost as if they were in tune with my thoughts. The feeling was new, like a fresh wound healing. It was a good kind of soreness, and it was strange how quickly they felt right. In the mirror I found two pairs of glowing eyes. Pyre, whose eyes were filled with a liquid amber now matched mine, which shone a brighter version of gold. I touched the skin beneath my eyes, finding that the face indeed belonged to me.

"A claiming and an ascension all in one day. Appropriately extraordinary," Pyre remarked. There was an over-whelming gleam in his eye as he surveyed me.

"A claiming... That's what we did, isn't it?" I asked, looking up to the one I'd chosen. Though the Fates had undoubtedly forged our paths together, I had made the choice to choose him. I chose to walk this path with him, and I would choose him over and over again. I knew it more than ever now as something biologically clicked into place within me.

"We did far more than that." He smirked, then I watched the shape of his lips grow more serious. "Yes, *Sōrza*. We did," he answered, his face so intense and full of emotion. I understood all that he was feeling. I was feeling it too.

"What does that mean for us?" I wondered, lifting a hand to cup his cheek. He leaned into the touch and closed his eyes, thick lashes brushing against my fingertip. I studied his features, admiring his strong jaw and sharply arched brows. The perfect cupid's bow that shaped the top of his lip had me leaning in to brush a light kiss to its center. He took a moment to breathe, before opening his eyes again.

"You chose me," he said, his throat bobbing at the affirmation.

"*You* are *mine*," I told him, a throb lingering in my gums, reminding me of the surety in those words.

"We have always been one another's fate, but now, we are mated in soul." I inhaled shakily, remembering how I felt in the moments before, during, and after biting Pyre. I'd claimed him as my soulmate without fully understanding it. Now that I understood, fully comprehended just how right it was, a sense of calm filled me knowing that he'd claimed me too. "What has occurred between us is called a Primal Claim-ing. As gods, finding our soulmate is very rare," he said, brushing a finger down my cheek. "Seeing as how a mate can both be a blessing and a weakness, most of the gods tend to turn a blind eye when it comes to finding theirs. With mating, there is only ever one, and to have such a big part of who you are live in the heart of someone else is a dangerous thing for gods. If an enemy were to harm their mate, or worse, end their life, a part of the god dies with their mate." Rage boiled within me at the thought of someone ever hurting Pyre. I didn't even want to think of someone trying to kill him. If anyone ever even tried to get their hands on him, I would tear their heads from their shoulders. "Easy, *Sōrza*," Pyre soothed, running a hand down my side. "It's all right, my love." I took a steadying breath and calmed my mind as I let him stroke my bare skin.

"If I were to die," I said, then felt Pyre tense. He relaxed again to keep the slow rhythm on my flesh, and I continued my train of thought. "If I died, would you be able to find another mate?"

"Never." He growled, his fangs visible beneath the skin of his lips. "There will only ever be you."

I didn't want to think of one of us dying, and I certainly didn't like the jealousy that roused within me at the thought of Pyre ever being with another woman. But it was a valid question that I had to get off my chest.

"Only me?" I questioned, looking for any hint of this only being kind words, and not the truest meaning of it. The way his eyes bore into mine sent shivers up my tender spine as I saw just how deep this claiming ran.

"Only you," he vowed.

I closed my eyes as he kissed my forehead, savoring the intense feeling this brought forth. I opened my eyes again and looked into the mirror at the two of us. Though seeing myself naked with another person present was new, and the change in features were hard to swallow, the two of us, side by side proved how much we belonged together. Dark feathers lifted behind us, a shadow to my bright, shimmering wings.

"This is so strange," I said, looking over my new features.

"Not at all, Goddess," Pyre answered, and pulled my hair back to better see my face. "You are only seeing what I've known you were made of all along."

"And what is that?" I asked, looking away from the mirror to him.

"The most awe-striking form of light. My salvation."

59

INSUFFERABLE

SHIVALRI

"Hello?" called a chirpy, girly voice from the doorway. A short, slender blonde stood with one foot through the door, holding a woven basket filled with clothes.

"Izra," Pyre greeted her. "Come in."

The young woman came floating through, her form light and airy as she walked. When she reached us, she bowed in curtsey and placed the basket on the tufted bench, which sat at the foot of the bed. When her head dipped down, I caught sight of her green, pointed ears peeking through her hair.

"There are snaps sewn into the back of the dress, fitting the same as your wardrobe. They should fit just fine, though if adjustments are needed, I am happy to alter." She lifted the red dress adorned with golden flower patterns and turned it so as to show the back. "See here?" she said, pointing to two slits where my wings were meant to go. "Simply step into the dress and pull it up to your waist. Lift it up, put your arms through from the front, and fasten in the back from the middle. There is a snap at the top, and one just under the slits where the material will meet with the bottom." I tried to wrap my mind around the movements and decided I'd let Pyre help me into it the first time. Or, perhaps, every time.

"Thank you," I said, taking the dress from the girl.

"My pleasure," she answered sweetly, curtseying again before turning on her heel and leaving the room.

"She seemed nice," I said, looking to Pyre.

"She is. One of the best spinstresses at the palace."

"She's quite pretty too," I added, lifting a brow at him, checking to see what he thought of her. I'd seen a few ladies since being at the palace, and the smallest, darkest corner of my heart tugged at jealousy when I thought of them living here with Pyre. But I wasn't too concerned about them now. Certainly not after what we had just shared.

"All feïnyr were made with beauty in mind," he answered, toying with a piece of my hair. His hand trailed down my shoulder, hooking under the towel I wore. "You, Shivalri, were made with *me* in mind." My face heated at his words as I allowed them to sink in. We were really in this. The God of the Dead and the Bringer of Death were finally united in a way like none other.

"Hey, Pyre?" I asked, removing his sneaky finger from my person.

"Hmm?" he mused, his finger finding perch at the hem of the towel.

I swatted his hand away and he grinned wide, grabbing me by the waist and dipping me so that his body leaned over me. His teasing eyes watched my lips as if anything I might say would be the beginning of a seductive game.

"What about Gerimor?" I blurted, and he looked at me, unamused, and set me back upright.

"He will meet with us this eve."

I looked at him in shock. "What for?" I wondered aloud.

"He's going to tell us what he knows."

"You trust him?"

"With my life," he answered. I remembered the oath that Gerimor had sworn to me at the Orsimm cave and felt a rush of curiosity come over me. He'd pledged himself to me and said that he had pledged himself to the king of the Under Realm. Swearing to protect me while here in this realm, I wondered just how binding that oath was. Especially after Pyre had sworn that same oath before we met the Fates.

"Did you ask him to swear an oath to protect me?" I asked, now wondering how much Pyre had played a role in the situation.

"I did not have to," he said, the brightness in his eyes heating. "He knows how important you are, not only to me, but to our realm. Gerimor is the God of Death. You might find that you two have a lot in common. In fact, I think when paired together, death will feel far easier."

"How do you mean?" I questioned, wondering how I might fit into Gerimor' life.

"If you are the Bringer of Death, and he is the one in charge of its order, there is a connection there. With Greivos, too, I presume."

"Who's Greivos?"

He walked over to the window, pointing out to the distance. "Do you remember when I told you of the river Ondalôr?" he asked. I met with him at the window, trying to see what he could. I found that when I focused, my eyes were able to hone in past the trees.

"I can see!" I exclaimed, then rubbed my hands over my eyes, making sure it wasn't just a trick. When I looked again, it was like a focal lens had been place in front of me, and I could zoom in. "I mean, of course I can see, but, what the hell? I can see without glasses. I can see better than when I wore my glasses. What is this?"

"Most gods have perfect eyesight. It is a skill given to all of us."

I stilled at that. "Wait just a minute…" I said, and popped a squat, not caring about the towel that ruffled around me. *If I could see better now, would I feel better?* "Ugh." I groaned, rubbing at my knees. I lifted my hands afore my face, turning them over and examining my wrists and knuckles.

"What's wrong?" he asked, a look of concern occupying his expression. I looked up at him through my fingers, a little disappointment settling in my gut.

"The pain," I answered grimly. "It's still there."

He grabbed my hands from the air and ran his fingers over mine. "Your bones still hurt?" he asked, checking me over. He rubbed my knuckles with gentleness. "Does this hurt?"

"It feels wonderful," I admitted, letting a laugh find its way out of a dark place. He squeezed my hands in his, pulling them up to his mouth to kiss the tops of each. "But yes, the pain in my bones is still with me."

"I am sorry to hear," he told me, kissing them once more. "If the trouble with your eyes was not caused by disease, godhood should heal such things. The magic that comes with ascension can heal wounds that are made by cause and effect. If your flesh is wounded by sword, it will heal. It is not known to cure disease. Though, I must say, I have never met a God with your condition, so perhaps we should not rule it out of question."

I shook my head, shrugging it off. "It's all right. It's always been a part of me. I've never imagined it going away."

"Even still, I am sorry. If I could take your pain from you, I would."

I smiled at his words of kindness, and he pulled me into a

hug. My entire being settled into his warmth like second nature. He turned us around and pointed to the river again. I let my eyes work their magic and found the water he'd been referring to. It wasn't very far away, but in general, my eyes would never have been able to see such detail from this distance. It was amazing to have this ability.

"That is the river that travels between realms. It is the only entrance into the Under Realm from the Earthly Realm, aside from the Gates. You may only pass through if you are deceased, and you may only travel into the Under Realm if you have the funds. Greivos works for memories and coin. He will accept either for passage on his skiff."

"And you think I have something in common with a guy who takes memories from the dead?"

"He is the ferryman of the dead; the one who carries death into the Under Realm. You are the Bringer of Death. Is that not quite similar?" he questioned, turning into me.

"I don't like it," I fussed, and exhaled dramatically into his chest.

He let out a low laugh and ran a hand through my silver hair. "I like you like this," he mused, then placed a kiss on the top of my head. This sweet gesture was becoming a habit, and I loved it. "However," he began, pulling away. "I think I much prefer you like this." In an instant, his hands were between me and the towel, throwing it to the floor and leaving me nude in front of the giant window.

"Pyre!" I scoffed, running out from the window's sight. He caught up to me far faster than I could ever imagine and lifted me into his arms. "What is wrong with you?" I teased, pushing against his chest.

"What can I say?" He growled into my ear. "I'm enamored."

"Put me down, you giant,"—he stopped me with a kiss,

leaving me breathless—"insufferable—" I panted, but he kissed down my neck, leaving a spark of heat at my collarbone, making me dizzy. "Beautiful, terrible, perfect fool."

"Perfect?" He growled, nipping at my shoulder. I jumped at the contact, and when I grabbed him with both hands on either side of his face, I kissed him until I saw stars behind my eyes. "Beautiful," he said, breathing heavily between kisses. "Insufferable, terribly perfect enchantress." I bit my lip at his words, letting him see my grin. "What spell have you cast on me?" I pulled him in again, not wanting any time between us wasted. Pyre laughed into me, and I tore my lips from his to see what the fuss was about.

"What?" I gasped through ragged breaths. He put his forehead to mine, inhaling deeply.

"Gerimor has excellent timing." He sighed, putting me down. "Let's get you dressed before the God of Death finds himself in the middle of a very heated spectacle."

"He's here?" I shrieked, trying to cover myself with the bed's blanket, which was the closest thing to me now. Pyre strode forward, grabbing the dress from the bench.

"He's not in our bedroom, as you can plainly see." He grinned, gesturing to the closed door. I marked how he'd said *our* bedroom, and stored that memory for later, knowing I'd be happy playing it over again when I was gone. The dimming sentiments of what was to come today washed over me, and I was suddenly feeling very unwell. I clutched the blanket to my chest, pressing the velvety material in my hands. Pyre held the dress out in front of me and lowered so that I could step into it. One after the other, my legs did what they were supposed to do, and Pyre lifted the dress over my hips. He opened the sleeves for me, and mechanically, I put each one through as he pulled it over my chest. The slight boning in the top kept my breasts supported, and I was thankful not to have to wear a bra with it.

Pyre made his way around me, and I heard the audible inhalation as he stared at my back. I felt a finger trace my skin and understood that he was looking at the scars I'd forced my magic to make. Where I'd normally be protected from my element, I'd been able to use my fire and allowed the barrier to come down as I pictured myself carving the words into my flesh. I would carry this reminder with me everywhere I'd go—*Abrôrta dhèjl Ôhrtum*—Bringer of Death.

60

SEED

SHIVALRI

"Gerimor," Pyre greeted as the God of Death met us in a large room fit for a king. The two gods clasped forearms, then fisted a hand over heart.

"Good morning, Lord Mortades." The golden-haired god bowed, making his white, wispy tendrils billow around him. "It is fine to see you well."

"And you," said Pyre, releasing the handshake and replacing his hand on the small of my back.

"And you, my... lady? What shall I call you?" Gerimor asked.

"She is called *Abrôrta dhèjl Ôhrtum* by the Fates," said Pyre, answering for me. Gerimor's eyes widened in time to mine as Pyre revealed this information so freely. I cleared my throat and took a step forward, asserting myself. That would have been my information to share, but I supposed if Pyre trusted this god enough to give him these details, then I would have told him either way.

"She is typically used to being called Shivalri," I corrected, nudging Pyre in the ribs. "And she can speak for herself." Gerimor grinned at the God of the Dead, eying the two of us as if enjoying the fire between us.

"She is good for you," Gerimor joked.

"She is vexing in the best of ways." The heat in my cheeks grew hotter at Pyre's words.

"Which is it, then?" Gerimor asked me, a tick in his eyes evidently entertained. Pyre sighed heavily, looking to me.

"My apologies," said Pyre, affording me a slight bow. "The gods are meant to use their ruling title or alias given by the gods before them, their creators. You, my *sōrza*, are an anomaly. The Fates gave you a title, but did not give you an alias; rather, your alias was given to you by the humans who raised you. Though you may prefer that one, the gods typically go by their fated names. You were given your title here in the Under Realm, so typically, that's what you should be called. Though I don't go by my primary title or alias willingly, it is what most call me."

"Your given name is Mortades?" I questioned, feeling a tingle on my tongue as I realized it was the first time that I'd spoken that name in front of him. He nodded, face unflinching. "Why did you tell me your name was Pyre Malum?" I wondered, finding it odd that only I would call him something different.

"Because when the gods named me Mortades, they'd declared my destiny as God of the Under Realm. I was deemed *Xïeuhre dhèjl zràhl Ôhrxe*—God of the Dead. I was created to do nothing more than rule over the dead. I never liked not having a say in my life." As he paused for a moment, I began to understand where he was coming from. To be born for misery would be a lifetime filled with sorrow. "When it was decided that the separate realms were to be created, the Fates, in preparing me for my role, spoke to me in all the world's languages, making sure I learned who I was for all the deceased. In their many prophetic verses, the one thing that was told boldly was that I was to be the fuel for evil. A Pyre for Malum."

"You mean to tell me I've been calling you fuel for evil all this time?" I shrank away in horror, throwing a hand over my mouth.

"*You* call me *Pyre*," he said, and I suddenly recalled him being upset with me when I'd used his full name. "I seem to remember you calling me *perfect* too." I slapped him in the arm and swore under my breath.

"I, for one, refuse to use that name," said Gerimor, pulling my attention to him. "He's very much a tortured soul. He castigates himself however he can manage, and I do not condone such things; therefore, I do not call him Pyre Malum." He turned to the God of the Dead and flashed a knowing smile. "You'll be sorry to hear I will not be calling you *perfect* either."

"Gerimor," Pyre warned, but the God of Death only widened his smiled.

"What shall I call you?" asked Gerimor, turning to me again. "It is up to you." I thought about it for a moment, considering this. Never before had I given my name a second thought. For a while now, I hadn't liked being referred to as Goddess, since I couldn't believe it was true. Yet, here I stood, silver haired and carrying a set of white, shining feathered wings. I'd liked the name my parents had given me, but now, Shivalri felt far away. *Abrôrta dhèjl Ôhrtum*, on the other hand, was engraved in my seared skin. But that was a mouthful, unlike the name Pyre had chosen.

"I would like to be called Shivalri," I decided, just giving my first name. My family would still call me Shivalri Acadia Grimsbane-Gray, for with them, that's who I'd always be. Here, in the place where immortality coursed through my veins, I would be what all realms needed from me, but I would do it with my entire heart, and that would require staying true to who I am. I would be the Bringer of Death, and I would do it in a way to bring peace to our world, keeping the cataclysm at bay. I would always be Shivalri.

I suddenly understood the similarity between Gerimor and me. He'd been described as the God of Peaceful Death, and I would do everything in my power to help him maintain that. I was also going to improve things, and he would benefit from it. My existence and fate all came down to a flip of the coin as to whether death would be chaotic on account of the world's end or become something fair for all souls.

"Shivalri," he chimed, his white tendrils dancing through my hair. "Lovely to meet you in godhood." He held out a hand and clasped my own, shaking it once in welcome. "Now that we've passed the pleasantries, let us convene in private."

I looked around, confused by the suggestion that we were anywhere near other people. The room was huge and empty, save for the three of us.

"She's here?" Pyre, scoffed. "Matrine," he called, a look of disgust lingering on his face. A tall, slender feïnyr appeared from behind a curtain, slinking toward us with the swish of her hips. Eyes like a snake and hair sleek and shining, the woman was absolutely stunning. The way her eyes roamed over me turned my curiosity into animosity the minute she sneered my way. She scoffed at me like I was a piece of dirt in comparison to her glittering, barely-there dress, which draped perfectly off her shoulder. The way her gaze belittled me would have been enough to make me dislike the woman, but the way she turned to look at Pyre set a flame so hot I felt it melting my bones.

"And who might this creature be?" The woman grimaced,

her tapered almond eyes, tiny nose, and angular cheekbones prominent in her loathing expression.

"Leave, Matrine." Pyre snarled, and the way she looked at him made me think there was far too much history between the pair. She flicked her straight hair over her shoulder, revealing prominent collarbones as she sluggishly made her way past us. Bumping into my shoulder hard enough to make me stumble, she turned around to look at me, and scoffed.

"Oops," she muttered, a play of innocence on her face. Pyre whirled, making to defend me. Before I could tell myself to stop, I threw out my magic, growing a lashing vine straight through the floor, and wrapped it around her ankle. I yanked it back with just enough force to trip her, finding that it took no effort at all. When she tripped, trying to find purchase, I let go of the vine and let it turn to ash.

"Oops," I said, smiling like a feline who'd caught its unsuspecting prey. Her face shone the shock and fear I'd known would come, and even though I felt a small piece of pity for the feïnyr, I did enjoy my fill of watching her leave in a haste.

"I quite liked that display," Gerimor sounded before passing to close the door behind Matrine. Pyre was too stunned to speak as he looked between the door and me.

"What?" I asked, feeling playful and far too powerful for my own good. "It was an accident." I shrugged, unable to hide the grin. Pyre's brows knitted together as he gawked at me. "Too much?" I asked, feeling a little guilty.

"Not in my lifetime," he answered, running a hand through obsidian hair. My grin turned to a smile, and I bit my lower lip, watching the God of the Dead consider me. I let my power rise again, ordering a new vine to lift from the floor. With Pyre looking at me, he didn't notice it sneak up behind him. I gave him a playful wink, then slapped his ass with the plant. He jumped, turned to find the vine, and swatted it away, turning it to ash as I had done to the other. Pyre shook his head and laughed as he took my arm in his, leading me to the table where Gerimor was waiting patiently.

Pyre pulled a chair for me, and I sat without hesitation. I was nervous to delve into Gerimor's knowledge, but I knew it was important we do so. It was the whole reason he'd come to us in the first place. With Pyre at my side, I sat up straight, feeling anxious, and waited for someone to start explaining. When I found that the two of them were staring at me, a wave of self-consciousness passed over me. Every time I met someone new, worse things were revealed. What was Gerimor here to tell us? Why was he looking at me like I was the answer to his problems? Why couldn't I breathe? I began panicking, my breathing coming in and out in short pants. I saw blurring stars cross my vision, and just past those stars, I found a shocked look on Gerimor's face.

"What's the matter?" I asked, concerned; the panic coming in stronger.

"You're glowing, Lady Shivalri," Gerimor said, and I caught Pyre looking tense in the corner of my eye. I lifted a hand in front of me and found that my skin had been illuminated from the inside out.

"Weird…" I muttered, lifting my hand to scratch at my tightening throat. Pyre took my hand from my neck and rubbed his thumb over my fingers. I watched as the glow slowly faded and realized my nerves had gotten the best of me. "Sorry," I apologized, feeling a bit uncomfortable.

"Don't be," said Pyre, reassuring me with each stroke he placed on my fingers. "I am worried too," he admitted, and my heart sank at the obvious display of sincerity and concern. "Whatever Gerimor has to say will only help us."

"I don't want to be scared, but I can't help think of what the Fates showed me."

"You went to the Fates?" Gerimor gasped, leaning forward so that his arms lay on the table in front of him.

"Yes," said Pyre. "That is how we know she is called the Bringer of Death. We now know more of what we're meant to face. The prophecy is real, and it's been in motion for quite some time."

"I see," said Gerimor, pondering as he studied me. "I can feel it." He was sombre and frank. "Either the end is near, or a new beginning comes. Regardless, death will follow."

"I know," I said, finding my voice. "There will be a great loss no matter which path I take. But with the new beginning, there's a better chance that death will be different, improved. If I can repair the veil, and keep the Gates closed, it will keep the realms safe."

"You are fully ascended; therefore, you do retain the power to do such things. You are officially the Triple Goddess." Gerimor's words sunk through me as all the doubt, unknown and wonder was finally put to rest. I had become the Triple Goddess in every way possible. I no longer waited to receive my affinities and Godhood. I was officially the goddess who ruled the three realms, made to keep them safe for all. "However," Gerimor said, interrupting my train of thought. "To repair the veil, you'll have to use all of your strength," Gerimor explained. "To repair the veil and close the Gates all at once is asking far too much."

"How do you mean?" I asked. I thought that after ascendency, after becoming a full-fledged Triple Goddess, I would have no trouble accessing these powers of mine.

"To survive depletion of power, to then open the Gates, pass through, and then close it with the spill of your blood... You cannot do it all in one day."

"It will need to be done immediately," Pyre started, frustration and worry taking over his features. "We do not know when or how my brother and the Orsimm will strike." The God of Death thought for a moment, tapping his fingers atop the table. He studied me with familiar eyes and relinquished the finger tapping.

"If she wishes to accomplish all of this at once, she will need to borrow the strength of another," said Gerimor, looking to Pyre. "Will this be you?"

Pyre nodded, squeezing my hand under the table. "She will repair the veil while in the Under Realm, and I will give her all my strength, so that she can lock the Gates Earthside after passing through." Suddenly, the gravity of this exchange felt far too real for my liking. I still didn't want to do it. I wished for more time to consider my options. I couldn't imagine myself sealing the Gates shut for good and leaving Pyre alone in the Under Realm. I knew that it was what I had to do because there were no other options. None that I'd been given as of yet. I had to put away my feelings, put away Pyre's, and consider the greater good of such an action. The connection between us would never go away, and I would have to live with the fact that I could never see him again. I would have to, because if I didn't, everyone else, living, and dead, would suffer the consequences. Perhaps I'd learn to travel between the realms unnoticed without disrupting the veil and Gates.

"Are you prepared?" asked Gerimor, turning to me. A shiver ran over me, a feeling of dread pooling in my gut.

"Prepared how?" I asked, looking between the two gods who watched me.

"Have all of your affinities manifested in you?"

"Oh." I nodded. "I can call upon all five," I answered, remembering the uproar at the Orsimm cave. It had been the first and only time that all my powers came to me at once, and it had been a startling affair. I hadn't asked my affinities to come to me, though I imagine that if I had, they might have come tenfold. With that knowledge, I knew that my power would be able to handle the tasks ahead. It was my heart that I didn't trust to follow through.

"Good," said Gerimor, taking a long, deep breath as he leaned back in his chair. "Now, about your brother." He sighed, looking to Pyre. The God of the Dead grew hot at my side at the mention of the god who'd marred his back. I, too, hated his brother.

"What do you know?" Pyre demanded, and I steeled my spine in preparation.

"He knows about the prophecy, knows about you, Shivalri," he said, grimly. "The Orsimm have been speaking with him through dreams for a long while now. It was Ombrose who was sent to find you. He was ordered to send you nightmares, in hopes to uncover your secrets and power."

"I knew it!" I hissed, remembering Ombrose's mistake. He had told me that nightmares were not given but slipped into by the sleeper. Yet later, he had accidentally said that he'd intentionally given me a nightmare; the two pieces of information clashed with one another.

"How do you mean?" Pyre asked, eyes wide in confusion and shock.

"Ombrose slipped up when we were talking about nightmares one night. He'd told me that he couldn't force nightmares upon people, but later said he'd *given* me a nightmare in order to help find me. That's how he knew I was at the castle, and evidently, how he came to find me."

"I cannot wait to feed him to his worst nightmare." Pyre growled, an unholy sound alive in his chest. I held his hand tightly, afraid that if I let go, he might leave to pursue that need.

"So, you've had your own suspicions about Ombrose as well?" Gerimor asked, redirecting my attention from Pyre to the problem at hand.

"Yes." I nodded, and realized that there were things even Pyre still did not know. If we were going to get to through this, I'd need to tell these gods everything, starting from the beginning.

"What is it?" Pyre asked, seeming to catch my thoughts in my frown.

"I didn't realize it at first." I exhaled, rubbing the spot between my brows that ached from the stress of the situation. "At least not right away. But I already knew Ombrose before ever having met him."

Pyre's eyes visibly widened in disbelief. "How so?" he asked, incredulous. I rubbed his hand under the table in reassurance.

"When he came to the castle, I recognized his voice. At first, it only sounded familiar, but as I came to understand who he was, and what he does as a god, I understood immediately." I paused, considering how to explain what Ombrose and I had shared, how we were connected. "When I was home, on Earth, I mean, I used to have these terrible night terrors. I was always living my worst fears, pushed to the point of exhausted anxiety. When the nightmare came to be too much, when I thought my mind couldn't take it anymore, I'd hear someone speaking to me, as if to sooth me. Once the words cleared the scarier visions away, my nightmare would always end in the skies. It was like a calming end to the storm. The nightmare would allow me peace in the final moments until I woke. When it was brought up in conversation, Ombrose explained to me that he's never been able to speak to someone through a nightmare, and that when he found me, saw that I understood his words, he kept coming back to me when I screamed for help or from fear."

"How is that possible?" Gerimor groused, brows furrowed in deep thought.

"Ombrose suggested it was because I wasn't entirely mortal. He said that when he visits the nightmares of mortals, he can't do anything but watch and try coaxing the dreamer into fighting their fears. But with me, it was always different."

"When did you begin suspecting that Ombrose had been deceiving you?" asked Gerimor. Pyre's chest rose in anticipation.

"Like I said, he slipped up. First, he was telling me that he felt bad for my nightmares and was trying to help me. Next, he'd accidentally admitted to intentionally giving me the nightmares." I stopped to think about this for a moment, the clues lining up with recent events. "I think he's been spying on me through nightmares for a really long time now."

"Spying on you for my brother, then," Pyre stated, without a fragment of doubt in his mind. "My brother has known of you for far longer than I ever could have imagined. He must have known of you far longer than I, if Ombrose was in your nightmares while you were on Earth."

"A very long time," I disclosed, feeling icky from knowing that he'd been watching me all this time. I had had a stalking god studying me in the most indecent, vulnerable way. I let him see my worst fears, and he thrived within them. I shivered at the thought and curled my hands around my arms, feeling unwell at the intrusion.

"The question that remains quite heavy on my tongue," started Gerimor, placing a thumb and forefinger around his blonde chin, "is how and why would the Lord of Sky know of you?"

"I imagine he's been searching for the Triple Goddess reincarnate since Shivalri's conception," said Pyre, reminding me that he, too, had been searching for me.

"Yes, but that doesn't explain how he could have known it was her." Pyre grumbled at this, because just as he didn't have any answer, neither did I or Gerimor. "There must be a connection. We just aren't seeing it."

"When my powers awakened in me, and the veil tore, the skies on Earth turned a ruby red. Perhaps that's what had alerted him to my rise?"

"Is that when you started hearing Ombrose in your night-mares?" Pyre asked, his eager face making my gut plunge.

"No." I faltered, realizing that he'd come just before. "It was before my mom died."

"It cannot be a coincidence," said Gerimor.

"I just don't understand. There's so much missing from the mystery that I can't seem to land on anything that could help us figure out what Ombrose plans to do with me." I frowned, remembering the game was far bigger than the measly God of Nightmares. "Rather, I don't know what your brother wants to do with me," I said, throwing a look at Pyre. "All I know is that whatever it leads to, looks like the end of the world if I allow him to do as he pleases."

"Which brings us back to the root topic," said Gerimor. "If you do, indeed, wish to prevent that from happening, we will have to work on repairing the veil."

"Precisely," said Pyre, making my skin grow cold and clammy.

"It is very simple, and I have seen our original Triple Goddess do this many, many centuries ago."

"What?" I gasped, an electric wave of shock passing over

me. "You knew her?" I gawked, then whirled on Pyre, who was wearing an odd look on his face. "Wait. You knew her too, didn't you?" I said, accusatorily. "Gods, I'm witless." Pyre let out a brief, quiet laugh, and lifted a hand to tuck a loose strand of silver hair behind my ear. "You told me that the Triple Goddess was made to create the split. The Fates allowed her the gift of all five elements, making her more powerful than most other gods. You were there when it happened, and she, herself, placed you in the Under Realm. Both of you!" I gasped, looking over the God of the Dead and God of Death in a new kind of way. I had been undoubtedly caught up in the whirlwind, always on the run and worrying what horrors might come with each passing day. It was easy to forget how old and how powerful the people I'd met down here were. Pyre had lived a million lives before me, and I was just getting started with mine. "Where is the Triple Goddess now?" I questioned, voice breaking wearily in tune to the quickening heartrate that thundered in my chest.

"Gone," said Pyre, and I found that with the close of his eyes, he felt sad for this.

"Sorceficia is at peace in the void. She is one with Pandaos, having served her purpose. It is because of you that she is reunited with her ancestors, finally able to rest."

"I don't understand," I said, feeling the lump in my throat forming. "She wanted this?"

"She did. She was made solely to divide and protect the realms. She took roll of guarding the realms very seriously, but she knew that eventually, one day, she would like to go to peace. Making a deal with the Fates at conception, she asked for a replacement, which would come whenever the Fates declared it time."

"The Fates are to blame for what's to come then." I held,

finding that I should have already understood this. I knew that the Fates were the cause of everything.

"There is no blaming the Fates, child," Gerimor warned. "Everything happens with reason. There is always a greater purpose in mind."

"Gerimor," Pyre finally said, breaking his silence. I hadn't realized his quiet until he spoke beside me. "Are you telling me that Sorceficia told you of the deal she'd strung with the Fates?" A moment of pause creeped over our table as Gerimor considered how much to divulge. When Pyre leaned forward, fists clenched atop the table, Gerimor let out a slow, heavy sigh.

"Did you think the love of my life would have kept her secrets from me?"

"You—" I stammered, not believing my ears.

"Yes, Lady Shivalri. My love is gone, and she has taken my heart with her."

"Gerimor." Pyre breathed, running a hand through his hair. "Why didn't you tell me before now?"

"Oh, Mortades… When one knows a piece of the future, they must not share it with others. You know this. We cannot alter what is to come by trying to prevent it with future's knowledge."

"Do you know how Shivalri was made?" he asked. I physically felt my body turn inside out at the mention of this. Pyre was referring to my parents, the ones who were my blood relatives. My heart ached at the reminder that my parents, the ones I'd grown up with, were not my real relatives. My mother birthed me, and I used to look like her before I fully ascended. And still, that was not enough to make her my bloodline. A sudden pang of regret welled in me as I pulled a strand of silver hair forward. I had been so eager to cover up the dark ginger tone that matched my mother's.

Now, it had been stripped away from me, revealing the true nature of my traits, which were hidden beneath a spell to better hide the fact that I wasn't mortal.

"Sorceficia's deal with the Fates was to have a replacement. When the time was right, she would be given a life seed in which she could use to enter Pandaos. I do not know from who the seed came, but it had to be made of godly immortals. She told me it was harvested from celestials."

"That explains her tie to the Celestial Realm, but what of the Under Realm?" asked Pyre for me. I was far too stunned to speak.

"As you well know, the Fates do not grant favors unless promised something in return," Gerimor stated. "The Triple Goddess had to give up all her powers, which are native to the Under Realm. They are the very powers that allowed her to create the separate realms and keep them guarded. Hence, the reason Shivalri now has all five elemental affinities, and is tied to the Under Realm. For Sorceficia to leave, she would need to be replaced, completely. When the seed was delivered, she spilled all of her magics into it and planted it in the first human witch she'd ever created. The witch, of course, was sent to Earth, giving Shivalri connection to the third and final realm. The seed was passed down from generation to generation, until finally, it was released into the world, bringing the prophecy to life." Gerimor looked away from the table, staring into nothing, which seemed to be everything to him. "Taking my love from me in the blink of an eye..." he added, before shaking his head and returning to us.

"I am sorry," said Pyre, voice far softer than I'd expected. He looked at me longingly, my heart breaking at the implication of his stare. "I can truly empathize."

I lowered my gaze, not willing to feel these things just yet. Not ready to give up the person my soul was bonded to.

61

GAME

SHIVALRI

"Your adrenaline is spent, seeing as how you've just recently ascended into godhood," Gerimor explained. "Though I do agree that it is imperative for you to repair the veil and seal the Gates, you will not be able to do so any time soon, even with my lord's aid. Certainly not today."

My heart and head fought tooth and nail to win the battle over my emotions at his declaration. I knew how important it was for me to get this done and over with. I understood the dangers of allowing more time for Pyre's brother and the Orsimm to strike. Yet my heart was doing summersaults in my ribcage, setting fireworks to life at the mere thought of my having more time with the God of the Dead, who was doing a very bad job at trying to hide the very same battle within himself. His clenched jaw and tight shoulders told me that he was at war with his molten amber eyes, which looked at me with such yearning, I wanted to reach up and kiss the lids of each right here in front of Gerimor.

"How much time?" asked Pyre, who seemed to look to the God of Death for answers often.

"Time will tell. You will know when you're ready," he assured me, giving me a knowing smile, which only put me in unease as it allowed the belligerent feelings to stir even further.

"Ombrose told me that I only had until nightfall to decide which role I'd play in this. What if he tries to attack?"

Pyre huffed a dry laugh, his feathered wings ruffling behind him. "Ombrose is the least of my concerns."

"She has a point, Mortades," said Gerimor.

"It is my brother we must worry for," Pyre stated, those beautifully golden eyes of his dimming into a touch of redness.

"That is precisely what I am referring to. Your brother, the Lord of Sky, has been in contact with Ombrose and likely all of the Orsimm. You know how I feel about Reaver, but I will not cross him off our list yet. Nevertheless, the Lord of Sky has given us enemies we once considered allies. And if he can reach them here, who is to say he cannot reach Shivalri?"

"I don't believe it works that way," said Pyre, leaving me curious and intrigued to find that he'd had an untold theory. "Ombrose was able to reach you on the Earthly Realm and in the Under Realm through your nightmares. After your nightmare last night, you told me that you believed Dramael and Tasphen to be involved. That leads me to believe that the Orsimm are able to seek out whoever they wish while they're at work in the minds of the sleeping."

"So, it's them who reached out to your brother, and not the other way around?" I questioned, piecing the theory together.

"I believe so. I think they do his bidding where he is unable to."

"Hmm..." Gerimor grunted, considering this as a valid possibility.

"It only makes sense," said Pyre, leaning back in his chair. I didn't miss how his wing spread out and touched the back of my own. In fact, I couldn't miss it even if I tried, as the new feathered entities attached to my back were unbelievably sensitive. A tingle ran through the boning of my new extremities, and I had to stop myself from uttering inappropriate groans. "They are in power to give all beings slumber, dreams, fantasies, and nightmares. What is stopping them from learning to communicate with him, just as they did with her?"

"I think you're right," I blurted, shuddering under the touch behind me. "What can your brother do if he's not the one playing the cards?" I wondered.

Pyre quirked an amused brow my way. "Oh, darling. He's dealing them."

I grimaced at his quick work to catch up with the idiom I frequently used when referring to the mess I was in. I'd always thought of it like a game, trapped within it like an unlucky pawn.

"Great." I rolled my eyes, finding that I was quite exhausted.

"That is why you will need to rest and gather all your strengths as quickly and healthfully as possible," Gerimor interjected. "You know what to do when the time comes?"

I nodded, having understood the basics of what would happen. "I'm supposed to call upon all five elements, and bleed somewhere, which will give me the power to repair the lifted veil."

"Not just anywhere," Gerimor corrected. "You will have to find a sacred space, somewhere untainted and safe for you."

"Where am I going to find that?" I asked, finding it hard to imagine a place in the Under Realm that would be untainted.

"You will build it, with my help," said Pyre. I looked at him in confusion. "Remember how I explained that the feïnyr were responsible for creating the fake forests here?" I nodded, not entirely sure where he was going with this. "You can produce *real* life. You've done it time and time again since being in the Under Realm. If we combine strengths, and you will it, you can grow a sacred space—your own personal garden. It is done with blood magic and the elements, and it will be far easier for you than any feïnyr, as you have all five affinities where feïnyr are only born with one each. With my blood, the Under Realm will accept the space as a part of it."

"Blood magic?" I squirmed in my seat, remembering all the bad that came with the High Council using blood magic against me.

"It is I who will bleed for you," he reassured. "You will only need to bleed to repair the veil and close the Gates."

I nodded, feeling utterly unsure, but still knowing that it was the price I'd have to pay in the end. "Is there some kind of spell I should learn to do it?" I asked, looking to the two gods, who looked every bit the opposite, though the kindness in their façade were a match. "My grandmother uses phrases to cast spells and enchantments. The High Council did too," I said, reminding Pyre of what had occurred during my last day in the Earthly Realm.

"But you are not a witch like them," he reminded me, though that didn't answer my question. "You shall simply will it, and it will answer to your call. You are the Triple Goddess now." I looked to Gerimor, who was far, far away from the conversation by the gaze in his eyes. I couldn't imagine what my replacing Sorceficia had done to him. How long ago had he lost her? How terribly alone he must feel.

"Okay." I swallowed hard, feeling the weight of my destiny tenfold.

"I will be with you," said Pyre, running a hand over my thigh, and giving a reassuring squeeze.

"I, too," said Gerimor. "You will need someone on guard, to make sure you are protected and safe."

"Thank you, Uncle," Pyre said, making me realize just how badly I was at sorting through realizations. Of course, Gerimor was his uncle. He had called Ombrose his cousin. And if Gerimor was Pyre's uncle, then Dramael must be too.

"Will the pythrants be at the ready in case of intrusion?" the God of Death asked.

Pyre nodded affirmatively. "They are aware of the situation," he ground through gritted teeth, and a flash of their battle in the castle wavered in the back of my mind.

"Are they working for Ombrose?" I wondered, thinking of Nor and his desperately hopeful eyes before he'd jumped onto my back, forcing me to fall, having already accepted his own death.

"They are not," he said. "Those who refused to understand are no longer in my service." I blanched at that. I had a sinking feeling that those who refused to understand no longer existed.

"It is settled, then," Gerimor spoke pragmatically. "When you relax from the ascendency's high, and are able to wield your elements without strain, we will begin." He stood from the table rather abruptly and fisted a hand over his heart in salutation.

"We will send word in time," Pyre told him.

Before Gerimor could leave the room, I left my seat to find him on the other side of the table and extended a hand to him. He looked from me to Pyre, as if questioning, and then offered me his hand. I looked up into the eyes, which were the color of my old ones and found a genuine man behind them. The God of Death was kind and peaceful, and I was glad to see it.

"Thank you, Gerimor," I said, and before I knew it, I pulled him into a hug. The god released a sharp inhalation, rigid beneath my touch. I pulled away from him, arms still wrapped around the light-haired god, and watched him settle into the affection.

"It is my honor, Goddess," he replied, knitting his brows together. "She would have liked you very much, I think." I caught the crack in his voice at the mention of his lost love and crumbled under the weight of his regard.

"For what it's worth, I will try to do right by her," I said, releasing him and taking a step back. "I'm going to fix what I broke. And then, when I'm ready, I will make the world a better, safer place."

62

VENTURE

SATYRA

One minute we were fighting back the drifting snow on the Canadian mountain peak, and the next we were on the doorstep of the most breathtaking palace I'd ever seen. I could never forget the first time I'd seen it through the eyes of Ember Blackwood. When he had shown me this palace through a see-walk, the true depth of its beauty hadn't been as clear as it was now as I stood in front of the guards who held long sticks with pointed ends. Now I knew they were spears, and very deadly when properly wielded. I had watched as Kaede and Wulfric trained together while using them, each of them a lethal warrior, capable of ending anyone who might cross their paths.

"This is where your father lives?" Raidan gawked as Nesrin stood ahead of us. She didn't answer him as she took the first step on the staircase.

"State your name and purpose," one of the guards demanded in a heavily Irish accent, his red beard moving with the motion of his words.

"Nesrin Mehra, reporting to General Mehra for council," she declared, loud and proud with shoulders tight.

"Lieutenant," the four soldiers said in unison, each bowing their heads and driving their spears into the ground.

"Welcome," said the bearded one as he lifted his head. "We are sorry not to have recognized you," he apologized, lowering his gaze for a moment in respects. "Your father will be waiting for you in the command core. I will escort you to him."

"That will be unnecessary, Baird. These are Ember Blackwood, Wulfric Hallows, and Kaede Rin."

"And what of the other two?" he questioned, holding his stance.

"I am afraid you and your friends do not have clearance to that information," Nesrin answered, command in her voice. Raidan gave me a look of awe as we listened to the exchange.

"Lieutenant," Baird protested, but hushed at the tilt in Nesrin's jaw. "Very well," he replied, clearing his throat before moving to the door and unlocking it with a loud thud.

"Come," Ember said to me as he took my arm in his. The messenger bag that was slung across his shoulders was wedged between our bodies. I would have objected had it not been for Raidan's arm being taken in the same manner by Nesrin just ahead of me. I understood that it was not done in a comforting gesture, rather, as a means of showing authoritative protocol.

Just as I'd seen through the see-walk, the bland, slate gray corridors were filled with men and women, all dressed in black leathers and watching eyes. The bodies moved out of our way, indicating that the group of rebels Raidan and I had walked in with were not to be provoked or disturbed.

"All of these people… They're rebels too?" I asked quietly into Ember's ear.

"Yes," he answered, gaze straight ahead and latched on the red door waiting for us.

SHANIA SCICHILONE

"Do they know who we are?" I wondered, making short eye contact with a man who passed by.

"Only some of us do," he replied, still focused onward.

"Why?"

He looked down at me from the corner of his eyes and gave me a warning look. "Later," he said, both silencing and promising. As Nesrin disappeared behind the red door, Raidan, Wulfric, and Kaede followed, Ember and I trailing after them.

Just as it was in the see-walk, the room was built rounded with a long table in its center, and a thick desk at the far wall. A hexagonal stained-glass window framed the back of the desk, casting cobalt blue and canary yellow lighting into the room. All the furniture was made of a dark stained wood, looking severely antique, yet here due to proper care and a decorative purpose.

"Princess," the tall, dark man greeted, clasping Nesrin's arm. "So good to see you, Daughter." She gave her father a firm handshake with both hands clasped around his. Lifting her arms above their faces, she bowed her head in formal greeting. I turned to find that Ember, Kaede, and Wulfric had their own hands clasped together and held above their heads, bowing to the general just as Nesrin did. I almost moved to do the same, but they all released their holds, preventing me from doing something awkward or offensive.

"General Mehra," Ember addressed. "Please, meet Raidan and Satyra Grimsbane." The general held our stares with a lifted, harsh chin, and in this moment, I saw the shared trait Nesrin had learned from her father.

"Grimsbanes." He held, straightening his already perfect garb. Running a hand down the yellow embroidery lining the buttons, the general exuded a certain self-possession I'd never seen before. He took a slow, measured breath as he studied us. I felt the pressure of his gaze, feeling the power he held with just a simple look. "I would say it is a pleasure to meet you both, though I find lies entirely unavailing." I swallowed hard, remembering that this was the leader of the congregation, the head of the rebellion, and more than ever, I needed to make a good impression. I knew that the rebels shared the same goal as me and my family, yet standing here with his powerful presence, I got the sense that Raidan and I would have to earn his help, earn his respect.

"It isn't a lie for us," Raidan said, surprising me with his boldness. "The circumstances are trying, but for us, meeting you means hope."

The circumstances are trying... Who was this guy and where did he learn this kind of wording? It quickly donned on me that Raidan spent a lot of time playing video games and watching high-fantasy films. This was probably like living in a version of one of those fictional scenes.

"I suppose it would," General Mehra replied, and reached a hand toward my cousin. With more confidence than I would have expected, Raidan took the general's arm, and the two exchanged acknowledgment. "And you," the man in blue turned to me. "Would you suppose our meeting is a means for hope?" The man came forward to greet me personally, and I kept my feet firmly planted to the floor, unsure whether I was allowed to move toward him. "Hmm?" he questioned further as he took his place before me.

"I suppose our meeting is a product of our mutual goals," I replied, finding my voice. The general's eyes darkened as he stared down at me.

"Which is what, exactly?"

"Save the world," I said, swallowing dryly. "Save my family. Put an end to the assholes who sacrificed my cousin and kidnapped my grandmother." Everyone in the room froze at my reply. Kaede, who was usually blasé, had bulging eyes as they and the others looked at each other, waiting for the general's reply.

The man's chin lowered, eyes narrowing before suddenly, a crack in his lips revealed a heavy, rounded laugh. It was my turn to freeze as I stood beneath the rebel leader, unsure of what to do. "They really are assholes, aren't they?" He grinned widely.

I heard Nesrin's sharp intake of breath immediately before she said, "Papa!" The rest of the rebels released their held breaths.

"What?" He chuckled, turning to face the others. "It's true."

Nesrin shook her head at her father, a small smile creeping in her cheeks.

"You're not supposed to swear in front of superiors," Raidan told me, scolding me with his eyes.

"Oh," I blew, feeling my skin bubble from embarrassment. "Sorry, General."

The man gave me a sheepish grin and patted me on the shoulder. "I've heard far worse, girl. Relax. You may speak freely with me, so long as you are not calling *me* those names. In fact, from now on, you may all speak with the same ease as this Satyra girl."

"Even me, Papa?" Nesrin teased. "I can say asshole?"

The general flicked her nose before walking past the group and sitting at his desk. He stretched out his hands before placing them on a world map. When he looked back up to his daughter, he gave her a childlike wink. "Don't push your luck, Lieutenant."

63

UNITE

SATYRA

After sorting through the reconnaissance Ember and Nesrin acquired before leaving the High Council, the group of us, along with the general, wrote out an extensive timeline of events to keep things in order. When any of us remembered vital pieces, we made sure to voice them, and add them to the list. We'd spent all day and all night telling one another about what we'd learned, though much of the knowledge we sought remained a mystery. It was nearing four in the morning by the time we got everyone's version of the last few months since Shivalri was taken. Nesrin and Ember had even more to discuss, as they had been the ones to plan her sacrifice with Moira, Sora, and Damek. The pages were numerous, dating back to far before I ever even met Ember Blackwood. In fact, while working with the High Council, Ember had been keeping tabs on my family ever since Shivalri's powers started to manifest.

Ember had told us that storms had been far stronger than usual, picking up across the world with enough force to assume witchcraft was involved. Within them, the feel of powerful magics were potent. Ember couldn't feel it, but

Moira Darkmore had sensed it. The minute the magic made its way to Moira's anticipatory nose, Ember was tasked to find the source of the magic, with the assistance of Moira's mind device guiding him along. Once he found Shivalri, he was tasked with the job of spying on her and forced to report back anything suspicious or of worth. He kept tabs on me, Raidan, Gram, and Aunt Eden, too, just in case.

As the sun's beams replaced the night sky and cast the blue and yellow light back into the command core, the creeping of a new dawn washed over me. Today was Shival-ri's birthday, and she was spending it in Hell. Though perhaps if she was already dead, the curse had gotten to her, and she was simply gone now. I let my mind wander through the information regarding my family's mysterious legend and felt the anxiety of the book's secrets working a path in my skin. Ember told me that I could choose to tell Raidan about it, and after thinking on it while we pulled this draining all-nighter, it became clear to me that it wasn't a question of *if*, but rather, *when* I would tell him. After seeing the general and Nesrin together, it reminded me of the importance of a united familial front. Raidan might very well be the last Grimsbane relative I have alive. He should know about the curse as soon as possible, just in case anything was to happen to me, and I wouldn't be able to tell him later.

I hadn't found the time to tell Raidan without the other people present, especially while the rebels clung to every word said. The grandfather clock next to the whiteboard rang six times to indicate the new hour change. We'd been in this room for twenty-two hours, and with each minute that passed, the more I knew I needed to get the Grimm's Bane curse off my chest. The longer I kept this secret to myself, the more the itching in my skin bit. Without having the book with me, I wasn't sure how I would tell him, nor how I could prove the story. It would have to be seen to be believed. Even after having read and understood what Ember explained, I had had a hard time digesting the information. *"Not only will Grimm retrieve your souls in the end, but you don't get to have an afterlife."* I shivered as I recalled those haunting words. I would have to break that news to my cousin, and it wasn't going to be an easy thing to say. At least Raidan seemed to be doing much better in this new lifestyle now, and I was sure he'd be able to handle it if he were given the time to chew and make peace with it.

I glanced over at him, and though the bruised look beneath his eyes expressed exhaustion, watching the way he stood with grandeur proved that Raidan Grimsbane had found his place within the rebellion. I knew that I had to be the one who told him about the legend. If he were to find out that I'd known all of this and kept it from him, I wasn't sure if he'd forgive me for withholding it. When Raidan looked to me, questioning my blatant stare, I tried to convey an urgent look in my eyes, hoping he understood that I needed to speak with him privately. He bobbed his head in recognition and stepped away from the group of rebels huddled around the general's desk.

"You okay?" he asked as we made our way further to the back of the rounded room.

"Yeah," I murmured, checking to see if anyone else had caught our exchange. The others, all busy pinning maps and logging information hadn't been aware of me and Raidan slipping away.

"What's wrong?" he asked me, my apprehension apparent. Moving two metal stools in front of me, Raidan gestured for me to sit, and I obliged willingly.

"I need to tell you something, and I'm not sure how you're going to take it," I confessed, beginning with this in a way to warn him that there was something important I needed to explain.

"Well, is it bad?" he questioned, then tilted a dark brow at me. "Is it something to do with Ember?"

"No," I spat and swatted the idea away. Then I remembered that it did involve the seer, but not in the way Raidan's taunt had suggested. "Well, yes, but—"

"Did you sleep with him?" He gawked, turning to look at Ember who stood at the whiteboard. As if feeling the heat of our stare, Ember's eyes met with mine, his eyebrows shooting up before turning away.

"Rai!" I hissed, slapping his knee. "No, I didn't sleep with him. And stop staring at him." I grunted irritably. Raidan smirked when he turned to face me again, but when he saw the seriousness beneath my blush, I saw the moment he understood how important it was for me to tell him what I needed to.

"What is it, Saty?" he asked in a hushed tone. I took a deep breath and leaned closer to my cousin. "Tell me," he said, finally giving me his full attention.

"Well..." I blew, trying to find the words to begin. "Apparently," I dragged, trying to come up with a way for this to make sense. Just as Raidan was about to motivate me into spilling the news with the shake of my shoulders, a knock sounded, pulling everyone's attention to the red door. The general stood abruptly, and Raidan let go of his hold on me.

"Red, red, like the blood of a mortal, sharp exterior to guard soft heads. What is born by the hands of gods, yet grows underground at the mercy of the dead?" General called from behind his desk.

I didn't miss the subtle way his hand fell to the small sword that hung at his waist. What was this? Some sort of riddle in place of a password? When Nesrin led us through the door, her father hadn't asked us anything of the sort. Then again, Nesrin hadn't knocked before entering General Mehra's room, so perhaps, she was exempt from answering one.

"Red are their petals, sharp are their thorns, through life and death, a rose is born." The significantly Scottish sounding person who answered was sure in his reply. I had to hand it to them; they were unquestionably brainier than me. I hadn't sorted through the first line, let alone the second. For them to answer so swiftly, they were either a genius, or this was the common question, and they'd had their answer ready before ever trying to solve the riddle.

"Enter," General said, moving away from his desk and closer to me, Raidan, and the red door. When Ember and Nesrin came to find us where we sat, Ember nudged my arm with his elbow. Bending to level his face to mine, he pulled at a soot-colored curl that lay atop my collarbone.

"Do you know why General made that riddle?" he whispered in my ear. I shook my head no in response and felt my hair brush the side of his face. "The answer to the riddle is the name of his daughter."

"What do you mean?" I asked, looking to Nesrin, who rolled her eyes shyly before emitting a small smile.

"My name means wild rose."

"That you are," Raidan mumbled under his breath, and I could have sworn the austere lieutenant blushed.

As the door to the command core opened, a tall, slim, bearded man with golden brown hair stepped through the threshold. Covered in mud and grime and smelling of body odor, the man in brown leathers looked as if he'd walked straight out of a renaissance fair.

"Mr. Galbraith," General chimed, and to my surprise,

clapped the man on the back. "Good to see you back in one piece."

The man smiled, revealing a handsome set of teeth with uniquely snaggled canines. "Always sending me out to do your dirty work," he answered wryly, and pat his filthy chest as proof.

"Nothing the great Cormac Galbraith cannot handle," said General Mehra, who was still grinning from ear to ear. When Cormac turned to look at the rest of us who were huddled where Raidan and I had been chatting, the man's face went from confusion to caution, and then to a hesitant grin.

"No one told me you lot were going to be here." Cormac chuckled. "What's with the party?" he asked, before pointing his eyes and at me and Raidan. "And who in the world are these bright dafties?" Before anyone could answer, a set of sharp footsteps clucked at the tiled floor, and everyone one of us turned our attention to the door which still hung open. "Right," Cormac drawled. "I forgot to mention earlier," he said, turning and extending an arm out to the door. "I brought a friend. Says she's been trying to reach ya, General, but the guards keep turning her away." Just as the general's glower festered, a haughty woman with the brightest ginger A-line bob came marching in with her shoulders back and a look that could kill. Arrogance oozed from her fists to her proud chin as she stared down the general.

"You have a lot of nerve coming here after what you put my girl through," General boomed as he towered over the sharp-eyed girl. "*Aap gaddaar*," he hissed, and to my shock, spat at her feet. The girl lifted her chin further, unflinching and calculating.

"*I* am not the traitor," she declared. Her emerald-green eyes visibly seethed as she gave Nesrin a sharp, irate death stare.

"Who's she?" Raidan asked, taking a protective step in front of Nesrin. The ginger-haired girl slowly swiveled her head to dissect Raidan, and scoffed smugly, apparently deciding that he was no match for her.

"Her ex," Kaede chimed with a whirl of their hand, their face passive, yet annoyed.

"Fallon," the self-assured visitor corrected. "I've heard so much about you, Cousin."

64

SŌRZA
SHIVALRI

Just before Pyre went out the door, following behind the God of Death, he had told me that Gerimor was apparently spending the next few nights at the palace with us as both a protection, and as a warning if any stirrings happened. Pyre had quickly informed me of Gerimor's usefulness before leaving me to wait for him in the bedroom. According to him, Gerimor was the only god capable of controlling the Doors of Death. His spirit element allows him to understand everything there is to know about death, making him able to sense when a person's time has come. He is solely responsible for opening the door for the souls to enter, and it is through his magic that the deceased pass on into light, or into darkness. Pyre had explained that Gerimor was also able to see a person's time a few moments before it would come. It was something that could be used to our advantage, in case of attack. Not that we would want any of Pyre's guards or soldiers to fall at the hands of the Orsimm, but if it were to happen, Gerimor would sense it and warn us immediately.

"A pair of trousers, like mine you've grown accustomed

to wearing, a tunic, and some undergarments," Pyre said as he came back to the bedroom with a new set of clothes for me. He'd gone down to find Izra, who had been hard at work, crafting me an entire wardrobe. I had a hard time accepting this when Pyre had told me, because I felt as if the work was being wasted on me. I was supposed to be leaving this place soon, but Pyre insisted that for the days I was here, I should have my own clothes. This only made me fight with myself, the selfish part of myself, on whether it was a sign I should stay a bit longer and bide my time.

Pyre quietly placed the clothing on the tufted bench, pausing to watch the wheels turn in my head. I sighed heavily, flopping on the bed before pulling a pillow over my face and letting it darken my vision.

"Thank you," I answered beneath the cushion, my voice muffled and mind feeling silly and distracted and all sorts of things. I felt the weight of the pillow lift from my face before opening my eyes. Pyre stood above me looking both amused and concerned at once. The fact that I could tell this simply by looking into his eyes was baffling to me, and I wasn't sure if I'd ever get used to it. I wasn't sure if I'd ever get the chance to.

"Are you well?" he asked, lip quirking to the side.

"Besides having ascended and now having..." I paused, turning my head to the side for my face to find purchase in white, fluffy feathers.

"Wings?" he finished for me.

I grunted, and this he found entertaining. I, on the other hand, was busy filtering through the millions of questions that bombarded my brain, bouncing off one another in my skull.

"How am I supposed to go to Earth now that I look like this?" I asked, frowning into my wings. He casually lifted a

hand and lightly brushed a single finger down the new boning
I'd grown within seconds of ascension. A flash of heat and
indelicate imagery burst to the forefront of my mind. Capped
with the touch of Pyre's fingers, the flush in my face was
tremendously warm as I replayed the events that ended in my
growing these wings. A shimmering gold and silver hummed
down the veins of my feathers, and Pyre pulled back his
touch, letting loose a breathy sigh. I looked from the shiny
wings to him, my eyes pinned to the teeth that bit his bottom
lip. He hesitated with his hand in the air, then found my face.
I knew I should have been embarrassed by what he saw in my
face, but instead of leaning away and into humiliation, I let
him study me. His gaze remained on me as he lowered his
hand again, and when his fingers triggered another shimmer
to pass over my feathers, I stared up at him through heavy
lashes, knowing my eyes must match his. I watched his throat
bob as he swallowed thickly, a wave of black hair curling into
the front of his face.

"*Mìèye salbïtà sōrza*," he spoke, his voice rattling from
deep within. It took me a few seconds to find my own voice,
my entire being content to spend eternity looking into the
liquid pool of his honeyed gaze.

"*Sōrza*," I repeated, the word so heavy on my tongue, my
insides wanted to burst from the declaration. I didn't even
have the time to blink before the God of the Dead held
himself over me, the pure burning need evident in the way his
body radiated over me. It was as if the universe had sighed
into the world, finally able to take its first breath. He and I
were irrevocably forged in a way only myths could conceive,
activating a prophecy long meant to awaken the true people
we were. That's what this was all along. Two souls meant to
find their way together, to become one.

The problem had been not knowing of my duty and carelessly lifting the veil for all to see through the realms. The goal had always been to repair the veil and to keep the world safe by locking the Gates, and guarding them forever. But the solution was never to go into this alone. It wasn't my family who were meant to help me either. Pyre Malum, God of the Dead, King of the Under Realm, was always meant to stand with me, share his strength, and rule in death at my side. It was our fate. We were each other's *sōrza*. And now, we were also mates.

"Please tell me what you are thinking in that moon-spun head of yours," Pyre purred, heavy eyes boring into mine without a hint of barrier between us. My heart throbbed at the proof that he'd torn down his walls, letting me in.

"Will you speak to me in your old language?" I asked, loving the way the word *fate* had felt on my tongue. "Please? Anything you wish." He stared at me for a long moment, rubbing a finger under his chin in contemplation.

"*Jéghô ôrvïx tyeūx zuàvhe zōhx bèhsras.*"

"What did you say?"

He offered me a smug grin, causing my pulse to skip. "You'll have to learn the language to find out," he supposed.

"Hey, that's not fair!" I scowled teasingly. The way he shrugged his shoulders at me made his hair fall forward into his face. I lifted both hands to pull his hair back, tangling my fingers in soft obsidian. "How am I ever going to learn if you don't teach me?" He quirked his lips, heat flooding my core at the temptation only inches away from my face. "Come on, Pyre! Tell me." I sat up on my elbows, coming closer to him as I tipped my head up.

"I told you what I wish," he granted, still wearing the sly grin.

"And what would that be?" I prompted, tilting my chin so our mouths were within reach. He cursed under his breath and made to get off the bed. "Hey, don't turn away from me," I said, stopping him at the edge. "Tell me what you said! You never know; if you tell me what you wish for, I may grant it." I winked. Pyre's hand flew to his chest as he flopped onto his back; his dark wings spread out wide on the bed, matching the velvety black of the blanket. I bent over him with hair tumbling into my face. He lifted a hand and twirled a loose strand between his fingers before placing it behind my ear. His eyes shone a warm gold as he looked up at me. From this angle, he looked the most harmless I'd ever seen him. His eyes roamed my face, landing on my mouth. I watched his jaw tick before his eyes slowly returned to mine.

"I wish to kiss your lips."

"Oh…" My breath choked, my sights set on the perfect shape of his mouth. His lips slightly parted; the cupid's bow lifting on his full lips as he took me in. He made to get up, but I stopped him, pinning his shoulders down.

"Don't embarrass me further." He grumbled, still watching me.

"Say it again." The plea tumbled out from my mouth before I could even consider it. He wore a moment of shock on his face before replacing it with a grin. He slowly dragged his teeth over his lower lip, as if toying with the knowledge of my desperate need to kiss him.

"*Jéghô ôrvïx tyeūx zuàvhe zōhx bèhsras.*" My heart thundered as I watched him lower his gaze. I lifted a hand, brushing my fingertip along his bottom lip, which I was certain had been crafted with the sole purpose of provoking my desire.

"*Bèhsras.*" I inhaled sharply, feeling the heat pool in my core.

"Yes," he murmured against my finger, the heat and vibration riveting. He licked the tip of my finger, causing me to shiver. His eyes darkened, and in an instant, he took me by the waist and lifted us both into the air, hovering above the bed.

"*Zōhx... bèhsras.*" I trembled, tasting the language on my tongue, settled in the hands of this striking god. A growl I hadn't ever known tore from my lips, a thunderous storm like fire and rain rapturing at the sight of him. Hot and cold, eager and fierce, our bodies melded in excruciatingly intoxicating bliss.

"Please." Pyre gasped between kisses. I raked my hands over his strong, corded back, not ever wanting a moment away from the heat of him.

"What?" I thundered, mind, body, and soul starving for more.

"Let me love you," he begged, his voice just as raw and penetrating as mine felt. The mere mention of him wanting to give me this kind of intimacy had me painstakingly undone, unraveling any hold I might have had on control.

"You want to love me?" I swallowed, feeling the torch lift to the words, waiting to set them on fire.

"With every part of me, I will love you into eternity."

My wings unfurled, and now, it was I who had us lifting in the air. Like a muscle memory I'd never known, I pushed us both down into the mattress with the strength of a thousand winds. When I had him strapped between my legs, breath panting and begging my lungs for oxygen, I grabbed the front of his shirt and tore it to shreds, leaving his chest bare, and eyes ravenous with hunger.

The need to delve into the passion was like a frenzy and taking the remaining clothes from off his body had been done without a thought. He was breathtaking in every way, the perfect depiction of blessing's paragon. He was all I never knew I needed, and now that I had him, I would take advan-

tage of our time together. This instance, this precious, unde-
termined time we had together was not something promised,
and we could soon lose the chance to live in these moments.

My craving transformed from raging, lustful desire to an
achingly desperate need of him. Of *all* of him. Not just in this
new, physical sense, but I needed to know Pyre, and care for
him in every way before the two of us were inevitably ripped
apart.

No. He was *mine*, and I would not let anyone take him
from me.

"Pyre…" I quivered, hands trembling atop his chest. He
sat up, his hands cupping under my knees as I held on to him.

"Yes, *Sōrza?*" My heart swelled at his affectionate use of
that tremendously meaningful word.

"Will you call me that always?" I asked, voice quiet and
warmth pooling in my chest. He closed his eyes and leaned
his forehead to mine.

"It will always be you." He exhaled breathily. Gently, his
lips brushed mine, the declaration of our truth electric
between our lips.

"I am your *sōrza*," I told him.

"Mine," he whispered, moving his hands from my legs to
the back of my neck. He lovingly stroked the underneath of
my jaw with his thumb. "Yours." His words, his tenderness,
was my undoing. I moved in to kiss him, and he gladly
receive my touch. His hands traveled over my body, caressing
in a way I've only ever felt with him.

"Your hands are so soft," I told him between heated
breaths. "I love how you touch me." Pyre smiled, a boyish
grin turning into affectionate awe. The inner corners of his
brows lifted, his lips parting slightly as he watched me, still
caressing me.

"And I love *you*," he whispered. My heart stopped, heat rushing over me.

"Truly?"

He lowered my face to his and kissed my forehead. My heart came back to life, spirited and uncontrollable.

"With all of me," he answered. I moved my hand to softly place it over his heart, and found that his, too, beat passionately.

"I love you, too, Pyre," I professed, the tension in my shoulders left as my confession was made. "I have loved you for a very long time, it seems. Even before I wanted to. I have always cared for you." Pyre shook beneath me, then pulled me so that our bodies were flush, his arms wrapped around me.

"You saw me and cared for me when I did not deserve it. I have seen you try your best to show me empathy, to charm me into letting my guard down. You have shown what it is to have a friend, someone to care for and to be cared by. I still do not deserve your kindness, but my *sōrza*, my light, I will work every day to earn it." *Oh*. I felt a tear slide quietly down my cheek. All this time he noticed what I was doing.

"Oh, Pyre," I murmured, and kissed the tip of his nose. It crinkled beneath my touch as he smiled. "It makes me very happy to know you've let your walls down for me. All I've wanted is to know you. I am so glad that I get to love you."

"And I, you." He wiped my cheek of its tear, and brought me in for a warm embrace, holding me closely, as we showed each other that love.

AFTER SOME TIME of lying completely exhausted yet entirely renewed, we had fallen asleep, a tangled mess of blanket and limbs plastered together in a nap. When I woke, my heart skipped a beat, remembering all that had played out today. So much had happened in such a short period of time. To say that I was filled to the brim with thoughts and emotions would be an understatement. The one thing I was now certain of, though, was that I never wanted to let go of these moments. Though it posed the question of when and if I would return to Earth and my family, I didn't want to think on that right now. I finally felt like I understood my purpose. I was happy, irreversibly feeling like my true self.

Pyre lifted his free arm from me, and I grunted, tugging his hand back around me. He laughed into my hair and kissed the top of my head. I blinked the sleep from my eyes, only to find my face mushed into Pyre's bare chest. I moved my head up to look at him, but I could barely make out his features. It was completely dark in the room, save for the fire lit upon arrival. Though it still shone, it was dimmer now as it was dying out slowly. We had been wrapped in each other's arms, neither one of us willing to let go all throughout the day and into the night. I felt giddy just thinking about it.

"Such a darling smile," Pyre spoke, voice deep and smoky from having slept. My nerves coiled at the sound of it, raising goose bumps over my arms.

"How can you possibly see me right now?" I asked, throat dry from sleeping in a room heated by wood stove.

"I have excellent vision," he said and curled even closer into me. I tensed at those words, only now realizing how naked and rumpled I must appear.

"Wait," I stammered. "Can you see all of me?" I shrieked, desperately pulling for blankets to cover myself. Pyre swatted my hand away, then grabbed a handful of my ass and squeezed. "Hey!" I hissed, shaking my head into his chest. He draped a wing over us both, and I couldn't help but curl into the softness of his feathers. My own curled underneath his, resting over his body.

"If it pleases you, I would like to continue looking at all of you." Pyre shrugged, my body moving with his. At that precise moment, I felt the hardening of him against my hip bone, and a jolt of tingles ran through my entire body. Pyre groaned into the top of my hair and tightened his grip on my back. "You know what that does to me," he murmured.

"What what does?" I asked, then pressed a light kiss to his chest.

"I know what you're thinking." He moaned, and it brought forth the tingling sensation in my core. "I can smell you from a mile away. Imagine what it does to me to have you here, in my arms, while you think your sultry thoughts." I smirked at his words, fully aware of the strange gift of scent he had. Only now, we both shared this gift in our immortality, Pyre unaware of my having it.

"You know…" I trailed, tracing a pattern over his stomach. "That gift of ours really is something."

He stiffened under me, abs flexed beneath my fingers. "*Ours?*" he questioned.

"Oh, yes," I trilled. "Didn't I tell you? Since I'm fully immortal now, I can smell that scent on *you* too." The smell of his smokey sugar and spice made my toes curl, and I bit the skin of his chest. Pyre flinched under me, and I burst into a fit of laughter, so thrilled to find him caught off guard.

"Why didn't you tell me?" He groaned, exasperated. Releasing his hold on me, he turned from his side to flop on his back.

"Oh, yeah. 'Cause that would've went well." I laughed

teasingly. "Hey, Pyre, I can smell the enthusiasm coming from your cock."

"Forgive me," Pyre said, and slapped a hand to his face.

"What for?" I giggled, still trailing a finger down his stomach.

"For ever having asked."

65

CHOSEN

SHIVALRI

"I have something I wish to give you," Pyre told me as he poked at the fire with a long, sharp iron rod.

"You do?" I questioned with a lifted brow. The blankets were still rumpled around me as I took up ample space on the bed. I watched as the God of the Dead, tall and lean, cut with perfectly carved muscles, lower to pick something from the floor. When Pyre turned to find me, still messy and snug in the tangled sheets, he shook his head, grinning.

"How?" he mouthed, roving over me with a pair of eyes that saw straight through to my soul. I blushed fervently, lifting the blanket up to my chest as I surveyed the man stalking toward me. He was all predator in the way he moved, all love in the way he looked at me. When he sat on the edge of the bed, shirtless and back bare for me to see, my own back tingled, reminding me that I, too, wore a set of wings and similar markings. More than anything, I wanted him to know that he would never be alone, whether I was physically with him or not. He would not wear heavy words on his own, and he would know what it feels like to have true companionship if it was the last thing I could do. I lifted a soft hand and placed it between the set of his wings, warming the spot that haunted him. When the tension in his shoulders relaxed, he turned to face me, his forehead puckered, a hint of sadness clouding his features.

"What is it?" I asked as I lifted my dress away from my legs and settled next to him on the edge of the bed. The corner of his mouth turned up in a weak smile as he toyed with a crimson velour pouch. Drawing the strings between his fingers, he handed it to me, gently placing it in my hand. "What is this?" I wondered, uncertain about the way his features contorted in a mixture of cold and warm.

"I wanted to give you something to remember me by," he began, looking up from his lap to watch my shaken appearance. "When you leave this place... I want you to have a piece of me." The dawn of tears filled my eyes and I closed them before my grief could get the best of me. I didn't want to leave him. I didn't want to rely on whatever this item was to remember Pyre. "As you are fully ascended now, I believe you'll be able to leave without my aid. You'll be able to fulfill the prophecy and find safety with your family on Earth." If Pyre's theory about my ascension was true, I didn't have to wait around any longer. I would be able to do as I was meant to whenever I was ready. The question being whether I would ever be ready.

"I wish so badly that I could have it both ways," I told him, lids still closed to the face I was sure emitted the same emotions. "I need to leave, but Gods... I *want* to stay. I want to stay with *you*." My voice wavered between the cracks in my sentence.

"If I could have it both ways, I would still wish you to go." I looked up at him now, angry with his response. He moved to twist my hair between his fingers, taking a moment to watch the way it twirled in his hands.

"How could you say that?" I was unable to comprehend this. What we shared between us was nothing like I had ever known. I knew with every part of me that he felt this as immensely as I.

"I wish for you to be happy, *Sōrza*. I do not think you would find happiness apart from your family."

I took a moment to let that sink in. "If the Gates weren't part of the issue—"

He stopped me, placing a hand on my cheek. "No, Goddess. You wouldn't choose to stay in this place. And you cannot travel to and from without the risk of having someone else slip between the cracks."

"I don't like it when you call me that." I grimaced, inadvertently folding into his palm.

"You *are* a goddess. One of the most powerful ever to live. But you are my *sōrza*, my beautiful, brave light, and I will always think of you as such."

My heart fluttered at his adulation. "So, call me that," I demanded. "You can call me Shivalri like my family does, or Shivi, the nickname my family uses for me. But I don't like to be called Goddess. I am both not enough for that, yet *more* than that. *What* I am is not the same as *who* I am."

"Fair," he replied, leaning to press a kiss to my forehead. "*Who* you are is far greater than *what* you are." I sighed into the space between us, enjoying how his lips lingered atop my head. "Will you open the bag?" I frowned, hoping and praying that our inevitable parting would only be temporary.

He kissed my head again as I opened the draw strings. I dipped my hand in the soft pouch and drew out the tiny object between two fingers. My hands trembled as I held the golden ring between us, staring with eyes wide. Pyre took it from my trembling hands, turning it over to show me an inscription carved on the inside of the band.

"*Mïèye Sōrza, Mïèye Xïvhe*," he whispered as the ring glinted in our firelight. "My Fate, My Life." As he took my hand in his, sliding the ring to fit perfectly around my finger, a chanting hummed in my ears, every part of me singing to life. A large black diamond, raw and glistening, sat in the center of a golden band made in the shape of flower stems. I had never seen a handcrafted ring before and never imagined in my wildest dreams to ever receive one as lovely as this.

"It's beautiful," I breathed, trying to fight through the emotions and thundering questions that twisted around my heart.

"I find you often touching the one on your right hand, and I imagine it's a source of comfort, reminding you of someone you love."

I nodded, reflexively reaching for the wedding band I'd worn since Mom's passing. "It was my mother's," I said, running my thumb over it.

"I had a feeling," he answered, taking both of my hands in his and rubbing his thumbs over the rings on each. "I give you this ring, along with my heart, to carry with you so that perhaps I can offer you comfort, even when I am not there to give it." I could barely breathe from the overwhelming bursts of sentiment. Pyre's sincerity and love was flooding my chest like a wildfire, and I couldn't help but question the ring's placement. It fit perfectly on my ring finger, the black and gold an evocative and welcome presence on my left hand. "Though you've refused my proposal on more than one occasion, I hope you understand that this time, I ask you with love in my heart, and a dire need in my soul."

"You're proposing?" I gasped, pulling my hand to my chest, feeling the weight of his words rattling between my ribs.

"I propose our souls remain intimate and intend for my

love to go with you into the Earthly Realm. I do not need you to bind yourself with me, and I do not ask you to give me your power. We are mates, and that is far more powerful, meaningful than any magic. I only ask that you allow me this one thing. This one blessing. To love you endlessly, in life and death and everything in between, for as long as we both live, and even after that."

I couldn't hold it in anymore. My body shuddered under the tender regard, his proposal having lit my world on fire. I could never leave him now. Whether he knew it or not, I would find a way to be with this man. My destiny begged me for it, my soul craving this closeness for eternity. The Fates had shown me a life at Pyre's side, ruling and caring for the dead in the Under Realm. It was not the end to a war; it was the beginning of a life together.

With quivering hands, I held his face in mine, the two of us leaving tear stains on the crimson pouch in my lap. I couldn't stand to see him like this. So achingly handsome, and so painfully desolate. I kissed each of his closed eyes, salted tears wetting my lips at the touch of his dark lashes. When he opened his eyes, I saw a man who'd had a thousand lives, but was painstakingly new to life. This rare, desperate, beautiful thing between us, had awakened the biggest part of him, and I was unbelievably fortunate to see it flourish.

"My Fate, My Life," I whispered. His eyes slowly opened, brows lifting in tender hope. "I'm yours, and you are mine—always."

With a kiss so delicate, I thought I might drown, Pyre took me up into his arms, holding me close enough to feel the heartbeat that raced at the same speed as mine. "I love you, Shivalri," he vowed between breaths as he wiped the tears from my face. "Thank you," he said, kissing me again. "Thank you."

66

RED
SHIVALRI

Dust fell from the ceiling above me as I woke. The palace rattled and the bed swayed as I bolted upright in the dirtied sheets.

"Pyre!" I exclaimed, frantically searching for my love. He was nowhere to be found in the darkness of the room. I was left alone in the remainder of firelight, drenched in sweat, and covered in sooty sheetrock.

Tripping over my feet, I burst from the bedroom and bolted down the hallway, where frantic people of all backgrounds hurried to and from rooms, most of them armored from head to toe. I caught the eyes of several pythrants, their eyes glowing yellow as we recognized each other.

"Goddess," one of them called out to me over the sound of heavy pounding. It had to be an earthquake. Did the Under Realm even get earthquakes? I clung to the wall as my knees clanged together beneath me. A tinge of fear sparked my senses, my magic singing in my veins, begging to be let out. My wings fluttered behind me; it was a new sensation that followed the emotions flooding me.

"Where's Pyre?" I demanded, fisting my hands at the

ready. I had a bad feeling about this; my intuition screamed at me to find the God of the Dead.

"He's in battle, Goddess," the pythrant bellowed over the rumbling. "You need to get back in your rooms now." He made to grab my elbow, but I threw my weight away from him, my mind angering in tune to my instinctual fury.

"What is happening?" I hissed, nostrils flaring, and face so set in command that I knew I'd been born for a moment like this. To stare in the face of a soldier with slitted eyes and forked tongue and demand he answer me. He nodded in understanding and placed a hand on the hilt of a sword.

"Obystrus has been unleashed. They've been ordered to take you." My gut fell through to the floor as images of vile creatures came to the forefront of my mind. This was what the Fates had shown me. They'd prepared me in a way, readying me for this moment. "It's not safe for you to leave your rooms, Goddess. My lord has charged us with protecting you and keeping you out of enemy's reach." The group of pythrants encircled me in the hall, and it took everything in me not to scream at them to move out of my way. This was my fight, my battle to win. Whether Pyre wanted me there or not, it was my fate. It was now or never.

"If you're charged with protecting me, then guard my back," I ordered, and called forth the fiery flames that fever-ishly formed in my core. As I stalked down the hall, a fire burning all around me, coating the entirety of my skin, I didn't know exactly what I would find outside these walls, but I knew that I was ready to face it. My wings expanded, creating a balancing, sturdy protection at my back as the pythrants slithered and hissed behind me. I didn't take a moment to turn and see if they were following me to protect me or to stop me. I only marched faster, needing my feet to take me to Pyre.

A large, booming tremor erupted from the ground as I stared out the palace door, frozen in my spot. Enormous, monstrous giants stomped down on the ground, crushing trees, rocks, and people beneath their feet. Strong, cumbrous arms plagued their bodies, each of them having three or more on each side. This was grim. As my eyes roamed over the shaking grounds, a shimmering light stood out around each being who fought for their lives. Most bodies were streaked with red, both from blood and this strange, glowing light outlining their figures. There were reds and oranges and dim whites all around. When my eyes fell to the black-winged god, who was swimming in a light of bright, liquid white, I shuddered at the sight. Pyre Malum stood ten feet above ground. A fire roared around him as he fought not one, but three giant men. Where these giants lacked in numerous arms, they lacked in eyes too. For these monsters only had two arms, and one singular eyeball strapped to the middle of their foreheads. When one of them landed a blow to Pyre's gut, everything inside me thundered to life, and a terrifying guttural scream tore from my throat, finding its way out to the crowd of monsters. I watched as they stumbled and fell, clasping their ears in delectable pain I knew I caused. I felt the warm pooling of blood drip down my neck, and just like before, I was elated with this strength I had inside me. I screamed again, and this time, Pyre covered his ears too, making me falter for a split second. It was just enough time for a six-armed giant to grab me in his fist and toss me into the air.

I flew hard like a whip, heading for the side of the palace building. Before my body could snap under the impact, my wings seemed to have a mind of their own, carrying me up and away from the blow. I smiled in satisfaction, revealing glinting teeth ready to rip the heads from the beasts in front of me.

"That wasn't very nice." I grinned, finding the army of giants who were all turned to face me. At once, a thousand limbs came thrashing forward, the ground beneath their feet crumbling at their wake. The pythrants came at them with such speed and agility, it was magnificent to see them fight. Where they hadn't been strong enough to beat the God of the Dead during the fight at Pyre's castle, they were doing a much better job against their new opponents. One minute they were slithering on the ground, and the next they were airborne, wrapping their scaly torsos around the necks of giants the height of the palace itself.

Like a feral animal finally released from captivity, I launched myself into the mess of chaos, taking my torrent of rage and flame as shield and weapon. There were other bouts of elements being spread across the battlefield as I flew between the bodies of my enemies. People decked in armor and skin in shades of blue and green ravaged the scene in a flurry of unforgiving water and earth. Vines snapped up and around the legs of monsters, while others were doused in a flush of glowing water, much like the Dhetrïan Pools fluids.

"*Shivalri!*" Pyre roared through the warfare, his voice enthralling me in a way so fierce, the pull between us drove me through the crowd until I was face-to-face with the King of the Under Realm. "You shouldn't be here!" he screamed through the noise; lips pulled back to reveal his pointed teeth.

"This is exactly where I need to be!" I countered with steely conviction, making him understand what this was. "This is what the Fates decided for me. I will not stand by and let you face this alone, just for it to come again and find me later."

"I will stop them each time this comes for you," he

declared, before pulling me back and away from the swinging monster who'd tried to get me.

"That's not our destiny," I told him, gritting my teeth, and forcing myself to face this truth. "We do this together, or not at all."

His brows dipped in insufferable sorrow as his golden eyes heated between us. Gerimor flew in the air, golden hair whipping across his face as he sliced at the heads of giants before of us. He took one look our way and set his jaw before nodding once. He was telling us to go. He was giving us the opportunity to leave while he fought at the sides of pythrants and feïnyr, so that we could go together and find a place to fulfill our destiny. This would give us our one chance to save the world and put an end to this. This was only a glimpse into the world's end, a warning that if I didn't get my act together, gods and monsters far worse than this would devastate our world until there was nothing left of it.

"I can't let you go!" Pyre's voice broke.

The hold on my fears and weaknesses shattered as the truth of this rang through. "You have to," I said, reaching out and grabbing his hand as we hovered several feet above pandemonium. "We have to do this now. We can't let them get me. Can't let them use me for whatever your brother intends." Conflict warred in the depths of Pyre's gaze as he desperately searched for another answer. I wanted the other answer to come. Wanted to put away this fighting and mayhem to live another day at his side. But we couldn't risk it. "We can't be selfish in this," I said, my throat aching from having to voice this truth. He pulled me in close, hugged me fiercely enough for spots to blur my vision, and then launched us both into the skies and away from the war that trapped the residents of the palace in dismay.

As the rumbling grew farther and farther away from us,

Pyre's panting matched the drumming within my chest. With wind whipping through our hair, a mess of night and silver, Pyre dove downward, his feet skidding over the ledge of a mountain as he jumped off its cliff. My guts flew into my throat at the pitching maneuver, my mind unable to keep up with the speed at which Pyre moved us. Down the mounds of sand we glided, falling to the bottom of a desert canyon.

"Are you all right?" He heaved, still holding me tight enough to crack a rib. "Were you injured?"

"Fine," I squeezed out, my howling lungs unable to take in air. He let me down without release as he looked me over to make sure I wasn't hurt. Other than being backhanded by a six-armed giant, my body was perfectly well. Pyre let go of me abruptly, pacing back and forth in a heap of sand. The drift of dry grain smattered against the two of us.

"There is absolutely no source of magic or life in this desert. It's the perfect place for you to create your own, as it will be only yours to wield. I'll keep you guarded," he said, looking to note our surroundings. I nodded, understanding that this was the part where I'd have to delve deep into my elements and forge a safe place to work on repairing the veil, before opening the Gates and sealing them shut behind me. "We're going to have to make this quick," Pyre said, making my skin grow cold in the heat of this wasteland. "Fucking gods!" he boomed, startling me as he thundered in the empty canyon. "Fucking Fates!" I watched him scream until his lungs gave out, and when he fell to his knees with tear-streaked eyes, all of my affinities came roaring to life at the sight of him. The sight of the person who had been threaded into the very depths of my soul. "I don't want to lose you," he choked, looking up at me from the gritty pit. As my breathing began to rapidly increase, the oxygen fed the fire, which slid up my arms in a frenzy. I looked at Pyre, seeing his bright-white soul glowing around him, and the spirit affinity took over my senses, centering on the pure psyche knelt in front of me. He is inherently *good*.

Falling to the sands in a heap of emotions, I stared into the eyes of the one I'd need for the rest of my life—the one I couldn't have. Tears flooded my vision as a typhoon of water came surging out from my sockets. It flowed and flowed until my legs grew wet in the river I'd created in this barren land.

"I'm going to come back!" I cried.

"You can't."

The aching in my lungs, skin, and eyes were entirely unbearable, but it was nothing in comparison to the destined loss I felt when acknowledging what we'd come here to do. I plunged my hands through scorching sand and clenched my fists at the surge of power I called upon. The amount of power required for this task was unnatural, demanding everything from me. Though I was destined to do this, all of me screamed to give up entirely. I would do this now, before it was too late. But I would find my way back to the Under Realm. I would find my way back to my heart.

Pyre fought his way through my outburst, ignoring the blast of heat from my fire, trudging through the rushing waters against the current of hard wind pushing every which way. His eyes never left my gaze as I screamed a bloodcurdling curse into the skies, reaching for my last affinity. When the God of the Dead reached me, he bit into his hand and held it over my mouth as I choked on the scream and hot blood trickling down my throat.

"Why did you do that?" I coughed, my voice ragged and barely functional.

"Whether you truly need it now or not, I will give my strength. Like you did for me, I will bare this burden with you." Grabbing me with one arm around my waist, and the other clutching the back of my head to tuck me into his chest, I called forth every bit of strength within me, leaning into Pyre for the immense comfort he provided.

"Will it, *Sōrza*," he said into my ear, pulling me in tighter until our bodies were flush in the squall. He gently flipped my palm skyward and carefully sliced the flesh, allowing my blood to drop into the sand. "Tell the universe what you want. Order the veil to restore itself anew."

"How?" I cried, tasting the mixture of blood, sand, and tears on my tongue.

"Tell it with your essence," he insisted as he moved his hand from my waist to the front of my stomach. "Build from your core," he said, then lifted his hand between my breasts. "Love from your heart." He pushed our heads together, gripping my head through a mess of lashing hair. "Claim with your soul."

Thousands of blades sliced my being into tortured scraps of nothing as I clung to the pressure building in my frame. I stood within the sun as the rippling of realms wavered in my hands, so incredibly fragile, so extremely prevailing. I could see the veil, see the matter made of *aēthre* blanketing the realms, wrapping itself around our world. A pain so starving, so agonizing, it ripped me to pieces as I heard the cries of those desperately clinging to the cracks in the veil I'd created on the day of my mother's death. Anger and despair, hunger and irrationality threatened to end me for trying to take their sliver of sight into other realms. I knew with every fiber of my being that I needed to ignore their terrorizations. I knew they could not hurt me in this plane, for they were not truly here to begin with. I focused on the slits in the cloak, imagining the threads coming back together. The wisps of *aēthre* followed my command, knitting itself into its larger whole and completing itself before my very eyes. I was holding on only by sheer will of the mind, my body having completely left me in this window to all three realms. When the final crack filled itself, when there was no more light spilling through fractures, I let my mind leave this place and came back to the aching body that slumped in Pyre Malum's hands.

"Pyre…" I coughed, mouth devoid of speech. He flattened sticky hair to my face as he caressed my cheeks in his hands.

"You've done it, my love," he whispered. His arms shook around me.

"Hello," a voice like silky night cooed from behind us.

Pyre whipped me up into his arms, standing us up to face the perfidious Orsimm gods. I leaned into Pyre, bracing myself for the fight of my life. If Pyre hadn't been holding me, I was sure I'd have fallen face-first into blistering sand. But I wouldn't let this moment of weakness deter me from finishing what I started.

"Do not make another move!" Pyre snarled, his fangs and claws elongating to strike. Ombrose took a teasing step forward, his grin flashing through the sandstorm that riled around us. Three sets of black eyes stared back at me with eager temptations. Wind and sand tugged at their clothes, their wings tucked behind them and away from the force. With my affinities on lock, my body received another surge of adrenaline, which gave me the strength I needed to make my escape and close the Gates behind me. I could tell in the way that Pyre held me, and the way that the Orsimm gods looked at me, that every one of them understood my intentions.

"Why are you here? Why are you doing this?" I thundered, facing my enemies with an all-consuming animosity.

"Promises were made," Dramael replied, flashing his teeth in a mischievous grin.

"What promises?" I asked, clenching my fists, and feeling the burn.

"Mortades," Dramael bellowed, his voice grating against my eardrums. He'd entirely ignored my question. "Think of the chances we will have once the goddess opens the Gates." He spoke as if Dramael could turn Pyre against me.

"You will sooner see Obystrus before stepping foot past the Gates." Pyre growled, his voice so violent I believed his words true. I had no doubt he intended to follow through with his threat.

"*Yrdôs*," the God of Sleep boomed, and I quickly remembered this command from the first time we met. Dramael had put me to sleep with one simple word, yet while my affinities were alive within me, he would not succeed.

"That's not going to work on me," I ground out, clenching my fists at my sides. Pyre leaned against me, stumbling slightly, but enough to put pressure on me. When I looked up at him, I saw the clear strain in the way his muscles pushed through the God of Sleep's command. "Is it affecting *you*?" I gasped, clinging to him, trying to free him of the Orsimm's grip. When Dramael had tried to use this power against me back at his cave, I'd been able to call upon my elements to strengthen myself against him and refuse to fall under. But Pyre's struggle was evident in the way he fought against the current. This was impossible. He was the King of the Under Realm. Surely the God of Sleep could not measure up to the power that Pyre wielded.

"I've given you my strength," he managed to grit out, and sudden understanding alerted me to the problem. If Pyre's power, his sheer life force, was now coursing through my veins, he was left defenseless. Now I wished I could give it all back. The bile in my throat argued with the rationality of my mind. Repairing the veil had taken everything of me.

Though I didn't ask him to feed me his power, he knew I needed to borrow it to do what was needed for the Gates and had done so anyway. But now, this left a weak spot wide open for the taking. "Go." He blew, wincing through the sleep clawing at him to fall. I didn't have a second to think. I couldn't fight what had to be done. Pyre propelled a shield of flame around us, and I amplified it with my own fire affinity, keeping the Orsimm at bay. Though it felt like I'd wrenched my own heart straight from my chest, I left Pyre's side and plunged my fists through scorching powder and let myself unravel, pouring my soul into the ground and willing the Gates to appear before me.

"I'm here! I'm doing what you asked of me!" I screamed, the fire around me growing higher. "Fucking work!"

A tremor rippled through me as the pain inside me turned to a pleasure so electrifying, I thought I might dissipate entirely. "Oh." I sighed. I liked this. This was freedom. This was raw, enticing power meant to be used only by me. This was mine. The realms were mine.

"*Abrôrta dhèjl Ôhrtum*," I heard them call to me.

"Let me pass," I demanded, and I felt my eyes roll into the back of my head as I sowed, cultivated, and raised a colossal tree from the barren lands of the Under Realm's desert. I saw now, through the eye at the center of my fore-head—a third, all-seeing eye guiding me toward my Gates.

"Fuck!" Pyre snarled. I didn't have to turn my head to see Dramael and Tasphen beating the God of the Dead into the ground. Though I wanted to go to him, physically felt an excruciating need to save him from this misery, the Gates lulled me forward, demanding I pass through as I'd intended. I dragged my feet through the mounds of sand. My heart, mind, will, and destiny pillaged me as I placed two hands on the trunk of the massive tree. Blood-red pomegranates hung from vibrant branches as I looked up into the foliage. They spoke to me in invocations, a chant accepting me as their creator.

"Not so fast, little kitten," Ombrose purred directly into my ear. I couldn't move to do anything to stop him. The pull of the Gates was strong within me, and they would not accept a refusal. Not now that I'd convinced them to open. Ombrose took hold of my wrist, trying to force me into taking him with me as I stepped into the light of the trunk's entrance. I felt my body moving forward with easy, unthinking strides; Ombrose attached to the left of me, following my every move. I wasn't entirely worried since I knew that no one other than myself could walk through the other realms and stay within them. Pyre had taught me that since I was born with the blood of all three realms, as the Triple Goddess, I would be allowed to roam freely through them all. Ombrose was made for the Under Realm. He couldn't possibly come through with me.

I felt a tug on my shoulder as my eye saw the scene from above. Pyre, who was battered and bruised, had Dramael and Tasphen tossed into a pile of fleshy rubble at the bottom of the canyon. Now, the God of the Dead clawed at the God of Nightmares, screaming and tearing at the leathery wings. I felt a sharp pinch in the crook of my neck as I witnessed Ombrose's teeth latch onto my skin. The wrongness of his bite had my entire biology recoiling from him. He was trying to take my blood, in the same way I had taken Pyre's to use his strength. This was Ombrose's way of getting enough of my magic to pass through. I had to stop him. I couldn't let him escape into the Earthly Realm. If he was awful enough to offer me up to the god who wanted to end the world, I couldn't imagine the havoc Ombrose could wreak on Earth. I would do everything in my power to detain this monster, but if I didn't succeed, my family wouldn't stand a chance against the God of Nightmares. No one would.

I felt the tearing of my skin under Ombrose's claws and teeth, as Pyre tugged to remove him from my person. Try as he might, he was struggling with every move. He was spent from having given over his power so that I could leave this place of gods and fire behind me. A blood-curdling scream tore from the dark-eyed god. I flinched within my mind, but my body continued into the trunk's entrance. I managed to move only my fingers, just as Pyre managed to remove Ombrose's left wing from his back. With a cry of agony, the God of Nightmares followed me into the Gates of all realms, leaving Pyre in the deserted mess of blood and pomegranate, the nectar running red like a river in the sands of the Under Realm.

67

TREASURE
PYRE MALUM

"**N**o!" The blood coating my throat slapped my teeth, following the snarl that escaped me. My *sōrza* was gone, and that retched nightmare had gone in with her. No, this couldn't happen. This was not how it was supposed to be! She was supposed to be safe. She was supposed to go to the Earthly Realm and seal the Gates shut behind her. Now she was there with the God of Nightmares with his teeth sunken into her shoulder. "Mine!" I bellowed, another surge of rage coursing through me. She was mine to claim, mine to keep safe, and I'd failed her.

The grit of the sands scraped against my palms as I clenched my fists, my sharp nails elongating in the process and cutting at my flesh. I stared at the tree trunk that displayed a splattering of her blood—red like the living, with a fusion of gold, glittering energy. The ichor in her blood marked her completely immortal. It would be okay. I would find a way to help her. I would find a way through the Gates and get her back into my arms.

It suddenly occurred to me that my mate, the new Triple Goddess, would have to follow through with her plans and take care of her responsibilities. She knew that she was meant to close the Gates and keep the world from coming to an end. Would she choose to close the Gates with Ombrose unleashed upon Earth? If she closed the Gates now, she would be shutting him out from the Under Realm, and me along with it. I had to get to her before she closed the Gates for good. I couldn't let her face the God of Nightmares on her own.

"Let me in!" I demanded, placing both hands to the base of the massive tree. Blood, fruit, sand, and dirt covered the entirety of the base. I could still feel her through the connection we shared, as if the string tying us together were a beacon in this desolate desert. "*Gârqhe èllrhe sâlvhe,*" I pleaded, the desperation to find my mate burning a hole through my chest. "Please, keep her safe. Let me in so *I* can keep her safe." With all the strength I could muster, I pulled my fist back and launched it at the tree, my knuckles cracking beneath the blow. Over and over, I beat at the tree till my knuckles were raw and bleeding. It was no use. The Gates wouldn't let me in.

I sank to my knees and felt the heavy weight of my wings pull me back as a gust of wind tore into me. A flash of something gold glinted in the sand, my inferno's beams a scornful ray of warmth. Through the desperation and defeat, I sifted through the sand and removed the piece of gold from the tainted ground. The ring I'd given her… A heart-wrenching sting drove into my face as the prickle of tears clouded my eyes. My *sōrza*, in her last moment in the Under Realm, had removed this ring and thrown it to the ground for me to find. A sign that we were not finished, I could only hope.

I wiped my face, ignoring the bite of dirt scratching at it, and clung to this piece of treasure. I recalled the fragility in her hands, the times I'd ran my thumbs over her sore knuckles. She'd played with her mother's ring anytime her emotions became too much, but with this one, the one I'd given her, she touched it when she felt happiness. I grasped it tightly and kissed the hot metal before placing it on my smallest finger. Though her hands were slighter than mine, I found a snug place to keep the ring safe, to keep it close to me.

"*Mïèye alôrhe*," I whispered, placing my hand on the bloodied trunk in front of me. "My love."

A zing of power bolted through my fingers and chased through every vein in my body as ancient essence illuminated the space where my hand pressed into the tree. Red-and-gold liquid danced in a swirling, slithering fusion as the blood of me and my mate intertwined. Where I held my open palm, gashes to the gate, the Triple Goddess's blood fused with mine. Just one drop of her powerful blood was all it took to revive me. I felt my fangs elongate as a protective need to bite into her flesh carved its way through my gums. And I *had* bitten her, and she me, on the day she ascended to full godhood and claimed me as her fated mate. There lies a new dawn in this kingdom of death, as we were already intertwined in blood and heart. The Gates only needed a bleeding to generate the magic.

I stood from my kneel and with tipped fangs, I bit into my wrist and allowed more of me to fuse with my *sōrza*'s blood. Pressing myself into the bark, the zapping current of magic grew stronger as I began to sense the Gates mastering my movement. My legs moved without my telling them to, and before I knew it, the light winked out, and I was engulfed by mist and shadows.

EPILOGUE
SABINE GRIMSBANE

"Lovely to see you again, Sabine," a voice echoed around me. I tried to open my eyes, but a tearing pain stopped me from trying. With hands bound behind my back, I felt along the floor and up to the wall I was propped against. It was cold and hard, a surface like rock. *Where in all the realms am I?* I thought.

Quickly, I recalled the last memory I had before waking here. There had been a storm of snow, and I'd been wading in it, carving a footpath for my grandchildren. I had made it to the porch, closed the door behind me, and began taking my coat off. I thought I'd heard the kids coming up the stairs, but when Damek Lagunov's boot perforated the front door, caving the wood until it split in two, I knew I was in trouble. Moira Darkmore, Sora Fujin, and Nesrin Mehra all stood boastfully, watching the water-wielder put me under. Now, I knew they'd taken me.

"Moira," I barked, and the furrowing of my brow caused my eyes to lance again.

"In the flesh."

I could hear her arrogant grin from wherever she stood. "Untie me this instance," I demanded, sharpening my jaw as irritation gnawed away at my skin. Clomping feet approached me where I sat, and I felt the breeze the body had brought with it toward me. Hands grasped my bound wrists, and the pull and tug between my hands proved a knife was working its way through the cords tying me.

When my hands were free, I tugged at my face, and with the grit of my teeth, I tore the piece of duct tape from my eyes. When I blinked the pain away, I scowled up at the pale, slender woman who toyed with the tip of a dagger between two fingers.

"I know, I know," Moira cooed. "This wasn't part of the plan."

I kept my gaze cool as I surveyed her. "Where are my grandchildren?"

Her grin instantly vanished into a scowl. "They escaped," she answered.

Escaped where? I wondered, as I looked around the Grimsbane sanctuary. Damek, who stood at the bookshelf nearest the cave's entrance, pulled through my book collection, casting flecks of dust into the air. Sora, who was standing at Moira's side, was using her affinity for air to push the dust out and away from her as she scrunched her nose. I searched to find Nesrin Mehra, the newest member of the High Council, but found that she wasn't in the basement.

"Where's Baaz's replacement?" I questioned, still sitting against the rock.

"We sent the tracker to find them," Sora replied. "The spy was seen escaping into the woods with both of your grandchildren."

"I see," I held, and dusted the dirt from my pants.

Keeping my guard high, I made certain they would not be alerted to my panic as I portrayed nonchalance. "And what exactly am I doing here?"

Moira's smile widened at this, as if she were waiting for that very question. "The Scythe has come to see you."